Flame

Books by Amy Kathleen Ryan

Glow
Spark
Flame

Flame

AMY KATHLEEN RYAN

MACMILLAN

First published in the US 2014 by St. Martin's Press

This edition published in the UK 2014 by Macmillan Children's Books
a division of Macmillan Publishers Limited
20 New Wharf Road, London N1 9RR
Basingstoke and Oxford
Associated companies throughout the world
www.panmacmillan.com

ISBN 978-1-4472-2012-1

1 3 5 7 9 8 6 4 2

A CIP catalogue record for this book is available from
the British Library.

Printed and bound by CPI Group (UK) Ltd, Croydon CR0 4YY

For my brother, Michael

Our most basic common link is that we all inhabit this planet. We all breathe the same air. We all cherish our children's future. And we are all mortal.

—Thomas Jefferson

PART ONE

Back to the Beginning

*If we open a quarrel between past and present,
we shall find that we have lost the future.*
—Winston Churchill

Outside

When the metal helmet of the OneMan suit closed over Seth's head, his ears popped. Sweat soaked his armpits and trickled down his sides. He'd performed only a few space walks before, and they didn't get easier. During the last one he'd almost killed himself.

"I'm not going to die," Seth told himself for the twentieth time as he enabled the thrusters and checked his fuel and air levels. The flight prep took him twice as long as it should because he had to do everything with his clumsy left hand. His right hand was badly mangled; two of his fingers twisted into ugly, agonized knots. He turned up the oxygen in his breathing mixture to compensate for the awful pain.

"If that Neanderthal can do a space walk, I can do it," he said through gritted teeth, eyeing the empty housings for two OneMen, which must have been taken by Jake Pauley and his horrible little wife. She had been the one to set off the explosions that destroyed the Empyrean, then she broke her husband out of the brig and they must have come straight here to escape the dying ship in OneMen. She'd shown no remorse for leaving Seth trapped in the brig to die. If not for Waverly, he would have.

And to thank her he'd sent her all alone to the New Horizon—a snap decision that he already doubted. What was the alternative? Bowing and scraping to the people who had killed his father and destroyed his home ship? With his bad temper he'd get himself thrown in the brig, and he was damned if he was going to spend another minute of his life trapped like a rat. If he made it to the New Horizon and found a place to hide, he might be able to help Waverly, and maybe even do something to get back at Anne Mather.

He engaged the thrusters on his suit and hovered over to the air lock. Once inside, he turned back for a last look at the Empyrean. The shuttle bay was cavernous, quiet, deserted. Already it felt like a ghost ship. How many had the Pauleys killed today?

"Not the little kids. They're okay," he told himself, shaking his head against panic as he pressed the button to seal the air lock for the last time. The outer air-lock doors yawned wide to reveal the infinity of the open sky—black nothing carpeted with stars that seemed to rush away from him in a dizzying expansion.

Seth eased the OneMan out of the air lock and engaged the thrusters. He had enough experience now that he knew what to expect and was able to slowly maneuver his craft up and over the hull. At first the skin of the Empyrean looked undisturbed, but up ahead he could see plumes of freezing gases escaping in a billowing stream. Toward the aft he saw a vast cloud of white gas trailing behind the ship to disappear in the dark, leaving thousands of miles of air and water vapor in a long line cutting through the nothingness. Beyond that lay the nebula they'd left behind months ago, pink and glowing, belching flashes of electrical charge at the fringes. Seth turned away from its menacing beauty.

The New Horizon rose over the wound in the Empyrean like a

deformed moon. Pieces of debris came into relief against the gray hull. Jagged bits of metal, pieces of furniture, plant matter, even a tractor—all fell away behind the ship with awesome speed. He turned toward the prow of the Empyrean to get ahead of the debris and gunned his thrusters.

As he circled, he saw objects in the distance hovering over the Empyrean, strangely stationary. Seth used the telescope attachment in his helmet to get a better look: four New Horizon shuttles. The nearest shuttle's cargo ramp was hanging open, and from inside came four OneMen, drifting out like fish.

They were sending in rescue teams, Seth supposed. Or maybe they were looking for something that they wanted from the Empyrean cargo hold. He turned off his outer lights to make himself invisible, then scrolled through his radio frequencies until he heard voices.

"God. The damage is...," a man was saying. "Why would anyone do such a thing?"

An image of Jake Pauley's demented face appeared in Seth's mind—the weird smile, the heavy bones of his browridge, his grimy teeth.

"That's what I'm saying. This is useless," another man said. "I don't know why she sent us out here."

To pick over our bones, Seth thought. He was so angry that he wanted to ram them, sever their air hoses, knock them spinning into space.

"I think she's losing her grip. Did you see the way Dr. Carver was looking at her during services?"

"This is an open channel, boys," a male voice warned.

They were silent for a few moments.

"There are still a few missing kids," said a woman. By her tone, Seth guessed she didn't much like her companions. "I'm glad to help look for them."

"In an explosion like that? It's amazing all of them didn't die," said a third man.

"I guess we have to look for them," said the first man, "if they're just kids."

"Noble of you," the woman said, and the other men laughed.

Once they were out of view, Seth started toward the New Horizon again, this time less hurried. He had time. The ship wouldn't leave behind its search teams, after all.

Seth kept his eyes on the hull of the Empyrean as he moved. As long as he was near the large ship he didn't feel so exposed, but when the hull of the Empyrean rolled away and the starscape widened before him, he gasped.

"Did you hear that?" a woman said in his ear.

Stupid! He was so *stupid*! He'd forgotten to turn off his radio. He flipped the switch, just as someone else said, "Feedback from the other team."

His heart galloped and he trembled in his suit. He couldn't make a mistake like that, not ever again.

His problem was exhaustion. He'd just finished a grueling journey through the dying Empyrean carrying Waverly on his back. Aside from his mangled hand, his brain was still sore from oxygen deprivation, and his thoughts were fuzzy. He needed to concentrate.

He kicked the thrusters harder. The New Horizon was miles away; the sooner he closed the distance the better.

Seth ran over the mental picture of the Empyrean schematics he'd spent his boyhood studying. There were small air locks for maintenance all over the ship—one of them had killed his mother, along with Waverly's father, in what had been called an accident. The New Horizon was practically a replica of Seth's home ship, so it shouldn't be too hard to find an air lock in a seldom-traveled area.

He decided to try the storage bays toward the lower levels. They were far from the habitation levels, so it was unlikely he'd be seen, but if he needed, there'd be plenty of places to hide.

Closing the distance between the two ships took almost an hour, even pushing his thrusters at maximum capacity. He heard only the hollow sound of his breath inside his helmet, and if he strained, he could hear the blood coursing through the veins in his ears. He entered a kind of trance, distant from the pain in his hand so that he could concentrate on keeping his course true.

When the air lock in the storage bay came into sight, an alarm light from the OneMan's guidance system warned him that he was going too fast. He gunned the reverse thrusters to slow himself, grimacing against the unpleasant pressure of the inertial force. The metal hull reared up before him, and he hit hard.

Frantic, he shot out his magnetic arm to keep from bouncing away from the ship and clung to the controls, panting and shaking, waiting for his heart to stop racing. His entire body was trembling, though he felt paralyzed.

"Last space walk ever," he promised himself.

He checked his air: only ten minutes left. He shouldn't have turned up his oxygen after all. Another stupid mistake!

He looked around for surveillance cameras on the outside of the ship, for surely he was in view of at least one of them. He found one about thirty yards away, but it was turned slightly away from him. There was a chance that he'd been observed on his approach, so he should hurry.

Seth engaged the outer air-lock control and the door popped open. He guided his craft inside, and as soon as the air lock filled with air, took off his helmet. The inner door opened, and he drifted inside and set the OneMan down on the floor of the storage bay. He was surrounded by huge storage containers stacked to the ceiling— rows and rows of them, full of equipment and supplies for colonizing New Earth. The planned arrival on the planet was so many decades away, Seth doubted he'd live long enough to see it.

He'd released most of the clamps sealing the suit along his chest when he heard voices.

"Hey!" someone yelled. Four men ran toward him, carrying guns. They were about three hundred yards away, closing fast.

Seth pulled at the last remaining clamp on his suit and, ignoring the pain in his hand, catapulted himself out of the lower portion of the OneMan and started running.

He was winded almost immediately, but he wove between the room-size shipping containers, listening for footsteps and voices, which sounded close at first but soon faded away. Despite his physical exhaustion he had the advantage of youth and natural speed. Seth slipped through the door to the starboard outer stairwell and ran up several flights until he found the rain forest level. He dove into the velvety humid air. It was warm here, and it smelled beautiful. He sprinted down the path until he found a patch of large ferns growing under a teak tree and collapsed into them. He sprawled, listening, panting, wiping sweat from his brow with the back of his left hand. No one came. He was safe for now. But only for now.

Return

Waverly tried to focus on the familiarity of the pilot's seat in the shuttle she flew, the comfort of the joystick in her hands, knowing this was likely to be the last time she'd ever fly a shuttle. If she kept her eyes on the control lights, she could pretend she would be coming back home soon. But then her gaze would drift to the rear vid screen, and she'd see the long, cluttered trail of vapor gushing from the Empyrean, and reality would come crashing back. No. It was over. The ship couldn't be losing air like that and still survive. Her home was dead.

There was only one place to go now: into her enemy's control on the New Horizon.

With one glance at Sarah in the copilot's seat—her blank stare and the pallor underneath her freckles—Waverly knew her friend had gone into a kind of numb shock. *Just like me,* Waverly thought. The loss of the Empyrean was so devastating that she couldn't take it in all at once. No more orchards, no more granaries, no more hall-ways filled with familiar faces, no more home.

She was enraged to see the New Horizon so pristine, not a mark on her, lurking up ahead. Beneath that metal skin waited Anne Mather and all her blind followers. *If I have to live there,* she thought, *I'll lose my mind.* The New Horizon air-lock doors were tiny in the distance, but they grew inexorably larger, and then suddenly they were huge enough to fit her craft, and they opened for her shuttle.

"You're taking it too fast," Sarah said.

Waverly *was* going too fast. She knew she was. "You think I should slow down?" Waverly asked, her voice muffled in her own ears. *If I ram them,* she thought, *I could decompress the shuttle bay just like they did to the Empyrean, when all this began.*

"Are you thinking about . . . ?" Sarah's jaw set with ugly menace, but the menace wasn't for Waverly.

Waverly didn't answer.

The com system crackled to life, and a tense woman's voice said, "Empyrean shuttle, slow your approach."

But Waverly didn't slow down. How many kids were on board her shuttle? Five? Ten? Probably every one of them would love to put a hole in the New Horizon, even if it meant dying.

"The shuttle bay is full of young children," the woman's voice warned.

The shuttle joystick waited between Waverly's knees. To slow down, all she needed to do was pull back on it. It waited there, but she didn't reach for it.

"Waverly," Sarah said. Waverly glanced at her friend and saw tears streaming down her face. "I'd do it if it was just us, you know I would, but . . ."

"I know," Waverly whispered, and she pulled back on the joystick. Both girls were pressed forward against their safety harnesses as the shuttle slowed for landing.

When the inner air-lock doors opened for them, Waverly eased the shuttle onto the deck of the New Horizon. The landing gear connected with the metal floor, and a metallic snap reverberated through the shuttle bay. Someday Waverly might stand on a planet with nothing but sky overhead, no metal walls and ceilings trapping her with these people she hated. *Forty-two years before we get there*, she thought. *I'll never make it.* Through the blast shield she saw Anne Mather crossing the huge bay, an armed escort trailing in two neat lines behind her. She frowned at Waverly as they drew near and crossed her arms to wait for the shuttle to empty out.

"There are no kids here," Sarah said, fatalistic and flat. "They lied."

"I can't do this," Waverly said. She felt sticky with sweat and exhausted. She'd spent the last two hours trudging through the Empyrean as the ship died, enduring oxygen deprivation to rescue Seth until she'd collapsed completely. He'd saved her life, carrying her up endless flights of stairs to safety, and then he hadn't even come with her on the shuttle! He'd abandoned her to face Anne Mather alone.

"We have to leave sometime," muttered Sarah from the copilot's seat.

"Will they take more eggs from us?" Waverly whispered.

"No," Sarah said, her upper lip rigid.

The girls jumped in their seats when they heard the shuttle's exit ramp extend onto the floor of the New Horizon. Waverly looked through a side porthole and saw her passengers trickling out of the shuttle, walking with jerking steps toward Mather and her sentries— the last of the kids to be evacuated off the Empyrean, looking dazed and traumatized.

"Should we go?" Sarah asked Waverly. "Instead of making her come get us?"

"Probably." Waverly disliked the flaccid tone of her voice. She looked out the blast shield to find Mather watching her. "You go ahead," Waverly said miserably, turning away from Mather to stare at her own cold hands.

Sarah stood, her face set with stony courage, and left the cockpit.

Waverly couldn't make her legs move. She watched as Sarah, with her boyfriend, Randy, walked bravely out of the shuttle and across the gray metal floor, hands held over their heads. Two of Mather's men patted them down for weapons, then led them away.

Waverly took hold of the pilot's joystick with both hands and imagined escaping into the void of space where she would choose a direction, punch the engines, and just go. She'd be alone, and safe, and no one could come after her. It would take her awhile to die, but if it got to be too much, she could just blow out an air lock and it would be over.

If she wanted to do that, she should have thought of it sooner. And she didn't want to do it. Not really. Not if there was a chance her mom was still alive.

"Get up," she told herself. "Go out there. Go find Mom."

But she didn't. She couldn't. Acid rose to the back of her throat and she swallowed. Her saliva tasted corrosive.

She saw movement from the corner of her eye and looked out. Anne Mather had broken away from the group of guards. One of them started to follow, but she held a hand in his face and he stepped back into formation. He was vaguely familiar to Waverly from her time on the New Horizon, always in the background, behind Anne Mather, or off to the side. He was tall, with a bulbous, crooked nose, thinning gray-white hair, and the kind of heavy jaw that looked like it had been chunked out of a boulder. When he glanced up at Waverly, she looked away.

She heard the scuff of footsteps on the floor behind her, but she didn't turn around. She knew who it was. "No one is going to harm you, Waverly."

God, how Waverly hated that velvety tone! Mather wasn't human. She was something manufactured, designed for manipulation. Waverly could smell her, that sickly sweet coconut smell that clung to the woman's skin like grease. Waverly pressed her hand to the hollow of her gut.

"Waverly, I want to start over with you."

"Take me to the brig," Waverly said distantly. "I want to be with my mother."

"I have a better idea," Mather said. Waverly heard the whisper of the woman's clothing as she moved toward the copilot's seat and sat down, leaning her elbow on the back of the chair. "Naturally I can't leave you loose on the ship," Mather said carefully. "But I could let you and your mother have one of the empty apartments. How would that be?"

"Where did you take Sarah and Randy?"

"Your friends are safe. They'll be well treated."

"What did you do to Amanda?" Waverly asked. Amanda, the woman Waverly had lived with her first time on the New Horizon, had taken up arms against Mather and her guards to help Waverly escape the ship. Waverly had worried Mather might have thrown her in the brig, or worse. "Did you hurt her?"

"For what?" Mather said with a disingenuous smirk. "You took her hostage. She had no choice but to help you escape. Isn't that so?"

Waverly studied Mather's composed expression and saw the truth. Amanda had told a lie to protect herself and her unborn baby, and Anne Mather had chosen to believe her friend's lie—or at least to pretend she believed. Mather was capable of loyalty, Waverly supposed, and even love, but that only made her crimes all the more monstrous.

"Waverly." Mather had the audacity to lean across the aisle and place a hand on Waverly's knee. Waverly looked at it, seething, and Mather removed her hand before Waverly could claw the bones out of it. "What we did to you was wrong. Absolutely wrong. I knew it then and I acknowledge it now. I wish I could explain to you my mind-set." Mather shook her head as she gathered her thoughts. "Every last woman on board this ship was premenopausal. We had to harvest your ova and make them pregnant as quickly as possible. If I'd tried to win you over first—"

"Stop talking to me!" Waverly screamed at the top of her lungs. Instantly she heard heavy boots stomping up the ramp of the shuttle and into the cockpit. Two men squeezed themselves through the doorway, aiming their guns at Waverly. She ignored them. "You got your way. The Empyrean is destroyed and we're all yours."

Saying these words finally broke her. Sobs shredded her, and she collapsed against her chair. Mather reached for her hands, but Waverly jerked away. She thought if that woman touched her again she might go crazy.

"Waverly," Mather pleaded. "I know how it looks, but I never ordered anyone to blow up the Empyrean. I'd never endanger the mission like that! Or children! Jacob and his wife acted alone."

"Stop talking to me," Waverly said again, and she sagged. It was all hitting her now. Her home was gone. How many kids must have died? Where was Serafina, the deaf little girl she used to babysit? She wouldn't have heard the explosions. She might never have known there was any danger! "Where are the kids? How many . . ." She gagged on the words, forced them out, "How many died?"

"Very few," Mather said. "Almost all of them were in the central bunker, waiting for word about their parents."

Waverly could imagine them huddled in groups on the bunks, holding hands, waiting for Sarek to come in from Central Command to tell them their parents had been found on the New Horizon and their families would be whole again. *When will we learn to stop hoping?*

"Come on," Mather said. "Let's get you settled."

Mather reached again to take her hand, but Waverly ignored her and got up from her seat. The guards backed up the aisle of the shuttle, keeping their guns trained on her as she walked down the spiral staircase to the cargo hold, then down the ramp where the rest of the guards were waiting.

They walked her through the corridors of the New Horizon in a parade with Mather and Waverly at the head, followed by a small army of men. They met no one. Waverly supposed they'd cleared this part of the ship to deal with the Empyrean evacuees. As they walked, the big guard massaged the wooden grip on his gun, crushing his teeth together as though he were chewing on something that angered him. Unlike the other guards, who wore plain tunics, he had a gold insignia on his shoulder in the shape of a dove. Waverly had no idea what it meant, but she knew he must have some authority.

"Here," Mather said to Waverly, indicating an apartment door in the middle of the hallway. "We'll have guards outside round the clock."

"So I'm under house arrest?"

"Until we know what we're dealing with," Mather said with a nod.

"Where is my mother?" Waverly asked.

"Inside," Mather said and went to the keypad to unlock the door.

The door slid open, and there was Regina Marshall standing in the living room, emaciated and grayed but whole and alive, and she opened her arms to Waverly, who ran to her.

"Mom!" Waverly sobbed and couldn't say any more.

"I'm here, honey," Regina Marshall said. She combed her fingers through Waverly's hair. "Your hair got long!"

Waverly tried to smile, but her face dissolved into tears.

"Oh, there now, Waverly, everything is fine!" Waverly leaned into her mother, letting herself be held up. It felt good to be a kid again, so amazingly wonderful to have her mother take care of her. She hadn't realized how much she missed this.

"What a beautiful sight!" Anne Mather exclaimed from behind Waverly.

Waverly whirled, furious.

"Thank you so much, Pastor Mather," Waverly's mother said with a serene smile. "We're so grateful."

"Grateful!" Waverly sputtered. "Mom!"

"You two have a lot to talk about, I'm sure," Mather said with a smile for Regina Marshall. "I'll leave you to it. You have a stocked refrigerator."

"That's wonderful," Regina said. "Thank you."

Anne Mather backed out of the room, saintly eyes averted.

When they were finally alone, Waverly studied her mother. Regina met her daughter's gaze uncertainly, as though she were eager to please but wasn't sure how. "You know who that is, right, Mom?"

"That's Pastor Mather," Regina said with a strange pride. "Who would have thought a woman would captain a ship like the Empyrean?"

"We're on the New Horizon, Mom. She led the attack on the Empyrean," Waverly said. She felt faint.

"That was a rescue mission," Regina said, shaking her head as though she were clearing up some minor point.

"No, Mom, it was an attack."

"Oh, Waverly," Regina tsked.

"That woman attacked the Empyrean and kidnapped me and all the rest of the girls! Most of the crew died in that attack!" Her mother's eyes trained on Waverly's lips, as though she were learning a lesson by rote. "She's kept you and the rest of the parents on this ship for months, holding you hostage—"

Regina interrupted with a knowing chuckle. "You're seeing all this in a very negative light, dear."

"Mom!" Waverly stared at her mother, horrified.

Regina started toward the kitchen, smiling as though enjoying some pleasant daydream. "Pastor Mather explained the whole thing," Regina said as she turned on the kitchen light. "It was all a misunderstanding."

"Did the Pastor tell you how she drugged me and harvested my eggs to make babies for her crew? The other girls, too!" Waverly pressed a hand against her abdomen, feeling the surgical scars under her thumb like wires. "Mom?"

Regina did not seem to hear her.

The apartment had the same layout as the home Waverly and her mother had shared on the Empyrean, and the kitchen was identical down to the blue and yellow color scheme, but there were no baskets on the countertop, no scratches on the table from when Waverly was a toddler, no handwoven place mats, no scuffmarks on the floor.

Regina opened the refrigerator and looked inside. "Oh! There's a chicken! And fresh herbs. I'll make a roast for supper, sound good?"

"The Empyrean has been destroyed, Mom," Waverly said. "Our whole lives, up in smoke."

"Nonsense," Regina said with a patronizing smile as she turned back to the refrigerator, rooting through the basket of herbs. "Those are *things*, Waverly."

Regina hummed an old song Waverly remembered from childhood, a faraway look in her eyes as she carried the food to the countertop. Regina carefully set the chicken right on the counter, then arranged onions and potatoes in a circle around it as though designing a still life. She appeared unsure what to do with the bunch of fresh parsley she held in her hand and considered for a moment before placing it parallel to the edge of the countertop, tilting her head as she nudged the stems into order with her fingertip.

"What did they *do* to you?" Waverly whispered. "You're acting so—"

"How would you like me to act?" Regina said, bemused. "I think I'll make a nice spice rub."

Eyes fastened to her mother's face, Waverly crept closer and studied her. Had she been drugged? "Don't you have any questions for me, Mom?" Waverly asked.

"How's Kieran?" Regina asked as she ground up garlic, sage, and rosemary with a stone pestle and mortar. The familiar aromas inundated the room with memories of home. Waverly limped to the table against the wall and collapsed into a chair.

"I don't know. Mather has him," Waverly said, only now realizing how much danger Kieran might be in. She wished she could get a message to him.

"He was always such a wonderful boy," Regina said. "I'm sure he's just fine."

"Yeah," Waverly said miserably. "Everything's great."

Damage

"What have you done with my crew?" Kieran demanded when Anne Mather came back into her office. He was still tied up on her chaise, guarded by an armed man who watched him with flinty eyes. "Where's Waverly?"

"I'll show you." Anne Mather held up the com screen for him. His eyesight was still spotty from the bright flashing explosions on the Empyrean that had blinded him through the porthole, but he could make out the dim images of Waverly and her mother. Regina was standing at the stove, stirring a pot, and Waverly was sitting slumped at the table. "I want you to understand that I'm true to my word," Mather said. "I said no harm would come to her, and I meant it."

"So you're letting the kids be with their parents?"

Anne Mather turned to Kieran's mother, Lena, who sat primly in a chair in front of Mather's desk, a bland smile creasing her face. "Those we can trust, like Regina Marshall and your mother."

"How dare you speak of trust?" Kieran snarled.

Mather blinked mechanically. "Kieran, I did not order Jacob Pauley and his wife to plant bombs on the Empyrean. I would never do that."

"You tried to destroy the Empyrean before!" Kieran spat. "You caused a nuclear meltdown in your first attack. You almost killed everyone on the ship!"

"Now, Kieran," his mother said disapprovingly. "We're guests here."

Kieran couldn't even bring himself to look at her.

"The Empyrean's reactor failure was an accident," Mather said.

"You're lying," Kieran said coldly. He wriggled his hands in their restraints, trying to get more blood into his numb fingers.

"You look uncomfortable," Mather said and nodded at the guard standing by the door. "Untie him."

"He tried to choke you," the man said, but he knelt to untie Kieran's wrists.

"My legs, too," Kieran said, massaging his hands. "I want to see the Empyrean."

Mather nodded at the guard, who untied the cord around Kieran's ankles.

Kieran staggered to the porthole and stared out, aghast. The Empyrean was a ruin. A gash half the length of its hull gaped into the black sky, running from the shuttle bay, through the habitation levels, the schools, the family gardens, the corn and wheat granaries, the fish hatchery, to end at the lower levels, and the brig, where Seth had been trapped.

So he's dead, Kieran thought, surprised to feel so much hurt over the end of his old enemy. He'd grown up with Seth, after all.

"Do you have a count of survivors yet?" he asked, his voice unrecognizable in his own ears.

"I have a list of missing persons, if you'd like to see it." She pushed the list at him. "It's remarkable more lives weren't lost."

Kieran picked up the paper and read: *Arthur Dietrich, Tobin Ames, Sarek Hassan, Austen Hand, Philip Grieg*... His dear friends.

"They might be trapped!" Kieran sucked in air, choked on his words. "You have to find them!"

"I've got several teams searching the ship, Kieran. If anyone is there, he or she will be found." She smiled reassuringly, but he heard a hesitation in her voice.

"What?"

Her face fell. "They've searched all the areas where people are likely to have survived. They're just not there."

"They have to be. Sarek was in Central Command and Arthur was on Waverly's shuttle, on the way back from trying to rescue our parents! He wasn't even *on* the Empyrean when the bombs went off! He'd have gone straight to Central Command to help Sarek with the evacuation. Tobin and Philip were in the infirmary... They were nowhere *near* the bombs!"

"The bombs we can see from *here*," Mather corrected him. "The infirmary lost power soon after the explosions. They'd have been totally cut off from the com system and life support. My crew is checking, but right now their survival looks doubtful. And the two boys in Central Command—Arthur and Sarek, was it?—could they have tried to rescue someone else? Perhaps they were trying to get to the infirmary to help and got caught in a depressurized compartment."

Kieran closed his mouth. If anyone was likely to get himself killed doing something heroic, it would be those two. And Tobin and Austen would have stayed with the sick ones in the infirmary, unable to ask for help. They probably waited too long, trying to keep their mothers and little Philip and the rest of them alive.

He turned to the porthole again and watched his bleeding ship.

I did this, he thought bitterly. *I was acting Captain. I should have protected them.* But he'd failed, and now his friends were gone, along with the only world he'd ever known. He couldn't make himself believe it, even though the Empyrean was dying right in front of him.

"I think you need a rest, am I right?" Anne Mather said, the picture of concern. To Kieran's mother, she said, "I've found a beautiful outer apartment for you to enjoy. Usually these coveted apartments are occupied by senior staff—"

"Hey!" Kieran cut in, disgusted. "I want to see my crew, *now.*"

"It's late, Kieran," Mather said. "The young ones are getting ready for bed."

"Tomorrow, then," Kieran said, digging his heels in for a fight.

To Kieran's surprise, Mather nodded. "I'll contact the host families and arrange for something soon. Now let me show you to your quarters," she said with a sweeping gesture toward the door.

Kieran looked at her warily. *She wants something from me,* he realized. Mather ushered his mother down the corridor, making pleasant conversation. He had no choice but to follow.

First Things

The first thing is not to get caught, Seth told himself as he pressed his body into the soft rain forest soil, cradling his mangled hand on his chest. He pressed the back of his head into the ground beneath him. It was spongy with moss, moist with dew, and it accepted his aching limbs lovingly. The air was heavy and close like a blanket. He closed his eyes, and when he tried to open them again, they felt stuck together with sleep. *Maybe I should just rest,* he told himself. *This is as safe a place as any.*

He was drifting off when an alarm blared through the bay, making the ferns over his face tremble. It was a single loud blast, like a clarion call, so different from the repetitive bursts on the Empyrean. A tinny voice came over the loudspeaker: "Attention: Inform Central Command immediately if you see an unaccompanied young man."

Seth heard a quick intake of breath from someone close by.

"Poor thing!" said a woman off to Seth's right. Seth dared to shift his head to peer through the undergrowth. He couldn't see the speakers' faces, but he saw a petite woman's brown hands about fifteen feet away. She had a basket over her arm, and it was full of star fruit and papaya. He couldn't see the man. "They're searching for him like a common criminal."

"He might *be* a criminal, Maya," the man said. "He must be up to something if he didn't come with the rest of the survivors."

"He's just a kid, Anthony!"

"I know," the man said, his tone softened.

"Poor boy," the woman said sorrowfully. "He must be so afraid."

Am I afraid? Seth wondered. He was suddenly aware of his laboring heart, his dry mouth and jangled limbs.

The conversation between the man and woman subsided. Seth knew he was well concealed, but he felt pinned by their proximity. He heard the door he'd come through open and the sound of heavy boots on the path—at least four or five people, moving fast.

"Have you seen a stranger today?" asked a man, his tone forceful.

"No," said the man called Anthony. "Nobody came through here."

"Really? Because we've got video of a fugitive entering the rain forest bay."

Seth kicked himself. Of course they'd have video of him coming here! How could he have forgotten that?

I'm tired, that's how, he thought grimly. *Can't think straight.*

"Well, Thomas, we haven't seen him," Maya said.

"Are you sure?"

"What is that supposed to mean?" she asked. Seth squinted through the brush and saw her cross her arms.

"I haven't seen you at services for the past few Sundays," the man said. "That doesn't exactly vouch for your attitude."

"There's no reason to attend services anymore," she said. "Not when the Pastor is such a hypocrite."

"Maya!" Anthony cried.

"What?" she said. "This is a free society, isn't it?"

"The Pastor deserves your respect," said the man she'd called Thomas. Seth heard a footstep, and now the man was blocking Seth's view of the woman. He wore a black jumpsuit with a utility belt, and there was an insignia on his shoulder that looked like a dove. "I suggest you keep your thoughts private."

"Is that a threat?" Maya asked.

Thomas took another menacing step toward Maya, and finally Anthony spoke. "Everyone is edgy right now. With the explosion on the Empyrean? Thomas? We're all just edgy."

"You should control her better," Thomas said from between gritted teeth.

Maya made an outraged squawk, but Anthony spoke over her. "We'll let you know if we see anything. Okay?"

"I'll know if you're keeping secrets," Thomas said.

"It won't work, what you're doing." Maya stomped a little foot on the ground. "You can't control people with fear for long."

"You don't listen well," Thomas said.

A second guard, shorter and stockier, said, "We're getting off track, here, Tom."

After a pause, Thomas said, "Close off the exits and call up more men."

Seth was trapped already!

Perhaps not yet, if he left before the exits were sealed.

His hand throbbed, but he set his teeth against the pain. He listened to their fading voices as the men spread out, headed for the various exits. He tried to make a mental map of the rain forest bay on the Empyrean, which would be identical to this ship. There were six doors total. There hadn't been enough guards to cover all those doors. If he moved now, he might still get out. It was inevitable the couple would see him, but that was better than getting caught by the guards. Bracing himself on his good hand, he stood up quickly and shot off through the foliage, running as fast as his tired body could go.

"Did you see that?" he heard Maya ask as he sped away through the dense growth, trying to make his way toward the port-side stairwell. He jumped over the root of a banyan tree, but another root caught his toe and he hit the ground with terrific force. He rolled onto his broken hand and screamed.

Footsteps approached. Seth felt a hand on his back, and when he looked up, he saw the man named Anthony crouched over him.

"What are you doing here?" Anthony whispered. "They're looking for you."

Seth was in too much pain to speak. The man looked at Seth's hand and leaned over him to whisper, "You need to get to the infirmary."

"No! Please!" Seth managed to say through shudders of shock.

Lighter footsteps stumbled into the clearing, and the woman Maya put a cool hand to his forehead. She was pretty, with the caramel skin and the lovely full lips of an African woman. She saw his hand and winced. That's when Seth noticed the bone of his pinkie finger poking through a small puncture in his skin. Purple blood pumped out through the wound in time with his wild heartbeat. He nearly fainted.

"Maya!" someone barked. Whoever it was sounded much too close.

Maya stood quickly and ran toward the voice. "Yah!"

"What was that sound?" It was the man she'd called Thomas. Seth could tell by his imperious tone.

"Anthony tripped," Maya said.

Anthony held up his palms, telling Seth to stay put. Quickly, he grabbed some garden shears from the basket of fruit and used them to make a hole in the knee of his pants. Before Seth could react, Anthony jabbed the sharp end of the shears into his skin and pressed the cut with his fingertips, forcing it to bleed. In seconds he rubbed the blood into the fabric of his pants, then patted dirt all over himself and stood up. He limped toward where Maya and Thomas were talking, arms raised. "I fell onto my garden shears!" he said, shaking his head. "Stupid."

"You two know the penalties for lying to the Justice of the Peace."

Seth lay perfectly still between two large tree roots, silently absorbing the agony of his ruined hand, breathing as quietly as possible.

"Of course," Anthony said breathlessly. "Thomas, you know me. I'm not going to make trouble."

This was met with terse silence until Maya finally broke it. "God! Thomas! The suspicion on this ship is going to tear us all apart! Anthony is a good man! He doesn't deserve this!"

Thomas still said nothing.

"Come on, Anthony," Maya said, exasperated. "Let's get you to the infirmary."

"Okay," Anthony said shakily.

Seth heard the two of them moving off toward the port-side exit. The big man didn't make a sound. *He's listening for me,* Seth thought, and he tried to hold his breath.

Thomas's walkie-talkie squawked, and a man's voice said, "Thomas, we've got tracks over here you should look at."

"I'll be right there," Thomas said, but he still didn't move.

Moments passed. Seth heard tentative footsteps picking through the brush toward him, and he braced himself. But suddenly, across the room, two gunshots rang out.

"What's going on?" Thomas shouted.

"Don saw something!" called a third guard. Thomas took off running toward the sound of the shots, leaving Seth trembling with relief, wedged between two snaking banyan roots.

He lay still, he didn't know for how long, trying to think what to do. He'd obviously missed his escape window, and now discovery was inevitable. Already he'd let Waverly down, but now he wondered what he'd thought he'd be able to do for her. Rescue her from the evil witch like some knight in shining armor? *Idiot. Idiot. Idiot.*

He didn't hear the footsteps until they were nearly on top of him.

He looked up to see black pants and two white hands holding a gun across a robust chest. The guard crouched over Seth, the muzzle of his gun pointed at the ceiling. It was the stocky guard he'd seen before, a man of fifty-some years, with gray hair at his temples, speckled stubble across his jaw, and light brown eyes that seemed somehow kind. "Can you walk?" the guard whispered.

Seth stared at him.

"We have two minutes before my commanding officer figures out I've left my post. Can. You. Walk."

Seth nodded.

"Get up. Keep your head down. And be quiet."

The Doctor

After a couple days alone with her mother, Waverly wanted to run away from the jumpy way Regina's hands fluttered when she worked at her small loom, or the way she smiled at Waverly with twitching lips when the two made eye contact. Far into the first night, Waverly had questioned her mother about the conditions of her imprisonment, but she gave only half answers that never added up to why she seemed so hollowed out. Today, Waverly avoided her, spending more time in her room hiding under blankets, trying not to think about Seth, the way he'd kissed her so deeply, so sweetly, and the way he'd left her all alone. Where *was* he? How could he abandon her here after the way she'd risked her life to save him?

It didn't matter that it seemed relatively safe here; she couldn't *feel* safe. Something had been done to her mother, something horrible. Waverly knew it.

When someone finally rang the doorbell, Waverly bounded up from her bed. She didn't know what she hoped for—Seth?—but as she ran into the living room she realized she didn't want to hide anymore. She had to do something to help her mom.

"Delivery!" her mother said, excited. A roly-poly woman came in pushing a cart full of more chicken, baskets of freshly picked turnips, parsnips, carrots, kale, salad greens, and two loaves of fresh wheat bread.

"Hey!" Waverly said to the small woman. "I want to know what's been done to my mother!" The guard posted outside the apartment scoffed, and she glanced at him through the open doorway. He was shaking his balding head, grinning. She ignored him, knowing better than to try appealing to one of Mather's men.

"Please." Waverly reached for the woman's plump hand. "Couldn't you just ask a doctor to come look at her?"

The woman slapped her hand away. "Doubt it."

"Waverly," Regina cooed. "I feel fine."

"You need to see a doctor," Waverly insisted. To the scowling little woman she said, "Can't you give the infirmary a message?"

"No messages," the woman said over her shoulder as she entered the kitchen. She pulled a browned apple pie from the center rack on the cart and set it on the counter.

"Wonderful!" Regina exclaimed and went into the kitchen to help put away the food. Waverly watched them puttering, feeling helpless and lost.

A voice from the doorway made her jump. "Waverly Marshall?"

She turned to see a strikingly handsome man leaning on the doorframe. He had coffee-colored hair, olive-toned skin, and intriguing eyes. At first his irises looked black until he held her gaze, and then she saw they were a deep navy blue. He smiled, showing two rows of gleaming teeth, though one of his incisors was slightly chipped, a defect that only made him more masculine. He was dressed in a plain blue shirt that complemented his eyes, gray pants, and leather boots. Everything about him was composed, careful, and lovely to look at.

She tried to stand up taller. "Who are you?"

"I'm Jared Carver. Feel like going for a walk? Someone wants to meet you."

"Who?"

"A friend," he said.

"Someone from the Empyrean?" she asked, hopeful.

"No, but I can give you news of them if you like."

Waverly glanced back at her mother, who was absorbed in putting away the food.

"Your mother will be quite safe here," the man said with a sweet smile.

Waverly studied him. His friendly composure didn't seem completely trustworthy. *If Mather wants to kill me, she could do it anytime,* Waverly thought. *I might as well see if I can find anything out.* She called to her mother, "Mom. I'm going out!"

"All right," Regina called, not a speck of concern in her voice. The old Regina Marshall would never have let Waverly out of her sight in a place like this.

Waverly walked past Mather's guard, who stood at attention now, his mocking grin wiped from his fleshy face. The handsome man—what had he called himself? Jared Carver?—led Waverly down empty, quiet corridors. She looked around, listening for signs of life, but there was no one around. On the Empyrean, people were always complaining about noise. She remembered the near constant classical music her neighbors, the Moreaus, used to play, blaring Brahms or Mahler so that the entire hallway buzzed with it. They'd been childless, and with a pang she realized they must be dead with no one to mourn them. She ducked her head, overcome with sadness, but quickly straightened up when she noticed the man looking at her.

"You okay?" he asked gently.

"It's so quiet here," she said. "Like no one lives here."

"Pastor Mather is keeping you and your mother isolated for the time being," the man said. "You're restricted to uninhabited areas of the ship."

"What did she do with the people who lived here?"

"This wing has always been empty. Due to our infertility we have a much smaller population than the ship designers anticipated."

She nodded, looking at her shoes and their slow, plodding steps. Of course. Even the Empyrean had many empty apartments.

"Where are the other kids?" she asked.

"They're safe, I assure you," he said. They turned a corner, passing a maintenance closet with the door hanging open. A cloud of ammonia hovered around the doorway, and Waverly rubbed at her stinging nose. "The Pastor wants to move forward to a peaceful future for all," Jared was saying. "Right now she's concentrating on healing wounds. At least," he added with a smirk, "that's the story."

"When can I see my friends?" she asked, choosing to ignore his odd slip.

"Not right away. After what happened the last time, I'm sure the Pastor is going to be cautious. Especially with a fugitive on board."

"Fugitive?" Waverly asked, her heart leaping. *Seth! He'd made it!*

The man hesitated. "A young man came aboard in a OneMan. Any idea who?"

She shrugged. "No."

The man gave a half turn but said nothing as he pressed the call button for the elevator.

In silence, they rode to the administrative level of the ship, and when the doors opened, Waverly was surrounded by people. Men and women in the uniforms of deck officers, guards, engineers, horticulturalists—all the different types of workers needed to keep the New Horizon running. Most of them brushed right by Waverly and Jared without a glance, but a few looked at her with surprise, and one woman glared at her. Jared passed what would be the Central Council chamber. The door hung open and she could see the domed glass ceiling of the chamber, just like on the Empyrean, and the same oval table, the same cushioned chairs around it. Until several days ago, she'd been a member of the Central Council on the Empyrean, steering straight for disaster without even knowing it. Jared walked two doors past the chamber, knocked on an office door, and waited until a rattling voice called, "Enter."

Jared opened the door to a cavelike room, long and narrow, swathed in shadows. At the end of it, sitting in a dim circle of light, was a small, decrepit person, fingers woven together on top of a leather blotter resting on an ornate oak desk. Waverly couldn't be sure if this was a man or a woman—age had stripped away all signs of gender. The back of the leather chair hovered over the tiny person like a pair of dark wings, and when . . . she? he? it? . . . smiled, wrinkles rearranged themselves to make room for an overwide mouth and unnaturally white, square teeth, giving the impression of an otherworldly creature.

"Dr. Wesley Carver," Jared said with a bow, "I present Waverly Marshall."

So he was a man. Waverly recognized what was so strange about him: He was far, far older than anyone she'd ever met. The oldest person on the Empyrean had been Captain Jones, and he'd been sixty-five at the time of the attack. When the mission launched, no one older than twenty-five had been allowed to board the ships, or at least that's what everyone had said. For the sake of the mission, the crews had been chosen for their robust health, intelligence, skills, and a capacity for longevity. Yet this person, this man, might have been eighty, he might have been one hundred. Waverly had no experience from which to judge.

Tentatively, Waverly stepped into the room. The walls were lined with hundreds of leather-bound volumes. She glanced at some of the titles: *The Prince* by Machiavelli, *The Art of War* by Sun Tzu, *Histories* by Herodotus, *Thus Spake Zarathustra* by Nietzsche.

"Are you a reader?" the doctor asked with a smile.

Waverly stood before the desk, watchful. "Novels," she said breathlessly.

He rubbed a hand over sparse white hair and indicated the overstuffed leather chair to Waverly's left. "Sit."

Waverly lowered herself into it. She glanced behind her, expecting to see Jared standing there, but he'd silently left the room.

"You ought to try philosophy," the old man said. "Nothing excites the mind like a good bit of logic."

Waverly didn't reply. She felt too out of her element. There was nothing this decrepit person could do to hurt her physically, yet she felt afraid.

"You're not one for small talk," the man said, nodding approvingly as he pressed a button at the edge of his desk. "Let me get you something to drink."

The door opened behind her and Jared carried in a silver tea service. Ornate scrollwork covered the teacups in the twisting shapes of grapevines. The teapot looked to be made from ancient porcelain, and it was painted with a scene from antiquity—water nymphs lazing by a pool, centaurs carving their arrows.

"Regency period, I believe," the doctor said, watching her. "Quite rare."

The guard, if that's what he was, poured a cup of tea for her. She accepted it quietly and watched as he dunked a biscuit into the old man's tea and handed it to him before padding back out the door.

"You have an appreciation for old Earth things, judging from what we were able to learn from your mother," said the old man. "You like historical novels, isn't that so?"

She squirmed to have this person know anything about her. "I suppose."

"Don't say 'I suppose.' It makes you sound wishy-washy. 'Yes' or 'no' is best."

Waverly took a slow sip of tea, then set the cup and saucer on his desk.

"I've called you here, Waverly, because you have shown mettle. I am a person who appreciates mettle. It is so rare a thing. Most people are simpering heaps of nerves." He smacked his lips distastefully. "You're a smart girl. But I wonder if you've noticed that Anne Mather's light is fading."

This got her attention. She looked at the man, tried to read him, but he was inscrutable in the way he grinned, one eye larger than the other, lips glistening with spittle.

"Few people know instinctively how to wield power," he said, tenting his fingertips together. "I saw that quality in Anne, and I must admit, she was able to sustain it much longer than I'd foreseen. But you . . ." He settled his elbows on his chair, making his shoulders into points. "You, Waverly, show promise."

Waverly's mouth went dry, and she picked up her teacup to wet her tongue.

"I saw the way you seized control of the room during services before you made your escape. That speech you made? You turned the tables on Anne in about four minutes, do you realize that?" He laughed gleefully. "She's had to defend herself ever since. You have made things difficult, but that was a master stroke."

"All I did was tell your crew how she'd attacked the Empyrean, how she was lying to them about it."

"I wonder if you'd indulge me, young lady?"

"What do I have that you could possibly want?" Waverly said, pulling her cardigan closer around her.

He leaned back in his chair, studying her. "I want what everyone wants: peace."

"Seems to me everyone wants power," Waverly shot back.

He tossed his head back. At first Waverly thought he was choking, but his eyes sparkled, and she realized that he was laughing—a desiccated rasp tore out of him. "Quite right! Quite right!" he said, clapping.

"What do you want *from me*?" she asked, trying not to show her apprehension.

His eyes glistened like beads pushed into cracked clay. Slowly he pushed his chair away from his desk, picked up a cane, and began to walk around the desk toward her. She drew away from him.

"Saint Anne has been discredited. Surely you must comprehend the position that puts her in, not to mention the rest of the crew. And the church elders."

"What position is that?"

"We're vulnerable now. To chaos. To unpredictability."

"So?"

"Predictability is what ensures the continuance of civilized behavior. *Un*predictability is the enemy of progress. Of productivity. Of wealth."

Waverly didn't know what he was getting at, but something about him was strangely fascinating. He looked utterly at home in this dark room, surrounded by what must be a priceless library. Behind him hung a gloomy landscape painting, nineteenth century, Waverly guessed, showing rolling hills under a cloudy sky.

"I think you might be the key we're looking for to make the future more . . . sustainable," Dr. Carver was saying.

"Who's we?"

"The church elders. They'd be known as the Central Council on the Empyrean."

"Are you one of them?"

"I am." He nodded humbly.

"What do you want with me?"

"Haven't I made myself clear?" the man said, amused. "We want you to help us destroy Anne Mather."

The room suddenly felt very still, very quiet. "What?" she whispered.

He laughed at the look of astonishment on her face. "As one of few genetic sources for our first generation of babies, Waverly, not to mention your performance on the day of your escape, you have a certain moral authority. I want to use this authority and grant you a forum to tell your story. Expose Anne Mather's lies."

She stared at him. "She'd kill me."

"She might try," he conceded.

"Why would I risk that?" Waverly asked.

"Name your price," he said evenly.

Waverly rubbed at her temple with cold fingers. The thought of putting herself in more danger exhausted her. She wanted to fade away, become part of the background, live a small life, help her mother get well . . .

"Jared called you Dr. Carver. What kind of doctor are you?"

"I am a neurologist, among other things."

"Can you tell me what's been done to my mother?"

He tilted his head in question.

"She's acting drugged, or brain damaged or something."

"Is her speech impaired?"

"No."

"Is she dizzy? Having trouble walking? Does her face look strange? Droopy?"

"No."

"It doesn't sound like a stroke, though I can't rule it out without an examination."

"Could you come see her?" Waverly asked eagerly.

"I'm retired," he said. "You should take her to the regular medical staff here."

"I can't trust them," Waverly said, remembering the doctor she'd taken hostage during her failed attempt to rescue the parents, the same one who had drugged all the girls and taken their ova. She didn't want to see him again.

"All right," the old man said, blinking slowly in a kind of smile. "I would be glad to look at your mother."

Waverly stood up from her chair, and he raised his eyebrows.

"You mean now?"

"Please," Waverly said, aware she was begging, but she didn't care.

The man pressed a small red button on his desk, and soon the door opened and Jared appeared pushing a wheelchair. With practiced moves, he helped the old man into his chair, then placed a crocheted afghan over his knees. The doctor waved a bony finger toward the darkened corner and barked, "My bag."

Wordlessly, Jared picked up a black doctor's bag from the floor and hung it on the old man's chair.

"You lead the way, Waverly," Jared said, and Waverly walked out the door with them close behind.

When they got to Waverly's lone apartment in the abandoned corridor, Regina was sitting curled on the couch in stocking feet, sipping at a cup of tea. "Waverly!" she said. "You brought company!"

"Hello, Mrs. Marshall," the doctor said jovially from the doorway. Jared pushed his chair into the room, gave Waverly a polite nod, then left to go stand in the hallway next to the guard, who barely acknowledged him. "I'm a doctor and I've come to have a look at you."

Regina looked at Waverly, confused. "I feel fine."

"Just routine," the doctor said and worked his chair closer until he sat directly across from her, their knees almost touching. "Follow my finger with your eyes, dear."

Regina obediently set aside her tea to give him her full attention.

The doctor had Regina repeat several sentences after him, checked all her reflexes, and had her remember long lists of objects. He ran her through simple arithmetic and asked her all about her history. Waverly sat in the armchair, watching. Her mother seemed to pass every test with flying colors, but that only frustrated Waverly. If the doctor couldn't see what was wrong, how could he fix it?

When finally the doctor turned to look wonderingly at Waverly, she rushed to explain. "It's her emotions. She's not bothered by anything."

"Like what?" the doctor said, visibly confused.

Waverly stepped forward and took hold of her mother's hands. "Mom. Remember how I told you the Empyrean has been destroyed?"

"Oh," Regina said, assuming a worried expression. "Oh yes. That's terrible."

"Aren't you upset about it?" Waverly asked.

"Of course, dear!" Regina said, no more touched than if they'd been talking about a ruined dress. "It's terrible."

Waverly looked at the doctor, who wrinkled his brow, perplexed.

"Regina," the old man said with authority, "I was very sorry to learn that so many of your friends were killed."

"Oh, I know!" Regina said, shaking her head as she took up her mug of tea again. "It's been very difficult." She took a sip, smiling anxiously at her daughter, hoping to please.

The old man asked another dozen questions, each more provocative than the last, probing for some emotional response. At last he shouted, "Some mother you are! Not caring that your daughter's home is destroyed! You must not love her. Someone ought to take her away from you."

"Oh no," Regina said, finally becoming agitated. "Please don't take Waverly away again!" She broke into tears and hid her face in her hands. "Please. I care! I know I do! I just feel so strange!"

Waverly sat down next to her mother on the sofa, a protective arm over her shoulders, and glared at the doctor.

"I'm sorry," he said. "But at least now we know she's still in there somewhere."

"What's wrong with her?" Waverly cried. "What did they do to her?"

The old man worked at the handle of his cane with his bent fingers. "I don't know," he said, bemused. "I'll have to ask around."

"Will you please?" Waverly asked. "Maybe you can fix her? If you find out what's wrong?"

"I'm sure there's some kind of treatment." He nodded.

Waverly laid her head on her mother's trembling shoulder. "It's okay, Mom."

"I didn't mean to make him mad," Regina whispered.

"You didn't," Waverly said. "No one's mad at you."

"Jared," the doctor said to the door, not bothering to raise his voice. Immediately Jared came back in and took his place behind the wheelchair. As the old man was wheeled out, he raised an eyebrow.

"Remember what we talked about," he said sternly. "I'm counting on your help." Jared pulled him out the door backward, and the old man kept his eyes steady on Waverly as he added, "Just as you're counting on mine."

Waverly looked at her mother's confused, wandering eyes, and with bone-chilling dread, understood exactly what kind of trade the doctor meant to make.

Reunion

Kieran walked into the central bunker, his hands crammed into his pants pockets, trying to control his anxiety. Mather had called him the night before to inform him that after four days of stalling, she was finally gathering all the surviving Empyrean children together for a breakfast reunion. The room was bright with flower arrangements and glass pitchers of fruit juices. Children had already situated themselves into the rows of metal chairs, arranged in front of a small riser where a microphone and a podium stood. Did Mather expect him to make a speech to the Empyrean kids? Did the kids expect it? Why should they, after he'd failed them so utterly?

"Kieran!" cried a squeaky voice. A group of little girls rushed up to him, gripping his hands and clothes, all looking at him with hope.

"My mommy isn't here!" cried Harmony Goia, hanging on to his shirttail. "Where is she?"

"Mine neither," cried Stephanie Horan, pulling anxiously on one of her red curls. "They won't let me look for her."

He looked from one little face to another, at a loss. Weeks before, Anne Mather had sent a complete list of all the parents held captive on this ship, which meant that any parents not on the list must be dead. As acting captain, Kieran should have informed the children, but what could he have done with all that grief? Now here they were, their hopes of finding their parents on this ship completely dashed. He could see the ravages of worry on their little bodies. Stephanie had pulled one lock of her hair so relentlessly she was making a bald patch in her scalp. Little Monica Reese was sucking on a red, infected-looking thumb. Teresa Pratt picked at bloody cuticles. They were all pale and fretful and too thin.

What could Kieran tell them? "I . . ."

"Felicity!" cried Stephanie, running toward the door, forgetting all about Kieran.

He looked up to see Felicity Wiggam coming toward him, a radiant smile on her face. Kieran tried to think of something to say to her, but she was already kneeling down to kiss the children. "I missed you so much!" she said to each of them. They barraged her with questions, and she held her hands up in surrender. "One at a time!"

When she'd finally appeased the little girls, she came to him, took both his hands in her own, and kissed his cheek. She smelled like vanilla soap. "Kieran, how are you?"

"I . . ." His mouth had gone dry.

"I heard about the Empyrean." She blinked tears from her large blue eyes. "I can't believe it."

"Me neither," he said quietly.

"Felicity." Stephanie was pulling on Felicity's light blue dress. "Have you seen my mommy?"

Felicity turned to the little girl, her smile wiped away. "No, my sweet girl. I have not."

"Where is she?" The little girl pulled savagely on her red curl.

"I don't see *any* adults here," Felicity said, looking around the room, then she turned to Kieran. "Have you seen my parents?"

Kieran opened his mouth to speak, but he couldn't make himself say it. He didn't need to. Felicity saw it all in his pained expression. She froze as the color seeped from her face.

"I'm so sorry," Kieran finally said.

"I knew it," Felicity said, swallowing as though she felt like throwing up. She pulled Kieran away from the little kids, who were watching her in fear, and whispered, "There've been rumors that most of the Empyrean adults were killed."

"They were sucked out the air-lock doors when Mather first attacked," he whispered, relieved to have someone to confide in. "Hundreds of them, but we never knew which ones until we got the list of captives from Mather."

"But they don't know yet," Felicity said, looking at the young faces as children wandered between the refreshments table and the rows of chairs, unmoored and bewildered.

More children from the Empyrean trickled in over the next few minutes. There were many tearful reunions between friends, little girls clasping hands, boys patting each other on the back, older kids wrapping littler ones in loving embraces. When Melissa Dickinson entered the room there was a general outcry, and she opened her arms to a wave of children. Barely taller than the kids she'd taken care of, Melissa had cared for the youngest children on the Empyrean, and they all adored her. She kissed each of them on the cheek, then herded them to the seats. The little ones still looked worried, but Melissa's soft, sweet voice had calmed them.

Waverly was one of the last to arrive, and with her was Kieran's own mother, holding hands with Regina Marshall. They'd been friendly with each other on the Empyrean but never close. Now the two women strolled together, speaking softly like best friends. Waverly found Kieran in the crowd and held up a hand. He wove through the milling children to get to her.

"Waverly." He resisted the urge to hug her.

"They're all asking about their parents," Waverly said. Her face looked drawn with lack of sleep, and her voice was throaty and weak.

"What do we tell them?" he whispered.

She shook her head, looking like a lost little girl.

"Tell them the truth," someone said, and Kieran turned to see Felicity next to him.

Waverly rushed at her old friend, and the two girls held each other, their faces hidden in each other's hair. "Why did you *stay* here?" Waverly asked her. "Why didn't you come with us when we escaped?"

"You know why. I didn't *want* to go back," Felicity whispered. Kieran wondered what she was talking about, but now was not the time to ask. "Oh, there's Sarah!"

Sarah Wheeler and Randy Ortega had just come in accompanied by two armed guards. Sarah spotted Felicity and wove through the crowd to give her a brief hug. "We all missed you," she said, but her words were clipped.

"Kieran!" yelled Jamie Peters, a blond little boy who had valiantly cared for his younger brother. "Where are the grown-ups!" His face twisted with intense anxiety, and he tore at his hair with his fingers. "Where's my MOM?"

All the kids turned to look at Kieran. They were in agony. He couldn't make them wait any longer. He walked to the podium with leaden steps. The room quieted as he took his place at the podium and turned on the microphone. "Hello, everyone."

"Where's my mommy!" shouted a little girl who, Kieran knew, had been orphaned. Several other children erupted into tears.

Kieran stared into the audience of hopeful faces, wishing desperately that he could give them what they wanted.

"Your mommy loves you," he managed to say. "Like my dad still loves me."

"Where *is* she?" cried a little boy whose mother had been sucked into space along with Kieran's father.

"She's with my dad," Kieran choked out. "She's watching down on you now."

The little boy looked eagerly up at the ceiling.

"No," Kieran began, but he could only hide his face in his hands. He should be strong enough to do this, but he couldn't lift his head to look at them. He felt a gentle hand on his shoulder, and someone guided him from the podium to sit in the front row. When he looked up, he saw Felicity had draped her arm over him. "Look," she whispered.

"MOMMY!" called a little boy.

There was a great shuffling, and suddenly a cacophony of cries and screams as the children rushed toward the door.

Filing into the room were the forty or so surviving adult crew members from the Empyrean. Children stampeded toward them, arms outstretched, wailing as they were swept into tight hugs. Mothers picked up little girls and twirled them. Fathers knelt down and wrapped their arms around children two and three at a time. Behind them all stood Anne Mather and several of her armed guards. Mather had such a look of tearful joy on her face that Kieran had to look away. He didn't want to believe she was capable of anything other than cold calculation.

He knew he should gather up the children whose parents had not appeared, but something was happening. Regina Marshall had knelt, her hand on the arm of Jamie Peters as she whispered into his ear. He melted onto her, crying helpless tears, and she wrapped him up in her arms. This scene was repeated over and over throughout the room as orphans finally received the news of their parents' passing, one by one, delivered by a loving adult.

Kieran looked at Felicity, who was crying, her blue eyes bloodshot, cheeks blooming pink. He opened his arms to her and held her while she sobbed. Over her shoulder he saw Waverly holding Serafina Mbewe, kissing her plump brown cheeks. Serafina's legs were wrapped around Waverly's waist, her ankles hooked, looking like she never wanted to let go. Waverly looked up and blanched when she saw Kieran with his arms around Felicity. He felt embarrassed, but not enough to let go.

"Murderers," someone muttered. It was Sarah Wheeler, her jaw rigid with fury. Neither her parents, nor Randy's, had survived. Randy was crying openly and without shame, and Sarah rubbed his bulky shoulder with a tenderness Kieran would never have guessed possible for her. But when one of Mather's armed guards walked by them, Sarah narrowed her eyes and shouted, "Murderer!"

Felicity pulled away from Kieran's embrace to watch. The guard, a tall man with a heavy, protruding jaw, rounded on Sarah. The glare he gave her was chilling, and several people took a step away, but Sarah looked up at the man with unvarnished hatred. "How many of our parents did you kill?"

The man made a fist, and he stared, challenging her to keep going.

"How many kids did you *orphan*?" Sarah shouted. More people turned to take in the scene. Randy reached for Sarah's shoulder but she jerked away.

"You're murderers!" Sarah shrieked. She shook from head to toe, and tears spilled down her cheeks. "We should kill you all!"

Randy's eyes widened, but he stood by Sarah, whispering in her ear. She pulled away from him.

"I don't care what he does to me! Let him kill me in front of everyone! Let him show what a murderer he is!"

"I'm warning you." The big guard lifted his fist, uncoiling one finger to point in Sarah's face.

"I've got this, Tom," said a short, stocky guard as he rushed between the big guard and Sarah. Before the man named Tom could react, the smaller guard picked Sarah up by the waist as though she were no heavier than a doll and wrestled her out of the room. She kicked him and scratched at his hands, but he never stopped whispering in her ear, trying to calm her down. The bigger guard seemed annoyed that the other had stepped in, and he clamped a hand on Randy's shoulder to push him ahead, out the door.

"Kill me! Go ahead and kill me! I don't care!" Sarah was screaming in the corridor, and she went on screaming, "I can't live here! I can't! I can't!" Kieran could no longer see her, but he could hear the sobs breaking her down. He'd never liked Sarah Wheeler, but he was filled with hurt for her.

"Kieran," someone said. He turned to see Harvard Stapleton standing by him, the brave man who had run through the Empyrean with Kieran on the day of the initial attack, when all this started. Harvard looked ten years older now, his hair grayed, his skin mottled and sagging, his back bent. "Have you seen Samantha?" he asked, voice wavering. "They said all the kids would be here, but . . ." He looked around the room, his gray-green eyes wide with bewilderment.

"Harvard . . ." Kieran said.

Felicity extended a hand. "Mr. Stapleton. You were always good to me."

"Have you seen Samantha?" he asked her, sounding like a man lost in fog. "I can't find her."

Kieran opened his mouth to speak, but Felicity shook her head. "Mr. Stapleton, she was such a hero. You would have been so proud."

"Where is she?" he begged.

"She gave her life so the little girls could get away." Felicity paused, then straightened her spine and looked him right in the eye. "The guards caught us when we were trying to escape, and one of them shot her."

"Please don't tell me that," the man begged.

"I'm so sorry," Felicity whispered.

"She can't be gone!" he wailed, shoving his fists against his eyes and collapsing onto the floor. Kieran looked on, feeling useless as Felicity knelt by Harvard, her arms on his shoulders, whispering in his ear that it was going to be okay.

But it wasn't.

Kieran remembered his former self, the young man who was so sure he was on a divine mission, that God had everything settled and determined, that he was on the side of Good and Right, and he couldn't fail. He'd thought that horrific catalog of unimaginable loss had to be for some kind of purpose, but now he knew: It meant nothing. All those sermons he'd given were lies, lies he'd told himself because he couldn't heal the destroyed families, the orphaned children, all their futures altered forever. There was no meaning. It was senseless, needless misery and waste.

A cold blackness filled him. He couldn't breathe. His knees buckled, and he knelt down, holding himself up with one hand, staring at his white knuckles as his palm pressed against the frigid metal floor. The awfulness of the last months seeped into his body. He couldn't hold it.

He'd been such a *liar.*

His throat swelled, and he gulped for air, his fist pressed into his abdomen.

A warm hand on the back of his neck.

A warm hand pulling him from the floor.

Mother.

Maya

Seth woke up on a bed—not a hard cot in the brig, not a damp bed of ferns, but a real bed. The last time he'd slept in a bed had been that night in Waverly's apartment when he'd been on the run from Kieran Alden, who had framed him for crimes he didn't commit. That night, Seth had been in physical pain all through his body. Now the agony was located mostly in his mangled hand, which lay over his chest encased in a thickly wrapped bandage.

"You're awake," someone to his left said. He turned to see the shadowy silhouette of a petite woman standing in the lighted doorway. "Mind if I turn on the lights?"

The lights winked on, and as he sat up, he became acquainted with a dull ache in his head he hadn't known was there. He hardly remembered coming here. The guard who had come back for him in the tropics bay had stuffed him into a produce cart, then covered him with mangoes and melons. He remembered being wheeled around for what felt like a long time until Maya whispered, "Hey. Come out of there."

Trying to protect his hand, Seth had pushed his way out of the pile of fruit, then Maya covered him with a hooded jacket and took him to this apartment, where he collapsed onto the bed with hardly a thought for who these people were or what they might do with him.

Maya turned on the light, and Seth shielded his eyes with his good hand. "You slept a long time. You must be hungry?"

Bewildered, he nodded, and she hurried out. He heard plates clanging against each other, smelled the gentle aroma of cooking eggs, and his stomach rumbled.

He looked around the small bedroom. The corner shelves were replete with volumes of poetry and old yellowing magazines from Earth that he guessed must be pretty sought after. The blue striped comforter on his bed was stuffed with warm feathers. Against the wall at the foot of the bed was a hulking rough-hewn wardrobe painted along the sides in a botanical pattern of grapevines and small white blooms. It gave the room a comfy, homey feel.

Maya came back in holding a tray.

"Here we are," she said as she set the rattling tray on his lap and sat down in the chair next to his bed. "I know you didn't have dairy cows on the Empyrean, but I hope you'll like cow's cheese—not too different from goat. And I got some cinnamon rolls from Mrs. Engols down the hall. She's famous for them."

The eggs smelled creamy and rich, and the pastry was so large the edges of it drooped off the plate. "Thanks," Seth said. He dug into his eggs, which were fluffy and delicious, then gulped down some juice that he judged to be a mixture of orange and carrot. He was aware he was eating like an animal, but he was famished. "Thanks," he told her again when he could pause, embarrassed.

When his eating slowed, Maya settled in the chair next to the bed, folding her legs under her. "Why didn't you come on board with the rest of the kids?"

Seth set his cup down. "First you answer questions. Who are you?"

"I'm Maya Draperton," she said testily. "Pleased to meet you. And you're . . . ?"

"Seth Ardvale," he said and launched into what he really wanted to know: "Do you know anything about Waverly Marshall? Is she okay?"

"You know her?" Maya asked, her hand moving over her middle. "Is she a friend of yours?"

"Yes," Seth said eagerly.

"She's on board," Maya said. "That's all I know. I'm sorry."

At least she's here and alive, he told himself, but that did little to quell his worry.

"My turn." Her leg jiggled, making her chair creak. "There are rumors that you caused the explosions on the Empyrean."

He'd been about to take another bite of eggs, but his fork stopped halfway to his mouth, and he set it down. "No," he said quietly.

"You didn't set those bombs?"

"Who started that rumor? Kieran Alden?"

"I don't know who started it. Mrs. Engols, the woman who made that cinnamon roll? She said the *fugitive*"—Maya made quotation marks with her fingers—"was the one who set the bombs."

Suddenly Seth didn't want his food anymore, and he settled back against his pillows. "It isn't true," he said. "The people who set those bombs came from this ship. Jacob Pauley and his wife."

At the mention of these names, Maya sighed, shaking her head.

"You know them?" Seth asked.

"For a while they were celebrities on board. How do *you* know them?"

"I was in the brig with Jake and I pretended to be his friend. I got a little information out of him."

This made her edgy. "Why were you in the brig?"

"I had a problem with Kieran's . . . style of leadership."

"And he put you in prison for it?" Maya asked angrily, suddenly on Seth's side. She was naive, but he liked that about her. He supposed she was a trusting person because she was trustworthy herself, and that made him want to tell her the truth.

"I was no saint," Seth admitted. "I led a mutiny against him. He had reason for doing what he did."

"Did you do anything violent?" Maya asked warily.

"Yes," Seth said quietly. But he reached out toward her, causing the plates on his tray to clang against each other. "Maya, I promise you: I'm no threat to you."

She studied his face. "Okay," she said, but with hesitation.

A knock sounded in the other room.

"Anthony's here," Maya said. "He wants to have a better look at that hand."

Anthony appeared at the door behind her looking warily at Seth through the round wire frames of his glasses. He was small like Seth remembered, but he was in good shape, which gave him a youthful air, despite patches of gray running through his thick dark hair.

"You sure he's safe?" the man said to Maya, appraising Seth with small dark eyes.

"I was about to ask you the same question," Seth said to him.

"I'm Dr. Molinelli." He crossed the room with an officious stride, picked up Seth's bandaged hand, and slowly unwound the wrapping. When his hand emerged, Seth winced at the sight. His fingers were blue, twisted, and swollen beyond recognition. The puncture wound in his pinkie looked red and puffy, and the skin around the edges was whitish. Maya looked at Seth's hand with unabashed horror.

The doctor shook his head. "I'm sorry I couldn't get away sooner."

"Where have you been?" Maya asked, sounding worried.

"I was being debriefed."

"*Again?*" Maya asked, suddenly fearful.

"About being taken hostage." He turned Seth's hand over and looked at the palm, touched the ends of each finger very gently. "They wanted to know all about the girl."

"Waverly?" Maya asked with a glance at Seth.

Seth froze and examined the doctor's face.

"I think Mather wanted me to say she's some kind of violent sociopath," Anthony said.

"And what did you say?" Maya asked.

"I said she's no sociopath, but . . ." With an uneasy glance at Seth, Anthony continued, "she's unstable."

"Is that your professional opinion?" Maya asked.

"It's my opinion as the poor bastard she nearly killed," Anthony snapped.

There was an uncomfortable pause, but Maya said quietly, "The poor girl was looking for her mother. She was desperate."

"She didn't have to shoot at me."

"She didn't. You said yourself. She aimed at the wall above you."

"I still pissed myself," Anthony said sharply, and Maya closed her mouth.

"Where is Waverly?" Seth asked through a groan. The pain as Anthony touched his hand, however gently, was making him weak.

"I don't know anything about where she is now," Anthony said. "She's a friend of yours?"

"If she is," Seth countered, "would that change how you treat my hand?"

"Not a bit," he said, but the needle he removed from his bag seemed inordinately long. He punctured a vial of liquid and drew in a huge amount of medicine.

"What's that for?" Seth said, apprehensive.

"You're going to feel a pinch." Anthony plunged the needle into Seth's wrist, and he cried out in surprise. "I'd rather do this in an operating room."

Seth watched the doctor's face. "Am I going to lose some fingers?"

"Not if I can help it."

"Comforting."

"You're weak, from malnutrition and exhaustion, I'd guess," the man said dispassionately as his eyes traveled over Seth's bony shoulders. Seth didn't contradict him. He tapped Seth's hand. "Feel that?"

Seth shook his head no.

"I'm squeamish," Maya said. She gave Seth an apologetic smile and hurried out of the room.

"Okay. I'm going to straighten these out for you." Before Seth had a chance to speak, Anthony took hold of his mangled pinkie and wrenched it into a straight position. Seth instinctively pulled away, but Anthony clamped onto his wrist and straightened out the ring finger more quickly than Seth could react. His hand was numb, but a ghostly ache rippled up his arm.

"I'm sorry," Anthony said as he smeared an orange ointment over the puncture wound in Seth's pinkie. "In an operating room I could've knocked you out."

"It wasn't too bad," Seth said weakly.

"That puncture is small, but it's inflamed. I'm not going to take chances. One quickie ought to do it." From his bag Anthony took a small curved needle and a short piece of black thread. Working quickly, he tied a single stitch in Seth's skin, closing the wound. Seth was surprised that this didn't hurt at all. Next Anthony held Seth's fingers against a splint, fastened them in place with white tape, and finally wrapped the entire hand in a thick padding of protective bandage. "Tell Maya if it starts to feel tight. She'll find me."

"I will," Seth said.

From his bag Anthony pulled a small bottle of little white pills and held them up. "Antibiotics. You *must* take one twice daily with food until they're all gone."

"Thank you."

"This is *important*." He squinted sternly through his pert glasses. "We've got a drug-resistant bug going around. The infection in your pinkie is small now, but if it grows, you could lose your finger. These pills will keep it attached."

"You guys all done?" Maya asked as she came back in, smiling weakly at Seth.

"He needs lots of good food and a couple weeks of rest," Anthony told her. "Sound good?" he asked Seth.

"Yeah," Seth said, grateful. Months in the brig had taken a toll on his health. Odd that he had to go to the enemy ship to get help. "Thanks."

"Just doing my job," Anthony said.

"I mean . . ." Seth pointed at the man's knee where he'd injured himself to cover for Seth. "Thanks."

"Oh. Well . . ." Anthony ducked his head, embarrassed. "I'll be back tomorrow to check on that hand."

"See you tomorrow," Maya whispered in the man's ear. Though he wasn't a tall man, she had to stand on her tiptoes to kiss him. He nodded at Seth, then left.

"He's a good guy," Maya said with a broad, lovely smile. Her teeth looked jumbled together, but the imperfection made her smile engaging and sweet. She seemed to consider something, then stood resolutely, her hand on the large wooden wardrobe Seth had noticed. "I inherited this piece of furniture from my grandmother. It was in our ancestral home in Massachusetts, on the Underground Railroad. Know it?"

"They used to smuggle escaped slaves into Canada," Seth said.

"For that, they needed tricky furniture, like this." She opened the wardrobe door and pushed on the back panel, which gave way easily to reveal a surprisingly roomy compartment. "See? It's a false back here. You hear anyone come into the apartment, get in. Okay?"

Seth studied her. "Why are you helping me?"

Maya sat in the chair next to his bed, leaning her elbows on her knee. "Because Anne Mather is looking for you. And I don't like Anne Mather. Neither does Anthony."

Seth nodded, taking another bite of the cinnamon roll. "Why not?"

"Mostly because of what she did to your families."

"Why should you care about what she did to us?" Seth eyed her. "We're your enemies, aren't we?"

"That might have been true before Waverly and the rest of the girls came aboard. When we saw the way Anne Mather exploited them, attitudes started to change."

"Oh yeah?" Seth asked. He watched her for any sign of pretense, but she seemed totally straightforward. "That didn't stop people from taking their eggs."

"Actually, that played a part in changing people's minds," she said. "Waverly and the other girls helped us make our babies. Our children will come from them."

"Okay," Seth said slowly.

"So in a way, Waverly and the rest of the girls are family to us. That means Anne Mather hurt our families."

Something in her voice gave Seth pause. "*Our* families?"

Maya hesitated briefly, smoothing the fabric of her tunic over her middle before finally saying, "I'm pregnant with one of Waverly's embryos."

The glass on his tray began to rattle against his stoneware plate; he was trembling. His gaze dropped to Maya's middle, and he saw that her tunic had camouflaged a small bump. He blanched and pushed the tray off his legs. Maya darted forward to catch it.

"Please," he said. "I need to be alone."

She stood over him, holding the tray, an expression of sorrow on her face. "I'm sorry," she mumbled and shuffled out.

Seth cradled his hand to his chest. He wanted Waverly so badly then, just to hold her. Just to hold.

Duel

Waverly had hardly slept since that awful reunion with the Empyrean kids. The way Serafina had clung to her, arms and legs wrapped around her, broke her heart. *I let her down,* she realized. *I was her babysitter before. I should have taken care of her, but I was too wrapped up in my own problems to think about her.* Afterward, she'd asked the guard outside her door if she could visit Serafina and the rest of the kids, but he'd flatly refused, and she'd slunk to her bed, feeling defeated.

She hated herself even more for the petty jealousy that haunted her. The way Kieran had held Felicity, his hands spread over the small of her back, his face in her abundant blond hair—that was how he'd always held Waverly, before. He could have sought Waverly out, wrapped his arms around her and held on, but he hadn't. He'd chosen Felicity, and though Waverly knew she had no claim on him anymore, it still hurt. Seeing this proof that Kieran had moved on had brought a debilitating homesickness down on her. Not homesickness for the Empyrean, though she missed her home with every part of her. It was homesickness for the past, for her old self, for her mother, and for Kieran the way she used to know him.

For the last several days, she'd given in to her depression, had hidden in her room, head under the covers, her mother bringing trays of food and taking them away barely touched. She was waiting.

She knew Mather would come for her. It was in the woman's DNA to invade, meddle, control. So when the knock came at the front door, Waverly jerked in her bed, listening to her mother greet the holy Pastor with utmost deference. Sighing, Waverly reached for a black cardigan that had been left in her bedroom closet along with a full wardrobe of the simple, somber clothes that people wore on this ship. She slipped it on and looked at herself in the oblong mirror hanging on her bedroom door. She didn't know the girl in the drab shift standing there with the ratty brown hair and the haunted eyes. Too thin, too pale, too wispy. Weak.

"Waverly!" her mother called from the living room.

She took a deep breath, walked the length of the hall, and found Anne Mather in the doorway, two armed men behind her. They held their guns across their chests, their eyes on Waverly.

"Hello," Mather said, betraying a nervousness in the quick movements of her hands that Waverly had never seen before.

Waverly did not return the greeting. She stood in the middle of the living room with her hands at her sides, waiting.

"I thought you might join me for a pot of tea and some treats?"

"I don't suppose I can refuse," Waverly said with a glance at the guards.

"You absolutely *can* refuse," Mather said. "I want a fresh start with you. That means you're free."

"Except for the guard posted outside my door," Waverly rejoined with a look at the snide, balding man she'd come to despise.

Mather dropped a beat. "Yes. I do need to worry about the safety of my crew."

"And your own safety."

"Yes." Mather flicked her chin up defiantly. "Well? Will you come?"

A small part of her was curious about what Mather had to say, so she kissed her mother, strode out the door past the armed men, and headed toward the elevators.

Mather caught up with her, stooped, struggling to keep pace. *She's short*, Waverly realized. She'd never thought of the woman's height before. Mather had always seemed beyond physical considerations, but now she looked small and weak. Maybe what Dr. Carver told Waverly was true: The Pastor was losing her grip.

Mather's office looked different since the last time Waverly was here, more disordered, like a war room. Papers were spread across her desk, and she quickly stacked them on a credenza in the corner. A woman carried in a tray laden with tea, biscuits, and fruit preserves, and nodded when the Pastor thanked her.

"Have what you like," Mather said, pouring herself a cup of tea. Waverly noticed that it was black tea instead of the chamomile Mather had always drunk before. Waverly refused any food or drink and sat in the soft chair across the desk from Mather, who sipped at her dainty teacup.

"Is Sarah Wheeler okay?" Waverly asked. She'd been worried about Sarah ever since she'd been dragged out of the central bunker by Mather's thugs. "And Randy Ortega?"

"Sarah . . . is she the one who caused the scene at the Empyrean reunion?"

"More like she suffered a breakdown."

Mather nodded sadly. "The poor girl has been through too much. She's being treated for depression now, along with her friend."

"With drugs?" Waverly asked. Is that what they'd done to her mother?

"Gentle ones," Mather said. "Harmless."

"Where are they?"

"I'll look into that for you," Mather said, but the disingenuous look of concern on her face made Waverly think the woman knew very well where Sarah was.

She wants to keep us separated, Waverly thought angrily.

"Well. How is your mother?"

"She's very . . . changed," Waverly said with quiet fury. "I know you're drugging her somehow. Why haven't you drugged me?"

"Drugs? No." Mather wrinkled her brow thoughtfully. "Your parents staged a hunger strike for a period of weeks before our rendezvous. It's likely your mother was weakened by it. A period of reduced calories can have an effect on the brain."

The assured way Mather told this obvious lie was the final insult. Waverly stared at her, so angry she imagined the liquid coating over her eyes boiling away.

"Knock, knock," someone called from the doorway.

Waverly turned to see the decrepit old man, Dr. Carver, standing there, his hands grasping his cane with what looked like preternatural strength.

"Hello, Doctor," Mather said with reserved politeness, though she looked discomfited.

"This is the famous Waverly Marshall, I presume?" the doctor said, looking Waverly up and down as though he'd never seen her before.

"Haven't you two met?" Mather asked with a tilt of her head.

The doctor hobbled in, leaning heavily on his cane, which was beautifully carved into the shape of two snakes intertwined, one white, one black. He extended a knobby hand. "I'm Dr. Carver," he said. "Pleased to finally meet you in person."

After a brief recovery from her surprise, Waverly shook his hand. "Hello."

"I heard you two were meeting this morning, so I dropped by, unable to control my curiosity." He motioned a hand for Waverly to move to the next chair. His imperious manner demanded immediate compliance, and she found herself obeying. He lowered himself gingerly into her vacated chair. "I've heard so much about you, Waverly, I wanted to come and see you for myself." His eyes twinkled as though he were enjoying a private joke with her.

"Tea?" Mather asked him with controlled courtesy.

He shook his head. "My old stomach can't take more than lemon water these days," he said. "Thank you."

"We were just talking about the hunger strike."

"Oh yes," the man said with a kindly chuckle. "I know you lost some sleep over that one, Pastor!"

"But we finally resolved it," Mather said cheerfully. "When they learned we were on a rendezvous course with the Empyrean, they started eating again. Thank goodness."

Waverly noticed the way Mather's gray eyes darted over the frail doctor. *She's afraid of him*, Waverly realized.

"So, Waverly," Dr. Carver said with a gleeful tap on the handle of his cane. "How are you liking your new life in the bosom of your enemy?"

Waverly stared at the old man with no idea of how to answer.

"Come, now. You must have thoughts on the matter."

"Doctor," Mather broke in, tapping a pen furtively on her desktop. "I'm not sure stirring up past resentments is the right way to build trust with Waverly."

"Resentments?" the old man said, his gaze trailing over the woven tapestry that hung on the wall behind Mather. "Is that how you'd put it?"

The Pastor looked at him, cowed.

"What word would you use, Waverly?" the man said quietly. "War crimes?"

"Atrocities," Waverly whispered, her sudden rage choking her. "Monstrosities."

Mather smoothed her smock with trembling hands.

"Come now, Pastor," the old man said. "You must embrace your mistakes to embrace your enemy."

"All right," Mather said quietly, looking at the old man first, then at Waverly. "You're right. What I did to you and your families was . . ."

"Unforgivable," the old man said.

"Yes," Mather replied, before Waverly could say anything.

"So how do we move on from here?" the old man asked Waverly.

Mather opened her mouth to speak, but Dr. Carver held up a hand to silence her, and to Waverly's astonishment, Mather obeyed.

"Waverly?" He looked at her expectantly. "What do you feel would make life bearable for you and the rest of the Empyrean refugees?"

"She would have to go on trial," Waverly said evenly, wondering if he actually had the power to make that happen. During her captivity on this ship, she'd thought the church elders were beholden to Mather for their power, but she was beginning to wonder if it was the other way around. "The Pastor and all her thugs would have to be punished."

"You mean to send them to the brig?" he asked. "Or perhaps you mean for the Pastor . . . to be executed?"

Waverly stared at Mather, unflinching.

"Listen, now," Mather began, holding up a hand.

"So you see, Pastor?" said the old man. "Your idea that we can all live on this ship as one big happy family is perhaps . . ." He waved a talon in the air, searching for a word. "Unrealistic?"

"No," the Pastor said. All the fear left her face, and she looked doggedly at Dr. Carver. "I don't believe that. Peace is always the better alternative."

"A rather odd thing to say," the old man said, "coming from the architect of the Empyrean Massacre."

"You're the one who wanted the rendezvous," Mather shot at him.

He waved a languid hand. "A meeting is what I wanted."

"*You* suggested the nebula. To surprise them."

"I raised many concerns about your plans. You assured us there would be minimal loss of life."

"Things did not go as expected."

"Ah yes. The fog of war." He chuckled. "Invoked by many a war criminal."

Waverly could not believe her ears. She watched the old man's profile as he sat back in his chair, grilling Mather ruthlessly, calmly, taking in every twitch and squirm as the woman shrank under his attack.

"What matters now is the future," Mather offered.

"Not to Waverly," the old man said. He turned to her, lifted his chin, waiting.

"You need to answer for what you did," Waverly said to Mather.

Mather stuck out her chin. "What about what your crew did to us?"

"Ah!" The doctor was shifting in his seat back and forth, as though he were at a sporting event. "Go on."

"Captain Jones and your . . . his scientists destroyed our fertility," Mather said, her strength restored.

"They paid for it with their lives," Waverly said. "What more do you want?"

"What?" The doctor looked at Mather. "Does the girl not know?"

Mather shook her head, barely perceptibly, but the doctor ignored her. "Your Captain is alive, Waverly."

Waverly felt as though the wind had been knocked from her body. When she looked at Mather, she saw the woman glaring at the old man as though plotting his murder. He stared back at her, fearless.

Waverly finally started to believe at least part of what the doctor had said. He wanted to topple Anne Mather. Judging from the way Mather was watching him, beads of sweat moistening the small hairs on her upper lip, he'd already begun.

Waverly looked at the old man sitting next to her, his maleficent glare, the way his fingers dug like claws into the wooden arms of his chair. Like it or not, whoever he was, Waverly had just cast her lot with him.

"Waverly," the old man said as he struggled out of his chair, "I wonder if you'd lend me an arm."

Waverly stood, feeling awkward under the watchful glare of Anne Mather, and took hold of his elbow. Under the rough fabric of his woven jacket, his arm felt surprisingly alive with wiry strength. "Good-bye, Anne," he said as he straightened his back and looked down at her in triumph.

"Good-bye, Wesley," Mather muttered. Her fear seemed to have left her, and she looked at him with a loathing that seemed rooted in a great deal of time and experience.

Waverly walked out with the old man, acutely aware of his thumbnail, thickened and discolored, as it dug into the flesh of her elbow. He steered her toward the elevators, holding up a single finger to the armed guards who started to follow them. To Waverly's surprise, the men went back to stand outside Mather's office door.

The old man said nothing, seeming to wait for Waverly to speak. "Have you found out anything about what's wrong with my mom?" she finally asked.

"I have." Carver glanced at her with jiggling red eyeballs. "As far as I understand, most of the Empyrean crew has been medically lobotomized."

With her free hand, Waverly wrapped her sweater around herself more tightly. "What does that mean, exactly?"

"A lobotomy severs the connection between the prefrontal cortex and the rest of the brain."

"*What?*" she shrieked just as they passed an open office door. A red-haired man seated at the desk looked up irritably from his portable reader.

"I said it was done *medically.*" He held up a finger, then pressed the elevator call button. "*Medicinally.*"

"With drugs," she said softly. "So it's reversible?"

"I might be able to design an antidote, given the right incentives."

Waverly wished she could pull her arm away from him. "Why didn't Mather do that to me?"

Carver smiled with half his face so that he looked distorted, as though she were watching him through a vortex. "She still might, I suppose. Unless you do something to stop her."

Waverly pressed her free hand into the pit of her stomach. "I feel sick."

"I don't blame you," the man said, feigning sympathy, though he looked delighted. "Don't you see, Waverly, why I want to put an end to these monstrosities? Don't you see how much we need you?"

The elevator bell sounded, and the doors slid open. From inside came three pregnant women dressed in farm coveralls, giggling together.

"You say you might be able to design an antidote? For my mom, and the others?"

He raised an eyebrow. "Depends."

"On what?"

"On you, Waverly. Anne Mather would hardly let me reanimate her flock of tamed doves if she remains in power. But if you give us the testimony we need . . ."

"Okay," she finally said. "All right. I'll do it."

"Good." He let go of her arm, and as she stepped onto the elevator, she felt the blood rushing into her fingertips.

He blocked the elevator door with his cane as he beckoned Mather's guards. They rushed to comply and stepped onto the elevator with Waverly. The doctor turned his back on her before the elevator doors closed.

The Devil You Know

Kieran had just finished shaving, a ritual he still performed though it seemed poignantly futile. He was still haunted by the reunion of the Empyrean children, unable to sleep, hating himself for being unable to help the orphans. As a leader, he was a complete failure. He rinsed his razor in the steaming water, then turned off the faucet. In the quiet, he heard laughter coming from the living room. Someone was here.

He opened the bathroom door to find his mother sitting with Felicity on the large orange couch, eating cookies and drinking fruit juice. Felicity had made his mother laugh, a lightweight giggle he hadn't heard in months, and Felicity smiled in a way that made her cheeks glow. When she noticed him standing in the doorway, she stood. "Kieran!"

"Hi, Felicity," he said and tripped on his own feet as he left the bathroom. He wanted to ask what she was doing here, but he couldn't think how without sounding rude.

"Do you remember that dance recital we were in together when we were little?" She asked. "I think we were . . ."

She looked at Kieran's mother, who said, "No more than seven."

"We were square dancing, and you and I knocked heads during the do-si-do?"

"I felt really bad about that," Kieran said, wincing at the memory.

"You helped me off the floor," Felicity said, her bright eyes wandering over his face. "You were always a gentleman. Even back then."

"He's a good boy," Lena said, smiling at her son. Talking about the old days had done her some good, Kieran could see. Her amber eyes glowed in a way he hadn't seen since before the initial attack, and she looked relaxed and easy in Felicity's company. "I'll leave you two alone," she said as she stood up. "Sit down, Kieran."

Kieran had never felt so awkward as he stumbled toward the couch, minutely aware that Felicity was watching him. Her eyelashes were blond, he realized as he took his seat next to her. He'd never noticed that. And her eyebrows were a shade darker than her light blond hair. His face burned as he realized he was staring, and he turned away to pour himself a glass of juice. He took a few sips to calm himself, but he hardly tasted it.

He was embarrassed to have Felicity see the opulent surroundings Mather had provided for him. A large oval porthole behind the couch where she sat showed a view of the galaxy, and the spacious living room was lavishly decorated with paintings and objets d'art. A thick rug in an ancient Persian design lay diagonally on the floor, leading the eye toward the bright kitchen and dining area. His own bedroom was even worse, with satin sheets, down pillows, and an original painting by Kandinsky hanging on the wall. As soon as he'd seen this place, he'd known Mather must be buttering him up for something, and it made him feel dirty to live here. Now, seeing it all through Felicity's eyes, he felt even worse.

"Pastor Mather is sending me around to Empyrean survivors,"

Felicity said, having recognized the question in his eyes. "I'm kind of an ambassador, I guess."

"Oh," Kieran said. "Because you've been here so long."

"I've 'successfully assimilated' is how she put it," Felicity said, not without bitter irony. She looked him over with frank concern. "How are you?"

"I'm fine. Of course. Just fine."

"Really?" She raised one eyebrow, her eyes moving from his tense mouth to his fidgeting fingers.

He laughed. "Don't look so skeptical."

"I won't, if you'll tell me the truth."

He leaned back into the couch cushions. Her candor stripped away his thin layer of pretense, and all the devastation of the past week flooded through him. *I'm not fine. How can I ever be fine again?* He didn't want to cry in front of her, but he couldn't speak without crying, so he said nothing.

"I'm sorry, Kieran," she whispered. "About everything."

"You lost everything, too," he managed to say.

"I've had more time to come to terms with it," she said with a sad smile. "I knew when I got off Waverly's escape shuttle all those months ago that I'd probably never see my family again."

He studied her. She'd lowered her face so that her golden hair hid her profile, but he could see in her weighted posture that she felt the loss of their home, too. "Why *didn't* you come back with Waverly?"

She sighed, long and heavy. "It's not always easy . . ." She stopped to laugh at herself, shaking her head.

"What?"

"I don't know how this will sound . . ."

"Go ahead," he prodded.

"It's not always easy . . ." She paused and raked her hair with her fingers. "Looking the way I do. I stand out. I always have. My hair, my eyes. People comment. And for someone shy like me, who doesn't like to be noticed . . ."

Kieran remembered when Felicity was just starting to bloom

into womanhood, Captain Jones had walked into their physics class to speak briefly with their teacher, and on his way out his eyes had wandered over Felicity in a way that Kieran hadn't understood. She had drooped under his leer, hiding behind her hair, back bent to make herself small. In fact, she was sitting that same way now.

"On the Empyrean," she said, looking at her hands, "I couldn't always escape the looks, or . . ." She swallowed as though she felt sick. "Or the hands."

He wanted to touch her then, a reassuring hand on her shoulder, but nothing could be more inappropriate.

"Here," she said, straightening up as though throwing off the memories, "people still look, and they comment. But it doesn't feel so . . ." She sucked in a breath and finally brought her eyes up to his. He could see her lashes were wet. "Predatory."

"Felicity . . ."

"I always wondered why they chose me and not Waverly."

"You can't think like that," he said to her, and this time he did touch her very briefly on the shoulder. "You're not responsible for someone else being a pig."

She smiled then. "You're right. I know it. I just don't know it all the way yet."

He watched her, wishing he knew how far it had gone, how much she'd suffered, but she'd said as much as she wanted to and pushing her wouldn't be fair. So he sat next to her, holding his cup of juice, looking out the porthole at the stars.

"I'm also supposed to extend an invitation," she said. "The Pastor would like you to come visit her this morning, if you're up to it."

"Visit," he said with an angry laugh.

"She claims it's your choice," Felicity said. "She told me your guards would escort you to her office."

"Now?"

"I think so, yes," Felicity said. She seemed as puzzled by the invitation as he was.

"Should I go?"

"What's the saying?" She set her juice down and stood up. Was she leaving already? He stood, too. "Know your enemy."

He nodded, confused.

"I'd better go," she said as she backed away from him. "I've got lots of stops to make."

"Okay," he said, but he didn't want her to leave. "Will you come back?"

She smiled, gave a single nod. "Sure."

He walked her to the door and, as he leaned to open it for her, became aware of a light fragrance of crushed rose petals that permeated her hair. He breathed it in as she walked past him and out the door.

The guard standing outside his door jerked his head toward the elevator. "Ready?"

Kieran angrily followed the man to the elevator, staring with loathing at the bald spot on the back of his head. Would he always be surrounded by men with guns?

"Thank you for coming on such short notice," Mather said, standing up from her desk chair as he hesitated outside her office.

With a half glance over his shoulder at the guard who brought him, Kieran stepped into the woman's office and took the chair she offered. The guard stayed just outside the door, his hand on the butt of his gun. Mather smoothed her tunic with hands that fluttered over the fabric as though looking for a safe place to land. They finally settled, fingers woven, on the desk before her. *She looks like a helpless grandmother,* he thought, *but that's not what she is.*

"Tea?" Before he could answer, she poured a steaming cup and handed it to him. "It must be nice to be with your mother again."

"No," he said, slicing a hand through the air in front of her nose. "Mom's acting crazy, and I want to know what's wrong with her."

"I was worried about that." Mather frowned with concern. "She suffered a rapid decompression and had some bleeding in the brain, in her frontal lobes. The doctors warned there might be lasting effects, but since she retained all of her higher functions, we thought she'd come through unscathed."

Kieran studied her carefully, looking for some chink in her armor, but she met his eyes with what looked like real sympathy. He still might not believe it if he hadn't seen it happen to her himself, that first day. He and his mother had both been in the shuttle bay when Mather's crew had rigged the huge air-lock doors to open and decompress that part of the ship. Kieran had barely gotten away with his life and had watched as his mother struggled into a shuttle to escape the vacuum of space.

"So the damage will be permanent?" he asked, fighting tears.

"I'll send a doctor to take a look at her," Mather said gently. "Okay?"

Determined not to be grateful, Kieran looked out the porthole so he wouldn't have to look at her. He could still see the Empyrean from here, though Mather must have turned the New Horizon because his home ship was much farther away now, its giant wound no longer bleeding gas and water vapor. So it was over. The Empyrean had no atmosphere. Those poor goats and sheep and fish. Poor chickens. Poor Arthur. Poor Sarek . . .

"You shouldn't have sent that lunatic," he said to Mather through gritted teeth. He remembered the man who destroyed his home—Jacob Pauley—the brutish size of him, his calloused hands, the simple expression in his piggish eyes.

"I didn't send him. There was too much chaos during Waverly's escape for me to come up with anything like a plan."

"Then why was he contacting you?"

She picked up a pen and played with the cap, pulling it off, screwing it back on. "I believe he wanted to brag."

"After the way you attacked us, why should I believe anything you say?"

"When I became Captain, the church elders pointed out that the nebula would be the only place we could hope to get near the Empyrean. What choices were left to us, Kieran? We were facing extinction! What would you have done?"

Kieran didn't want to get sucked into this game.

"I want you to consider something." She fingered the padded arm of her chair, picking at the fabric with an oval fingernail. "You were the leader of the Empyrean for a few short months, were you not?"

"Yes." Kieran sighed. Why couldn't he wake up from this nightmare?

"Did you never cross the line yourself?"

"You mean did I kill anyone?" he asked angrily.

"Tell any lies? Compromise your morals? To get yourself out of a tight spot?"

Kieran tried to be impervious to what she was saying, but his mind picked at the time he'd told his crew that Seth Ardvale had turned traitor and was working with the terrorist Jacob Pauley, a statement Kieran had known to be untrue. Was he really in a position to judge Anne Mather?

I never killed anyone, he reminded himself, *but to get Mom back in one piece, with her brains right? I would. I'd kill this liar with my bare hands.*

"What do you want?" he spat. He felt he was in a trap, but he couldn't see the walls or feel the chains, as though Mather had somehow gotten him to lock himself in.

The smile faded from her lips. "What do you mean?"

"You're not making friends with me because you're lonely. There's some reason you're cozying up to me."

She pinched the end of her index finger as she considered him. "Okay, Kieran. The truth is, I've lost some credibility with my people. I've given them everything they wanted, but their enthusiasm for my leadership has faded."

"They probably think you're a hypocrite," Kieran spat.

"Maybe I am a hypocrite. Does that satisfy you?" she snapped. "I've racked my brain trying to think of a way to unite our two crews. You've been a leader through dangerous times. You understand the need for a common purpose." She bobbed her head at him, willing him to agree. "I believe you and I can work together to bring peace to our people. We both have a duty to make certain that our crews can live together safely. Can you agree to that?"

He didn't want to work with this despicable woman. But was there any other way to protect the Empyrean crew? He nodded and made himself say, "I can agree in principle."

"I want you to help me lead them to peace." She appeared absolutely earnest.

The room was so quiet he heard the air moving through his nostrils as he studied her. "Do you expect me to believe that you're offering me power on this vessel?"

"Not right away," she said, a hand held up to slow him down. "As a *start*, for now, I'm offering you *influence*. Your influence will be unavoidable, actually."

"What are you saying?"

"I want you to come to services this Sunday so I can introduce you to my congregation. Eventually, you could become a kind of junior pastor. And when I'm either ousted, or . . ." She waved a hand grimly. "You'll be poised to take over as the pastor and hopefully captain of the New Horizon."

For long moments all he could do was stare at her before he said, "Is this a joke?"

She smiled indulgently. "I assure you I'm serious."

"I don't see why you want *me*."

"*Don't* you see? After what Jacob Pauley and his wife did to your ship? The only way to incorporate your crew into ours is to give a representative from your vessel a leadership position here."

Kieran started to shake his head. This was a trick. It had to be.

She placed her palm on the desk between them. "Kieran. Think about it. My generation is aging. Your parents' generation has been at war, with a long list of grievances on both sides." She pointed a finger at him urgently. "Your generation can give us a fresh start. And if you haven't noticed, there aren't many of you. Given how remarkably well you've done on the Empyrean, you're the logical choice to take this crew forward when my time comes to step down."

Kieran looked at Mather's large desk, the way the intercom rested within a hand's breadth of her seat, the artful tapestries hanging behind her. He'd never imagined himself in the Captain's chair of the New Horizon. Was God working through Mather, trying to reach him? Had this been the plan all along to unite the two crews under one banner of leadership? He shied away from these ideas. This kind of thinking had gotten him in trouble before.

"We'll have to play our cards right," she was saying. "The church elders no longer believe that a faith-based government can peacefully lead a blended crew. They are actively working to minimize the political power of any pastor on this vessel." She tented her fingers, staring at him over the steeple shapes of her hands. "I'm convinced they want to enforce atheism. We can't let them destroy our faith."

"Which would destroy you, too," he pointed out.

She nodded, not even trying to hide her fear. "I want to use what's left of my leadership to shape the path forward. Despite my mistakes, I believe I'm the only person who can." Mather raised her eyebrows. "Will you join me?"

"If I don't?"

"You and your crew will become a powerless minority."

"Then I have no choice, do I?"

"Get used to it. The longer a leader is in power, the fewer choices we have. What do you say? Can we learn to work together?"

Kieran took in a long breath through his nose. He felt as though he were about to plunge off a cliff. "All right," he said quietly, hating himself. "I'll work with you."

"Thank you," she said, looking visibly relieved. Her com station beeped, and she read a short text from someone.

"I'll have a guard escort you back," she said, raising her finger, indicating for him to leave.

"I can find my own way, " Kieran said to test her.

She contrived a quick smile. "I'll contact you later, then."

"All right," Kieran said and walked out the door, right past her guards and down the hallway. As he passed by Central Command, the door slid open, revealing, for just a moment, the empty Captain's chair.

Spies

On the Empyrean, Arthur Dietrich crouched, hidden inside a ventilation duct, watching the crew chief from the New Horizon do his work. Arthur was sweating profusely, so his glasses kept sliding down his nose. He pushed them up with his knuckle, afraid even the faint rustle of his shirt sleeve would give him away. He'd been hiding here for nearly a full day, his only protection a flimsy vent screen. He was thirsty and starving and his back hurt him horribly, but he had no idea what they would do to him if he were caught, so he stayed put.

For most of the morning, Central Command had been bustling with activity, but most of the crew had left for maintenance tasks in various parts of the ship. Right now there was only one man here—the crew chief named Chris. He sat at Arthur's old post near the Captain's chair, using Arthur's old com screen.

"Pressure in the conifer bay is still dropping," Chris was saying into his headset. Everything about the man was square shaped—his shoulders, his blockish head, his cropped haircut, his jawline, his big meaty hands. "There must be at least one more pinhole in the bulkhead."

"My sensors aren't picking it up," said a woman over the com system. Her voice had the muffled quality of someone speaking from inside a OneMan.

"Okay, then, Marcy. I'll need you to go outside and look for it from there."

"There's no air lock between here and outside. I'd have to go all the way around, through the orchards, and then up through the hatchery."

"I know," Chris said. "Some of those trees might be the last of their kind in the universe."

"Thanks for the guilt trip, Chris."

"Sure thing," Chris rejoined before sitting back in his chair, rubbing his palms on his knees.

You're thirsty, Arthur thought at him. *You need to go to the bathroom! You need to leave! Go!*

But Chris started flicking through options on his com screen before holding the mouthpiece to his chin. "Hello, there, Greg. You in yet?"

From the other end came what sounded like a group of children moaning. Arthur stifled a gasp. He thought he and Sarek had gotten all the children off the Empyrean! "Yeah, Chris," a man answered, "we're in."

"How are they looking?"

"Skinny. We've got several goners, but most of them seem healthy enough."

Arthur shoved his fist in his mouth to keep himself quiet.

"Can you make a path to the granaries? Let them graze in there?"

Arthur suppressed a sigh of relief. Those weren't children crying;

they were goats and sheep! He was surprised any of them were still alive.

"We're already working on it. We've just got to fix a fist-size hole in the bulkhead to pressurize the corridor. Should take an hour or two."

"Those animals don't sound happy. Is the water system working?"

"By drips and drops, Chris. And someone left a whole mound of hay in here. I think that's what's kept them alive this long."

"Okay. Well, get to work."

"Will do, boss," the other man said, and after a brief burst of static, the link was severed.

Chris was silent for a long while, tapping at a keyboard, then started flipping through video views of the ship, but he paused at one screen and leaned in for a closer look. Arthur could see only about half of the screen from around the man's shoulder, but it looked like the corridor outside the infirmary. There was no light whatsoever coming from inside. Next Chris flicked to a display for the sensor readings.

"Hey, Greg," he said into his headset. "Where are you?"

"I'm knee-deep in chicken crap, Chris."

"You're a couple levels under the infirmary, right?"

"Yeah."

"Have you detected any signs of decompression on that side of the ship? Any pinholes?"

"Nah," Greg said. "So far so good here. But the infirmary's been showing no signs of life support, right?"

"Right," Chris said thoughtfully and peered closely at the screen.

Arthur racked his brain. Had Sarek evacuated the infirmary? He must have!

"You want me tracking chicken crap all the way up there, Chris? Because when I say knee-deep . . ."

"Nah," Chris responded and flicked through different displays, all of them showing stats on the infirmary level. "Low priority. I'll put it on our to-do list, okay?"

"Yeah, Chris. Put it at the bottom."

Chris sighed, rubbing the back of his neck, and then to Arthur's great delight, he stood up from his chair. Arthur was surprised to find that though Chris was broad and strong-looking, he was actually quite short.

"Got to see what's doing," Chris muttered to himself, patting his belly as he limped out the door in the stiff way of an adult who had sat for too long.

Arthur listened for a minute more, but he was too thirsty to wait any longer. He worked the ventilation screen out of its casing and wriggled onto the floor of Central Command.

Hiding in that cramped space had been horrible, but he'd been lucky to make it into the duct before Chris and his helpers had come in that morning earlier than usual. Arthur had had just enough time to back his way into the duct and pull the grate in after him. There he'd sat, all day long.

Now Arthur's back complained painfully as he stretched. He could hardly stay on his feet, he was so stiff. He reminded himself of his father, the way Hans Dietrich was always a little hunched from working into the wee hours on his various projects. This brought a pang of guilt to Arthur's middle. *Dad probably thinks I'm dead. Mom...* He wouldn't let himself finish the thought. His mother's name hadn't been on the list of survivors on the New Horizon, and there had been no video from her among the communiqués from the captured Empyrean crew. She was probably gone, but he couldn't allow the thought into his conscious mind.

Arthur missed his parents with every part of him. Once upon a time he'd felt smothered by his mother, but now he'd give anything for more of her tireless love. His father was even dearer to him. He would let Arthur stay up late reading to indulge his interests in writers like Proust, Hawking, and Goethe. The two would spend hours talking about existentialism, quantum mechanics, or the ancient Greeks. What Arthur learned during his time in classes was minuscule compared to what he absorbed on a daily basis from his brilliant father. There was no one in Arthur's life he enjoyed talking with as much as his dad. He had to get him back. And maybe his mother *was* still alive on the New Horizon . . .

He was tempted to hack into the com system to see what he could find out, but he didn't dare linger. He'd come to do one simple thing and get out, and that's what he had to do now. From his pocket he pulled a walkie-talkie and knelt under the com desk that Chris used. It was a simple matter of hooking the unit into a power source, then connecting the transmitter up to the audio signal that came through the computer. Once it was in place, Sarek and Arthur would be able to monitor all the voice communications that went through Central Command. Arthur was just finishing wrapping electrical tape around the loose wires when he heard Chris's voice in the corridor outside.

"I know that, George," Chris was saying, "but the Pastor wants us to secure that equipment first."

Arthur stood to look at the video screen that monitored the corridor. Chris was holding a small tray of emergency rations, standing just on the other side of the door.

Arthur broke into a cold sweat, too scared to move.

A second went by, and another, and Chris didn't open the door. He was distracted by his conversation.

Arthur scrambled back to his old com station and pounded on the keyboard. What could he do? Quickly he opened the software controlling the alarm system and set off the siren in the central bunker. On the video screen by the door, Arthur saw Chris startle, then go to investigate.

Arthur flipped the com screen back to the one Chris had been looking at, darted out the door, ran as fast as he could to the port-side stairwell, and sprinted down to the habitation level. He dove into the first apartment on the left, where he knocked Sarek to the ground.

"Hey!" Sarek cried from underneath him and hit Arthur with the flat of his hand. "Where have you been?"

"I got trapped," Arthur told him, adjusting his glasses on his face as he struggled to his feet. "In Central Command."

"Did they see you?"

"No," Arthur said breathlessly.

"What happened?" Sarek asked as he scrambled to his feet and followed Arthur into the kitchen. Arthur turned on the sink and put his lips right to the tap. He drank and drank.

"Arthur!" Sarek said, stomping on the floor. "Tell me!"

When he could pull himself away from the water, Arthur said, "Don't worry. Everything's okay."

"You planted it?"

"Yes. The goats and sheep are alive!" Arthur said. "I don't think the destruction was as total as we thought."

A rare smile crossed Sarek's face.

Arthur sat down at the kitchen table. Sarek went to the refrigerator and pulled out a plate of flatbread with hummus, olives, dried figs and dates, and set it down. Arthur smeared the bread with the hummus and took a big bite. Delicious. He'd worked with Sarek for months in Central Command and had never known what an excellent cook he was.

"Any news about our families?" Sarek asked.

"I didn't have time," Arthur said distractedly. "Did you evacuate the infirmary?"

Sarek looked at him blankly. "Yeah. I mean, I told them to evacuate."

"Did you hear back from them?"

"Yeah," Sarek said, looking slightly horrified. "Tobin said I had to be kidding."

"And you said . . ."

"I said I wasn't, that he had to get everyone out of there."

"And did he?"

Sarek's face was a blank.

"Because the sensors are showing no life support there," Arthur said.

Sarek's eyebrows dropped. "But that whole side of the ship is pressurized. It should be fine."

"I know." The two boys stared at each other, thinking.

"Where are the repair crews right now?" Arthur asked his friend.

Sarek put on his headset and tuned into the audio signal Arthur had just established. He had to listen for several minutes before he could finally say, "Most of them are with the animals. A few are in the conifer bay . . ."

"Nowhere near the infirmary."

Sarek stood up. "Let's check it out."

The two boys peeked into the corridor and, finding no one, ran to the central stairwell and started the climb up to the infirmary. They'd chosen this apartment for its proximity to the stairwell, and because there was no surveillance camera trained on the door so they could come and go without fear of detection. The ship felt enormous, deserted, and ghastly. Arthur didn't like walking the bare corridors, hearing the strange echoes of the repair crews' machinery groaning through the ship.

Staying behind had been Arthur's idea. He had come to Central Command looking for Sarek just as the last escape shuttles were leaving. He'd found his friend staring with trepidation at his vid screen: Four New Horizon shuttles were headed for the Empyrean.

"What do they want?" Arthur had said. "Should we hail them?"

Sarek hadn't answered; he hadn't moved toward his com system, either. The two boys had simply watched, helpless, as the shuttles docked not thirty minutes after the last of the Empyrean kids abandoned ship.

"Let's go, before they catch us," Sarek had said. "I don't want to talk to them."

"I want to know what they're doing," Arthur insisted. The two boys had stayed in Central Command as long as they could, watching the movements of the crew on the surveillance system.

When the crew started approaching Central Command, the two boys retreated to this apartment. Every day Arthur and Sarek talked about going to the New Horizon, but there was always some new repair happening, something to keep them here, watching the salvage crew, like ghosts protecting an old home.

In all this time, never once did it occur to either boy that maybe there were other Empyrean survivors on board. And the infirmary would have been the first place to look.

Arthur kicked himself for this oversight as they cautiously entered the corridor outside the infirmary. A surveillance camera was pointed away from them, straight at the infirmary doors. "What do we do about that?" Sarek asked.

"Lift me," Arthur responded.

Sarek wove his fingers together to make a step for Arthur, who stretched up to the camera and yanked out the wires from the back. The light winked out. He hoped no one would notice, but if someone did, he'd probably assume it was the same problem that had darkened the infirmary in the first place. Now the two boys could approach the infirmary without fear of detection. The glass windows embedded in the doors were completely dark, and it looked like the entire complex of rooms had lost power. But as they got closer, Arthur thought he saw a certain grain to the darkness.

"Curtains," Sarek said wonderingly. "Someone hung fabric to block the light."

"So it would look dark to the surveillance camera," Arthur said. He recognized the fabric from his recent stay in the infirmary. "This is one of the curtains they hang around the beds to block light so patients can sleep."

"What do we do?" Sarek asked, perplexed.

Arthur shrugged and knocked.

Almost immediately, Tobin Ames, the fourteen-year-old boy who had taken over running the infirmary, opened the door. "What the hell are you guys doing?"

PART TWO

Plans

Politics would be a helluva good business if
it weren't for the goddamned people.
— Richard Nixon

The Elders

Waverly passed the days in suspended animation, trying to read, trying to weave, trying to bake . . . willing time to pass more quickly. Every day was filled with plodding conversations with her mother, trying to make her see how desperate their situation was, getting nothing in return but comments like, "Everyone seems so nice . . . I'm sure it's not as bad as you think . . ." Waverly finally gave up and let her mother remain in her muffled, safe world. Doing so made the day-to-day existence peaceful, but it made Waverly feel even more alone, and more worried she might never get her real mother back. What if the doctor couldn't find a way to fix her? What then?

And where was Seth? If he really cared, how could he have left her alone like this. When Kieran was her boyfriend, he would never have left her side if he thought she was in danger. But she'd made certain he'd never be there for her again, hadn't she? She'd practically become his enemy, showing him nothing but doubt and mistrust and criticism ever since she got back from the New Horizon. And why? Because he'd used religion to give solace to the bereft children on the Empyrean? Was that so terrible? Kieran was a good person, one of the best she'd ever known. She'd treated him like dirt, and now she had no one.

She couldn't even dream of the past, or of Seth. Instead of comfort, sleep brought her nightmares of blood and revenge. She'd killed Anne Mather so many ways, so horribly, that she woke in the night, her feelings a mixture of horror and a disturbing joy that made her wonder if she was losing her mind.

She spent more and more time in her room, in a twilight state, still and quiet under her blankets. That's where she was when she heard a knock on the front door. She went into the living room to see who had come and found Dr. Carver's handsome assistant making small talk with her mother.

"Remember me?" he asked as he stepped neatly into the living room.

"Hi, Jared," she said, wondering why he made her feel timid.

"Want to go for a walk?" He swept his arm toward the door.

He smiled as she wordlessly reached for her black cardigan that she kept hanging next to the door. The flabby, snide guard who stood perpetually outside her doorway looked at Jared with apprehension but made no motion to stop him from taking Waverly.

"Why is he letting me leave?" Waverly asked when they were out of earshot.

"He can't interfere with the church elders," Jared said.

"Where are we going?"

"The doctor has been laying groundwork. Now he wants you to meet his colleagues." The elevator doors opened, and Waverly stepped on with him, careful to leave plenty of distance between them. He smelled earthy, like rich soil and sage, a masculine, primitive fragrance.

"Do you know anything about my friends? The ones who were taken away from the Empyrean reunion? Are they okay?"

"I'll see what I can find out," he said conspiratorially. "All right?"

"Thanks," Waverly said.

The elevator doors opened onto the administrative level of the ship, and Jared led her down the hallway to the Central Council chamber. The room looked just like the council chamber on the Empyrean, though it was filled with religious icons. Most of them were Christian, but Waverly recognized a Muslim crescent and star, a laughing Buddha on the ledge below the large dome of windows, and a Shiva sitting on the credenza by the door, cross-legged, many arms stretched like a fan around his head.

"Waverly!" called Dr. Carver, waving from his place at the head of the table, around which sat five other people who looked almost as elderly as he did. She nodded, uneasy to suddenly be in front of an audience. "Everyone," Dr. Carver said, "please introduce yourselves."

A tiny, withered woman held her chin high as though she expected to be admired and said, "Miranda Koch." She fingered a necklace of white beads around her neck. Beside her was another woman, much larger and plumper, with lots of rouge rubbed into her swollen cheeks. She smiled at Waverly and held up a hand, disturbing dozens of gold bracelets around her wrist. "I'm Selma Walton. Welcome." Across the table from the women sat two men, identical from their unnaturally brown hair to their crooked noses, and angular shoulder bones poking up through gray cardigan sweaters. Twins, Waverly realized. She'd heard of twins, though she'd never before seen any. They looked at her steadily, and she blushed, embarrassed to be caught staring. One of them lazily lifted a finger and said, "Wilbur Murdoch," and his brother muttered, "Raymond." Next to them, Waverly recognized Deacon Maddox, the stooped figure who always sat on stage with Anne Mather during services. Now he was sitting perfectly still, eyes closed. Waverly thought he must be sleeping, for he made no move to introduce himself.

"On the Empyrean there are seven council members," Waverly mumbled to the room.

"I'm number seven," Jared said, smiling with good humor. "Don't I look dignified?"

Waverly returned his smile, and suddenly she didn't feel so alone.

"Ladies and gentlemen," said Dr. Carver with ceremony, "I present the key to bringing down Anne Mather. After that, we can put anyone we like in the Captain's chair. Jared, for instance."

Jared humbly bowed his head.

"Isn't the Captain chosen democratically?" Waverly asked, small voiced.

"He will be," the doctor said, looking around the room, garnering support. "Most people want a leader to make them feel safe, offer them a vision, make them proud of who they are. I can show Jared how to achieve that, the same way I showed Anne. The crew will love him, and for that, they'll choose him. That's how democracy works, after all."

"That's just artifice," Waverly said, aware she was challenging him, a little afraid of what he'd do. "It wouldn't be real."

"A little artifice is necessary," Dr. Carver countered. "People need leaders."

"Maybe it's the leaders who need followers," Waverly said.

The doctor laughed, but it didn't feel sincere to her. The rest of the elders watched him; none of them seemed to be in on the joke.

"Leaders and followers need each other," he finally said as he dabbed at the corner of an eye with his sleeve. "But first things first. We need your testimony."

Waverly took a deep breath. The mere mention of the word sent her heart fluttering, and her fingertips trembled as she pressed them together under the table.

The doctor studied her. "Don't tell me your resolve is weakening."

"I don't blame her for hesitating," Selma said, drawing the

doctor's glare away from Waverly. "You want to use this girl to deal the final blow to Anne."

"It *has* to be her. No one else has the moral authority Waverly has," said the doctor.

"I'll do it," Waverly said quietly. "I'd kill Mather myself if I could."

Seven sets of eyes turned to her.

Dr. Carver thoughtfully stroked his upper lip. "If we call Anne Mather's transgressions crimes against humanity, Anne would be subject to impeachment."

The table was silent as the council considered this.

"What does that mean?" Waverly asked.

"It means that the church elders would become her jury," Selma said quietly. She was looking at the doctor now, her face unreadable. "We wouldn't need the Justice of the Peace to be involved."

The doctor raised his eyebrows as he looked around the table.

"Wesley," said little Miranda as she rattled her beaded necklace. "Are you proposing that we fix this trial?"

"*Fix* it?" He pounded his cane on the floor. "We *know* she's guilty!"

"There were mitigating circumstances . . . ," began Deacon Maddox, opening his eyes lazily. "You know that, Wesley."

"She has botched *everything*, Maddox!" The doctor raised his voice so loudly it reverberated against the glass dome over their heads. "Let us fool ourselves no longer! The woman has become a monster and she needs to be deposed!"

The table went silent, so still that Waverly could hear the rattle in the twins' throats as they breathed.

"It's dangerous," Selma said warningly, and Waverly realized the plump woman was addressing her. "You understand that, don't you?"

"You saw the way she turned the congregation against Anne the day of her escape," Dr. Carver insisted. "This girl is formidable."

"Are you prepared for this, little girl?" For the first time Deacon Maddox looked totally present and awake. "Are you ready to take on Anne Mather?"

Waverly glared at him so that he could see she was anything but a little girl. He looked away, raising his eyebrows, hiding one veiny hand under the other. Then she stood. "Destroying Anne Mather is the only thing that will make life on this ship tolerable for me."

"Huh." The sound came from Selma, something between a bemused chuckle and an exclamation of surprise.

"Thank you, dear," said Dr. Carver, and he patted Waverly's wrist. She stared at him until she understood she was being dismissed. Jared had stood, too, and nodded at her in a deferential way, extending a hand to usher her out of the room.

Once the door to the Council chamber closed behind them, he turned to her with a smile. "Want to go for a walk?" he said.

"Don't you have to stay for the meeting?"

"Dr. Carver will fill me in. And he wants you to get some exercise." He raised a finger in the air and stooped over. " 'She needs exercise and mental distance from her captivity,' " he said in a nearly perfect imitation of the old man.

Waverly laughed in spite of herself.

He rested his eyes on her, those dark blue eyes that were so unsettling, then took hold of her elbow and led her gently. She pulled away. Each time he touched her, or looked at her, she wanted Seth, missed him more. Where *was* he?

I should forget about him. He's obviously forgotten me. And so has Kieran.

"Where would you like to go?" Jared asked her.

"I don't care," she told him honestly. He held out a palm, indicating for her to choose the direction, so she continued down the hallway. She walked slowly, unsure whether she was matching his pace or he was matching hers. She didn't look at him, but she was intensely aware of his presence and his scent. Soil, sage, and something more—cardamom and garlic, maybe.

They entered the stairwell and descended several flights in silence. When he opened the door for her, she found he'd taken her to the family gardens, a fabulously lush and beautifully kept acreage. They walked between rows of huge cabbages, overgrown squash plants, pumpkins so large she could have sat on them, tomato plants hanging heavy with rich red fruits. He turned left, passing perfectly straight rows of uniform corn plants, then stopped at a large arched trellis bursting with purple clematis and sweet pink honeysuckle. A small path led from the trellis to a petite stone bench upon which he sat. He patted the seat next to him, and Waverly took it, leaning away because the heat coming from his body made her uneasy.

"Do you like it?" he asked her, waving his hand over the herbs and flowers growing in patches all around them. The colors were perfectly arranged: fragrant lavender next to pale green sage, golden saffron framed by white chamomile.

"Did you plant this garden?" she asked him.

"I've been working on it my whole life."

"It's . . ." She tried to find the right word, one that wasn't too generous. "Nice."

"*Nice?*" he said, comically outraged. "Decades of my life boil down to *nice?*"

"What do you want me to say?".

"It's a work of art!" He threw up his hands theatrically. "Are you blind?"

"Okay, Jared," she said condescendingly. "It's a work of art."

"Better," he said, squinting at her with mock anger. He was funny, she had to give him that.

"You grow a lot of herbs. Do you take them to the processing plant?"

"Oh no. These are for me. I dry them at home. I don't share."

"Never? Not even a tiny bit of thyme?"

"I have no thyme to spare."

She looked at the huge patch of the herb growing in a tangled knot. "You must eat a lot of soup."

"I do. I eat a *lot* of soup." He looked at her sideways with mock suspicion. "Not that it's any of your business."

She was laughing again. How did he do that? She was trapped, miserable, and she'd lost everything, but this strange man was cheering her up. She hated herself for relaxing, but she couldn't help it. *I can't be miserable all of the time, or I'll die.*

Maybe he knows that, she thought. She snuck a glance at him. His nose was narrow and straight except for the end, which bulged out slightly, but it was a nice nose, a friendly nose. His skin was very smooth for someone who must be in his forties, and she wanted to ask his age, but she held her tongue. His hair was still thick, though it was salted here and there with specks of gray. He turned toward her, but she looked away quickly.

"You must have questions," Jared said. "About the doctor?"

"Why do you work for him?" Waverly asked.

"He's my father, kind of." Jared swung his feet casually, his attitude completely different from the rigid discipline he showed around Dr. Carver. "He took me in when I was just a kid. My mom . . . she didn't deal well after the launch. Being cut off from Earth, never to return. It kind of made her . . ." He twirled a finger near his temple. "A lot of people were affected that way at first. Most of them got better. Some of them, like my mom, didn't." He was silent for a moment, as though caught up in a memory. "Dr. Carver said he liked the way I played with the other kids. I guess something about me seemed smart. Or self-sufficient. So he took responsibility for me."

"He raised you?" Waverly asked. She couldn't imagine that wily old man loving anyone, not even a child.

"Not in a traditional way. He brought me into his household. He saw to my education. He hired women to care for me. I was kind of raised by a bunch of people."

"That sounds . . . difficult," Waverly said, remembering her own mother and how she used to be—totally reliable, always on Waverly's side, and absolutely loving. If Waverly had gone without that kind of love as a child, she didn't know how she might have turned out.

But Jared shook his head. "I got lots of attention, from all kinds of people."

"And that's because of Dr. Carver?"

"Yes. And I'll be forever grateful."

She dug her heel into the soft garden soil, enjoying the fragrant smell of loam and tender roots. "Do you remember Earth?" she asked as an indirect way of learning his age.

"No. My mother was pregnant with me when she boarded the New Horizon. I was born a few months into the mission. So I'm not *so* old," he said with a knowing smile.

"Well . . ." Waverly grinned while she calculated. "You're over twice *my* age."

"Thanks for the reminder." He laughed.

"My pleasure." She thought she should remind herself, too, because she felt guilty talking to this handsome man, laughing at his jokes when she had no idea where Seth was, or if he was safe.

Why *should* she feel guilty? Was some part of her being loyal to Seth? Why should she be loyal after the way he'd abandoned her? But even if she wanted to forget about Seth, she couldn't. Despite her anger, deep down she knew he was staying away so that, when she needed help, he'd be able to do something. If he were under Anne Mather's control, or Dr. Carver's, Seth would be as helpless as she was. And Seth *did* care. She knew he did. The way he'd kissed her, like he needed her so much, communicating everything that he felt with an openness that couldn't be mistaken. Not even Kieran had ever kissed her that way.

But she kept these thoughts trapped deep, in the back of her mind, because if she let herself feel Seth's caring, if she felt her own caring for him, she'd have to miss him.

She'd have to worry about him. She'd be *sick* with worry.

Her hand moved over her stomach and she swallowed down her queasiness. *Please please please let him be okay.*

If he's not . . .

"Your mother is probably wondering what happened to you," Jared finally said. He stood and extended a hand to help her up.

Waverly picked her way between rows of basil and sage, searching her mind for a topic of conversation. A tobacco plant ahead gave off its heady aroma, reminding her of the corncob pipe Captain Jones often held between his teeth. "Dr. Carver told me Captain Jones is alive."

"Don't worry. He's well treated," Jared said, but he put a hand to his forehead, embarrassed. "Oh, I'm sorry. I forgot you wouldn't exactly be his biggest fan." He opened the door for her with a great show of courtesy. "I'm sure you don't want to talk about all that."

"All what?" she asked, pausing on the landing.

He touched her shoulder lightly as they started up the stairs. "The business with your father, and . . ." He paused. "How he died."

"How do you know about my father?" she asked sharply.

He stopped climbing the stairs and looked at her, surprised. "The doctor mentioned it to me yesterday."

"What did he say?" Her voice echoed down the endless metal stairwell. "Tell me the precise words he used."

"He said your father had been executed—"

She grabbed his wrist. "What?"

He blinked, surprised. His eyes looked black in the dim light of the stairwell. It was as though he had two faces, one blue-eyed and friendly, and one black-eyed and mysterious. "You didn't know?" he said.

"By who? Why?" she shrieked.

"Captain Jones," Jared said, hands held up to calm her down. "Are you telling me you didn't know about this?"

"They called it an accident," Waverly said.

Jared shook his head, dropping his hands to his sides. "It wasn't an accident."

"So my father *was* murdered." She made a fist.

"He was *executed*," Jared said, looking confused. "For what he did."

Waverly's pulse thudded inside her ears as she whispered, "What?"

He stared at her for a long moment before saying, "Your father was the one who sent the bastardized formula to the medical team here. Him and two others."

Her legs gave way, and she lowered herself to sit on the stairs.

"Galen Marshall was the architect of the whole thing," Jared said gently, his hand on her shoulder. "He created the poison that sterilized our women."

Waverly's vision blurred. She lowered her head between her knees, panting. She felt two strong hands on her shoulders, and his warm breath as he said into her ear, each word laced with regret, "I'm so sorry. I thought you knew."

Congregation

Kieran and his mother arrived for services early as Mather had requested. He was surprised to see a long line of people waiting to get into the large granary bay where services were held. He didn't know what was taking so long until he reached the front of the line, and two armed guards patted him down, then swept a sophisticated-looking detection wand over his body to search for weapons before sending him in.

The granary was huge, one of the biggest bays on the ship. To Kieran's left, a soft carpet of mulch had been laid on the floor, and there were rows of hundreds of chairs facing a stage draped in enormous swaths of fabric appliquéd with scenes of a harvest celebration. The setting was splendid, Kieran had to admit, and the huge room with its high ceiling had a stately air, like the cathedrals of Old Earth he'd seen in history books. To his right, behind the last row of the chairs, the cornfield began. Tall stalks reached up toward the lights in neat furrows that stretched away from the stage until the rows met in the vanishing point, far away at the central bulkheads. The beautiful spacious room made it impossible not to think of eternity. Such an effect could never be achieved in the little auditorium with its low ceilings and gray walls.

Kieran and his mother sat in the front row, where the guards directed them, and he snuck a peek at her to make sure she was okay. Mather had been true to her word and had sent a doctor to look at Lena. Dr. Jansen, a middle-aged woman with a knot of gray hair at the nape of her neck, had done a series of neurological tests, and her opinion had been maddeningly noncommittal. "I can find no sign of the original trauma, but decompression effects can be unpredictable." She'd smiled sadly at Kieran. "I'm sorry I can't give you more."

Mom still enjoys life, he reminded himself now, looking at her profile as she took in the spectacle of Anne Mather's church. *For that I should be grateful.*

Anne Mather herself, wearing gleaming white vestments, mounted the steps to the stage. She wore a colorful embroidered stole over her shoulders that glittered as she moved. A spotlight caressed her face so that she glowed with an otherworldly sheen, making her beautiful and awful at once. The lighting, the garb, even the choreographed way Mather moved—all of it conspired to create a perfectly crafted atmosphere. This was a level of theatricality that Kieran had attempted in his services but never achieved.

Slowly the buzzing of the crowd subsided under Mather's loving gaze, and the choir began a lilting hymn accompanied by effortless guitar playing. The lights over the stage faded, leaving a sole cone of light over Mather, who lifted her arms, miming an embrace of the crowd. She called out with a clarion voice, "Peace be upon you!"

"Peace be upon you!" the crowd repeated.

The music faded away. "Welcome to all on this, the two thousand three hundred and thirty-first Sunday of our mission to New

Earth. Joining us for this celebration we have several new crew members. Aidan Johnson was born on Wednesday, a beautiful nine-pound-four-ounce baby boy!" Kieran was shocked. Had enough time passed for the Empyrean girls' eggs to grow into babies? He counted back and realized more than ten months had passed since the New Horizon first attacked. Kieran saw a couple in the middle of the congregation, huddled proudly around a little bundle of wriggling legs and arms. The crowd erupted into applause and the couple beamed.

"Also joining us are some young people who have made the difficult journey from the Empyrean to join our crew. Could you all please stand when I mention your names, children?" Anne Mather called out name after name of young children who had survived the Empyrean explosion, and each of them stood, looking around uncertainly. Kieran wished he could gather them up, protect them somehow.

". . . And Kieran Alden!" Mather called, her hands held over her head. Kieran stood up, head down while Mather heaped on the praise. "This remarkable young man, leading a crew of children, managed to maintain the Empyrean and keep her on course, all the while cultivating crops and livestock with a level of professionalism that is truly incredible. Kieran, please accept our warmest welcome!"

Hating himself, Kieran turned to wave at the congregation. The crowd was on its feet instantly, and those nearest to him patted his back, jostling him, saying, "Good job! . . . Amazing! . . . Welcome aboard!" Kieran nodded and was made even more uncomfortable when he saw the familiar faces of Empyrean children in the mix, some of them clapping, some of them staring at him in confusion.

"Kieran, come up here," Mather said to him. "People want to get a look at you." She waved him up the stairs to join her behind the podium. Once he stood by her, he saw the large guard who had searched him standing off to the side, his hands wrapped around the body of a rifle, watching the edges of the cornfield with grim focus. What was he afraid of?

"Why don't you say a quick hello?" Mather said, offering Kieran the microphone. Kieran tried to wave it away, but the crowd had quieted and waited for him to speak.

"Thank you," Kieran said into the microphone. Mather raised her eyebrows, nodding him on. Clearly she had sensed the enthusiasm of her congregation and wanted Kieran to take advantage of it.

"Uh . . ." He looked at the Empyrean kids, who were poised watching him, waiting for a sliver of hope. "I can see that my crew and I have found a safe port." His voice was shaky, but no one seemed to notice. Several people in the front row smiled at him. "We've lost everything," he went on. He spotted the blond Peters brothers sitting with an austere-looking couple. The boys looked at him as though hoping for some secret message. He felt Mather shift uncomfortably behind him. This was more than a quick hello, but she couldn't stop him, not if she wanted to uphold the illusion of a united front. "To the families who have taken in our orphaned kids, I thank you kindly. And I ask that you do your best to treat these kids with compassion and understanding. The loss of our parents has been"—his voice broke—"devastating. If some of us are difficult, or angry, please respond with love and patience." He looked at the austere couple with the Peters brothers. The woman's face was hard, but the man was listening to him, so he spoke directly to him. "Be kind, even when some of us might be difficult to deal with. It's the only way for us to live together on this ship as one crew."

The man nodded, and Kieran saw several other people nodding in agreement throughout the audience. The Empyrean children still watched Kieran, waiting for a message just for them. He saw Mather's hand reaching for the microphone and gave a quarter turn away from her.

Inspiration struck, and Kieran plunged forward without care for consequences. "And to you Empyrean kids, we're setting up a way for you to see your friends and have some fun. Soon you'll see a lot more of each other. How does that sound?"

A great cheer rang out, and dozens of little fists pumped the air.

He turned to see Mather's tight smile. "We might have discussed this," she said.

"You said I could have influence," he said as he handed her the microphone.

He expected her to be furious, but she looked out over her congregation and saw how happy the children were. "No, you're right," she told him. "They need this. We'll set something up."

Surprised, Kieran returned to his seat.

"Wonderful, honey," his mother said, rubbing his back as though he'd had a starring role in the school musical, then turned to watch Anne Mather, who was standing behind the podium, smiling down at her people.

"Love your enemy," Mather said into the microphone and waited for her congregation to think about the familiar words. "In all of Christian Scripture, it is perhaps the most difficult tenet to live up to." Kieran squirmed in his seat, suddenly reminded of who these people were and what they'd done to his family. Why would she awaken such emotions *now*? Mather smiled that relentless smile of hers and asked, "How could Jesus expect us to love those who cause us harm?"

The room was deathly silent.

"You see," she said with tilt of the head, "Jesus wanted more than to create a religion that embraced God's loving nature." She shifted her stance, carefully placed her hands on either side of her podium, and looked out over her people—because that's who they were. Judging from the way they gazed at her, expectant, hungry for her guidance, eager to hear her next thought—they were *hers,* body, mind, and soul. "Think about it. If we all loved our enemy, wouldn't we live in a beautiful world?"

She let these words hang in the air, drifting like soft snow.

Her tone changed to one of warning: "But you and I know that even if we desire peace, war can still be visited upon us. Indeed, the war for the future has already begun." The room had been silent before, but now Kieran thought everyone must be holding their breath. "There are those on this ship who hate our way of life. They destroyed the Empyrean, and now they're coming after us."

Mather lifted her chin and intoned, *"Blessed be the LORD, my rock, who trains my hands for war and my fingers for battle.* Many of God's chosen people were called to defend their faith, and we may be no different. The wolves are circling, my friends, and they call themselves the church elders. Look around you! Do you see any of them here?"

The tension in the room climbed, and Kieran heard murmurs moving through the crowd as people looked around.

"They're coming. They're coming to depose me, strip this room of its vestments, and plow over our church! I ask you, brothers and sisters, will you stand with me if we are attacked?"

Kieran heard the creaking of chairs and saw that already people were standing up, looking determined.

"Will you put down your spade and pick up the sword, if the forces of darkness threaten to swallow us?"

Several more people stood. Kieran's stomach dropped and his pulse quickened. What *was* this?

"We shall not be silenced!" Mather's voice sailed over the heads of her congregation, electrifying the air. Her crew answered with raised fists. "We will defend our faith, and we will be victorious, for we stand on the side of the LORD! And the generations hereafter will remember us as the great generation, the stalwart founders of our home on New Earth, forever and ever!"

"Amen!" the congregation answered and erupted into a cacophony of cheers, pounding feet, and clapping hands. Kieran had to fight his instinct to hide his head. Most people fixated on Mather, but one woman to his right looked at him through narrowed eyes.

Through it all, Mather held her hands over her head, drinking in their adulation, a light in her eyes that he recognized. *I've felt that elation,* he thought to himself, sickened. *After a sermon that went well, I felt like she does now. Like a god.*

He never wanted to feel that way again.

After services, Kieran stood next to his mother, staring at the floor, going over Mather's sermon in his mind, marveling over the contradictions that no one else seemed to notice. He jumped when he felt a hand on his shoulder and looked up to see Felicity Wiggam smiling at him. She wore a dark kerchief over her bright yellow hair—that must be how he'd missed her in the crowd. Her skin was creamy, and fiery color touched her cheeks, highlighting her pale eyes.

"How are you?" Felicity asked him.

He nodded. "All right, I guess. You?"

"I'm doing well," she said, looking around furtively. "What did you think of the sermon?"

"She's a skilled speaker," Kieran said honestly.

"Yes," Felicity said carefully, then leaned in to whisper, "But I'm tired of war."

"Me too," Kieran said. Admitting this brought a wave of drowsiness over him. If only he could hide away under the covers of his warm bed. "I'm still trying to understand how she can say love your enemy one second and raise the battle cry the next."

Felicity only looked at him with her fringed blue eyes. She was afraid, he could see. He had the sudden, irresistible desire to know her, to learn every part of her past and her hopes, to see the world as she saw it. His gaze dropped to her long, tapered fingers, and he noticed a ring on her left hand where a wedding ring should go.

"Are you . . . ?" he began, taken aback.

"Married?" She laughed and lifted the ring for him to look at. The setting contained a blue stone that flashed under the lights. "I'm engaged."

He tried hard to hide his shock. "To who?"

She turned and pointed to a group of laughing men. A handsome, smallish man with thick hairy arms waved at her, and she smiled. "His name is Avery," she said and tucked a lock of hair behind her ear. "He proposed a few days ago. He's making the rounds, telling everyone."

"But he's so . . ." Kieran shook his head.

"Old?" She shrugged. "I'd like to have a family of my own. And there isn't anyone our age available anyway."

"What about me?" he blurted before he could think how it might sound.

She laughed nervously, shaking her head as though he'd made an inappropriate joke. "You're with Waverly."

Kieran stared at her with his mouth half open, unsure what to say.

Felicity read his expression. "Did you break up?"

He gave a small nod, embarrassed into silence.

"Honey!" The man Avery held out a hand to Felicity. She hesitated, looking at Kieran, obviously reading everything he was feeling as he wilted under her gaze. She saw his embarrassment and, kindly pretending not to notice, turned and went to her intended, letting the man wrap his arms around her and press his nose into her cloud of pale hair. She looked over her shoulder at Kieran and held up a hand to wave good-bye.

He nodded.

They looked away from each other, and the moment passed.

Next

Seth sat on his bed wearing short black pants and a loose-fitting tunic, clothes he'd borrowed from Anthony. On his feet were espadrilles woven of goatskin that creaked every time he flexed his toes. Tonight his fate would be decided. He'd spent two weeks in Maya's care and now was strong enough to be moved. That morning Maya had told him to expect a "family discussion" about where he should go from here. His stomach had a fluttery feeling, and he forced himself to take deep breaths to slow his skittish heart. He thought he could probably trust Maya, but he knew Anthony would do anything to protect her, including turning Seth in.

Soon Maya appeared in the doorway to his bedroom. "Ready?" she said.

He got up, feeling shaky on his feet, and went into the living room. He was surprised to see several strangers seated on soft-looking chairs draped with colorful African prints.

"This is Seth," Maya said to the room at large, patting his shoulder.

Anthony stood from a rumpled blue chair and, without ceremony, started unwrapping the gauze on Seth's hand. "I'm just going to take a peek. How's it feel?"

"Sore," Seth said with an uncertain glance around. He didn't like being examined in front of strangers, but the rest of them were involved in quiet conversations and weren't even looking.

"Bones feel okay," Anthony said, turning his hand over. "But that wound looks red." He touched Seth's fingers gently. "I think I'll start you on a stronger course of antibiotics."

"Should I be worried?"

"Nah," the doctor said. "I'll get you the strong stuff." Anthony rewrapped Seth's hand with fresh tape and gauze. It felt sturdy and comforting.

Seth sat in a stiff wooden chair and looked at the faces of Maya's "family." It took him a moment to recognize the guard with the barrel chest who had helped him out of the tropics bay that first day. He took up an entire chair with his stocky frame, his light brown eyes trained on Seth, and he held up a hand in greeting. "I'm Don."

"Thanks for, uh . . ."

Don waved away his words. "Don't even."

"This is Selma Walton," Maya said, holding a hand out to a plump old woman, maybe the oldest person Seth had ever seen, with a sagging neck and thick forearms that were covered with glittering gold bracelets.

"Seth." Selma smiled, lighting up. "Welcome."

"And this is Amanda." Maya pointed out a very tall woman sitting folded in a chair in the corner. She was wrapped in a brightly colored shawl, and she smiled warmly.

"Maya tells me you know Waverly," Amanda said to him. "I helped her escape, along with another woman named Jessica Eaton."

"Is Jessica still . . . ?" Maya began, looking at Don.

"Still in the brig," Don said quietly.

Seth expected this to be a disappointing answer, but everyone in the room looked relieved, and he realized they'd feared she might be dead. This, more than anything they'd said, told him how great a risk they were taking in helping him.

"Have you heard from Chris?" Anthony asked Don.

"Not yet," Don said, shifting uncomfortably in his seat.

"Who is Chris?" Seth asked.

"He's Don's brother," the tall woman answered. "No one has seen him for over two weeks."

"I have an idea of where he might be," Don started, and everyone looked at him, but he seemed unwilling to say more.

Maya picked up a large earthenware teapot. "Darjeeling, anyone?"

Without waiting for a response, she poured tea for each person, handing small egg-shaped cups to her guests. Amanda sipped distractedly while Selma took in the aroma, her hands folded over the warm cup. "A real treat, Maya."

"Maya always gets the best stuff," Don said to Seth, feigning resentment.

"She wheedles," said Anthony, sending a loving jab at her. "And people give her things."

"That is because I am irresistible," Maya said, handing Seth his tea before plunking onto a beanbag chair with a grunt.

"Careful," Anthony told her. "You don't want to shake that baby loose."

"Anthony," Maya said warningly.

"I have a question about that," Seth said.

Judging from the way everyone turned in unison to look at him, they were surprised he'd spoken at all. "Waverly left this ship months ago, but you can't be that far along."

Maya's hand went to her belly. "This little one came from a frozen embryo."

Seth braced himself. "How many babies came from Waverly, then?"

Anthony looked at him steadily. "We were able to divide several early embryos. We got a total of, I think, thirty-two from her. The total, from all the girls together, is about one hundred and eighty, not counting the ova Felicity Wiggam has been very generous to provide. We can only hope they all come to term."

Seth was stunned at the number. "Did any of you think to ask Waverly how she felt before you took her eggs?"

Amanda ducked her head with a guilty glance at Maya but said nothing.

Anthony sliced the air with a fine-boned hand. "Anne Mather told me Waverly and the rest of the girls had given consent. Believe me, I wish I had talked to the girls myself before I took their eggs, okay? I lose sleep over it."

Seth studied Anthony, who shoved his small round glasses up the narrow bridge of his nose. The man seemed to be telling the truth, but Seth still couldn't forgive what he'd done to Waverly. "If it bothers you so much, why are you still using the embryos?"

"Should we let them die?" Maya said, her manner much more shy and hesitating than usual, which showed how mixed her feelings were. "And what about the rights of the men who donated their sperm? They don't want the embryos of their children destroyed."

"Where *is* Waverly?" Seth asked. "Do any of you know?"

"I've seen her," said Selma, "but I don't know where they're keeping her. I can tell you she's pretty feisty, and she looks okay."

"*How* did you see her?" Seth asked. "Can you get me to her?"

"Impossible. The church elders are considering taking testimony from her. Until she's on record, she's being kept sequestered."

Seth didn't like the sound of that. "Can you get a message to her?"

"I don't even know where they're keeping her," Selma said. "Don, could you try to find out?"

Don nodded deferentially to the woman, who seemed to have the kind of authority that comes mostly from a strong personality.

Seth looked around the room at each careworn face and decided he liked these people. He instinctively trusted them. If he was going to help Waverly and the rest of the kids, he needed their help.

"Look," Seth said, and he stood up to get their full attention. "Maya hasn't told me anything, but I know who you people are. You're part of a resistance organization, and I want in."

Amanda's cheeks puffed out. "Resistance! That's rich."

The other people in the room tittered.

"It's not a joke," Seth said, and the room quieted. "You *are* the resistance. Even if you haven't done anything yet, that's what you are." Maya's eyes shone with fondness as she looked at him. "Anne Mather and her friends killed our crew, hobbled our ship, stole our girls, and used them horribly. Is this a government you support?"

"I think everyone here agrees with you, Seth, but what do you propose we do?" Amanda set her small teacup on the side table. "Anne still has a lot of loyal followers."

"Do they know the truth about her?" Seth asked.

"They know everything we know," Anthony said as he adjusted his glasses on his nose, "but we seem to be the only ones who have a problem with what's going on."

"Not true," Seth said, surprising himself with his certainty. "Others *do* have a problem with it. It's *got* to be nagging at the backs of their minds. What they need is someone to bring it to the fore."

"How do you do that?" Selma asked with a grin.

"You put it into words," Seth said. He'd thought about this while he was healing under Maya's care. The only way to get Anne Mather was to foment rebellion, and every rebellion in history was based on a few choice slogans. "Give them a battle cry."

"Articulate it for them," Maya said, nodding as she tucked a leg underneath her, adjusting a yellow crocheted blanket over her knees. "Frame it."

"That's what we've got to do," Seth said. "Right? We convince them."

The adults all looked at each other, worried.

Seth sat back down on the wooden chair and picked up his mug, looking thoughtfully into the mirrored surface of the black tea. "On the Empyrean, the kids would draw graffiti if they weren't happy with Kieran Alden."

"Like cartoons?" Amanda asked. Of all of them, she seemed the most interested.

"Sure," Seth said. "Slogans, that kind of thing."

"How do we do that without getting caught?" Anthony asked, seeming irritated by the idea.

"The kids always wore hooded jackets to hide from the cameras," Seth said.

Suddenly the room exploded with the sound of knuckles rapping on the door. Seth tensed up, sending a throbbing needle of pain into his hand.

"Maya?" called a husky voice. "Open up!"

"It's Thomas!" Maya whispered.

"Hide!" whispered Selma, shooing Seth out of the room. "Don! Come with me."

Selma and Don sneaked into the bedroom where Seth had been staying. Selma hissed and tried to beckon him, but he knew all three of them would never fit inside that wardrobe, so instead he ducked into Maya's bedroom just before he heard the door being forced open and heavy boots stomping into the room. Seth dove into the master bedroom closet and closed the door behind him.

"Is this a meeting?" said a booming voice.

"We're a group of friends gathered for tea, Thomas," Maya answered bravely. "Is there something wrong with that?"

There was a pause, then Thomas said, "I count six teacups here."

"Some of my guests left a few minutes ago," Maya said quickly.

"Search the place," Thomas said to someone.

With his good hand, Seth pulled at the paneling at the back wall of Maya's closet, creating a space just large enough that he could crawl into the narrow passage behind the wall. He sidled in, pursued by the sounds of her bedroom being ransacked, and pulled the panel closed just as he heard the closet door open and hangers screeching along the pole.

"Nobody here!" called the guard.

Another guard called the same thing from the other bedroom, where Selma and Don had hidden. Seth exhaled long and slow, leaning against the ductwork that surrounded him. He thought he might pass out from fear.

"Are you hiding the fugitive here, Maya?" Thomas said in the living room.

There was a pause before Maya recovered enough to say, "No!"

"You've been taking a lot more food from the stores than usual."

"I'm pregnant," she said. "Eating for two, you know?"

"Stand up," said Thomas.

"What are you doing?" Maya cried.

"Anthony's going to come with us now."

"What for? He didn't do anything wrong!"

"Maya," Anthony said in a warning tone.

"When did this start?" she cried. "When did we become a society where guards barge into people's homes and take away whoever they like?"

"What are you *doing*?" Anthony yelled in the midst of a scuffle.

"She's coming with us."

"Maya didn't do anything!" Anthony said.

"Then she has nothing to worry about."

"T-Thomas . . ." Amanda stuttered, "Maya is p-pregnant. You can't . . ."

"Shut up for once, Amanda," Thomas said, and Seth heard heavy boots leave the apartment.

Every cell in Seth's body wanted, *needed* to know what had happened. But if he went back into that room, he could get them all killed. So as quietly as he could he crept through the narrow passageway that snaked behind apartments, tripping over electrical boxes and squeezing past plumbing and ductwork, his heart in his mouth, with no idea of where to go.

Hearing

"Mom," Waverly said, then knocked on her mother's bedroom door. She poked her head in to find her lying on the mattress, a washcloth across her eyes. "Another headache?"

"This one isn't too bad," Regina said, beckoning her daughter.

In the dark room, with her mother's familiar smell, Waverly couldn't resist lying next to her and laying her head on her shoulder. Regina had always suffered from migraines, and this familiar scene felt almost like home. Tears pooled in the corners of Waverly's eyes as she gave herself up to the sensations of her lost home, her lost mother.

Lately Waverly felt more distant from her old life than ever, after what Jared had told her about her father and his supposed role in sterilizing the New Horizon crew. She didn't believe it. It couldn't be true of the man whose warm heartbeat had once lulled her to sleep.

"You're quiet," Regina said and tightened her hold around Waverly's shoulders. "You okay?"

"I heard something about Dad," Waverly said. She hadn't planned to ask now; it just came out of her. "To do with phyto-lutein."

She felt her mother's body tense up. "Your father developed the formula for phyto-lutein. He was a hero. He saved the mission."

Waverly could only whisper, "Someone told me Dad was the one who poisoned the women on the New Horizon and made them sterile."

"Whatever Captain Jones is saying now, it's to cover his own hide." Regina spat, palpable rage bubbling out of her—so different from the muffled, distant woman of recent weeks.

She's having a real emotion! Waverly realized. *Am I waking her up?* She reached for her mother's hand, but Regina drew away. "So you're saying the Captain framed Dad for it, and then killed him to keep him quiet?"

"That's why Seth's mother and Dr. McAvoy had to go, too. See? If the Captain was to blame your dad for everything, he had to get rid of witnesses."

"But then he covered up the whole thing," Waverly said. Something about it still bothered her. "No one on the Empyrean knew the New Horizon crew was infertile. So what's the point of framing Dad? And how did Captain Jones get *you* to keep quiet?"

Somehow, this was the question that frightened Regina the most. She got up from the bed, knocking Waverly away, and started pacing the room.

"Mom?" Waverly asked, bewildered.

"Was that a knock?" Regina rushed out as someone pounded on the front door. "Oh, Waverly," she called from the next room, "look who came for a visit!"

Waverly groaned. It could only be someone making further demands, exerting more pressure. She covered her head with her mother's pillow, but then she heard a familiar voice. "Is she doing okay?"

Felicity Wiggam? They'd let her come? Waverly dragged herself out of bed and went into the living room, squinting against the bright lights. Felicity gave Waverly a hug.

"How are you?" Felicity asked as she rubbed Waverly's back.

"A handsome man has come calling for her," Regina said teasingly, but when she saw Waverly's face, she wiped her own smile away. "But I'm sure Kieran will come see her when—"

"Mom," Waverly interrupted. She couldn't bear another display of her mother's delusions. "Felicity and I are going to my room, okay?"

"Oh, sure," Regina said, but she looked hurt. "You two have lots to talk about."

The two old friends sat on Waverly's soft mattress, silent until Felicity ventured, "I saw Kieran a few days ago."

Waverly pounced on this. "Is he okay?"

"Physically, yes," Felicity said slowly. "Emotionally, he's about how you'd expect. He's safe, though."

"For now, anyway," Waverly said, wondering if her old friend thought she and Kieran were still together, not sure she even wanted her to know the truth.

"I'm sure he's worried about you," Felicity said with a forced smile.

I'm sure... Obviously Kieran had expressed no such sentiment. Waverly didn't want to talk about it. "You seem to be doing well here."

"I'm with someone." Felicity demurely tucked her hair behind her ear, and Waverly noticed a ring on her finger. "He's a little old, but he's gentle and sweet."

Waverly studied her friend. "I'm glad for you."

"Me too," Felicity said, but with her furrowed brow and her darting eyes, she looked muddled at best. "I needed to feel a part of something when you all left. And Avery was willing to take things slow."

"He sounds nice," Waverly said, choosing to ignore her friend's obvious doubts.

"He's helped me make the adjustment to life here. That's why I told the Pastor you and Kieran need each other . . ."

"You *told* her?" Waverly studied her friend. Did Felicity have some influence with Mather?

Felicity smiled. "Don't look so suspicious. She only talks to me because she wants me to talk to all the survivors, smooth things over, try to get you to cooperate."

"You've seen others? What about Sarah?"

"I haven't seen her," Felicity said, her blue eyes troubled. "You and Kieran are the only older kids I can get to. I can't find anything out, either."

"*Could* you?"

"I'll try, but I don't think the Pastor trusts me much more than she trusts any of you." To Waverly's questioning look she said, "I think she can tell I'm not her most enthusiastic supporter."

Waverly lifted a finger to her lips and pointed into the air to indicate their conversation might not be private, but Felicity waved this away.

"I'm no insurgent," Felicity said, flashing a sheepish smile. "You know me. I'm not brave enough for that." This led to an embarrassed silence between the two girls as they remembered Felicity's unwillingness to help Waverly escape the New Horizon. Felicity's eyes darted around, but she seemed unable to make eye contact as she said, "I stayed here partly because I didn't think you'd make it back to the Empyrean. I thought you and the rest of the girls were on a suicide mission."

"We almost were."

"I have regrets." All Felicity's pretense was gone, and she looked levelly at Waverly in a way she hadn't done since they were very young girls. There was something different about her, Waverly realized. "I'm sorry I didn't help you. I wasn't a very good friend." Felicity reached for Waverly's hand, but she was interrupted by a small knock at the door.

"I made some cocoa," Regina said as she set a small tray on the desk. "I thought you girls might like . . ."

Felicity stood. "I wish I could stay. I've got a lot of people to see today." She pulled Regina into a hug and kissed her on the cheek. "It was good to see you."

Regina hugged Felicity back as she said, "Your mother would be so proud of how strong you've become."

"I've just been telling Waverly how weak I feel sometimes," Felicity said. Waverly looked on, silently agreeing with her mother. Felicity seemed straighter, more solid. Avery must be good for her.

Or maybe she just needed time to heal, Waverly thought as she watched her friend pull away from her mother's arms and walk out the door.

Waverly looked at her own reflection in the mirror over her dresser—drawn, pale, hunted. "I have regrets," she whispered. For a few minutes, she let herself stare at the defeated person she'd become. She let herself hate her.

Another knock sounded on the front door, and Waverly went to the living room to answer, thinking Felicity must have forgotten something. When she opened the door, a hand reached into the apartment and yanked her out.

"What!" she shrieked. She found herself looking into Jared's dark blue eyes.

"Something's happened," he said. "We need to get you on the record right now."

Waverly stepped on something soft and looked down to see her guard on the floor, unconscious, snoring through a bleeding nose.

Jared reached into his waistband and pulled out a small black object Waverly didn't recognize. "What is that?"

"A handgun," Jared said. "An antique. The doctor is fond of old things." From his jacket pocket he produced a large knife, which he held in the other hand. The way he moved reminded Waverly of videos she'd seen of Old Earth—extinct giant cats that stalked the jungles.

Jared motioned to Waverly with his knife. "Stay *right* behind me." He ran to the stairwell doorway. His swiftness caught Waverly by surprise, and she ran to catch up. He gave her an admonishing look, and mouthed the words, *Stay close.* He slowly pushed the stairwell door open. Waverly followed so close behind him she could feel the dampness of his shirt on her cheek.

"Come on!" Jared said. He started to pull her into the stairwell, but Waverly jerked from his hand.

"Wait! What about Mom?" she said.

"She doesn't know anything. She's safer here," he said and pushed her ahead of him. "Up!"

She hesitated, but the frightened way Jared was looking around convinced her that she had no choice but to trust him. She ran up the stairs two at a time, with Jared right behind. "What's happening?"

"Mather got wind of the doctor's plans to put her on trial. She's gathering up witnesses."

"Witnesses?" she rasped, already out of breath.

"People who can speak against you." He caught her arm and pulled her back, his eyes fixed on a point above them, sensing danger. Waverly stopped, watching his face, trying to breathe quietly.

The stairway landing looked empty, but the quiet was menacing. Waverly tensed just as a dark shape dropped on Jared from the landing above. A percussive sound exploded all around her. Suddenly she was in the corner of the stairwell, shielding her head with her arms as Jared slammed backward into her, ramming her shoulder painfully into the wall. She couldn't see anything, but she heard Jared grunt as his weight shifted, then he was off her.

When she could look around, she saw a gray-haired man sitting on the stairs, his hand wrapped around his forearm, which was bleeding. There was so much blood that for a moment Waverly couldn't look at anything else.

"Waverly!" Jared yelled. He was wrestling with a second man.

Where had he come from? The man was red faced, groaning, sweat dripping from his chin as Jared tried to pull his gun away from him. A gunshot exploded through the air, and Waverly ducked. Jared jerked the barrel of the gun upward as a second shot ricocheted off the stairs. Jared rammed his forehead into the man's nose, and the man's face burst into a bloody mess. "Behind you!" Jared managed to say to Waverly as he wrestled the man to the floor.

Waverly turned just in time to see a third man coming at her from downstairs, pointing a gun at her face. Another shot blasted in her ears, and the man crumpled into a heap on the landing, lingering just a moment before rolling down the stairs.

Moving slowly as if in a nightmare, Waverly checked herself for bullet holes.

"He didn't get a shot off," Jared said as he tucked his handgun into his waistband. The man he'd been wrestling lay at his feet, dazed. Jared stepped on the man's face as he jerked the rifle out of his hands and then he pushed Waverly up the stairs. "They'll be coming," he said, out of breath. "Hurry."

She didn't know how many more flights they ascended. She moved up the stairs barely aware of her surroundings. Her ears rang from the gunshots, and she felt weak from shock.

She looked at Jared's sweat-soaked back as he pulled her along. She hadn't known who he was or what he was capable of. No wonder the guard outside her door acted afraid of him.

When they finally reached the door he wanted, he pulled it open, peeked through, then shoved Waverly across the corridor and through a door. Suddenly she was standing in front of the church elders. They sat around a folding table in a nondescript office.

Selma stood up, horrified at the sight of her. "What happened to this girl?"

Waverly looked down to find she'd been spattered by blood all over her arms and chest. "Oh my God," she said and rubbed at her skin, smearing the oily red around.

"Jared?" Dr. Carver made a fist on the table and tried to stand, but his legs failed him.

"It didn't go well," Jared said before collapsing onto a chair by the door. "I had to shoot a guard."

"Unacceptable!" The old man pounded his cane on the ground.

"Jared saved my life," Waverly said.

This mollified the old doctor, though he still pouted.

"Are we safe here?" Waverly asked, disoriented by the contrast between this peaceful room and the violence in the stairwell.

"Don't worry," the doctor answered. "Your route to this room cannot be tracked by surveillance. We planned carefully."

"Do you know why you're here?" asked Miranda as she fingered a long string of pearls that rested over the folds of an elegant silk blouse.

"To testify," Waverly said, sinking into a folding chair, her hands at her temples, pressing, trying to get herself under control. "But Mather's men just tried to—"

"Capture you to keep you from talking," the doctor said. "Once we have you on record, you'll be safe again."

"Mather will just get more angry. She'll come after me—" Waverly felt panic rising in her chest. "Or my mom."

"No," the doctor said, one bony hand held up. "Once you testify, she can do nothing to you without admitting guilt. You'll be under the protection of the church elders as a chief witness, and anyone who tries to harm you will be charged with interfering with our investigation and could be imprisoned on that basis alone. Even Anne Mather. When we're done here, you'll go back to your life with your mother. If you don't testify"—he tilted his hand, palm upward—"I can't protect you from her."

Can't, Waverly thought, *or won't?* She didn't trust the doctor or his colleagues. She wasn't even sure she trusted Jared. So what choice did she have? If she didn't cooperate with these people, there'd be no one on this ship to protect her or her mother. "All right," she whispered.

"Begin recording." Dr. Carver lifted a finger from the handle of his cane. Jared limped to a com station in the corner of the room. Waverly saw a light blink on above her and realized a camera had been turned on.

"Waverly," Selma said, her many gold bangles clanging as she rested her elbows on the table. "We need you to tell us everything you remember about the first attack on the Empyrean."

Waverly nodded and began.

At first, talking about that day was difficult. She hated reliving the horror of her friends' parents being shot in front of her, remembering how she and the rest of the girls had been taken to the New Horizon, and all the lies Anne Mather had told them, trying to get them to believe they'd been rescued instead of kidnapped. The more Waverly talked, the angrier she became. The elders asked her questions of greater and greater detail, regarding who pulled triggers, who killed whom, whether she'd seen Anne Mather order anyone to shoot.

They couldn't let this point go.

"You're certain you didn't see Anne Mather until *after* the shoot-out in the shuttle bay?" Selma asked. "Could you have *heard* her ordering people to shoot?"

"I never saw her face until we were away from the Empyrean."

There was a disappointed silence as the elders looked at each other, worried.

"Think, Waverly," Dr. Carver said. Waverly turned to him and he raised his eyebrows. "Remember, this is your chance to show that Mather is a war criminal."

Did he want her to lie?

"I . . ." Waverly paused. If she lied, couldn't Mather put her in jail for perjury? It was better not to give her an excuse. "I didn't see her during the fight."

The doctor looked at her, seething. "That is too bad," he said slowly.

"She did so much more," Waverly said. "She took our eggs without our consent . . ."

"Let's get to that," the doctor said, twirling a finger impatiently. "How did you learn she had taken your eggs?"

"It was after I'd been shot."

"You were shot?" Deacon Maddox said, opening his eyes. "When?"

"When I was trying to see my mom, in the storage bay."

"I've interviewed the guard," Jared said. "He claims he thought Waverly was an escaped prisoner. He says he had no idea she was one of the young girls."

"That is plausible," Selma said thoughtfully.

"And there's no way to pin it on the Pastor, who wasn't even there," the little woman said, sounding bored. "Get to the eggs. That order certainly came from her."

Waverly told them how she woke up after being shot to learn that her ova had been harvested to help create the next generation of New Horizon crew members. The entire council, the women especially, listened with sympathy, but at the end of the story, the doctor tapped his cane against the edge of the table, looking annoyed.

"Waverly. Did you ever *witness* Mather giving orders to harvest those ova?"

Waverly shook her head. "All that must have happened while I was unconscious."

"Think!" he insisted.

She racked her brain, but Waverly could think of no clear proof that the orders to harvest the ova had come from Mather. "She justified it afterward, though. She told me how lucky I was to be helping the mission by giving up my eggs."

"She'll say she didn't realize Waverly hadn't given consent," the tiny woman, Miranda, muttered. "She'll blame the doctors."

"So there is no *proof* that you can think of that the doctors were acting under her orders?" Selma asked, clearly crestfallen. "None?"

Waverly looked down to see that she'd been pressing her palms into the cold plastic table. When she lifted them, her sweaty fingers left behind a misty outline that faded away. "Can't you ask the doctors?"

Selma looked at Dr. Carver. "Does she not know?"

"Mather has Dr. Molinelli, the one who worked on you, in custody," Dr. Carver told her. "He was arrested last night, along with some known opponents to Anne Mather. She's holding them in the brig, and we haven't been able to gain access to them."

"How can she get away with that?" Waverly pounded the table with a fist.

"She has a great deal of power," Dr. Carver said. "That is what I've been trying to tell you. The situation grows more serious every moment."

"So you see, dear," Miranda said, rubbing at the chains that covered her throat in glittery gold, "if you can provide us with nothing showing that Anne Mather is a war criminal, I'm afraid there is very little we can do to protect you. Or anyone."

They wanted to get Anne Mather. All of them. They wanted it badly.

"It's *my* neck on the line," Waverly said slowly.

"Play the martyr all you like, dear," said the tiny old woman through a sneer. "We just need your testimony."

Who did these people think they were to use her in this way? Waverly looked from face to face, all of them staring at her, impervious, betraying not a hint of concern for her situation—all except Selma, who worried at her bottom lip with stained teeth as she watched Waverly. *At least one of them is human*, Waverly thought ruefully.

"Well?" Dr. Carver prompted her.

"I'm no martyr," Waverly said through slitted eyes. *If they're going to use me*, she decided, *I'll use them, too.* "I want something in exchange."

"We already have an agreement," Dr. Carver said menacingly.

"So you found an antidote?"

"Antidote to what?" Selma asked with surprise.

"Selma," the doctor said irritably. "Let *me*."

The old woman squinted angrily at him, but she closed her mouth.

"I'm still working on it, Waverly," Dr. Carver said. "I need more time."

"Then I'm amending our agreement. I want to know what happened to Sarah Wheeler and Randy Ortega. I want to talk to them."

"That can be arranged—" Dr. Carver began, but Waverly cut him off.

"And I want to talk to Captain Jones. Alone."

Glances flew around the room, from eye to rheumy eye.

"Why?" The doctor finally asked.

"I have my reasons."

"That could be difficult," Deacon Maddox said.

"Not impossible," Jared volunteered, only to earn a furious glare from his . . . employer? Father? He sank back into his chair, angry but cowed.

"You'll find him changed," warned Miranda. "He won't be useful for anything you might have planned."

"This trial"—Waverly lifted her arms to indicate the council themselves and what they were about to do—"is my only plan."

"You'll give us what we're looking for," Dr. Carver asked, pointing his chin at her, "if we promise to let you see him?"

"I'll say what you want me to say," Waverly said quietly. Anne Mather was as guilty as anyone could be. Waverly knew it in her bones, and she didn't care what she had to do to convince the rest of the crew, even if it meant bending the truth. *If I can't kill her with my bare hands*, Waverly thought bitterly, *I'll have to settle for this.*

The doctor looked at Jared. "Can you arrange this?"

Jared nodded.

"You'll see your Captain," the old man said. "And your little friends."

"Okay, then," Waverly said with a grim smile, "I'll give you what you want."

Dr. Carver smiled. "Jared, erase what we have thus far and begin the recording again," he said with a lift of his finger.

With a grim sigh, Jared limped to the com station and did what he was told.

Agitator

Seth crouched in his cramped hiding space in the janitor's closet. He was taking a chance being here, but there wasn't room enough to turn his head in the maintenance passage behind the apartments, let alone work on a stencil. He cut another letter out of the cardboard he'd torn from a box of cleaning solution. It was difficult with only one hand and no better tool than the dull kitchen knife he'd managed to steal from someone's apartment last night, but it was worth it; the stencil would enable him to paint his graffiti much more quickly.

Since the night Thomas raided Maya's home, Seth had hidden in the tight passageway, entering apartments when no one was home, and only for minutes at a time, to steal clothes and food. Once a day he'd dart into the corridors to quickly paint graffiti on the walls before slipping back into this janitor's closet, always ready to disappear behind the wall panel if need be. As on the Empyrean, there was no camera trained on the closet door, but when he was in a corridor he was exposed. He quickly wrote his messages, spending only about thirty seconds in the hallway before he ran back to his hiding place. Any more time and he was certain to register on the surveillance system, but still, it was only a matter of time before they caught him. He'd already taken too many chances.

He didn't even know how long he'd been hiding back here; he had no clocks, no corridor lights to help him gauge the passage of time. Judging from the effect on his body, he'd been hiding out for at least a week. His back ached horribly from being squeezed between the ductwork, but that pain was nothing compared to the agony of his hand. Already his gauze bandage was gray with dirt and grime, and Seth was tempted to unwrap it to see if the wound on his finger had gotten worse, but he didn't dare. He wished he could somehow get to Anthony for more antibiotics, but that would be too dangerous, not only for Seth but for everyone else as well. Though he burned to know if Maya was okay, he knew he could never contact her or her friends again.

He held the stencil up to look at it in the narrow shaft of light that shone around the edges of the door. He'd gotten the idea to do the graffiti this way when he'd stumbled into the apartment of a model maker. The apartment was stuffed with small trains, airplanes, frigates, and battleships, and the guy who lived there had tubs of paints lying around. Seth had taken a large pot of black paint that he hoped wouldn't be missed, along with a wide paintbrush. He'd also nabbed a loaf of bread along with a big hooded jacket and slunk back into the passageway. He'd managed to do it all in less than five minutes, but every second he spent in someone's apartment was another second his life was on the line.

He'd made rules to protect himself from being impulsive. Before entering any apartment, he'd listen from behind the closet walls, straining his ears for any sound at all. Even when people were alone in an apartment, they made some noise eventually. Most of them talked to themselves, or sang, or whistled. When he found a quiet apartment, he'd wait a long time, and if he didn't hear anything, he'd slowly work the back paneling open and steal into the closet. There he'd crouch, looking through a crack in the door until he was certain no one was home.

My days are numbered doing this, he told himself. It was true. Sooner or later he'd walk in on someone. Or Mather's people would simply figure out where he was.

That was why it was important to get as much graffiti done as he could.

He'd almost completed the stencil. When it was finished, he'd only have to press it against the wall and run the paintbrush over it quickly, leaving behind the cut-out letters. MURDER IN OUR NAMES was the slogan he'd chosen. He thought it might cause guilty feelings among the crew, make them think about how they'd created their families at the expense of so many others.

His stomach rumbled. He remembered the delicious aroma of roasting chicken he'd smelled the night before on the other end of the corridor. It had been a salty, garlicky, greasy scent, and his mouth had watered. That's what he needed—some good protein. He'd heard only two muffled voices talking in the apartment as they ate the chicken—a man and a woman. Two people couldn't have eaten that entire bird in one night. It was worth checking out.

Now was a particularly quiet time on the ship, so he folded up the stencil and started squirming toward the apartment. A cramp cinched between his shoulder blades as he worked his way over, and his hips ached from lifting his legs over pipes for toilets and sinks. Twice he banged his foot against the wall and froze, listening, but he never heard anyone.

When finally he reached the apartment, he could still smell the garlicky chicken lingering in the air. He waited as long as he could stand, listening to the silence. Then, with his good hand, he worked his fingernails into the groove in the paneling and carefully pried it open. He poked his head into the closet, which was neatly ordered with somber-colored clothing, and waited. Not a peep from anyone.

Quickly, he stumbled into the apartment. It smelled of the chicken, garlic, lemon peel, and a chemical odor that he couldn't identify. He dashed to the kitchen and opened the refrigerator. The chicken was sitting dead center, and there was still so much delicious-looking meat on the bird he groaned. He knew he should take only a small quantity that might not be missed, but he couldn't help himself. He took the entire bird, grabbed a decanter of what looked like orange juice, a loaf of bread, wrapped it all in a dish towel he found, and turned to leave.

When he reentered the living room, a familiar pair of deep eyes peered at him from over the couch. He froze, blinking at the unreality of it.

Waverly. It was the perfect image of her, those luminous brown eyes, her strong fingers, her long neck. She was looking at him from a painting that hung on the wall.

"How?" he said out loud.

"Who the hell are you?" someone yelled.

Seth whirled. He was standing face-to-face with a slight man holding what looked like a guitar, loose metal strings twirling away from it, quivering.

"How did you get in here?" the man demanded as he glanced at the locked front door.

"I'm sorry," Seth stalled. The man was smaller than Seth, and skinny, but that guitar looked heavy enough to do serious damage. And with his hand this way, it was all over, unless . . . "Why do you have a picture of Waverly?"

The man tilted his head. "You know Waverly?" He gave the guitar a little shake as though judging its potential as a bludgeon.

"Yes. She's my . . . ," Seth began, but he didn't know the word he was looking for.

"Is she okay?" the man asked. He was beginning to relax a little.

"I was about to ask you the same thing."

"Sit. And keep your hands where I can see them."

Embarrassed to be caught stealing, Seth held up the chicken to show he carried only food, no weapons. He moved slowly toward the couch, keeping his hands and the greasy bundle on his lap as he sat.

The two men looked at each other, neither one moving or making a sound.

"You're the fugitive," the man finally said.

"Yes," Seth said.

"I should turn you in."

"Why don't you?"

"I should," the man said again.

Suddenly the front door opened and in walked a tall middle-aged woman with a baby wrapped in a swath of fabric around her middle. She stopped short. "Seth!"

"Amanda!" Seth cried. It was Maya's tall friend, the one who said she'd helped Waverly escape. The puzzle pieces fell into place, and Seth sighed with relief.

"Where have you been?" she hissed as she closed the door behind her.

"Hiding out."

Seth turned to see that the man was again holding the guitar like a club, keeping one eye on Seth as he asked his wife, "How do you know this kid?"

"He was staying with Maya." Amanda noticed the chicken Seth held in his lap. "You're hungry."

Seth shifted the chicken in his lap, swallowing hard. "I'm sorry."

"Don't be," Amanda said. "Josiah, put that down. It's okay."

Reluctantly, her husband lowered his weapon.

"Is Maya okay?" Seth asked her.

The couple exchanged a glance, and Amanda said, "I can't find out anything."

"Why didn't they arrest you?"

"Anne use to take care of me when I was little. She cares for me a great deal," Amanda said. "So she tolerates my misbehavior."

"To a point," Josiah growled.

The couple watched Seth appraisingly, then looked at each other, seeming to have an entire conversation in a glance.

Finally, Josiah spoke. "We can't help you."

Amanda didn't seem as certain as her husband, but she held the baby closer to her chest and looked down at the tiny face. Seth could hear little sucking noises as the baby worked its lips against a tiny fist.

"All I ask is that you pretend you never saw me," Seth said to the couple.

"How did you get in here?" Josiah asked him again.

Seth paused, eyeing him, and said, "I really can't say."

"Not the front door," Josiah said slowly.

Seth simply looked at him, revealing nothing.

"I heard something in the master bedroom," he said. "I thought Amanda had come home."

"The back conduits?" Amanda said.

"No," Josiah said. "No one could possibly fit back there."

"It's tight," Seth agreed, "but I'm skinny."

Josiah stomped into the master bedroom. Seth could hear him moving clothes aside in the closet and pulling out the back panel to look. He came back in, shaking his head. "You're right. There's just enough room to squeeze in. I doubt anyone actually goes in there, but they'll figure it out. Sooner or later."

"I know," Seth said, his heart sinking. He shouldn't have come here. "I'm just trying to stay out of the brig as long as I can."

"There's an unoccupied apartment," Amanda said all in a rush, pointing. "That way, three doors down."

"Amanda," Josiah said under his breath.

"Okay," Seth said, standing up.

"Don't come here again," Josiah warned. He was angry, his lips pulled tight against his teeth.

"I won't." Seth tucked the chicken under his arm again and got up to leave.

Amanda stood, too.

"I'll leave some food for you in the closet," she said to Seth. "Every day."

"It's too risky," Josiah said to his wife.

"He's still growing!" Amanda said.

"He's tall enough," the short man said resentfully. Seth almost laughed. "We've already got a child to take care of," Josiah said to her, more softly.

They stared at each other. Seth watched them. Amanda was soft and sweet-tempered, he could tell. Her fingernails were stained with blue and green pigments. He figured she was the artist who'd painted Waverly's portrait, and her paint must be the chemical smell he'd detected. She looked pleadingly at her husband, and Seth liked her for that. The baby she held made a little cooing noise. The tiny face was scrunched, and fat fists pressed against a little mouth, perfect ruby lips curled around plump fingers.

He recognized the shapes of the face, the eyes, the lips, the fingertips.

"Is that . . . ?" Seth pointed at the child, then looked at Waverly's portrait again.

Amanda stared at Seth, her face locked in an unreadable expression. Then she relaxed and finally said, "Our daughter came from Waverly. That's why I want to help you."

Seth looked at the infant, her tender mouth as she worked at her soft, little fingers. Seth indicated the bundle of food he held. "You've already done enough."

"You need *help*," Amanda insisted.

"You need to be safe." Seth nodded toward the baby she held. Waverly's baby.

Amanda looked at the child, studying the little face with an attentiveness that made him miss his own mother, whom he hardly remembered. With her ring finger, barely touching, the woman stroked a thin lock of brown hair that rested against the baby's forehead and whispered. "Yes. Okay." She looked at Seth's hands, which were stained with model paint, and she brightened. "You're the graffiti artist. I thought so."

Seth said nothing.

"You know, they're cleaning your paint off pretty easily. It just takes a good scrub. None of your stuff stays up for more than a night."

"People see it, though, right?"

"You should use a metal patina," she said with a mischievous gleam.

"Amanda," her husband warned.

"I've got some. I went through a metal sculpture phase. It'll oxidize the metal walls, make them black. They won't be able to erase it."

In her excitement, she rushed from the couch and went to the back bedroom, holding the baby to her shoulder, a protective hand on her tiny head. Josiah glared angrily at the floor, his fist clenched around the neck of his guitar. Quickly she came back carrying a small metal can in one hand and offered it to Seth. "It'll last if you use it sparingly. A thin coat will do."

"Thank you!" Seth took the can from her.

"What if he's caught?" Josiah fumed.

"I'll say I stole it." Seth got up to leave, but with a start, he turned back to Amanda. "Did you ever find out where Waverly is?"

"Oh! Yes." Amanda smiled. "She's with her mother, thank goodness, and they're being kept one level above us, in a wing of unoccupied apartments."

Seth nodded, grateful to finally have a lead.

"I don't want to see your face again." Josiah's hands balled into fists, his jaw set, seething with fury.

"You won't," Seth assured him, looking him in the eye to show he meant it.

"Now leave," Josiah said. "Go the way you came."

Seth got up and went back to the bedroom closet.

He could hear the couple quietly arguing as he sidled along the passage toward the vacant apartment Amanda had mentioned.

He broke through the back paneling of the bare closet and stepped into a bedroom with only a bed and a dresser in it. He crouched on the floor and ate every last scrap of meat, skin, and gristle off the chicken, followed by the entire loaf of bread and the decanter of juice. With a full belly, he became suddenly exhausted. He crawled onto the bare mattress and stretched out, every joint in his body loosening. Much better than the floor of a janitor's closet.

I'll just sleep a little while, he told himself. *And when I wake up, I'll find Waverly.*

The Captain

Waverly hadn't expected the doctor to let her see Captain Jones, yet here she was, on her way to the brig, standing in the elevator with Jared on one side of her and one of Mather's guards on the other. After the violence she'd witnessed on her way to testify, she was amazed that they let Jared and her walk the halls at all.

Choice tidbits of her testimony had been released to the crew only minutes after she had finished. The doctor had called Anne Mather to inform her that Waverly was now a protected witness of the church elders, and Mather had accepted this news with a single, chilling sentence: "So be it." Jared had escorted Waverly back to her apartment, where a thinner, more disciplined guard was posted outside her door, and their lives had resumed as if the violence before her testimony had never happened. Days passed with the same monotony she'd grown accustomed to, until Jared appeared at her door this morning to pick her up. Mather's guard let them leave without comment. Some of the New Horizon crew members they passed in the hallway had glared at her venomously, but most of them pretended not to see her at all. The day of her testimony had taken on a dreamlike quality in her mind, as though Jared hadn't beaten those men in front of her, and as though she hadn't testified at all. The only remaining vestiges of the incident were the fevered nightmares that vanished the moment she opened her eyes.

And to add to the unreality, Waverly was about to speak to the man who had killed her father and whose policies led to the destruction of everything she'd ever loved. The elevator doors opened, and she and Jared stepped off. They walked down the long hallway toward the admittance desk for the bridge. Now that she was about to see Captain Jones, she realized she had no idea what to say.

Jared and she stood at the desk, and the flabby guard sitting behind it looked at them as though he'd been expecting them. He waved them in with a languid hand. "Twenty minutes," he said over his shoulder.

"Surveillance?" Jared asked with a glance at the camera above.

"Darnedest thing," the guard said with a smirk. "Stopped working a couple minutes ago."

"Thanks," Jared said.

The brig held a stale odor of food and ancient human sweat. Jared led her into the first cell to the left. Waverly looked around and gasped.

Standing shackled in the corner was a skeletal, stooped, ancient man who couldn't be Captain Jones.

But it was.

The Captain had always been paunchy and physically substantial, but this man's stomach was a concave, and his wrists were bony and frail looking. His beard had gone completely white, and his hair had grown past his shoulders. His hands shook with palsy, and he smacked his lips together as though he were terribly thirsty. His eyes danced over the cell as if he were expecting some kind of animal to jump at him from above, but then they landed on Waverly, and he blinked as a man waking.

"Captain?" she asked tentatively. She felt the wrongness of addressing him by his formal title. Calling him *liar* or *murderer* would be more fitting. But he was so pathetic, she couldn't find it within herself to attack.

"Waverly Marshall," the man said. Even his voice had lost weight, become wispy and weakened. "God, it's good to see you." His knees knocked, and the chains around his ankles trembled and clacked. Slowly, the Captain approached her and sat down at the end of the cot. "They wouldn't tell me why they were shackling me," he said with a nervous laugh. "I thought my time had finally come. I never thought I might have a visitor! How are you?" the Captain asked eagerly. "How are the rest of the children?"

"All right," she said, meek and unsure.

"We've been so worried for them." He seemed to be holding back tears.

"We?" Waverly asked in a whisper.

The Captain pulled himself together enough to look over at Jared, who stepped out to give them privacy.

"Gunther Dietrich, Kahlil Hassan," the Captain whispered. "I know for sure they're here. They're still resisting the deal."

"Deal?" Waverly shook her head.

"They refused the *pills*." The Captain looked around furtively, then leaned in close. His breath was unbearably rank. "Your mother took them so that she could be with you. Almost all the parents took the deal."

"Did they say whether the pills do permanent damage?" Waverly asked as she sat down on the cot next to him, suppressing tears. "Or what kind of drug it was?"

"I don't know what it was," the Captain said. "I just know it's bad. *Bad*," he repeated. "It's been very hard being here, unable to see anyone or know what's going on."

"I—" Waverly began, but he interrupted her.

"And your parents?" he asked, lunging toward her, grasping for her hand. She pulled away from him, scooted to the edge of the cot. "How are they?"

"My parents?" Waverly shook her head, and finally her rage surfaced. "You mean my father? Who you killed twelve years ago?"

The Captain's face fell. "Galen," he said, as though just learning his friend had died. Was he senile? "Oh, Galen."

"You sent him out an air lock with Seth's mother and Dr. McAvoy!" Waverly pointed a finger in his face. He shielded his eyes. "You killed them to cover up what you did!"

The Captain studied the webbed skin over his palms, looking as though he were trying to recollect what she was talking about. "I'm sorry," he finally muttered. "Tell your mother I'm sorry."

"For killing her husband?" Waverly spat at him. "You're *sorry*?"

"I couldn't let him go!" the Captain pleaded. "Not after what he'd done!"

"You killed him to protect yourself!" Waverly said. She stood up, her hands stretched toward the Captain's face as if to scratch, but she backed away until she felt the cold metal of the iron bars against her hip. "Tell me why." The desperation in her voice alarmed her; she'd begun to cry. "Why did it have to be *my* dad?"

He blinked at her. "We can't choose our parents, dear," he said. He reached toward her, but the chains around his wrists stopped him. "You must remember him as your daddy. Try to forget what he did."

"*Forget?* He discovered phyto-lutein!"

The Captain stared at her, reading her expression, then nodded emphatically. "That's right. He was a hero. That's right."

"And you *killed* him."

He nodded. "Right. Right."

She shook her head, flummoxed. She'd expected some defense, some rationalization, or more lies. This . . . it didn't make sense.

"What are you not telling me?" she said slowly.

He waved his palsied hands in the air. "Ask your mother. This isn't my place."

"Tell me what *happened*!" Waverly flew at the Captain, but a firm hand closed around her arm. Jared must have been listening just outside the door, and now he held her back, folding himself around her until she dropped her hands, and he finally let go. "I want to know the truth."

The decrepit, ruined man looked at her with pity. "I'm sorry, child. You were never meant to know."

"What do you mean?" she whispered.

"Your mother and I. We only lied to protect you."

"What are you *talking* about?"

He studied her from beneath bushy white eyebrows, then reached a hand toward her shoulder. "I suppose you had to find out sometime," he said wistfully. "We tried."

"Please." Waverly breathed. She didn't have the strength to make her voice work. "Just tell me."

He shuffled back to the corner, shifting his weight from one foot to the other in a kind of nervous dance. "Ask your mother, Waverly. Ask her."

"Time's up," Jared said in her ear, and she realized he was holding her again. "We have to go or Mather will find out we were here."

She let Jared pull her out of the cell, but her gaze never left Captain Jones's confused, wandering eyes.

Jared led her back to the elevator and pushed a button—she hardly cared where they were headed. Why had she thought seeing the Captain would bring her anything but regret? When had she ever gotten what she wanted since this dreadful turn in her life began?

In a daze of disappointment and sorrow, she followed Jared off the elevator and down a corridor at the midship level. He seemed to understand she didn't want to talk and didn't push her. In silence they walked back to her apartment. Waverly watched her feet take one step, and another, hardly aware of where she was going until they arrived at her door.

"What is this?" she heard Jared say sharply.

She looked up to see he was addressing the guard outside her door—the pudgy one was back, recovered from his fight with Jared except for a bruise on his forehead. An insolent smile pasted across his face, he stood with his hands behind his back, his chest swelling with smug pride. To his right, just over his shoulder, was a picture of Waverly. It was a black-and-white drawing of her, all in bold lines and dark shadows, and underneath in huge black letters was written a single word: LIAR.

Fear coiled in Waverly's stomach. She wrung her hands, squeezing her fingers to calm their trembling. "What is that?"

"You weren't meant to see this," Jared said, shaking his head angrily as he ripped it off the wall. He shot an angry look at the guard, who's face fell in confusion. Jared moved to tear the drawing in half, but Waverly ripped it out of his hands to look closer. It wasn't a drawing. It was a printed copy. "How many are there?"

"Oh . . . ," Jared stalled.

"Jared!"

He sighed regretfully. "They're hanging all over the ship, I'm sorry to tell you."

"Mather?"

"I think so. The Pastor has publicly ordered that they be taken down, but they keep reappearing. I think she's trying to create the illusion of popular condemnation against you."

"People hate you," the guard said to Waverly with an ugly grin.

Jared stuck his finger in the man's face. "You shut up."

The guard's face went blank with fear, and he stared at the wall opposite him.

Jared pushed her through the door to her apartment, pulled her into her bedroom, and closed the door. She sat on the foot of her bed, her legs too unsteady to support her.

"Some people believe me. Right?" Her voice sounded puny.

"Yes," Jared said with a nod. "But . . . Mather is charging you, me, the doctor, and the rest of the elders with attempted mutiny."

"Mutiny," Waverly whispered. That could bring the death penalty, she knew. "What about the trial?"

"There'll be a hearing," Jared said with an apologetic smile, "in front of the whole crew."

"Will I have to testify?"

"We're hoping your video testimony will be enough because . . ." He trailed off.

"Because," she prodded.

"Mather's attack dog is quite good at pulling witnesses apart."

Waverly remembered the large man with the dove insignia on his shoulder. The thought of facing him in an interrogation chilled her blood.

"Be alert," Jared said to Waverly as he opened the door of her room. "Don't talk to anyone. *Anyone.* That comes straight from the doctor." He bowed his head to make hooded eye contact with her. "The safety of all the elders is in your hands. Understand?"

Waverly nodded, breaking eye contact with him too soon, knowing she was giving the impression of weakening resolve but unable to help herself. *I'm not strong anymore,* she realized as he closed the door behind him. *I'm starting to be nothing at all.*

Conjugal

Kieran watched, annoyed, as Mather picked up a mug from the tea tray his mother had prepared and poured herself a cup, making herself perfectly at home in Kieran's apartment. She'd shown up just as he and his mother were putting away the dinner dishes, unapologetic about the late hour. Now she huddled her fingers against the hot stoneware, tipping her nose into the steam, breathing it in before saying, "Something has happened. The church elders—" She scoffed. "What a joke to call them that now, after what they've done."

"What?"

"They're using Waverly against us."

Us. Inwardly, Kieran cringed, but it was crucial that Mather tell him everything, so he raised his eyebrows in a show of interest.

"They've released a video of an interview they conducted with her, and it has caused quite a stir with my crew." She pivoted the com unit toward him and flicked a button with her index finger. Waverly's face appeared on the screen. Her cheeks were ruddy, her hair disheveled, and she looked confused and exhausted.

A voice came from off camera: "You say you heard Anne Mather give the order to start shooting Empyrean crew members as they tried to save you girls?" The speaker sounded sickly, but the tone was forceful and angry.

Waverly nodded. "She was inside the shuttle, behind her crew, and she was shouting, 'Shoot to kill.'" Kieran detected something unnatural in Waverly's monotone.

"Did you *see* her giving orders to kill people?" the interviewer asked.

"Yes," Waverly said firmly.

Mather furiously turned off the com station. Her cheeks flared bright pink, and her breath sounded ragged and shaky. "She's lying, Kieran. None of that is true. I have an audio recording of my transmissions to my crew through their headsets during the gun battle." Mather tapped some commands into the com station and Mather's voice came over the speakers. "Please! Come aboard! Stop shooting and come aboard!"

In the background of the recording was gunfire, and people shouting or crying out in pain. Very faintly, Kieran heard his own panicked voice calling, "Waverly! Waverly!"

He remembered all of it—every gunshot, every scream, his own cries, begging Waverly not to get on the enemy shuttle. He was shaking with the reality of it.

"Kieran," Mather said, and waited until he could look at her face. "I'll release this to the public, and it will help, but as you may know, Waverly's testimony could be quite damning for me."

"What does any of this have to do with me?"

"That's your voice on the recording, calling her name. I know it. You could help me prove this recording is real."

"I . . . ," Kieran stumbled. "I don't remember that day."

Mather studied him for a long, uncomfortable span of time, letting him know she saw through his lie. "Then can you at least appeal to Waverly? Get her to recant her false testimony? I know you're not together anymore . . ."

"*How* do you know?" Kieran asked, suspicious.

"It's obvious. Forgive me, but neither of you has even asked to see the other. It's clear you've split, but . . ." She leaned toward him, her eyes betraying a deeply buried anxiety. "You were once very close. You might be able to influence her."

Kieran made a sweaty fist, letting his chewed-up fingernails dig into his palm.

"Remember the future, Kieran. We've got one ship." Mather held up a finger. "We have *one* chance to make it to New Earth. If this crew erupts into civil war, we won't survive."

He hated her in that instant, because he knew she was right. The survival of everyone depended on peace. Kieran didn't think Waverly's lies would lead to anything but more violence.

"Walk me to the door," Mather said, standing up from the com station. "Will you?"

He laughed, amazed at her presumption, but he still found himself following her. The rules of decorum were hard to abandon, especially around someone like her—a grandmotherly woman with a careworn face.

"Kieran, I can see you're torn by your feelings for Waverly. I understand that. But right now she's perjuring herself. Once I prove she's lying, she'll be charged with attempted mutiny."

Kieran regarded Mather with deep anxiety. *She's implying that Waverly could be executed for this.*

"There is another option," Mather said slowly. "If you told Waverly you plan to testify that she's lying, that would give her good reason to withdraw her testimony now, before I'm forced to pursue legal actions against her."

They'd reached the door. Mather turned to wait for his reply.

He could never do that. He'd hate himself forever.

Mather saw his hesitation. "Then convince Waverly to recant however you can, and I won't have to put you on the witness stand."

He saw the trap she was setting: If he lied to protect Waverly, he could be charged with attempted mutiny, too.

"Or you could simply step down," he said quietly, hoping there was some core of decency still left in her. "Save everyone by retiring."

"You think it's so simple? I have a strong and loyal core of followers." Mather clenched her jaw as she stared at Kieran. "Many of them would die for me."

"You'd let them start a civil war? Compromise the mission to defend yourself?"

This made her angry, and she jutted her jaw at him, but when she spoke her words were slow and cold. "I've had to choose between assuming the personal pain of difficult choices, or letting my flock suffer the anguish of knowing that their happiness depended on the destruction of other people. It might not seem it, Kieran, but everything I've done has been a personal sacrifice."

"Oh. So you're a martyr."

"That's right," she said, her gray eyes flickering with a warning. "And the only thing more dangerous than a living saint is a dead one."

Kieran was taken aback and remembered the fervor of her congregation, how they'd taken up her battle cry at the mere suggestion their faith was threatened, and he shuddered.

If their prophet were killed, they might never stop fighting.

"Will you talk to her, Kieran? Try to convince her?" Mather prodded. "This can only end in blood."

"Yes," he finally whispered, "I'll talk to her."

Mather smiled at him, opened the door, and stepped aside to reveal Waverly standing in the hallway, looking dazed. She was thin and pale as she stood back from Mather, her expression wary. Two armed men stood on either side of her, and the big one with the dove insignia on his shoulder held her by the elbow, looking like a giant. When Waverly shifted her weight, he watched her with unmistakable menace, and for one panicky moment, Kieran was afraid the man would break her arm.

He could, Kieran thought. *He could snap her bones with a flick of his wrist.*

"Come, Waverly," Mather said. "You're among friends here."

The man let go of her arm, and Waverly stepped into the apartment, looking around furtively.

"You can wait out in the corridor for Waverly, can't you, Thomas?" Mather asked him. With a nod, he placed himself just outside the door, his back to the corridor wall. Mather followed him out and reached to close the door behind her. She knew better than to exchange even a glance with Kieran, lest she give away the meeting's true purpose.

He felt oily and sneaky and wrong.

Kieran turned to see his mother just releasing Waverly from a warm hug. At one time, Waverly and Lena had been close and had even belonged to the same book club. They used to laugh together at one witty novel or another, giggling at passages, eyes alight as they imagined the green pastures of preindustrial England.

"Can I whip up some cookies for you two?" Lena asked Kieran.

Waverly shook her head, but Kieran said, "Yes. Gingersnaps, please. Thank you, Mom."

"Coming right up," Lena said and jogged to the kitchen.

Waverly looked at Kieran, waiting until he beckoned her into his bedroom and closed the door behind her.

"How did you make this happen?" she asked, her voice wavering with barely suppressed panic. Having Mather come for her with armed guards had scared her badly.

"This was Mather's idea," he said.

Waverly seemed stunned by this and sat slowly on the bed. She passed her hand over the silk comforter and satin sheets, and Kieran felt once again embarrassed by his opulent surroundings. He sat down on the foot of the bed, leaving plenty of space between them. They looked at each other, each waiting for the other to begin.

Once Waverly started talking, words flooded out of her. She told him about the church elders led by an old doctor, how they were using her in a power play against Anne Mather. She mentioned a younger man who was also on the council, and how he seemed friendlier, though she was unsure he could be trusted. Then she hesitated for a moment, and with a glance at the bedroom door, whispered, "Your mom seems off."

"It's from decompression syndrome," he said.

Waverly shook her head. "That's a lie. Mather gave all the parents some kind of drug to make them docile."

He felt like the breath had been knocked out of him. It was almost a full minute before he could speak. "How do you know?"

"Dr. Carver told me. He's working on a cure . . ." She paused midsentence, her eyes darting around the room, searching for a listening device, Kieran assumed.

He took a portable reader from the desk and typed into it, *As long as we don't transmit, this should be safe.*

She took the tablet from him and typed, *Dr. Carver is a neurologist. He said he might be able to cure our parents.*

Kieran's heart leapt at this. *Would he give us the cure if you didn't testify against Mather?*

I don't think so, Waverly typed.

That's why she was giving false testimony. If he could have his own mother back, he'd perjure himself, too. He wanted to believe there was a cure, but he had misgivings, and he could see that she did, too. Only a truly despicable human being would force a girl to give false testimony before helping her brain-damaged mother. If the doctor was capable of that kind of blackmail, he was certainly capable of lying about a cure.

But then, Kieran suspected, Waverly knew that. She was willing to risk being executed just for the slim hope that a hateful old man might help her mother. In that moment, Kieran loved her again.

Waverly collapsed sideways onto his bed. He watched her abundant brown hair fall around her face and remembered how it used to feel in his hands when he kissed her. "I'm so tired," she said with a groan. "This place makes me tired."

"Me too," Kieran muttered. He wondered if he should tell her what Mather had said about making him captain, but what if Waverly misconstrued it?

"Have you seen anyone?" she asked him. "Felicity?"

"She's getting married," Kieran said, failing to keep the longing out of his voice. By the searching way Waverly looked at him, he knew she'd noticed. "Did you know?"

"She mentioned something. Are you"—Waverly's voice quivered—"interested in her?"

"Nah," Kieran said, shaking his head. But Waverly saw. She knew. She'd always been able to unlock his secrets just by looking at him.

She smiled at him then, sadly and—was he imagining it?—wistfully. Did she want to get back together after everything? He'd thought that door was closed forever. In the tense silence, part of him wanted to reach for her, pull her in, but something held him back.

"You know . . ." Waverly lay on her back, her eyes dreamy on the ceiling. "That day, before you left to come to this ship to negotiate with Mather? And I didn't know if I'd ever see you again . . . I'm sorry," Waverly said. Her voice sounded small, and when he looked at her, she seemed shrunken. "I was wrong about so many things on the Empyrean. I think I forgot who you are."

"Who *am* I?" he asked with a shake of his head. "On this ship, I don't know anymore."

She looked at him as though waiting for him to say something more, but he could only look at her. If he couldn't tell her what Mather's plans were for him, what *could* he say? Finally she dropped her eyes with visible disappointment.

If Mather was listening, and he thought she probably was, shouldn't he try to talk to Waverly as she'd asked? Whatever happened, he needed to *seem* like he was on Mather's side, at least until Waverly was able to get the cure from the doctor, if there was one.

"Waverly," Kieran knelt on the floor in front of her. "I need to talk to you about something."

"What?" She gave a half turn away from him, casting her face in shadow.

Kieran took up the portable pad and typed, *Mather might be listening. This is a performance. Understand?*

She sat very still as though bracing herself.

"When you testified for the church elders," Kieran said, "Mather says you were lying." He took in a deep breath, put his hand on hers firmly, willing her to feel his friendship in his grasp. *"Were* you?"

Her face took on a rage so rapid and intense he instinctively leaned away. "Did Mather set this up with you? Are you supposed to talk me out of testifying?" She looked around the room as though she were already caged.

Kieran nodded slowly and mouthed the words, *Play along.*

"I'm afraid you're walking into a trap," he said aloud. "Because *if* you're lying, you're giving Mather a reason to come after you."

"I'm. Not. Lying," she said steadily, then took the pad and typed, *Mather is weak right now. This is our only chance to bring her down.*

Kieran bit his lip and typed, *She's stronger than you think. Her followers are zealots.* "I just want you to be careful."

Waverly stood abruptly and spat, "I can't believe I trusted you."

Kieran stood, unsure about whether she was putting on a show or if he'd really offended her. She marched out of his bedroom but stuck her head into the kitchen where Lena was still measuring out ingredients for the cookies. Kieran saw an immense heap of white flour in the mixing bowl—enough to make a dozen batches.

Waverly looked back at Kieran with sadness. He took a half step toward her, but she was already walking to the front door. She closed it behind her without looking back.

Kieran went back to his room to lie down, and then it came to him.

I made mistakes on the Empyrean, too. That's what she'd expected him to say in response to her apology: *I was wrong, too. I'm sorry.*

He should have said that. But he hadn't.

Doubt

Seth stretched on the bare mattress, slowly emerging from sleep, then jerked awake with a start. He'd intended to sleep only a couple hours before leaving to find Waverly, but he could tell that he'd slept a lot longer than that.

He put on his hooded sweatshirt, shouldered his bag of painting supplies and the new can of metal patina, and squeezed back into the conduit behind the apartment, snaking his way past plumbing and electrical wiring until he reached the maintenance closet. He listened a long time at the door before he dared to crack it open. Finding the hallway empty, he darted across to the central stairway, sprinted up a level, and slipped into the maintenance closet across the hall.

This ship was identical in design to the Empyrean, so his entire route ought to be camera free. No one knew he'd come here.

He squeezed along behind the apartments, pausing to listen every few feet until he heard someone singing softly to herself. It wasn't Waverly's voice, but it might be her mother's. He was about to enter when he noticed unmistakable red, yellow, and white surveillance wires snaking into the com system units from behind the kitchen wall. So they were spying on her. He angrily yanked them from their housing and let them dangle loose, then eased into the closet in the master bedroom. He waited until he heard the occupant go into the kitchen, then he sneaked down the hallway to the smaller bedroom and shut himself in.

A quick look around told him this was definitely Waverly's room. There were historical novels on the bedside table, and the sweater draped over the chair smelled like her. He even found a picture of her on her desk, a bad photocopy of her, and underneath her face was written LIAR in bold black letters. He wrinkled his brow, worried. This was definitely something to ask her about.

Then he had nothing to do but lie down on her bed to wait for her.

Only an hour passed before Seth heard Waverly enter the apartment. She said something soft to her mother, her tone of voice sweet and loving. He heard her footsteps come down the hallway, and the door opened, and there she was, standing in the doorway, staring down at him. He'd surprised her. And she'd surprised him, too; she was so beautiful that for a moment he couldn't breathe.

"What are you *doing* here?" she finally hissed. It was worth all the worming around, the sneaking, even the pain, just to see her face.

"Surprised?" he whispered. She closed the door behind her, but she didn't act happy to see him. She stood with her back to the wall, staring, shaking her head. She looked skinny, too skinny, and her eyes had a darting, haunted look that made him think she must be too scared to sleep at night.

"Once I knew where to look for you, it wasn't that hard," he said to her, then wished he hadn't. It sounded like bragging. "I wanted to see you."

"Where the hell have you been?" she spat.

He was shocked by her anger. "I've been hiding out," he said, detesting how small his words were. Small—that's how he used to sound when he tried to explain himself to his father at the beginning of an interrogation. Seth had always known how talks with his father would end: cruel words and fists, then being locked away in a dark closet for hours. These punishments never scared him like they were supposed to; they only enraged him. Now, looking at Waverly, the way her lips glowed red, her eyes pink with veins . . . he had no idea how this conversation would end. That *did* scare him. "I've been looking for you."

"So you could do what?" She folded her arms over her chest, tapping her heel against the floor with an exaggerated movement that jerked her whole body. "*Rescue* me? There's nowhere to go."

A knock sounded at the door. "Waverly?" her mother called. "Everything okay?"

"I'm just watching a vid file," Waverly said through the closed door, her eyes never leaving Seth.

"Okay," her mother said doubtfully, but she shuffled away.

Getting here had been the easy part, Seth was beginning to realize. Getting Waverly to forgive him would be another story.

"What do you want?" Waverly whispered, her eyes burning coals.

"Just . . ." He'd had no hopes for anything tangible, he just needed to see her, hear her voice, be near her. He'd been thinking about her all this time, missing her, wanting her. He'd taken a real chance trying to get here. Anger flared inside him. "I've been trying to help. Finding out things. You should be grateful."

"*Grateful?* Your presence puts me in *danger*," she hissed. "They have surveillance cameras in this apartment. They might be watching us now."

"I pulled all the video wires before I came in. There's no video coming into or leaving this apartment. So you're welcome."

"Then they'll come here to fix it." She shifted on her feet, looking around the room, near panic. "You always thought you were so much smarter than Kieran! He'd never be so stupid."

Seth felt as though he'd been punched in the chest. He stood up.

"Princess Waverly doesn't want me here," he said, hating the words as soon as they left him, but hurt flooded through him, warping everything. "I'll go."

"Don't call me that again." She took a half step to block his exit, her eyes narrow, bottom lip trembling. "You need to learn how to fight without burning bridges."

"Or what?" he said, and God help him he sneered at her scornfully, knowing full well he was making a mistake but unable to control his hurt and rage.

"Or you'll be alone forever," she said, her voice rumbling.

The room was small enough that he got a sense of how much taller he was than her. He looked down at her for one heartbeat, two, three . . .

The old tactics, the power plays, the sarcasm and name-calling, all the old tricks he'd learned from his father—none of that would work with Waverly. Did he want to be the freak his father had made of him, or did he want to be with her?

The old rage fell away.

You're right, he ought to say. He knew it. He tried, opened his mouth, made a fist, tried to say it, but . . .

A long moment stretched between them, long enough for him to see what a terrible mistake he'd made, abandoning her to face these people alone. Had he actually said she should be *grateful*? Now what choice did he have but to stay hidden and separate from her? Maybe forever.

She lifted a hand to her brow, and he could see her fingertips trembling. She was scared. Terrified, he realized. "What have they been doing to you?" he said, realizing this should have been his first question all along. He picked up the picture he'd found of her and held it up. "What's this?"

"Nothing," she said as she swiped it out of his hand, balled it up, and threw it in the waste bin. He thought he saw tears forming, but when she looked up at him, her eyes were icy. "You cast your lot when you decided to come alone. Now you have to stay hidden, and I . . ."

"Waverly," he whispered, his throat swollen and thick. *Put your arms around her,* he told himself. *Say you're sorry.*

He took a half step toward her; she took a half step away. He couldn't find his voice to apologize, so he did the only thing he could think of. He pulled her to him, cradled her head on his chest, and held her, held her, held her, the both of them rocking back and forth. Her body was like a rope pulled too tight, but gradually he felt her muscles releasing, and slowly she melted into him. She gulped air, and he felt her tears soaking through his shirt. "Waverly," he whispered.

A knock sounded at the front door and they both startled. She jerked away from him, looking more scared then ever. "Hello!" her mother said to someone, and a silky male voice responded, though Seth couldn't hear the words.

"You have to go!" Waverly said to him. "*Now!*"

Waverly went out, motioning for him to slip away through the master closet. He stayed just long enough to swipe the balled-up paper she'd thrown away and shove it in his sweatshirt pocket. Then he slid into her mother's bedroom closet where he'd left the paneling loose, and into the passageway.

He didn't like the way she'd jumped at the knock on the door. He needed to know who it was that scared her so. With no regard for silence, he frantically crawled past pipes and ductwork until he spilled back into the maintenance closet, knocking over a jar of a yellow liquid. It smelled strongly of ammonia, but he hardly noticed.

"I'll be fine," he heard Waverly's mother saying to someone in the hallway. "You go have fun," she said.

Fun?

"Okay," Waverly said. Seth picked up the bag of supplies he'd left on the shelf and hastily draped it over his shoulder. He didn't dare open the door yet, so he pressed his ear to the cool metal to listen.

"What's going on?" Waverly asked the man who'd come for her.

"Something happened," the man said, sounding urgent. "The doctor wants to see you right away."

His heart pounding, knowing he should stay hidden but unable to help himself, Seth eased open the closet door and stepped into the hallway. The closet was on the inside corner of the hallway so, with his back to the door, he could peek around the corner to watch the front door of Waverly's apartment.

A few doors down a guard stood at attention, the picture of military discipline. Waverly emerged from her apartment with a svelte man in his early forties and walked with him to the elevator. The man pushed the call button and Waverly nervously fingered the hem of her sweater, working at the stitches as though trying to make a hole. She stood with her profile to Seth and rubbed at an eye with the knuckle of her index finger, looking stressed and worryingly exhausted. With all his heart Seth wished he could tell her he'd be back, that he hadn't abandoned her.

The man reached out a hand, snaked it around Waverly's shoulders, and gave her a gentle shake. He whispered something in her ear and she smiled, nodding as she tugged on a lock of her hair. The blood rose to Seth's face, and he pressed his fist against his thigh. The man kept his hand on her shoulder until the elevator bell sounded, the doors opened, and they stepped aboard.

All Seth could do was stare at the place where she'd been, his illusions broken. That guy was good-looking, he'd had his hand on her shoulder, and she let him keep it there. No, she didn't seem to mind it one bit.

She doesn't love you, a voice inside him whispered.

"Hey!" The word smacked him into reality, and he turned to look down the corridor behind him, blinking with disbelief.

A group of four guards were running toward him!

"Stop right there!" one of them yelled, pulling a gun from his holster.

Seth jumped across the corridor, jerked open the stairway door, and ran down the stairs. Only a few seconds passed before he heard the guards enter the stairwell above him, one of them shouting, "He's headed toward the biosphere levels!"

Seth had a six-flight lead at best. He slid down the handrail and landed with a bang. Above the door he spotted something that didn't belong: A surveillance camera had been set up. They were monitoring stairwells now, too? A long wire snaked from the back of the camera, across the top of the doorframe, and into a freshly drilled hole in the corner—a jury-rigged connection into the com system.

They'd probably seen him come here on surveillance after all! Waverly was right to call him stupid. He'd put her in danger.

Seth jumped up and swatted at the wire, his bag of supplies banging painfully on his hip. The camera came away from the wall and bounced on the stairs behind him, leaving him holding a wire about ten feet long. He could hear the guards a mere two flights above him, closing fast. With a stroke of inspiration, he wrapped the wire first around one handrail and then the rail opposite it, tying it down so the wire stretched across the staircase.

Don't let them see it, he prayed as he started running again. A few seconds later, the stairs above him exploded with the sound of heavy male bodies falling, yelling in frustration.

He rounded the next flight, his ears tuned to the men above him. They'd hurt themselves, he could tell from how long it took them to get back up and how much slower they were now. He'd bought himself a lead of about eight floors, but how could he use it?

At every other stairwell landing he encountered another jury-rigged camera, and he pulled the wire out of each of them. This might be futile—a disabled camera was as much of a clue about where he went as a video image. Unless . . .

He sprinted down eight more flights, yanking the wire out of each camera as he went, listening for his pursuers. They were about twelve floors above him now, but surely they were calling in reinforcements.

He pulled out the last wire from the camera eight floors from where he started pulling wires, but then doubled back up two flights and slipped into the corridor. Now they'd have to search eight whole floors for him.

He slipped into the first door he came to, not even aware where he was going, and stopped short. He was in some kind of lab, a small one, not one of the big main labs in the administrative levels. A man in a white coat was standing with his back to Seth, focused on his work. Without looking up the man said, "Can you bring me those CBC slides, Em?"

Seth ducked behind the row of counters that ran down the middle of the room and peered at the man through a small space between two metal storage cabinets.

"Emily?" the man called out, turning to survey the room. When he saw no one, he switched on a centrifuge. At first it ran silently, but once it sped up, the vibration rattled the dozens of glass beakers and test tubes on the shelves above.

Seth crawled along behind the rows of counters, hoping the noise from the centrifuge would mask his passage. He slipped past the end of the counters and into a shower stall at the back of the room, concealing himself behind the curtain. Water soaked into the seat of his pants. His pulse was birdlike, and he dropped his forehead onto his knees. He heard the centrifuge slow down, then stop, leaving the room silent enough that Seth could hear the scientist counting under his breath.

Who was that guy with her? Seth wondered, now that he could think. *Why did Waverly smile when he touched her?*

He remembered the picture she'd thrown away, and as quietly as he could, he pulled it out of his pocket. Though crumpled, he could see the picture of Waverly was drawn with strong lines in sharp relief. It showed her in profile with her mouth open as though about to speak. And those bold letters: LIAR.

Something had happened with Waverly. Something serious that scared her badly. Maybe that guy was a part of it. But she hadn't *seemed* scared of him. It hurt Seth to admit that to himself, but the truth was she seemed to like him.

A door squeaked open. Seth froze.

"Hi!" the scientist said to someone, sounding alarmed.

"We're conducting a search," said a deep male voice that sounded familiar to Seth. It was the big guard, the man named Thomas, the one who had arrested Maya and Anthony. Seth tried to make himself small. Few people frightened Seth, but that man did.

"Did anyone come in here?" Thomas asked.

This was it, then. Seth tried to keep his breathing under control. He put his bag on the floor in case he needed to fight.

"No," the scientist said. "It's just me here."

"Mind if we look?"

Seth heard footsteps approaching and made a fist as the shower curtain was yanked aside. He almost punched the guy, but stopped when he found himself face to face with Don, Maya's friend. Seth closed his eyes in relief.

Don blinked at him once, twice, before recovering enough to say, "All clear back here, Thomas."

"Thanks for your time," Thomas said.

"No trouble," the scientist said, sounding intimidated.

The front door of the lab opened and closed, and the two guards were gone. Maybe Don would come back later when the scientist went home.

Seth rested his head against the damp wall, trying to breathe calmly. He was so thirsty he could barely think, but running the shower to drink would make too much noise. He'd have to wait until the scientist left. He put his thirst out of his mind, trying to remember that moment just before he and Waverly had been interrupted. He'd held her close, she'd relaxed for just a moment, but on her face there'd been . . . He replayed the scene over and over in his mind, rewriting it until he could believe she'd smiled a little before she left, like she might forgive him, like she might even let him kiss her again . . .

He woke up trembling in darkness several hours later, soaked by the dripping showerhead. The lab was completely still and quiet. Seth stood to drink directly from the shower. Water ran down his face, soaking his shirt, but it felt heavenly.

Once he'd had all he could drink, he sneaked out of the shower stall and made a careful once-over of the laboratory. In some lockers at the back of the room he found clean lab coats. He slipped into one of them. The material was scratchy and irritating, but it was better than a wet sweatshirt. Next he looked for food. In the refrigerator he found half a container of some kind of soup that smelled okay, so he ate it cold. There was an apple on the desk, and Seth bit into it, licking juice from his fingers as he looked through the drawers for what he'd need for his next graffiti project.

He found some scissors in the middle drawer and a large piece of cardboard that he ripped from a box of test tubes stacked in the corner of the room. He went back to the shower stall and sat back down to wait for Don.

While he waited, he worked on a new stencil.

Waverly's smart, he reminded himself, trying to quell his worry. *She won't let that guy do anything to her.* He couldn't stop himself from adding, *if she doesn't want him to.*

Nebula

Waverly's blood whistled like high-pressure steam through her veins as Jared pushed the elevator button, and her stomach lurched when the floor dropped beneath her. Her conversation with Seth bounced around in her brain, and she searched her memory, trying to find some hint of where he planned to go, what he planned to do, or if he'd ever come see her again, but there'd been nothing she could latch on to.

"Where are we going?" she finally asked Jared.

"First to the doctor. Then," he said with a teasing tug at her sleeve, "I have a surprise!"

The elevator doors opened to the administrative level. Jared led her to the office where she'd first met the doctor and opened the door to the darkened room. The old man sat behind his enormous wooden desk, just as he had before, swathed in shadows, surrounded by his priceless books from Earth. She had the feeling as Jared closed the door behind her that she'd entered a kind of sepulcher. She lowered herself onto the chair in front of his desk and waited.

"We've fixed a trial date, you'll be pleased to know." The doctor attempted a grin, but it only made him look menacing. "Next week, on Monday, we will begin Anne Mather's impeachment proceedings in the granary bay in front of the entire crew."

She breathed a huge sigh of relief. "What about Mather's charge of mutiny against us?"

He smiled grimly. "Our charges were brought first. So the trial decides two things at once: Is Mather a war criminal, or are we mutineers? It all depends on our linchpin."

"Which is?" she asked through a constricting throat.

"You," he said with a smile. "If you're willing to work hard to prepare for your cross-examination."

The chair beneath her felt suddenly insubstantial. "I thought you were keeping me off the witness stand."

"You just saw Kieran Alden, about an hour ago." He smiled grimly and swiveled his com screen so she could see it. Her mouth dropped open in horror. Before her was a frozen bird's-eye image of Kieran Alden's bedroom, with the both of them seated at the foot of his bed. With controlled rage, the doctor tapped a button, and Kieran's voice filled the room. "If *you're lying, you're giving Mather a reason to come after you.*"

"*I'm. Not. Lying.*" Then her video self took a portable reader from Kieran and typed something. At this point, the video image froze and, to Waverly's shock, zoomed into the reader's screen. It said: *Mather is weak right now. This is our only chance to bring her down.*

Waverly felt her heartbeat all the way down to her fingertips.

"Did Jared not tell you," the doctor asked as he turned off the video, "I said not to talk to anyone?"

"Yes," Waverly whispered, but she couldn't look at him.

"*That is practically a confession!*" he screamed.

Waverly shook in her chair, her ears ringing. The doctor's jowls trembled with rage. Kieran's voice whispered through her mind, *You're walking into a trap...*

"It isn't a confession," Waverly said, small voiced. "I never admitted to lying."

"That is what you'll say when Mather countersues you for perjury and mutiny."

"Mutiny," Waverly whispered. She knew a mutiny charge could bring the death penalty. Then what would happen to her mother? She could feel the walls of her cage tightening around her. If she was going to help her mother and the rest of them, she had to do it now. "I've cooperated with you so you'd cure my mom . . ."

"I made no promises," the doctor spat.

"What research have you done?" To this he said nothing. "Have you found my friends? Have you even been looking for them?"

"These things are delicate. They cannot be forced."

"Well, neither can I."

His face elongated into a condemning frown. "What are you saying?"

"I want to see my friends and make sure they're safe, and I want my mother and all the Empyrean crew treated for their brain damage, or I'll withdraw my testimony." For the first time since she'd met him, the old man looked nervous, and this made her brave. "If you don't, I'll tell Anne Mather that you blackmailed me into giving false testimony."

"I did no such thing."

"Yes you did. You said you'd only help my mother if I did what you wanted."

"Prove it."

"Prove you didn't."

They glared at one another. Waverly's pulse thrummed in her neck, insistent, warning. She was playing a dangerous game with a killer, she knew. *So you be a killer, too,* she told herself.

"Are you giving me an ultimatum?" the doctor finally asked quietly.

"Yes," she said, refusing to allow even a hint of fear enter her voice, though her body buzzed with it.

The doctor wove his fingers together and looked at her over the mass of his fists. "All right, Waverly."

She was taken aback. "You'll do it?"

He typed briefly into his com station, and though she couldn't see the characters, she guessed that he'd sent a text message. She was unsurprised to hear the office door whisper open just before Jared took his place at her side. He raised his eyebrows at the doctor, who waved them both away in disgust. She turned to leave the room, but she heard the doctor say as the door closed behind her, "Good-bye, Waverly."

Her breath snagged in her throat as she started down the hallway with Jared. What had she done?

Jared scowled comically. "Somebody's got his panties in a bunch."

She tried to laugh, but she couldn't find the breath for it.

They stepped onto the elevator once again, and Waverly noticed the basket Jared carried. "What's in there?"

"Goodies," he said teasingly. "Hungry?"

She couldn't answer.

Jared started humming an old Earth song that she'd once heard played at the Harvest Cotillion back on the Empyrean. She remembered the adults flocking to the dance floor when the song started, and was delighted when Kieran had stood and held out a hand to her mother to lead her to the dance floor, twirling with her under the lights. She'd noticed Seth looking at her from across the room, half hidden in the shadows, always watching, never participating, but when she made eye contact with him he looked away quickly. That was when she first knew Seth wanted her. It was a lifetime ago, but Waverly could see it all so clearly she thought she could reach out a finger to find the thin membrane between this time and that one, and step through it.

She opened her eyes and was surprised to see the elevator had dropped below the biosphere levels. Where was Jared taking her?

The elevator doors opened to reveal the vast storage bay. This was where she'd been shot the first time she'd tried to rescue the parents. They'd been held in a livestock crate down here, and she'd been able to steal only a few words with her mother before she'd been discovered by the guards, chased, and shot in the leg. Her heart beat double time at the memory. With a smile, Jared took a light hold of her elbow, and she followed him with halting steps.

"You okay?" he asked with a puzzled expression.

She gave a slight nod, her mind spinning on a wheel. All her instincts told her that she was running out of time. She put a hand on Jared's arm. "Do you think that Anne Mather is really going to jail?"

"That's what we're all betting on."

"Can you get me in to see her, like you did the Captain?" Waverly asked. He heard the heaviness in her voice and looked at her searchingly. "I want to be alone with her."

"What for?" he asked.

She tried to sound harmless. "I want to talk to her."

He seemed to recognize something in her eyes and took a half step back. "You want to kill her."

Waverly lowered her eyes. "Of course not." It was a stupid idea anyway. They'd lock her up for good or execute her, and then what would happen to her mom?

They walked on, silently, side by side. She thought she'd shocked him, but then he looked at her sideways, a playful smirk on his face. "You're a little tiger, aren't you?"

She was too embarrassed to respond. He'd read her intentions so easily she felt totally unnerved, and his nonchalance about the whole idea confused her.

Jared led her to a large air lock at the end of the room, and she stopped dead in her tracks. "What are you doing?" she asked, her eyes on the air lock. That was how Anne Mather killed the Empyrean crew in the first attack. She'd blown out the air lock. And her father—that's how Captain Jones killed him.

Without hesitation, Jared went to the air lock and opened it.

Waverly cowered, expecting an explosive decompression, but the door opened onto the cargo hold of a shuttle.

"I should've told you!" Jared laughed and reached out a calming hand. "This shuttle has been docked here since we left the nebula."

"Why? Where are we going?" She took a deep breath to quiet her nerves.

"Don't you trust me?" His eyes traveled over her tense body. "I just want to show you something. We're not going anywhere. The shuttle will stay docked the entire time."

She watched him, not moving, saying nothing.

"I'll leave the air-lock doors open. I promise."

"Then why are we going in there?"

"You'll see as soon as we go up to the cockpit." He held out a hand.

Arms folded over her middle, she scuffed onto the shuttle and moved through the empty cargo hold, which was sterile and metallic like any other empty shuttle. She followed Jared up the spiral stairs to the passenger level, then down the aisle between seats to the cockpit.

She gaped.

The nebula they'd left behind months ago stretched across the star-pricked sky, its spiral arms glowing pink and amber, flashing with lightning. It was shaped vaguely like a kind of fish that used to live in Earth's oceans, a squid or an octopus, with tentacles that reached toward the ship.

"Isn't it beautiful?" Jared said from right behind her, close enough she could feel his breath against her hair. But this time instead of tingles, she felt her skin crawling, and the muscles of her back tensed in warning. "I thought you'd like it."

She did not. She would always remember that nebula as a graveyard for so many of the crew of the Empyrean, people she'd known her whole life. *That's where I died, too,* she thought. *Waverly Marshall the innocent is buried there.*

Jared gently pushed her toward the copilot's seat, then took the pilot's seat for himself and started unwrapping the food he'd brought. He prattled as he laid out sliced fruit, soft white cheeses, smoked salmon, crusty bread, and a decanter of what smelled like ripe red wine. "It was Dr. Carver's idea to park a shuttle here, facing aft so we can still see the nebula. People can reserve it for dates and . . ." He stumbled on the word, made hooded eye contact with her, continued as he spread white cheese on the soft bread. "Or whatever. You know. I'm the one who got to pilot it down here and dock it. It was the first time anyone had docked a shuttle with one of the air locks. I was honored to be the one to do it."

"That's . . . nice," Waverly said.

"I was excited," he was saying as he laid thin apple slices over the cheese and handed it to Waverly. "As the doctor's assistant, I don't often get much glory."

Assistant. To hear Jared talk, he took care of an old man and grew herbs, but in reality he was a church elder, and the doctor had called him his son. The way he'd beaten up those guards: He'd taken on three men at once and had incapacitated them inside of a minute. Who was he really? He poured her some wine and handed it to her in a dainty crystal chalice. She took a sip automatically. It was fruity and sweet, but it settled bitterly at the back of her throat.

"Good?" he asked her.

"Yes," she whispered but didn't take another sip.

"Waverly, what's wrong?" Jared said, seeming finally to acknowledge her reluctance. "You can tell me. I'm your friend."

"I'm your prisoner," she muttered, looking at the vast pink cloud.

After a brief, surprised silence, he said, "That's not my doing."

"Mather's guard lets you take me places."

"That makes me your jailor?" he asked angrily.

She gripped her bread so hard part of it broke off and fell on the floor at her feet.

"Waverly, I hate how they're treating you. If there was anything I could do to change it . . ."

She watched him as he spoke, looking for signs that his heart didn't match his words, finding none. But did that make him truthful or just a good liar? He leaned toward her, hands cupped together, dark blue eyes searching her own.

"Why do you spend so much time with me?" she asked him.

"Isn't it obvious?"

She shook her head.

"I like you."

"But the doctor wants you to keep an eye on me, right?"

He groaned. "Okay, yes. But I don't *have* to spend so much time with you. And I don't have to enjoy it."

For want of something to do, she took a small bite of her mangled bread.

"Waverly. Look at me." He moved closer. It was a matter of inches, but she could feel the heat from his body moving through the cold air to find her. "There aren't a lot of single women my age on this ship, and none of them are particularly . . . attractive. You might have noticed."

She looked at her hands. Her fingers were white and trembling.

"But you." He held up his hands in a gesture of helplessness. "You're very mature for your age. And you're so beautiful."

She looked into his eyes, those mysterious beautiful eyes, and found she didn't want to look away. She could smell him intensely—a mix of fresh male sweat and musky perfume. "I think I'd better go," she whispered.

"Why won't you let me in?" Jared pleaded.

"Can we go?" She stood up and waited for him to do the same.

Jared stood, arms at his sides. She moved toward the door but he stopped her with a hand on her arm. If she moved even a millimeter farther, he'd let her go, she knew, but she hesitated.

He pulled her in before she knew what he was doing, his fingers winding in her hair, his strong arms wrapped around her. He pressed his lips against hers, his tongue working its way into her mouth.

He was adept at breaking through her defenses, and at first she let him. She wanted to forget her fight with Seth, forget Kieran, forget all the childish things that kept her holding on to the past. She melted a little.

He was powerful.

He's more powerful than me, she thought.

She liked it. She liked being held in his hands like a precious, fragile object.

But.

But . . .

This isn't right. A small part of her realized it as he was drawing her down to the floor, his hands already under her tunic, fingertips skidding along the smooth skin of her back.

Seth's kiss hadn't been anything like this. It had been so tentative, honest, halting, so . . . inexpert, and beautiful. He had shown her only naked wanting and passion. There had been none of this . . . skill.

Manipulation.

"Jared," she whispered. *Don't make him mad.* "Please. I'm not ready."

She tried to stand, but he pulled her back down.

"Really, I can't," she said and pushed him away. "I'm confused."

He still came toward her, pulling at her clothes, wetting her lips with his tongue. She pushed him away once, and again, and a third time as hard as she could until he lost his balance and fell away from her.

"I need to go," she told him. *Find Seth. Get to Seth. Make things right.* She got up, brushing her hair out of her face with trembling hands, pulling her tunic down to cover herself. Jared ran his hands up her calves, but she kicked him away. "I need to be alone," she said through her teeth. "Don't follow me."

He didn't look at her face. He turned away.

She ran down the spiral stairs to the cargo hold and across the storage bay to the port-side stairwell. She vaulted through the door and headed up the stairs, a single thought in her mind—Seth!—when she was hit from behind by a wall of muscle.

An iron fist clamped around her shoulder. She looked up to see the twisted mask of Jacob Pauley. A scream exploded inside her throat, but a meaty hand was wedged over her mouth and nose, confining the scream to the inside of her head, piercing her brain and rattling her ears. She tried to shake loose of his hold, but his grip was machinelike. He locked another hand around the back of her head and held on while she wriggled. *I can't breathe I can't breathe I can't breathe!!!* were the final words to bloom in her mind as her eyes fluttered closed.

Surviving

Arthur Dietrich slid along the corridor of the Empyrean, his eyes on the door to the infirmary where he knew Tobin, Austen, and all their patients were waiting. If everything was working correctly, Sarek was watching him on the com screen from the apartment they'd commandeered. When Arthur reached the infirmary doors, he knocked, two quick raps, then another set of three slower knocks. Almost immediately the doors opened, and Tobin greeted him with a pat on the shoulder. "You made it."

"How is everyone?" Arthur said.

"Stable," Tobin said. "Hopefully," he added, worrying the inside of his cheek with his teeth.

Arthur and Sarek had tried many times to convince Tobin to turn himself in and transport the patients to the New Horizon, until Arthur heard a conversation between the crew chief, Chris, and one of his repair crew. "I've been thinking the infirmary might have life support after all," said a woman over the com signal. "It might just be a malfunction in the sensors."

"As soon as we seal all the bulkheads," Chris had answered, "the infirmary is next. We're breaking it down and bringing all the equipment and meds to the New Horizon."

"What if there are survivors hiding in there? I heard rumors there were comatose patients," she persisted. Arthur liked this woman; she was always looking out for the animals on board, too. "Maybe we should have a medical team on standby."

"The Pastor told me no doctors will be allowed to come on board," Chris said, sounding angry about it. "She's short on medical staff as it is, and she's not willing to risk them when there's probably no one to help anyway. If we find any, we'll just have to hope they survive the journey to the New Horizon without help."

Rattled by this new development, Arthur and the rest of the boys decided to hole up on the Empyrean for as long as possible to give the coma patients, including Tobin's mother, a chance to heal. That meant they had to move everyone out of the infirmary to avoid discovery, and today was the day for it.

"Ready?" Arthur asked Tobin now. They had a lot of work ahead of them.

Tobin nodded distractedly as he tucked bags between his mother's legs and the safety rail on her gurney. She'd been in a coma for months now, the result of severe decompression trauma and radiation sickness. Her hands had curled up against her sides, her legs bent, her spine twisted. Tobin had insisted on keeping her on life support until a real doctor could see her, and Arthur knew he'd do the same thing if it were his own mother. But now, would there ever be a doctor?

Austen walked into the room carrying a large bag filled with bed linens and plopped it on the floor.

"Hey," Arthur said to him.

"Hi," Austen muttered distractedly as he shoved the linens into a cloth bag and hung it at the foot of one of the gurneys.

Each patient's gurney was loaded with bags of medications, but Tobin and Austen had also stuffed every available wheeled cart with medical equipment and supplies. This was going to take hours.

"The patients first," Tobin said as he gripped the railing of his own mother's gurney. "Austen, you stay here for this trip. Arthur, you take Philip."

Arthur moved to the head of the little boy's gurney. Philip Grieg looked pale as he slept, totally insensible of the activity around him. In the weeks since his injury, the bruising around his eyes had faded, and he looked peaceful, though his left hand twitched as he dreamed. "How is he?" Arthur asked quietly.

"The same," Tobin said wistfully. "As far as I can tell, anyway."

"There are other planets," Philip whispered. His head turned on his pillow and he was quiet again.

Arthur looked sharply at Tobin. "I thought you said he couldn't talk!"

"He can't when he's awake," Tobin said as he rubbed at the back of his neck. He looked sore and tired. "Philip says all kinds of stuff when he's sleeping."

"Well, that sounds like a good sign," Arthur said.

"It might be." Tobin looked doubtful. "Victoria doesn't know what it means."

Arthur looked at Victoria Hand, the sole remaining medical practitioner aboard the vessel. She was sleeping now, but she looked almost like her old self except for the downy fuzz of grayish hair growing over her skull. She used to have thick brown locks that coiled around her face, but they'd fallen out months ago from radiation sickness.

"Let's get going," Arthur said. Sarek was probably already wondering what was taking them so long.

Tobin and Arthur pushed the loaded gurneys down the dark corridor. Arthur hoped that Sarek was able to mask their progress on the surveillance system by sending prerecorded video of their route to the system in Central Command. Arthur wasn't convinced that the person manning the surveillance system would ignore the blinking of the screens as they switched from one image to the other, but that couldn't be helped. He was impressed that Sarek had figured out how to do this at all.

When they reached the apartment that would serve as the infirmary, Sarek opened the door for them, smiling. "It worked," he said. This was as close to bragging as the young man had ever come.

Arthur slapped him on the shoulder. "Good work."

Tobin quickly plugged in the equipment for the patients and collapsed onto the sunken couch that had been pushed against the wall. "I can't believe we have to do this another dozen times."

"We better hurry, then," Arthur said. The two boys left to begin the process again.

It took all day. When they were finished moving all the patients and equipment, the apartment was stuffed full of gurneys lining the wall, piles of medical equipment, bags of medications and syringes, gauze, alcohol rubs, and latex gloves. They'd left a few token machines and gurneys in the infirmary, hoping the New Horizon crew wouldn't notice anything amiss.

That night, after a long hot shower to soothe his aching muscles, Arthur lay on his bed wrapped in a terry-cloth robe he'd found in the closet. Sarek knocked on his door. "You awake?"

"Yeah." Arthur kept his eyes on the book he was reading. "What's up?"

"You think they're going to find us?" Sarek said.

"Eventually." Arthur nodded and turned the page. He'd always been able to do this: carry on a conversation and read at the same time. It had always unnerved his mother. "The only reason they haven't found us already is they're not looking for us."

"I've been thinking." Sarek rubbed his chin thoughtfully. "They're not just salvaging equipment and species . . ."

Arthur nodded. "They're working on saving the ship."

"Which means they think it's spaceworthy."

"For a while maybe."

Sarek's eyes looked black in the dim light from Arthur's bedside lamp. "Which means maybe we can take it back from them."

Arthur closed his book and gave Sarek his full attention.

"There aren't many of them here," Sarek said. "If we're going to take the ship back, we should do it before more of them come."

"But what about our parents on the New Horizon, and the rest of the kids? Do we leave them behind?"

"Of course not." Sarek pressed the heel of his hand to his temple. "That's the part I can't figure out: how to get them here."

"I wish we could talk to Kieran," Arthur said. Sarek and Arthur made a good team, but it was really when Kieran was with them that things worked well. Something about Arthur's broad knowledge, Sarek's technical skill, and Kieran's creativity made the right chemistry.

Sarek shook his head with frustration. "All our plans to deal with Anne Mather until now have been pretty—"

"Useless?" Arthur finished the sentence with a mirthless chuckle.

"What do we even have to bargain with?"

Arthur held up his hands. "This ship. That's all we've got."

The two boys studied each other in silence. When Arthur saw Sarek raise his eyebrows as an idea struck him, he thought he knew what his friend was thinking.

"No way," Arthur said. "We're not good enough pilots."

"Arthur," Sarek said patiently as he turned to go. He was a last-word hog. That was another thing Arthur had learned about him. "Think about it. What do we have to lose?"

That night, despite his exhaustion, Arthur lay awake, listing the Empyrean losses in his head. The fish hatchery. All those salmon and trout and shrimp and mollusks, gone forever, but their eggs were probably frozen. They might be able to bring some species back. Entire wings of the granaries had been lost, but the emergency pressure doors that cut through the center of the ship had held well enough that most of the fields on the port side were intact.

The nursery and the school were completely depressurized, and the starboard-side living quarters were uninhabitable. His own apartment had been there, and now he could probably never go back for his diaries, his photographs, his computer, his beloved books. Sarek's apartment was lost, too, though Arthur had no idea what his friend missed from his former life. Sarek rarely spoke of heartbreak.

Arthur rolled onto his side in this unfamiliar bed. There should be a way to make it right. There must be.

A partial map of the galaxy hung on Arthur's bedroom wall, glowing faintly in the darkness, and he turned on the bedside lamp to get a better look at it. Someone had plotted the course of the Empyrean with pushpins. In relation to the rest of the poster-size map, the ship had traveled fewer than two inches. Arthur shook his head. Forty years of unimaginable speed and they'd only gone two inches.

He looked a little closer and saw that the ship was headed for a particularly dense cluster of stars. The closer distance couldn't be perceived out the portholes with the naked eye, but judging from the map, the Empyrean was within a dozen years' journey of several hundred star systems.

He wondered if any of them had been surveyed.

He went into the living room, fired up the com console that sat on the table, and called up the nav system. He knew he was taking a chance doing this, but he suspected that the repair crew didn't have time to monitor com usage on the ship. They barely had time to keep track of each other.

He called up the approaching cluster of star systems and started going through them one by one, looking for any information. To his surprise, the vast majority of the systems were labeled "Insufficient Data." He read farther in the comments and learned that the nebula the Empyrean had just traversed had distorted the readings on these systems, making their data unreliable.

Now that they were on this side of the nebula, though, there was nothing stopping Arthur from performing a survey of his own.

PART THREE

Monsters

It is only in folk-tales, children's stories, and the journals of intellectual opinion that power is used wisely and well to destroy evil. The real world teaches very different lessons, and it takes willful ignorance to fail to perceive them.

—Noam Chomsky,
"The World after September 11 (2001)"

Snare

Kieran lay burrowed under a mound of satin sheets. After seeing Waverly the day before, he'd crawled into his silky bed, getting up only to relieve his bladder and sip at cups of tea his mother worriedly pushed at him. He couldn't eat—couldn't swallow anything past the lump in his throat. He couldn't even have the light on—it hurt his eyes. He wanted to sleep forever and forget about Anne Mather and Waverly and the constant question that nagged at him: Had he betrayed Waverly, or had he tried to help? He drifted in and out of a flaccid doze, relieved of his self-loathing only when he slept.

"Kieran." A soft voice entered the room, changing the composition of the air. "Waverly's missing."

It took him a moment to realize he hadn't dreamed that voice. He peeked out from under his pillow to see Felicity looking down at him. Her hair was pulled into a loose ponytail at the nape of her neck, and it lay over her shoulder like silk.

"What do you mean?" Kieran sat up, regretting the stale smell of his room. He pressed on his eyes, willing himself awake. "She's *missing*?"

"I just came from her apartment. Her mother says she never came home last night. Has she been here?"

"Not since yesterday afternoon." Kieran shook his head. He just saw Waverly! How could she be *missing*? Kieran threw his covers off. "Let's go talk to Mather."

He paused to run his fingers through his matted hair, then went out of his room to find that Felicity was already opening the door and walking out of the apartment. He ran to catch up.

The elevator on the way up to the administrative level felt very small to Kieran. Felicity stood close enough that he could smell her floral shampoo, making him painfully conscious of his own stale shirt.

"I liked what you said at services about getting the Empyrean kids together," she told him. "The Pastor arranged a school for the little ones to attend every day, did you know?"

"I guess that's something." Now that Waverly was missing, all else seemed small and petty. "Mather has the power. All I can do is ask for things."

"You did more than that," Felicity said. "You said it in front of the whole congregation. Mather needed to do *something*, or it would seem strange."

Kieran glanced at the surveillance camera trained down on them from the ceiling. "Shouldn't you be careful of what you say?"

Felicity shrugged. "I didn't say anything bad."

Kieran studied her. She smiled at him, crinkling the bridge of her nose in the most adorable way.

The elevator doors opened onto the busy corridor. Kieran sidled out of the elevator and, with Felicity right behind, went to Mather's office. Two guards stood outside the door. The big one with the dove insignia on his shoulder eyed Kieran with suspicion. "The Pastor is busy."

"I only need a moment of her time," Kieran said steadily, though the man made him feel pinned and vulnerable.

"Please?" Felicity said softly from behind Kieran. The man glared at her so coldly Kieran felt the need to step between them.

"It's important," Kieran said to him, trying to make his voice forceful.

"Is that Kieran?" Mather called from inside her office. The door opened, and Mather smiled. "Felicity, too! Come in."

"Waverly is missing," Felicity blurted, refusing the chair Mather pointed to. She stood over the woman's desk, dancing nervously on her feet. Kieran resisted the urge to put a hand on her shoulder to calm her.

"Yes, we know," Mather said, composing herself as she settled into her chair. "Waverly evaded her guard yesterday afternoon and ran away under her own power."

"Is Jacob Pauley still on the loose?" Kieran asked.

She nodded once. "He is."

"Did you know he has already tried once to kill Waverly?"

Mather rested her elbows on her desk, knitting her fingers together. "No."

"He attacked her on the Empyrean, which is what led to his capture."

"I hear your concern, Kieran," Mather said coolly. "But I think it's more likely that Waverly is in hiding."

"There's no way Waverly would leave her mother," Felicity said, her voice soft but strong. "She's very protective of her."

"There's no telling *what* she might do," Mather snapped.

"I'm telling you," Felicity said, taking a step forward, "Waverly didn't run away. Not without her mom."

Kieran looked at Felicity's profile, the way she stared at Mather, though he could hear that her breathing was quick and frightened. *Waverly always described Felicity as spineless,* he thought, *but it took courage to contradict Mather.*

"You and I see Waverly very differently," Mather said with a kind smile.

"Please listen to me, Pastor," Kieran pleaded. "Jacob Pauley will hurt Waverly if he finds her before you do."

Mather blinked, once, twice, and understanding flooded Kieran.

That was exactly what Mather was hoping for. She didn't want to find Waverly. Mather wanted Pauley to kill her.

"I'll make an announcement, Kieran, that Waverly has evaded her guard." She spoke slowly, like a schoolteacher soothing a child. "Would that help?"

A shudder went through Kieran. "But an announcement would only inform Pauley that Waverly is alone."

"What would you have me do?" Mather said, her eye twitching with annoyance.

"*Look* for her," Kieran said. "Send out your guards. Comb the ship! You can't let that lunatic get her!"

"You'd like me to serve justice by finding Waverly?" Mather narrowed her eyes. "But you won't testify in my trial to defend the truth?"

Kieran's throat went dry. In the corner of his eye he saw Felicity's mouth drop open. She looked at Kieran, her eyes wide and frightened.

All along, he thought, *she's been waiting to spring her trap to get what she wanted from me.*

The room was quiet. With the tip of her ring finger, Mather straightened her blotter, a row of pencils, papers sitting on the corner of her desk, then she lifted her eyes to Kieran and waited.

"I'll testify," he finally said in a whisper, "at your trial. I'll tell the truth if you find her."

"Thanks for this talk." Mather stood up and held a hand out to the door.

They were being dismissed.

As they walked past Mather's guards in the hallway, Felicity looked sidelong at Kieran, but neither of them spoke. Felicity nodded her head toward the central stairwell, and the two started down the cold metal stairs.

"She isn't going to do anything for Waverly," Felicity finally said, her voice shaking with anger.

"I know," Kieran said grimly. "I'm going to Dr. Carver."

"The church elder?" Felicity asked, confused.

"He's the one using Waverly against Mather," Kieran whispered. "He might help. But I don't know how to get in touch with him."

"I'll have Avery send a text through the com system to the elders chamber. He has access." Felicity lightly stepped down onto another landing and opened the door for Kieran. He felt awkward walking through ahead of her.

"I'm here," Felicity said, pointing to a door to her right. Unlike the deadly still corridor outside his own apartment, he could hear the sounds of people living behind these doors—the laughter of a man and woman, the clink of silverware on stoneware plates, the strumming of an instrument. It sounded like home, and not home.

"Do you live with . . . ," Kieran began, but he stopped, hating how the question sounded.

"With Avery? Not yet." Felicity smiled, biting the tip of her tongue between her front teeth—an odd quirk of nervousness that made her painfully endearing. "Living together without being married isn't really allowed here."

"Oh," Kieran said with an embarrassed nod.

"Waverly's smart," Felicity said, reaching toward Kieran's hand with her own, just enough to tap him on the wrist. "She's a survivor."

"Yeah," Kieran said, but his stomach tightened. *Please just let her be hiding in the rain forest. Or the orchards. Please let her come home.* The thought of that man finding her and what he might do to her made Kieran tremble. He didn't want Waverly anymore, but he would always care for her, and he'd do anything to help her.

Night

Seth woke gradually, confused by his surroundings until he understood he was still in his hiding place in the back of the lab. Some kind of loud noise he couldn't identify at first—the intercom—had woken him. He moved to rub his eyes, forgetting about his hand, and was paralyzed by a pain so severe he curled into a fetal position and endured shooting needles emanating from his finger and up into his forearm. His hand was worse, much worse.

The next thing he became aware of was a creeping chill moving over his spine and into his aching limbs. It felt like more than cold. It felt like fever.

So this was it. He had an infection.

He peeked through the gap in the shower curtain to find the lab lights were turned off. The scientist must have left. He shoved the bag of graffiti supplies out of the stall along with his new stencil, turned on the shower, and drank from it, then pulled the shower curtain aside.

Arrogant, Waverly had called him. If he'd gotten on that shuttle with her, he'd have received medical attention and his hand might be healed by now. Instead he hid out for a few useless weeks until his wound got so bad he was going to have to turn himself in anyway. Because that's what it had come to. If he didn't want to lose his fingers, or his whole hand, for that matter, it was time to turn himself in.

Everything Waverly said to him in that awful fight, every single vicious word, had been the truth. It wasn't the whole truth, though. He'd had one noble motive for this ridiculous escapade: to deserve her, even if he couldn't have her. He still wanted that.

"So, Ardvale," he asked himself through his teeth, "what are you going to do with your last night of freedom?"

Seth picked up his sack, which held only a few tubs of paint, a wide paintbrush, and the metal patina solution that Amanda had given him. He examined the stencil he'd made. It wasn't perfect. The curve of her nose was slightly off, and so was the shape of her left eye, but it was unmistakably Waverly.

"I'll make it up to you," he whispered.

He limped to the door of the lab and peeked into the corridor. There was no one around. The clock on the desk by the door read 1:07 A.M. There probably wouldn't be too many people moving about, but there'd still be a night crew in Central Command, and someone would be watching the surveillance video.

He'd have to move fast.

He found a lab coat in one of the lockers at the back of the room and a white cap that looked like something a surgeon would wear, probably to keep the scientists from contaminating samples with shedding hair. It would likely take a few minutes for anyone observing surveillance to recognize him. A few minutes would be all he needed.

He left the lab and took the stairs up two at a time, ignoring the way each impact jarred his poor hand. Once he reached the habitation level, he bolted through the doorway and held his stencil against the wall with the forearm of his hurt hand, careful to protect his splinted fingers. He soaked the paintbrush in the tub of metal patina and, with a few strokes, smeared a thin coat over the stencil. The whole process had taken less than two seconds. The patina solution was a charcoal gray color, and he could smell it already working on the metal it touched, corroding it, changing its color, leaving behind an image of Waverly that mirrored the posters of her hanging everywhere.

Only under Seth's version was a single word: TRUTH.

As he worked his way down the hallway, he ripped the awful posters down. He didn't pause in a single hallway for more than a minute or two before he moved on to the next. Within five minutes he'd coated an entire level, and he hadn't run into a single person. He sprinted to the stairwell and went down to the next level. He ran out of the metal corrosive after his third hallway and moved on to royal blue paint. By the third habitation level, all he had left was red. This made the most striking image of her: Waverly in the color of blood, the color of prophets, Waverly the truth teller.

He'd covered all three habitation levels with her image by the time he ran out of supplies. Hopefully the New Horizon crew would believe the graffiti had been done by one of their own so that those who doubted Anne Mather might feel brave enough to come out of hiding. It was small, but it was all he could do.

He sent the empty paint tubs and the stencil down an incinerator chute and ran back to the stairwell. He estimated his project had taken no more than thirty minutes, but he was certain they'd be on his trail by now. He took off at a run, pushing his body as fast as it could go. His feet felt as though they were attached to hundred-pound weights. His heart felt weak. His lungs felt clogged. His face was throbbing in time with his pulse. *I'm breaking down.*

All he wanted was to get to the rain forest level. He wanted to smell that soil again, breathe in that fresh oxygen, bury his face in fern fronds, just one last time before they took him.

They were waiting for him on the next landing: five guards, armed with guns and Tasers and iron fists. Seth stopped on the landing above them, hands above his head. "I'm unarmed."

They rushed at him en masse, and a hand shot out, slamming him in the ribs. Seth buckled. Hands pulled on his clothes, his hair. He covered his hurt fingers with his good arm. "I give up! I give up!"

They didn't stop. He felt kicks on his legs, rough hands pulling on his clothes, a harsh grip on the back of his neck that paralyzed him with pain.

"I give up!" Seth cried again. His voice reminded him of the thousand times he'd defended himself to his father. The thousand times he'd insisted he hadn't lied when he had. "You don't have to do that!" he said as hard fingers on the back of his neck forced him to his knees.

"Try anything and we'll finish you here." The speaker's lips were close to his ear, the breath moist and sickening.

"I won't!" Seth said. He raised his hands over his head and screamed when someone behind him took hold of his twisted fingers. "It's broken! It's broken!" he pleaded.

"Owie," someone behind him mocked, but they let go of his hand and jerked him to his feet. Then he had to endure having his wrists bound behind his back. He was face-to-face with the big guy, the mean one. He held a nightstick, which he shook in Seth's face as he growled, "Just try and get away."

"Say please," Seth managed to whisper before he was pushed forward, up the stairs. Two men walked ahead of him, another two on either side, and the mean guy behind. All of them were quiet. All of them looked to be twice as strong as he was. None of them was Don.

"I need a doctor," Seth said to the one on his left. "My hand's hurt. I think it's infected."

The guy behind him jabbed him in the ribs with a nightstick.

"Where are we going?" he asked.

"Shut up," the guy behind him said with a blow to the spine that was even harder. After that Seth didn't try to talk to them.

When they emerged from the stairwell Seth recognized the corridor outside Central Command. It was disorienting to be walking openly in the public areas of the ship. The corridor was crowded with freshly showered morning crew members reporting for duty as the tired night crew waved good-bye and headed home. A woman, petite though soft around the middle, stared at him as she passed by on her way to Central Command. He wanted to cry out to her, ask for help, because she looked like a nice woman who would feed him some soup.

In that moment, he missed his mother. He missed her so much it was like a frozen block of ice inside his chest, one that could never be worn away or lightened, not even by Waverly Marshall. As the guards pushed him into the Captain's office, he understood finally what his life had been about: revenge for his mother's death. To be a hero. To save her. To undo it somehow. To bring her back.

Was this clarity or delirium? His fever ate through his thoughts. When had it gotten so bad?

"No wonder I'm so fucked-up," he said under his breath as the tall office chair at the desk swiveled around and he was face-to-face with a matronly, plump old woman who could only be Anne Mather, the antimother.

"You've led us on quite a chase," she said.

"I hope you had as much fun as I did," Seth said breathlessly, becoming aware that his throat was sore. The guard pushed him toward a chair and forced him down.

"You're unwell," Mather said appraisingly.

"At least I'm not old."

Her gaze lingered at his hairline. "What have you been up to, young man?"

"You know. Stealing pies off windowsills. Your basic Huckleberry Finn—type stuff."

"You like Twain?"

"Never met him."

"You're coy," she said without a hint of humor.

"Yeah. I like him," Seth said. *Huckleberry Finn* had been one of the few books in English class that hadn't felt like a waste of time. He'd had an affinity with Huck, who had a mean dad, too. After that he'd read everything Twain ever wrote. "Probably the best writer to come out of the United States of America."

"I've always been partial to Hemingway."

"Never heard of him."

"You'd like him. He's very"—her eyes narrowed with the word—"male."

"So what are you going to do to me?"

"Who are you working with?"

"I'm alone."

"Jacob Pauley?"

"That lunatic?"

"Have you seen him?"

"Not since he left me to die on the Empyrean."

"What about Waverly Marshall?"

"Haven't seen her since she *rescued* me."

Her eyebrows tweaked upward. "You're Mason Ardvale's son."

Seth stiffened at this. "So?"

"Your father was a bully."

This enraged Seth beyond reason. He didn't know why, since he agreed with her. Still, he was so angry all he could do was stare at her forehead, willing it to split.

She smiled. "I trained with Mason on the space station before the mission launch. He had a reputation among the women on board."

Seth tried to think of something witty to say, something to make her think she hadn't drilled to his core, but he was too tired. He stared at the blotter on her desk—it was pristine, perfectly aligned with the row of pencils that lay to one side, lined up with the intercom to Mather's right.

"Wow," he remarked distantly, "you're really anal."

"I beg your pardon?"

"Retentive," Seth said. "I read Freud, too."

"Young man, do you appreciate your situation here?"

Seth sighed. All he wanted was to sleep. He felt used up, aged. "I tried to be a hero. I failed. Can I see a doctor?"

"We're not finished. Why have you been hiding?"

"I thought I'd be able to help Waverly."

"Help her do what?"

"Nothing." Seth looked out the porthole. He hadn't seen the stars in such a long time. "Just help her."

"What is your relationship to her?"

"I'm not exactly sure. Why don't you ask her?" He rubbed his eyes with his thumb and forefinger. A gray film had grown over his vision like a layer of mold.

"Because I don't know where she is," Mather said.

"She ran away?" Seth blinked his sticky eyelids.

Mather studied him carefully. He stared back at her, letting her see his surprise and his gladness. Waverly got away. Good for her, once again proving she didn't need Seth Ardvale. Or anyone, for that matter.

"Of course you'd *pretend* you haven't seen her," Mather finally said.

"Look." He waited for Mather to make eye contact with him. "If I'd known Waverly had slipped away, I wouldn't have turned myself in. I'd be looking for her myself, and"—he smirked—"I'd probably help her kill you. But I don't know where she is. And I need a doctor. That's why I *let* you catch me."

Mather tapped her chin with her finger. "Maybe Jacob Pauley has her after all."

"What?" Seth's heart skipped. "You can't let Jake get her. He wants to kill her."

"Yes, I know," Mather said with a grim smile.

"Please," Seth said, but then he found he didn't know what to ask for. "You can't let him hurt her."

She raised one eyebrow. "Waverly wants to kill me, you said?"

Seth froze.

"And Jacob wants to kill Waverly."

Seth opened his mouth to speak, to plead for Waverly, defend her. But he couldn't find the words.

"Why should I do anything?" Mather spat.

Seth said the only thing he could think of: "To prove you're not a monster."

She nodded to someone outside the door. The big mean guard came in, holding his gun across his chest. His jaw protruded weirdly, as though he'd once been punched so hard that his whole face had been knocked out of alignment. *This guy probably had a mean dad too*, Seth mused.

"To prove I'm not a monster," Mather repeated fondly, "when we find Waverly's body, I'll hold a memorial in her honor. There will be flowers, and a choir, and I'll make a sermon about the sin of wrath." She motioned to the guard, who pulled Seth up by the armpit. "Take him to the brig."

"You can't leave her," Seth said weakly. "You can't let him . . ."

But Mather had picked up a portable reader to peruse, tapping her chin with her finger as the big man pulled Seth out the door.

The Dark

As she woke, Waverly became aware of a horrible ache at the base of her skull. It was dark, so dark that at first she couldn't be sure her eyes were open, but she could feel her lids moving over her eyeballs. The inside of her mouth was stuck together and sour. Sweltering heat pressed against her skin, and a droplet of sweat ran down the side of her nose. She wanted to wipe it away but realized she was tied up, her arms wrenched behind her, her legs bent back, her wrists bound to her ankles. She couldn't move at all. Her shoulders were horribly sore. Her neck, her back . . . she tried to roll onto her stomach, but she couldn't throw her weight over, and after several tries she gave up.

She heard a snort, near enough to her ear that a puff of air disturbed the hairs at her temple. She froze, tried to quiet her breathing, and listened. Another body moved in the darkness.

Someone sniffed—a man. He sounded close.

She reached back in her fuzzy memory. She'd been running. Running on the stairs away from Jared. Running to Seth. Then someone had closed a fat hand over her nose and mouth, smothered her until she'd fainted.

Jacob Pauley.

A paralyzing terror overtook her, and she gulped a mouthful of air.

"Shut up," said a voice to her right, and a hand clamped over her mouth. A woman's lips pressed against her ear, "You'll live longer if you make things easy."

Waverly whimpered, and the woman's hand pressed the back of her head against the hard metal floor. "He wanted to kill you right away."

Waverly could hear someone snoring in the darkness. The woman released her grip over Waverly's mouth.

"You're his wife?" Waverly whispered.

"I said shut up," the woman said.

A light switched on, and Jacob Pauley's groggy face appeared over Waverly, huge and looming. The corners of his mouth were pulled down, the nostrils of his hooked nose flared, the pores in his skin oversized and cruddy. His bloodshot eyes bored into hers.

"Jakey," the woman said in a warning tone. "Light the Bunsen burner."

His gaze shifted away from Waverly, then back again.

"She's more useful alive," the woman insisted. She was small and mousy, with angry, darting movements and sallow olive skin. Her hair was disheveled and greasy, and she wore a heavy wool coat despite the heat in this . . . room? Waverly looked around. The three of them were crammed into a tiny space. To their right was a wheeled vehicle Waverly recognized from training videos—a rover designed for travel over the surface of New Earth. On her other side were boxes of rations and jugs of water. At her feet was a corrugated metal wall, painted bright blue. This must be a shipping container in the storage bay, miles away from anyone.

Her heartbeat coalesced into a tiny point in her neck, tapping against the inside of her carotid. She was going to die here. It was going to hurt.

Jacob knelt in front of a cardboard box and turned the valve on a small propane tank until a hiss sounded in the close air. A blue flame sputtered to life. He dropped a handful of what looked like oats into a small metal bucket, poured water over them, stirred the glop with the tip of his finger, and set it on a metal frame over the fire.

"We got big plans, I keep having to remind him." The woman glared with contempt at her husband's broad back before turning her attention back to Waverly. "They're going to have you testify, right? At Mather's trial?"

It took Waverly a while to process the question. "Yes," she said. Did this mean they were going to let her go? "Do you want me to do something? I'll do it."

The woman laughed sardonically. "We got a long list of grievances, and it ends with you, honey. It all begins with Anne Mather."

"I hate her, too," Waverly said through her teeth.

The woman spat on Waverly. She felt the spittle trickle from her ear and along the hollow between the tendons of her neck and larynx.

"I said shut up," the woman snarled. "I'd like to kill you, too. Just give me a reason."

Waverly couldn't stop the tears. They stung like acid as they squeezed out from between her lids. She bit her bottom lip to keep from making any sound. She hated crying in front of them. She hated the way they looked at her through the sides of their eyes, smug and satisfied.

This was the worst thing that could have happened, and it had never once occurred to her that it might. How could she ever be safe if she couldn't see the terrors coming?

A sudden knock on the wall of the shipping container made Jacob and his wife jump in their skins. Waverly held her breath.

Please let it be Jared. Please.

"Jake? Ginny?" came a gruff male voice. "It's Tom."

The wife, Ginny, he'd called her, picked up a large jagged-edged knife and pointed it at Waverly. She held a finger to her lips.

"Jesus, you scared us," Jacob said. He crawled over the landing vehicle to a sliding door at the end of the container and opened it a crack. "What are you doing here?"

"Brought water. Some fruit."

Waverly spied the man for half a moment, and her breath caught in her throat. It was Mather's Justice of the Peace, the one with the iron jaw and the insignia on his shoulder. His gaze skirted over the interior of the container, but Jacob slipped between him and Waverly, blocking his view.

"Hiding something?" Tom asked.

Jacob sniggered.

"Because some people would be interested to know if you've run into anyone."

"Nope," Jacob said.

There was a pause. Waverly looked from the door to Ginny, to the knife she held. Ginny shook her head at Waverly, slowly, meaningfully.

"Waverly Marshall went missing," Tom said. "I thought you might want to know that."

"Oh really?" Jacob said, feigning slight interest. "When?"

"It's been about twelve hours now."

"Haven't seen her. Wish I had. I'd like to get my hands on her."

"Yeah," Tom said, stretching the word out.

Through all of this, Waverly's mind raced. If she opened her mouth, Ginny could stab her right now. If she kept quiet, she might live longer, but . . .

"Help!" she called, almost before she'd decided.

With lightning speed, Ginny darted to a crouch over Waverly and pressed her blade against her neck. Waverly nearly fainted from fear. The room turned orange, then gray.

"You have her," the man said. "I knew it."

She heard the door sliding open, a brief scuffle, and suddenly Mather's big guard was standing over her. She stared at him, panting like an animal. *Please.*

"What are you going to do with her?" Thomas said. The way he looked at Waverly, with complete detachment, deepened her terror. *He's as bad as they are.*

"None of your business, Tom," Ginny spat. "She's ours, fair and square."

"I don't care," Tom said, holding up his hands. "I'm just telling you. If you're planning on trading her, you won't get anything from Anne. The Pastor hates her as much as you do. So you may as well . . ." He drew his thumb across his neck.

"We're not trading her," Ginny finally said. "That's not why we took her."

"What for, then?" Thomas lifted one corner of his mouth in a confused sneer.

Ginny stood and pointed a finger at the big guard's chest. It was almost comical, seeing a tiny woman trying to push around a huge man, but something about her scared Thomas, because he took half a step back. "It's none of your concern, Tom."

"Anyway, you guys are safe here for a while yet," Thomas said. "But it would sure help me protect you if I knew what you were planning."

"Oh, you know," Ginny said casually. "We're just trying to help the Pastor out. Get back in her good graces. Show we can be useful, you know. For the mission."

Waverly was confused by this, since Ginny had just avowed her hatred for Mather, but she knew not to contradict.

Thomas nodded. "Well, anything you need from me . . ."

"Food is all we need," Ginny said briskly.

"Any news?" Jacob asked.

Thomas rubbed his chin as though trying to recall. "Oh! We found that kid."

"Seth?" Jake asked eagerly.

Waverly froze.

Thomas nodded, and Jake punched the air and laughed. "I told you he'd get out of the brig, Ginny!"

"Yeah," Ginny said and rolled her eyes.

Waverly felt as if the life had gone out of her. Mather had Seth. Kieran was Mather's pawn. She'd won. There was no point in fighting anymore. *Except Mom,* Waverly thought as fresh tears came. *What will happen to Mom?*

"He's hurt," Thomas said, watching Jacob's expression. "Want to get a message to him?"

"Hurt how?" Jacob asked warily.

"His hand. Bad infection."

Waverly remembered Seth's mangled fingers and the dirty bandage he'd had on his hand. She hadn't even asked him about it.

"You can't do nothing for him?" Jacob asked. "Get him a doctor."

"Pastor didn't say to." Thomas pulled a sloppily rolled cigarette out of his breast pocket, tapped it against the back of his hand, and picked up the Bunsen burner to light it.

"Did she say *not* to get him a doctor?" Jake asked. "Specifically?"

Waverly looked at Jacob. Genuine concern had softened his features, making him look boyish and strangely kind. When she looked at Ginny, the woman glared at her. She dropped her gaze to the wheel of the landing vehicle and tried to go to a place inside herself.

"Anyway." Thomas set the Bunsen burner back under the tin of oatmeal and took a long drag on his cigarette, eyes shifting lazily between Ginny and Jacob. "I'll be off."

"When will you come back?" Ginny asked gruffly.

"Don't know. You've got food for a few days."

"Yeah," Jacob said.

"I'll check back with you." Thomas stepped out of the container.

The couple glared silently at each other as they listened to Thomas's footsteps fade away, then Jacob sat back down on his box. "I don't like lying to him."

"Jake, sometimes you're so stupid I can't even believe it."

"We can *trust* Tom. He and I used to play together in grade school."

"He's not a kid anymore, unlike you. He's loyal to Mather. He'd try to stop us."

"Maybe not," Jake offered, "if I promise to make him my right-hand man when I'm captain."

Ginny sneered. "He's just keeping an eye on us for Mather. He thinks we're stupid, that we don't know he's working for her. And we'll let him think that until the time comes to make our move."

"You're wrong about him," Jacob said, staring into the flame of the burner. "You'll see."

"Right," Ginny said grimly, then glanced angrily at Waverly. Without warning, she kicked Waverly in the leg with the toe of her boot.

"When I say quiet," she growled, "you keep your mouth closed. Understand?"

"Yes," Waverly whispered.

"*Understand?*" Waverly felt a handful of her hair being grabbed and her head wrenched backward. She could smell the woman's sour breath as she sobbed. "Because you don't seem to learn very fast."

"I'm learning," Waverly pleaded. "I am."

Allies

"Thank you for seeing me," Kieran said to the ancient man sitting at the mammoth oak desk. Dr. Carver rested his knobby hands on the handle of his beautifully carved cane and stared at Kieran with pinpoint eyes as he worked his jaw around a prune. He picked up a cup and clumsily spat the pit into it, then leaned back in his chair. So this was the evil doctor. He looked to be at death's door.

"I was curious to meet you," the man said, lifting his chin. "Mather's little friend."

Kieran squirmed in his chair, which squeaked embarrassingly. He heard a movement behind him and glanced back to see that the doctor's assistant stood with his arms folded over his chest, looking at Kieran coldly.

"You are concerned about Waverly Marshall, I gathered from your text," the doctor said.

"I think Jacob Pauley might have found her," Kieran said.

"That's what worries us," the old man said thoughtfully with a glance at his assistant. "That's why we're using all our resources to find her. But I'm afraid I must tell you, young man, we are not holding out much hope."

Kieran's heart sank. This man didn't seem remotely concerned about Waverly. "Where have you looked for her?"

"We've given the ship a thorough going over."

"She was last seen in the storage bay," Kieran said slowly. "So if Jacob Pauley came across her there, he could be hiding her in a shipping container."

The doctor laughed. "So all we need to do is search every container. There's only, what? Ten, fifteen thousand of them . . . We'll find her within the year."

Anger surged through Kieran. "What about surveillance? They must be coming and going for supplies."

"Mather won't let us near the video system."

"We could set up cameras of our own." Kieran turned to look at the assistant, who was watching him. "Hook them into a computer network wired separately from the central com system. Mather won't even know about it."

The old man pulled on the end of his nose a couple times. "All right. Jared, will you see to it?"

"Of course," the assistant said quietly. The old man turned toward his computer screen, shooing Kieran away.

"There's one other thing," Kieran said in a rush. "Waverly told me you're a neurologist? That you might be able to cure our parents?"

The old man squirmed, but he arranged his withered features into a regretful smile. "I made no promises."

"Can you help?" Kieran said with barely controlled rage. "My mother is very . . . damaged."

The doctor lowered his eyes in a dim imitation of sympathy. "I'm sorry. I have been . . . unsuccessful."

"What have you tried?" Kieran pressed. "What kind of drug did the damage?"

"It's all very technical," he said with a wave of the hand. "I couldn't explain it."

"I'm very smart," Kieran said slowly. "Why don't you try?"

"I haven't explored all the avenues," the doctor replied. "I'll know more soon."

Kieran watched the old man's nose twitch once, twice. *He's lying,* Kieran suddenly knew with murderous certainty. *He's doesn't care about helping our parents. He doesn't care about finding Waverly. He's been lying to her all along.*

"I can understand the Pastor's interest in you," the doctor was saying to Kieran, nodding toward the door. "You're an intelligent, passionate young man."

Kieran stood, eyeing the doctor with unvarnished hatred, but immediately the assistant moved next to him. Jared was slightly taller than Kieran, and light on his feet. He looked wiry and strong, but his subservience to this weak old man was puzzling. Jared gestured toward the door and Kieran followed him through it. Jared kept his pace even with Kieran's, and when they reached the end of the corridor, he opened the door for him, cocking his head toward the stairs.

They walked down a flight together before Jared finally spoke. "If we want to help Waverly," he said quietly, his head turned away from the camera, "we'll have to do it ourselves."

Kieran stopped, but with a glance at the security camera over them, Jared pulled Kieran down to the next level. Kieran didn't see a microphone attached to the camera and guessed that Jared had taken him here so they could talk without anyone else hearing.

"The doctor doesn't want to find her?" Kieran asked.

"I don't think so," Jared said. His voice was gravelly with fatigue, and he rubbed at his red eyes with his thumb and index finger. "Anyway, he's not too concerned."

"So he *was* using her."

"Like Mather is using you," Jared said out of the side of his mouth.

Kieran was silent as they descended the next flight. When they reached the level where his apartment was, he turned to face Jared. "Why are you telling me this?"

"I want Waverly back," the man said.

"Then what are you going to do about it?" Kieran challenged, choosing for the moment to ignore Jared's odd choice of words.

The man's face hardened. "Can you get out of your apartment tonight?"

"Probably. I'm not under guard."

"Wait for my text." Jared opened the door for Kieran. "We're finding her tonight."

"How?" Kieran asked.

Jared looked surprised. "Your plan. It's a good one. I'll set up the cameras. Be ready."

Kieran went home with butterflies in his stomach. The apartment smelled of fresh rolls, but when his mother served him one, it tasted as though it had a pound of salt in it. He spat it out and watched, astonished, as his mother ate her own roll eagerly.

"Mom," he whispered.

She looked up, surprised. Crumbs from her roll clung to the corners of her lips.

He couldn't speak, so he wrapped his arms around her and held on. She laughed at first, tried to pull away to look at him, but finally gave in to his embrace and held him.

Still my mom, Kieran told himself. *Even if there's no cure.*

Later, they read in companionable silence, an ancient recording of the Bach piano inventions playing over the com system. Kieran looked out the porthole just as a shooting star whizzed by. It wasn't really a star—that was just what the adults called a stray particle that was ignited in a collision with the hull. It happened very rarely, so whenever anyone saw one, he or she'd always call out, "Make a wish!"

"Let us find her alive," Kieran whispered under his breath.

"What, honey?"

"Nothing." What point would there be in telling her? So Anne Mather could interrogate her later?

Lena smiled absently and went back to her reading.

At bedtime, Kieran went to his room to wait. His com screen showed a short text from Felicity asking, *Any word?*

No, Kieran wrote back, choosing not to mention his plan with Jared, for her protection. *How are you?*

Worried, she responded almost immediately. *Scared.*

Me too, he responded. *Don't take any chances, okay?*

You neither, she wrote back. And that was the end of it.

It was getting late when Kieran lay down on his bed, the crook of his elbow over his eyes, waiting for Jared's text. He was in a light doze when he jerked awake to the *ping* of an incoming message. He sprang to his feet and clicked the message icon.

Storage bay, central stairwell, now was all it said.

Kieran crammed his feet into his shoes and ran out the door, relieved that Mather still hadn't posted guards on him. Once in the stairwell, he slid down the metal handrails, holding his arms out for balance, swinging around as he hit each landing. He hadn't gone very far before his heart started beating madly, and he had to stop to catch his breath to keep from fainting.

Running down the stairs would be even worse, so he kept sliding and swinging around, his heart pumping painfully, his fingertips tingling. "Thank God," he cried aloud when he saw he was nearing the storage bay level. He was swinging around to the final landing when a dark shape whirled at him.

"Quiet!" Jared hissed. "They might hear."

Kieran wanted to ask if he'd found Waverly, but he couldn't speak. He collapsed onto the stairs, hanging his head between his knees. His stomach heaved, and he threw up a thin, bubbly phlegm and spat it between his feet. What was *wrong* with him?

"You okay?" Jared asked in a whisper.

"Not really," Kieran said between ragged breaths. "I have a weak heart, I think."

He felt a hand on his shoulder. "You should have told me."

Kieran could only nod.

Jared knelt and whispered in his ear. "They know me, they know my voice. They won't talk to me. That's what I need you for. I want you to knock on the door, pretend to be alone. Get them to open the door. I'll handle the rest."

"What if they won't talk to me?"

"Make yourself sound vulnerable and alone. They'll open up if they think they can shut you up themselves."

"Okay," Kieran said doubtfully.

"Come on," Jared said, pulling on Kieran's shirt.

Kieran got to his feet, swaying a little, and followed Jared. They crept along a row of shipping containers, hidden in the shadows where the lights didn't reach. Jared counted under his breath, pulling Kieran behind him until he crouched abruptly, leaning against the heavy metal side of one container. He knocked on the door.

Not a sound came from inside. Jared looked at Kieran and raised his eyebrows.

"Um. Hello?" Kieran called. "Jacob Pauley? I know you're in there. It's me, Kieran Alden."

No response.

"I'm alone. I just want to talk to Waverly. I need to know she's all right."

Silence. Jared looked at Kieran from under heavy black brows. His jaw was set at a square angle, and he held both hands out, facing the door, ready to pounce. He looked every inch a killer.

"Jacob," Kieran said, his mind racing, "I'm telling you, right now I'm alone. If you don't open the door I'll call Central Command and tell them where you are."

Kieran thought he heard a whimper escape from inside, and someone muttered under his breath. The latch on the door turned, and the door slid open a couple inches.

"You alone?" Jacob Pauley growled at him.

"Yes," Kieran said.

It was so dark in the container that Kieran could see only Jacob's outline—his nose, some stray hairs caught in the light as he peered out from the darkness.

"Because if you're not alone . . . ," Jacob said.

"You think I have a lot of friends on this ship?" Kieran said.

A brief exchange of hisses sounded from inside the container, then the door squealed open and Jacob poked his head out.

With stunning speed, Jared leapt up and hooked an arm around Jacob's neck. He rammed the big man's throat against the edge of the doorway with such violence that Kieran hid his face. Jacob collapsed, hacking and spitting. Jared took hold of his hair, jammed his head into the side of the container, and held it there. Jacob fought for breath on his hands and knees, sputtering.

"Ginny!" The name came out of Jared like a howl, ending with a sneer of such contempt that Kieran took a step backward. "I've partially collapsed your husband's larynx, darling. A punch in the throat will kill him. Understand?"

A woman screamed out of the darkness: "Let him go, you *murderer*!"

"What I do next depends on whether Waverly is still alive." There was a brief pause, then the sounds of bodies moving around inside the container, and finally a thin, terrified voice called out, "I'm here."

Waverly. Kieran closed his eyes with profound relief.

Jared said, "You may have just bought your husband's life, Ginny."

"I'll kill her if you hurt him."

"So we each have something the other wants."

Jacob tried to stand, but Jared pushed his head harder against the side of the container, and Jacob went limp.

"How did you find us?" Ginny snarled.

"I'll tell you a secret, you little idiot," Jared said. "We've known where you were all along."

Was this true? Kieran glanced at Jared and tried to read his face, but the man was encased in darkness.

"That's . . . ," Ginny began.

"The truth, Virginia. They've all been waiting for your plan to reveal itself. Mather. The doctor. Your friend Thomas. Until you took Waverly, they were just waiting for the moment to squash you like a couple of roaches."

The woman was silenced by this. Kieran could feel her thinking in the dark. "Thomas and Jakey are friends," she finally said.

"Thomas isn't anyone's friend, Ginny."

Waverly cried out in pain, and Kieran stiffened.

"You're lying!" the woman screamed, and Waverly shrieked. "Why would the doctor change his mind now?"

Kieran started to feel an uncomfortable doubt worming through the back of his mind.

"The doctor has nothing to do with this conversation," Jared said. "If you want to live through the night, you'll listen to me."

"If everything's over like you say, why should I talk to you? I could kill this little bitch and be done with it!"

"I'm not here to take you down."

Again, silence.

"What are you talking about?" The woman, Ginny, was trying to sound strong, but Kieran could hear tears in her voice.

"You've got nothing to bargain with, Ginny. Mather *wants* you to kill that girl. She was going to let you do it."

"You think I wanted to trade her?"

Jacob had stopped coughing, though his breath was still whistling in his throat.

"Whatever your plans for Waverly were, they're done," Jared went on. "Regardless, I know there's no easy way to get Waverly out of this container alive."

"That's right!" the woman shrieked.

"That's why I brought two things to offer you."

Kieran squirmed.

Jared held up a small, glowing com unit, a type Kieran had heard about but never seen. It was small enough to fit in the palm of Jared's hand, and it glowed with an ethereal blue light.

"Where did you get that?" Jacob whispered in awe.

Jared gripped Jacob's hair in his fist and knocked his head into the container. The man swayed on his hands and knees.

"Ginny, are you listening?" Jared asked.

"I'm listening," she parroted.

"When you let Waverly walk away, I'll give you darkness."

"What?"

"A blackout. This device disables all the lights on the ship for thirty minutes. As long as you avoid the infrared cameras at the air locks, you'll be invisible."

After a pause, the woman said, "Interesting. But you said two things."

"I brought you Kieran Alden."

Before he saw Jared move, Kieran felt him land on his back. Kieran fell onto his stomach, kicking at the air and trying to pull his hands free, but within seconds a cord was pulled tight over his ankles, wrapped once around his neck, and then bound around his wrists. If he tried to pull his wrists or legs free, the cord tightened against his throat. In a matter of seconds he'd been totally immobilized.

The struggle had given Jacob Pauley enough time to stand up and rub his head, but Jared pulled a small gun from a leather holder around his waist and pointed it at Jacob's heart. The man lifted his hands, glaring.

"Why would I want Kieran Alden?" Ginny asked.

Kieran lay perfectly still, hoping Jared was bluffing. *But if this is a bluff, why wasn't I in on it?*

"Because," Jared said, drawing the word out, mocking her intelligence, "Anne Mather wants Kieran Alden. Alive. Now you have something to bargain with."

There was another pause while Ginny thought about it. "Is he going to testify at Mather's trial?"

"He's on Mather's list of witnesses," Jared said hesitantly, as though he didn't quite understand the question.

"Where's my darkness?"

"I want Waverly first."

"Fine," the woman said, irritated.

Jacob grunted in frustration. "Ginny! No!" His voice rattled in his injured throat.

"We'll get her later," Ginny said.

"Waverly?" Jared called.

Kieran could hear halting footsteps from inside the container. As Waverly emerged, she sobbed and collapsed onto her knees next to Kieran. Her hands fumbled over his body, clawed at the cord around his wrists. A corona of wild hair glowed around her head in the dim light.

"It's okay," Kieran tried to tell her.

"No. No. No." She shook her head as she desperately worked at the knots that bound him.

A motion caught Kieran's eye, and he turned just in time to see Jared lift the small com unit and tap the screen. The lights in the storage bay went out with a resounding boom. Kieran wriggled, but the cord tightened around his neck, swelling his face with blood until he felt woozy and he had to lie still to keep from passing out. "You son of a bitch," he hissed at Jared.

In the shine of the com unit, Kieran saw Jared's dark shape pull Waverly away.

"No!" she screamed. "You can't leave him!" She clawed at Jared, kicking, but he lifted her by the waist and disappeared behind a shipping container. Kieran could hear her screaming and fighting until her voice disappeared behind a heavy-sounding door.

"Let's move," the woman growled. "Can you walk?"

"Yes," Jacob said, though he was hoarse.

"Carry him," the woman said.

"I'm choking," Kieran rasped.

"Cut the cord," Ginny said irritably.

Kieran felt an increase in pressure, heard a blade slide though the cord that bound his neck to his feet, and he could breathe again, though his hands and feet were still tied.

Kieran felt himself being picked up in the man's arms. He tried to memorize the number of steps, the number of turns, as Jacob stumbled through the darkness behind his wife. He thought they were headed to the starboard side, and he lifted his face to try and get his bearings. Without word or warning, something crashed down on his head, sending sparks across the backs of his eyes, and he couldn't think anymore.

Seth

The smell in the brig was unbearable. Usually with a stink, you could get used to it, but not this one. The cells were all empty, except maybe for a few in the back, and the brig looked clean to the eye. But a rank, putrid smell invaded every square inch of the air.

And his hand . . . the pain was so total it erased everything else. All he could do was concentrate on breathing, in and out. *Stay alive and breathe,* he told himself. *Don't think about your hand.*

He had gangrene. He could feel it in the way his blood scalded the insides of his veins. His head buzzed, his chest felt weak and loose, and his heart was fluttery. He knew he had a high fever, but what he felt was horrible, bitter cold that overtook his body in spasm after spasm.

"They're going to let me die." He said the words to himself, under his breath, moving his tongue behind his teeth to form the word. *Die. Die. Die.* He was trying to get used to the idea.

He'd always assumed he'd end up a skinny old man like his father, though he'd hoped for a better life. He'd even thought he might try being a dad himself and treat his kids with the kindness he'd never had. Some abused kids went on to be good parents, didn't they? But he'd wanted more than just a family. He wanted to be the best deck officer there was. He'd be so good that his dislike of Captain Jones wouldn't stop him from someday piloting the ship. He'd make himself someone his kids could be proud of.

That was the future Seth had imagined before everything started.

Then, after the attack, Kieran had taken over the Empyrean and proceeded to endanger everyone on board. Watching Kieran's mistakes and miscalculations had brought out Seth's own brutal nature, and he'd turned into a worse brute than his father had been. That's when Seth had seen how unrealistic his dreams of having a family were. He was too angry to be a loving father, or even a decent deck officer. Seth's internal darkness would always engulf him; he'd always be unlikable and vicious.

So he'd landed himself in the brig on the Empyrean. His months there taught him to let go of his dreams, to accept a far humbler future, to disappear into a lab or a field somewhere. No woman in her right mind would want to raise a family with him, he'd thought; he'd just be grateful for his freedom, even if he was alone forever. He'd do his humble work, and live a solitary life. That seemed to be all he was good for.

Then Waverly came back to the Empyrean. And they talked. And hope came back. Maybe he could have his dreams after all . . .

Through all those imagined versions of the future, through all those compromises, he'd never considered he might not have a future at all.

Footsteps.

Footsteps were coming up the corridor, falling like feathers on the hard metal. A short, skinny woman with brown hair knotted at the nape of her neck peeked around the wall at Seth.

"Oh God," she said under her breath. She was dressed in the gray-green scrubs of a nurse.

"Huh-huh-help," Seth croaked through his cracked throat.

"I need access to this cell now!" she screamed down the corridor at someone.

"You don't have to yell," called a man irritably.

"How could you let him suffer like this?" she snarled at someone who was coming up the hallway, his heavy footfalls sounding like the beat of a drum. "*Anyone* could tell he's seriously ill!"

"I've got other things on my plate, Nan," the man said, but when he turned to look at Seth, his fat face fell. "Oh boy," he said.

"Yeah," she snapped at him. "Open the door!"

The guard rattled through his key chain, the woman shaking her head furiously as he fumbled. When finally the door slid open, she ran to Seth.

"I'm a nurse. My name's Nan," she said as she pressed fingertips against his wrist. "Can you speak?"

Seth nodded, tried to say "Yes," but all he could get out was "Yuh Yuh Yuh Yuh . . ." The tremors from his fever shook him into silence.

"I can't help him here," Nan said to the guard. "He needs the infirmary."

The guard shook his head. "Strict orders from the Pastor he's to be kept in solitary."

"She doesn't know how sick he is!" the woman yelled. "Call her! Tell her I'm down here. Tell her it's an emergency!"

The guard shook his head again but took a walkie-talkie from the belt around his sagging middle. "Central Command," he said into it, and waited.

"Go ahead, brig," said a woman's voice.

"I've got a request to speak with the Pastor. Nan McGovern says it's an emergency."

"Wait," the voice responded.

The woman pulled a long needle from her case along with a vial of clear liquid. "Are you in pain?" she asked Seth.

The simple, compassionate question nearly made him weep, and he nodded.

"This is going to fight your fever," she said as she wiped a cotton swab on Seth's inner elbow. The smell of alcohol stung his nose. "Hold still." She waited for a pause in Seth's spasms before she pierced his skin and injected the medicine into his bloodstream. Then she unwrapped his hurt hand and turned it over, keeping her expression neutral and businesslike. Seth thought for a moment that the nurse's face was glowing with an orange light, but he blinked and she looked normal again. Now the orange light seemed to come from the guard, near his swollen belly. Seth stared at it until it faded away.

"Nan," came Anne Mather's voice. She sounded so smooth, so kind, so understanding.

"Yes, Pastor," Nan said. She spoke the title with deference, as though she'd always dreamed of having a private word with her hero and was finally getting her chance. "I've got a young prisoner here who needs emergency medical attention."

"Who gave you access to him?" the Pastor asked, lilting.

"Jared Carver escorted me here. He's waiting outside."

There was a long pause before Mather spoke again. "Nan, that boy is dangerous. We thought it best to keep him in isolation."

"Pastor, I'm telling you. He's not dangerous to anyone. He's at death's door."

Another pause.

Nan rushed to speak. "I only say so because I know you wouldn't want a young man to die, even if he did make mistakes. Everyone deserves a second chance, isn't that so? Isn't that what you say in your sermons?" Nan bit her lip, and Seth felt sorry for her. She wanted to believe in Anne Mather. She *needed* to.

"All right," the Pastor finally said. "You're absolutely right, Nan. If you think he's in danger, we must help him. Mustn't we?"

"I think so," Nan said. "Shall I call the infirmary?"

"I will," Mather said. Her voice was comforting, motherly, and Nan let out a long sigh, as though she'd been afraid that good was bad and up was down. "Sit tight, Nan. Try to make him comfortable."

Nan took a wad of gauze from her bag and held it under the tap, soaking it with water. When she held it to Seth's forehead, he started to cry.

"Hush, now," Nan whispered. She smoothed the hair out of his face and wiped his brow, then pressed the cool cloth to his cheeks and his neck.

Soon two men dressed in white came with a gurney, and Nan helped them lift Seth onto it. As they wheeled him down the corridor, he was struck with a wave of horrible dizziness, and he had to close his eyes or he might fall off.

His next thought was that the brig was too bright. Someone pulled on his wrist while a middle-aged woman shined a penlight into his eyes. Her breath smelled like garlic, and a small speck of tomato sauce clung to the corner of her mouth.

"Can you speak?" she asked Seth. She moved slowly and deliberately, as though she were incapable of panic.

"Yes," Seth managed to whisper.

"How long ago did you hurt your hand?" the doctor asked him.

He couldn't form words to answer her.

The doctor nodded. "Doesn't matter. Looks like broken fingers to me?"

Seth nodded.

"Okay, buddy," the doctor said, sitting down in a chair right next to Seth's head. He trusted her absolutely—was it real, or only because he needed to trust her? "Here's the deal," she said. "You can have your arm, or you can have your life. You can't have both."

Tears squeezed from under Seth's eyelids, and he bit his lip.

"Are you a brave lad?" She kept her eyes on his. Green eyes, unwavering.

Seth could only look at her.

"Will you let me help you? I have your permission to do what I need to do?"

Seth looked down at his hand. The smell from the brig had followed him here.

Of course, it hadn't been the brig that stank.

Seth nodded at the doctor, who patted his shoulder.

"Good man. Good decision." She nodded to someone who stood at Seth's head, and a mask was fitted over his nose and mouth. "Breathe in deep, okay?" the doctor said.

"Okay," Seth said into the mask. His own voice sounded as though it were coming from the bottom of a tin can, a nice, comforting, small tin can where he fit perfectly. *One day I'll go back to that tin can*, Seth thought. *I'll bring Waverly to show her... if she isn't with that creep. Her and me in a tin can.*

He shook his head to clear it, but the hand with the mask stayed firm on him.

That's crazy was the last thing he thought.

He woke up to a dark room, immensely relieved to feel his right hand searing with pain. They hadn't amputated after all! He lifted his hand to look at it, but it was invisible. He could feel it, he ought to be looking right at it, but ... He was suddenly attacked by intense vertigo and a horrible pain in his upper arm that nauseated him.

He took deep breaths, holding perfectly still, until the nausea subsided.

Then, with a sinking feeling, he felt with his good hand along the side of his body.

He didn't have a right hand anymore.

He didn't have an elbow.

He didn't have an arm.

He still had a shoulder.

"He's awake," he heard a soft female voice say from the shadows. He felt woozy, and he blinked. He was lying in a pool of light surrounded by darkness. The light had a strange hazy quality, as though a thin smoke were lingering in the air, but there was no smell of smoke. It was his vision that was smoky, he guessed. He should tell someone. He opened his mouth to speak but found it difficult to breathe.

"Don't," someone said. He got a whiff of some kind of flower, and he turned to see a bouquet of lilacs being set down by his bed on a little table. "Stay still."

"I can't—" he gasped.

"You still have a high fever," said that soft voice from the darkness. Seth blinked as a thin oval face moved into the light next to him. Suddenly everything hurt a little less.

"Waverly," he whispered. All his jealousy and doubts melted away.

She kissed his cheeks, his forehead, his mouth. She nuzzled her nose against his neck. He tried to put his arms around her and felt almost as though he could. He knew his right arm was gone, but he felt it so clearly.

"Don't move. You're weak," she said. She was crying, and she draped her body over his, holding his good arm down with the weight of her torso. "Just rest."

"I'm so sorry . . ."

"Shush." She placed cool fingers over his lips, then kissed him again, warm, soft. Oh, he loved her. She put her head on his chest and lay there a long time, crying softly. Her tears soaked through his bedclothes and the thin gown he wore. He kissed her hair again and again.

When she'd cried herself out, she lifted her head and smiled at him, but it wasn't a happy smile. It was a brave smile. She swallowed, preparing to tell him something hard.

"I know my arm . . . ," he began and lost his breath.

"Okay," she said and covered his mouth with her fingers. He loved that. He kissed them. "Seth, your infection . . . it's bad."

He nodded. He could feel it, like tiny bugs jiggling all through his body, from his veins to his muscles to his skin.

He couldn't see her face. She hid it behind her hair, a thick curtain of mahogany waves.

"They said you were missing," Seth whispered. "Where you been?"

A shadow passed over her face. "Looking for you."

"How did you find me?"

"I had help," Waverly said with a glance at the doorway. Seth could see a dark male shape standing just outside the infirmary. "As soon as I was able to, I came to the brig for you. While you were in surgery, I checked on my mom and came right back."

"Who is that guy?" Seth asked, his jealously gone. *She's mine*, he knew. *We belong together.*

"I used to think he was my friend but . . ." She chewed on her lip as she looked at the man. "I saw pictures of me in the corridors. They said *truth*. Was that you?"

He smiled weakly.

"Thank you."

He thought over what she'd just told him about his infection and worked up the courage to ask, "Am I dying?"

She looked at him sharply. "Don't talk like that."

"Waverly," he said.

"They're throwing everything they have at it."

"Tell me."

"I can't," she shrieked. The room, the darkness outside their pool of light, was jarred by her voice.

Seth heard a chair being pushed across the floor, someone getting up, soft footsteps, and then the nurse who'd saved his life came into the light. She frowned at Waverly. "You need to keep it down. There are other people here."

"I'm sorry," Waverly cried, panicked and trembling. "Please don't send me away."

Before Seth's eyes, Waverly fell apart, no more composed than if she were made of loose powder. Her hands caught in her hair, pulling at it in handfuls. Something was wrong with her. Really wrong.

The nurse softened a little, but her words were hard. "Now you know what it's like to be a hostage."

"I recognize you," Waverly said tearfully. "You were on the medical team we took hostage. I know I scared you. I just wanted my mom back."

"You almost killed Anthony."

"I never wanted to hurt him." Waverly pulled on the woman's shirt like a little girl begging. "Please. Let me stay."

"I will if you let me give you a mild sedative. You're hysterical and you're disturbing the other patients."

"I know." Waverly nodded, her eyes dancing over the floor as though she were remembering something, or trying not to.

"Wavey," Seth whispered. He'd meant to say her full name, had faltered with his tongue. "What did she mean . . . hostage?"

Instantly she was calm. "How do you know to call me that?"

He crinkled his eyebrows in question as he panted. He was sweaty. His sheets were soaked, and he was overtaken by a sudden falling sensation, as though his bed were being lowered by increments.

"My daddy used to call me that," Waverly said, smiling through her tears. "I'd forgotten."

"What *happened* to you?" he managed to ask just as his bed fell again.

Her face crumpled. "I'll tell you sometime. But right now, just don't talk about dying. Okay?"

"Okay," he whispered. He motioned her over with his right hand, with what should have been his right hand. He felt it moving, beckoning her. The movement made a horrible pain in his shoulder. *Oh God, stop moving my hand. Stop moving it,* he told himself, but he couldn't stop. That ghost hand kept beckoning to Waverly, over and over and over.

As though she'd seen the missing gesture, she climbed onto his bed, her body tucked along the length of his. She didn't move a millimeter when the nurse plunged a needle into her shoulder.

He put his arms around her, the real arm and the missing one, and he held her as long as his strength let him. It wasn't long, but it was enough for now.

They slept like that a long time.

The Devil

Waverly jerked awake and looked at the clock. She'd slept for hours! She had to go!

Seth was still sleeping, though his body shuddered with every breath and droplets of cold sweat glistened in his hair. She eased off his mattress, tucked the blankets around him, and put a palm to his forehead. He was blistering hot, and he shuddered with every breath. He looked so ill she was afraid to leave him alone, but she'd stayed too long already. Those lunatics had Kieran and she had to do something.

She was about to leave the room when something caught her eye: The glass vial of tranquilizer that the nurse had given her still lay on the counter next to Seth's bed, nearly full. The nurse had called it mild, but that must have been a lie. It was powerful, and it had acted fast.

Waverly glanced around. The nurse was at her desk at the front of the room looking through a file drawer. Jared was still in the corridor outside the infirmary, dozing on a chair. Careful not to make a sound, Waverly opened the top drawer of the cabinet by Seth's bed and peeked into it. Nothing. The next drawer down had what she needed. She chose the largest syringe she could find, pierced the skin on the vial of tranquilizer, and drew in as much medication as she could. Then she placed the vial back on the counter, capped the needle, and slipped it into her pocket. With one last look at Seth, she started toward the entrance.

She stopped at the nurse's desk, waiting for the woman to look at her. "Will you please tell Seth I'll come back as soon as I can?"

"If you're so worried," the nurse said through pursed lips, "why don't you stay?"

"Someone needs my help," Waverly answered.

"My, aren't you important."

Waverly left without another word, walking right past Jared down the hallway. He jogged to catch up to her.

"How many times do I have to say I'm sorry?" Jared said through the side of his mouth. "It was Kieran's life or yours."

"I've seen the way you fight." Waverly made a fist. "You didn't have to use Kieran. You gave him to those maniacs because the doctor wanted to hurt Mather and save me!"

"Right," he said with a chuckle.

"What?" Waverly said with a half turn of her head. Jared looked away, embarrassed about something, as though she'd struck close to home without meaning to. "What are you hiding?"

"Nothing." Jared tried to laugh. "You've been through a lot—"

"Don't." She held up a hand. She didn't want any mention of her time with the Pauleys. She studied Jared now, trying to understand why he looked . . . guilty? No. Embarrassed, as though she'd caught him in a lie. She searched her memory and lighted on something Ginny Pauley had said. "Ginny asked you if the doctor had changed his mind about something. What did she mean?"

"Don't overthink this." He lifted up his handheld com unit, and Waverly watched his thumb fly over the small keypad. He typed in a password: *mynx101* or *mynx1901* . . . something very close to that. She lifted her eyes to his, hoping he hadn't noticed her watching. "The cord I used to tie Kieran up?" he said. "It's got a tracking device in it, no bigger than a pencil eraser." He rounded on her so that they stood toe to toe, and she could feel his breath caressing her cheek. "I could help you find him, but you've never even thanked me for saving you."

"You're right," she said as she took a step back. The easygoing Jared had been replaced by a callous, hard man who matched up a lot better with the violence she'd seen him do. "I'm grateful that you helped me. Really. I . . . I just need to help Kieran. Okay? Can you help us?"

"It's just that," he said, his eyes perfectly still on her, weirdly still, "I love you. But all you care about are these little boys of yours."

She could only stare at him. "What are you talking about?"

He turned away from her abruptly, walked down the corridor.

"So you're tracking them?" Waverly asked, trying to make her tone curious and friendly as she jogged to catch up. "You know where Kieran is right now?"

"Yes," Jared said distractedly. He pushed the button for the elevator, tapping at his leg impatiently. "It doesn't matter to you that I love you?"

She hesitated. She didn't know how to have this absurd conversation.

"It doesn't matter that I saved your life?"

"For that you have my gratitude." She allowed no trace of emotion into her voice.

Jared looked at her flatly until the elevator doors opened, then he stepped on, his body taut with anger. There were other people already on the elevator, and a man quietly stepped forward and pushed a button for the next floor. The other people stood in the corners, their eyes fastidiously trained on the floor indicator until the elevator stopped for them, and they stepped off, but as they left a woman looked over her shoulder, first at Jared and then at Waverly. There was an unmistakable fear in her eyes.

The elevator doors closed, and Waverly was once again alone with him. "Why are people afraid of you?"

"People aren't afraid of me," Jared said, small voiced.

She said nothing.

"Why do you think they're afraid?" he asked quietly.

"It's the way people look at you," she said. "The women especially."

"You think you have a reason to mistrust me?" A droplet of spittle flew from between his lips. "I thought we were friends."

The elevator shook slightly, and Waverly realized she didn't know where he was taking her.

Jared laughed. "The doctor always warned me about pretty girls," he said and raised one finger, bending it into the twisted shape of an old man's talon. " 'If they're too pretty, they'll expect you to bend over backward to please them.' "

His impersonation of the doctor was flawless, but this time it was chilling.

"I don't expect anything from you," Waverly said quietly. Was he taking her to the habitation levels? She watched the counter above the elevator doors, calculating the levels in her mind. They went past the floor where she lived with her mother, descending deeper into the ship.

"I was once popular with women," Jared said as they passed the granaries and headed for the forests. "But I sure am striking out with you, huh, Waverly?"

"Maybe you should try someone your own age," she said.

He punched the elevator wall. "What's a guy gotta do if saving your life isn't good enough?"

Waverly wedged her shoulders into the corner. "Why did you help me find Seth?"

He held up the com unit, flicked a button, and Waverly's voice filled the air. "*Seth, your infection... it's bad...*"

"You were *recording* us?" she asked, stunned.

He grinned. "The doctor likes to know who all the players are."

"Otherwise you'd have let him die?"

Jared shrugged.

"Seth's too sick to do anything," Waverly said, afraid of what the doctor might have planned for him. "Please don't hurt him."

"Please don't hurt him!" Jared whined at her. "Poor little Waverly is worried about her boyfriend!"

What *was* this? Waverly tried to understand, but there were too many moving parts and she was too scared to think.

"You think that Ardvale kid is better than me, *Waverly*?" he spoke her name with sneering scorn. Waverly shrank farther away. She thought of the needle in her pocket, but there was no way she could get it without him seeing. "Do you think *anybody* on this godforsaken ship is better than me?"

She jammed her jaw shut, afraid if she spoke she'd only enrage him further.

"This is a ship of *murderers,* honey. Okay? Your parents. My parents. His parents. Killers." He nodded at her self-righteously. "They pretended this was a democratic mission so the engineers and the metalworkers and the scientists would work with them. *Thousands* of the greatest minds on Earth cooperated for a chance at a lottery that *never happened*!"

Waverly shook her head—tiny little motions. "My father was a botanist."

"You don't even know who you are! Your father was the heir to billions! Marshall Oil Refineries in British Columbia. Those were your people."

"He discovered phyto-lutein," she said, her voice tiny. "He saved the mission."

Jared laughed out loud. "It only took him twenty-six years! Ask me how many Nobel Prize–winning botanists he killed so he could get on the Empyrean."

Waverly had nothing to say to this. Jared's body was shaking with rage now, and he spat as he talked. "Daddy dearest? No better than me, sweetheart. Not by a long shot!"

"You're right," she started to say, but he punched the wall again.

"You know the best part? Your daddy and all his billionaire friends? They were the ones who ruined Old Earth in the first place! They could have protected the planet. They had the power to clean it up! Do you know why they didn't?"

Waverly's eyes felt stuck open, and she stared like a doll.

He sneered. "It was *cheaper* not to."

The back of Waverly's throat felt swollen. She looked at his profile, that perfectly formed nose, those chiseled cheekbones, the angled jaw. He was calming down now, but something about his calm was terrifying.

"Where are we going?" she finally asked. The elevator doors opened onto an empty corridor, deep in the innards of the ship. Jared closed a hand around the tender part of her elbow and squeezed. "That hurts," she said.

He tightened his grip. "When the doctor needs something done, I do it. I don't question. I don't *worry* about it. I've been given a role in life, and I fulfill it."

He jerked her in front of him, pushed her down the hallway. She stumbled but regained her feet and started to run.

Because finally she knew what this was.

Too late, a sneering voice like Jared's whispered in her mind.

"So, Waverly," Jared said as he caught her wrist, twisting it until she crumpled to her knees. "What should I do with you?"

"What?" she could only whisper as she looked up at him. His eyes looked black and bottomless, his breath rasping and dry, his lips yellow and cracked as he smiled.

"The doctor was . . . annoyed . . . when he found out I saved you."

Long seconds passed as she took this in, staring at his twisted features in horror.

" 'Take her to the shuttle,' " Jared quoted the doctor. " 'Do what you like with her. Record her saying that she lied. Then let her go . . .' "

Understanding filled her. "You *let* the Pauleys find me?"

Jared only stared at her.

"Then why save me?"

"You ran off before I could get what the doctor wanted!"

"What does he want?" she whispered. The insides of her mouth stuck together like gum. "I'll do it."

"He wants you to admit," Jared cajoled, "that you *lied* during your testimony."

"The doctor *wanted* me to lie!" she pleaded. His grip on her arm was robotic and immovable. The human spark had gone out of his eyes. "*You* wanted me to lie!"

"Just say it, Waverly." He pulled his small com unit out of his pocket, flicked a button, and aimed at her. "Say, 'I lied.' "

"Why? Did the doctor cut some kind of deal with Mather?"

Jared turned off the recorder and bragged, "Mather gets to keep her pulpit, we get the Captain's chair."

"You mean *you* get the Captain's chair."

"If I do one last errand for the good doctor." He pressed the Record button again and held it in her face. Was he making a video? "Now admit that you lied."

She stared at him as comprehension flooded her. "They're going to blame the impeachment on me. Everyone gets to stay in power."

"Because you lied about the whole thing." He bent down and screamed in her face, "Admit it!"

"They're getting me out of the way."

"Say it."

"Then *why*?" she wailed. "Why did he try to impeach her at all?"

"She grew a conscience and stopped cooperating. '*No, I won't kill the Empyrean survivors,*' " he whined sarcastically. " '*I don't want to go down in history as a murderer!*' "

"So she lobotomized them instead," Waverly whispered in horror. "Or was it the doctor . . . ?"

"Little idiot." Jared hammered on her head with his knuckles. "Who do you think designed the drug in the first place? What do you think killed Captain Takemara and his allies? Food poisoning? No. The first batch of the doctor's little cocktail. He's made some refinements since then. Goes down easier."

This was too much. Waverly hung her head and sobbed, "Please don't hurt my mom."

He let go of her arm, pulled the gun out of the waistband of his pants, and held it in her face. "Do as I say"—he cocked the gun—"and I won't kill your mommy."

"I lied," she said through tears.

"Good girl. Now say, 'I lied during my testimony.'" He waved the muzzle of the gun in a circle, mouthing the words for her.

She repeated, "I lied during my testimony."

"Now say, 'I lied during my testimony against Anne Mather.' Say *that*, honey, and I won't hurt Mommy."

"I lied during my testimony against Anne Mather," she whispered.

He cocked an ear toward her. "I can't hear you, sweetheart. Say it again. Louder."

"I lied during my testimony against Anne Mather," she cried.

"Good *girl*!" He flicked a button on the com unit and slipped it into his breast pocket. With one hand he gripped her wrist, with the other he pointed his gun at her face. "Now! What do you suppose the doctor would like me to do with you?"

She was so scared she had to fight not to collapse. "I don't know."

"Oh, I think you *do* know, Waverly. I think that's why you're so scared."

Her eyes fastened onto his.

"Now," he said with mock officiousness, "I *could* follow orders like I usually do . . ."

"But you won't," Waverly said quickly. She tried to get to her feet, but he twisted her wrist again, and she slumped to the floor.

"Why shouldn't I?" Jared asked. "You already told me you can't be mine."

"Because . . ." Waverly's mind raced. "Without you pushing people around for him," she said, "he's nothing but an angry, weak old man."

"Don't underestimate him," Jared warned.

"It's *you* people are afraid of. What can the doctor do without you?" She realized her long hair was hiding her right hand from his gaze. She shook even more of her hair over her arm and fumbled in her pocket for the needle as she spoke, holding his gaze. "You don't need him."

"I owe him. He raised me."

"He *used* you." Her fingers swam through the fabric of her pocket, which was twisted and tight against her body. She touched on the plastic cap over the needle and pulled, but the cap came off, leaving the needle still wedged in her pocket. "Do you think the doctor *loves* you?"

"Manipulative little . . ." He twisted her wrist a little farther.

"You don't have to be a murderer," she whispered as she worked the needle free.

His expression changed. "What are you doing?"

She jammed the needle deep into his calf and plunged the syringe in one motion.

"Ow!" he screamed, and his hold on the gun loosened long enough for Waverly to bat it out of his hand. He saw the syringe sticking out of his leg, let go of her wrist, and backed away from her. "What did you *do*?"

She tried to get to her feet, but he tackled her to the floor so quickly he knocked the wind from her body. As she sputtered, he sat on her back, holding her between his knees. She felt his hand in her hair and tried to pull away, but he twisted her head around.

"You little bitch! I saved you!" he said and swung at her face with his left fist, his hand passing harmlessly through her hair as he slid to the floor. She rolled away and stood over him, watching him fade.

"Whaddid you give me?" he slurred. "Whad issit?" He smacked his lips.

She waited until his eyelids started to sag, then reached down and pulled the tracking device from his pocket, picked his gun up off the floor, and ran to the central stairwell, glancing once over her shoulder at the surveillance camera in the corner, which must have captured the whole thing.

The Plan

The first thing Kieran saw when he opened his eyes was the woman, Jacob's wife—Ginny, he'd called her. She had a cruel little face, and the way she scowled gave her the aspect of a pouting child. She was bent over some kind of craft project, shoulders hunched, gloved fingers working with fine precision. She tilted a spoon full of what looked like black pepper into a small balloon, then tied it off with her teeth.

"Where are we?" he croaked. He tried to sit up, but he was still bound by tight cords. He licked his lips, trying to moisten them, but his mouth was dry.

"Never mind." She laughed as though he'd just asked the stupidest question she'd ever heard.

Kieran looked around, considering his situation. They'd taken him to a small, nondescript room with a single buzzing fluorescent light overhead. Bare of furniture, the walls were lined with unlabeled cardboard boxes. He guessed they were in a storage room, and, judging from how far away the engines sounded, they were at about midship level.

He looked again at her project. She gently placed the little balloon, which was the size of the upper joint of his thumb, onto a small pile of identical balloons. There were about ten of them.

"You getting ready for something?" he asked fretfully.

"Anne Mather's trial's, today." She chuckled. "These are a little gift."

Today? He'd been so worried about Waverly he'd forgotten that he was supposed to testify today at Anne Mather's impeachment. Is that why Jared Carver had traded him for Waverly? So he couldn't testify?

A shuffle sounded from the front of the room, which was obscured by stacks of boxes, and Jacob appeared, looking irritable and tired, carrying what looked like a fifty-pound flour sack over his shoulder. He dropped it on the floor with a thud and glanced at Kieran. "How long has he been awake?"

"Just a few minutes," Ginny said.

Jacob crossed the small room to pick up a walkie-talkie and dialed through the channels, his ear to the speaker, smiling at what he heard. Kieran couldn't make out any words, but he heard all kinds of different voices, both men and women, all of them sounding routinely officious. "They're looking for you," Jacob said. He put the walkie-talkie on top of a box. "I didn't hear anything like this for that little bitch."

"Anne Mather must like you," Ginny said with a distrustful look at Kieran.

"I suppose," Kieran said.

"That woman's a serpent," Ginny said.

"The serpent in the garden," Jacob singsonged.

"She'll wrap herself around your legs till you can't walk no more."

"And she'll whisper in your ear, confuse you," Jacob said, nodding.

"So you can't listen to her," Ginny said. "Because the more she tries to make you her friend, the more of an enemy she becomes."

"I'm no friend of Anne Mather's," Kieran said. "She killed my father."

"That so?" Ginny jerked her chin upward. "My father was gut shot on our way to the launch. He drove me in his jeep to the launch site, bleeding from a hole in his tummy. Got us on board, but the launch killed him."

"Who shot him?" Kieran asked Ginny. He thought if he could make friends with them, they might have second thoughts about whatever they had planned.

"Someone who wanted his spot on this ship," Ginny said. "Lots of people died like that."

Jacob grunted in agreement.

Ginny tied off the last of the balloons from her pile, and Jacob rolled one between his thumb and forefinger. "No way he can swallow that. It's too big."

"What?" Kieran asked, but they ignored him.

"Sure he can," Ginny said, nodding toward Kieran. "He's a big kid."

Jacob held up the small, tightly packed balloon. "Can you swallow that?"

"I'm not swallowing anything," Kieran said, trying to control his growing panic, because he was beginning to suspect what those little bundles were.

"You love those little kiddies, don't you?" Ginny snarled. "The ones from the Empyrean?"

Kieran's body turned to ice.

"You might've figured out we're not nice people," she said through a rank grin, then looked at her husband and cocked her head at the large sack he'd brought in, which was still sitting by the door. "Jake."

Jacob obediently heaved the sack across the floor and set it at Kieran's feet.

"Show him what you brought, Jakey," the little woman said.

Jacob untied the mouth of the bag and something spilled out.

No. Please don't let it be... Kieran closed his eyes. He didn't want to see.

Serafina Mbewe lay facedown on the floor. Kieran recognized her immediately by the puffy pigtails over her ears, her coffee-colored skin, her skinny little girl legs and arms. She groaned and wriggled into a sitting position. Her eyes rolled in her head as she took in her surroundings. They'd tied her up, her arms bound behind her back, thick surgical tape over her mouth. She looked at Kieran, eyes wide with terror.

"If you hurt her...," Kieran snarled, pulling against the rope that bound his own wrists. He wanted to kill them.

Ginny pressed her knife to Serafina's cheek, just under her eye, and grinned at Kieran. Serafina's body shook with spasms of terror, and a stain of urine spread over her pants.

Kieran hated these people. He'd never hated anyone like this.

"It's your decision," Ginny said to him as she pricked at Serafina's cheek with the blade. A bead of blood formed on the knife edge, and Serafina whimpered.

"I'll do it!" Kieran screamed.

While Ginny held the knife to Serafina's throat, Jacob put a balloon in Kieran's mouth, then tilted some water at his lips. He tried to swallow but he gagged on it, so Jacob brought a jar of butter and rubbed each capsule with it before feeding it to Kieran. They went down a little easier then, but they landed in his stomach like boulders and sat there in a painful, immovable lump.

Next Ginny produced what looked like a transmitter of a type Kieran had never seen before. It had a blinking red light and an antenna. She held it up, squinting at him with her beady rodent eyes.

"This sends *and* receives. Can you guess what it'll send to me?"

"My location."

"And your *words*," Ginny said. "Everything you say, to anyone, and what everyone says to you, I'll hear it. Understand?"

Kieran nodded. He glanced down at Serafina, who was shivering and glassy-eyed.

"*And* it's a receiver," Ginny said.

"I'll be able to hear you?" Kieran asked breathlessly.

"No. But the payload will," Ginny said, pointing at his swelling stomach.

"So I'm a bomb? You made me swallow a bomb?" His voice rose in a shriek.

Without warning, she ripped a hunk of Serafina's hair out of her head. The little girl cried out. Ginny held it up to Kieran's face—a puff of curly black hair. Oh, he despised her. "Swallow it, or she'll die bald."

Jacob took the receiver from Ginny and placed it in Kieran's mouth. It felt jagged and too big, but Ginny was winding another hank of Serafina's hair around her finger, getting ready to pull. Frantically, Kieran gulped it down, ignoring the way it tore his throat as he swallowed and swallowed and swallowed. Jacob handed him another grav bag of water and Kieran drank, forcing the device down his esophagus until it finally scraped its way into his stomach. God it hurt.

"Okay, then. We're ready," Ginny said. "Get up."

"What's going to happen to her?" Kieran asked. Serafina was staring at him, her teeth chattering. He wanted to wrap his arms around her and hold her close, but tied up as he was, all he could do was mouth the words *I'm going to get you through this*, hoping she'd be able to read his lips. She stared at him, trembling.

"Stay here until it's time," Ginny said to her husband in a warning tone, ignoring Kieran's question.

"Why? What's *she* going to do?" Jacob said, tilting his head at the little girl. "She can't walk, can't move, can't talk, can't *hear* nothing."

"I don't want you going after that kid," Ginny said, and the dark look she gave her husband made Kieran shudder. "Check the hall."

Jacob opened the door a crack and peeked out. "All's clear," he said. He picked up a black jacket and threw it to Ginny, who caught it with one hand. She handed her knife to Jacob, who trained it on Kieran and Serafina while she slipped the jacket on and fitted the hood over her head. Next she picked up a pillow from her bedroll and stuffed it under her shirt so that she looked pregnant. To the surveillance cameras, she would look like half the women on board.

Ginny stood, waving her knife at Kieran to stand up, too.

"At Mather's trial," Ginny said, "you're her chief witness, isn't that right?"

Kieran gaped at her.

"We'd better get you there," Ginny said as she tugged at the rope that bound his wrists. To Kieran's surprise, he felt the rope loosen, and suddenly his hands were free. "Let's go."

"Let Serafina go first," Kieran said as he massaged his wrists, which were deeply grooved by the rope.

Ginny laughed at him. "You're funny."

"I mean it. I'm not going anywhere until she's free."

"Get *going*." Ginny pressed her knife into his ribs and he took half a step forward. "Or I'll kill her in front of you."

Kieran recognized the powerlessness of his situation. There was nothing he could do but look back at Serafina, who watched him go, stretching her neck after him, pleading silently not to be left alone.

"Wait here," Ginny said to Kieran, as though she'd just remembered something. She went back to her husband, and the two of them stood over the cowering little girl, having a vicious whispered conversation. Kieran couldn't make out the words; he could only look at Serafina, who watched the two adults talking over her, shivering with fear. Ginny spat a final command at her husband and handed him something that Kieran couldn't see. Jacob sat down on a box, nudging at Serafina's leg with his boot, pushing her body aside to make room for his feet, as though that sweet little girl were nothing more than a pile of garbage.

Ginny poked Kieran in the back with her knife, pushing him out the door. Hating himself for leaving Serafina alone with that lunatic, Kieran walked down the corridor slowly, conscious only of the woman behind him and the knife she held. Ahead he could hear the surreal sounds of playing children, and laughter.

"Please," he said as they approached a door. It hung ajar, and he could see a woman sitting on a stool at the head of a classroom holding up an illustrated edition of the Holy Book. Surrounded by two dozen little kids from the Empyrean, she told the story of Noah and the flood. That had always been Kieran's favorite as a child because he imagined the Empyrean was like the Ark. The kids sat in a circle around her, rapt, their little faces lifted toward her. They were round and pudgy and dear to him, infinitely dear.

"See that basket?" Ginny said. She pushed up behind him; he could feel her hard little breasts pressing into his side, and his skin crawled. He saw a wicker basket full of fruit sitting on the teacher's desk. "It's full of explosives."

"No!" he began, but she pushed the tip of her knife into his ribs, and he quieted.

"Your little friends will survive the day if you go to the trial, get to Anne Mather, and tell her you were never kidnapped. You just needed some time alone to think about your testimony, so you went to the forests. You didn't even know they were looking for you. You get on that witness stand in front of everyone and these little ones will be okay."

"You think using me to kill Anne Mather will get you what you want?" Kieran's legs went weak and he almost fell down. Was this real? Was he going to die today?

"Anne Mather dead *is* what I want," the little woman said.

"I could just run," Kieran said.

"You wouldn't get more than two steps before I kill everyone around you, *and* these little ones."

Kieran looked into her eyes—eyes that showed no feeling, no compassion, and no concern for the future. There was no reasoning with her.

"The trial is in the corn granary," she spat. "Get going." She spun on her heel and jogged off without a glance back.

For long moments Kieran stood in the hallway outside the classroom listening to the sweet, soft little voices. He'd known each of them since their birth, and if anything happened to them, he'd never forgive himself. No. There was nothing to do but follow that hateful woman's orders.

He could hardly feel his feet hit the floor as he walked along the corridors. With each turn, the sound of a large crowd grew, until finally he reached the entrance to the granaries, full of people waiting to be searched for weapons. He took his place in line, hoping his terror didn't show on his face.

One of the guards searching people noticed him with a start. "What are you doing here?" he said to Kieran.

"I'm ready for my testimony," Kieran said breathlessly. Not ten feet away two women were talking and laughing together. One was hugely pregnant, and the other held a tiny baby to her breast. If Ginny blew him up now, they'd all die. *It's a nightmare. I'm in a nightmare.*

The guard lifted a walkie-talkie to his lips and said, "Kieran Alden is at the door."

A man's deep voice sounded over the speaker. "I'll be right there."

The guard motioned Kieran over to the side to wait. Kieran leaned against the wall, concentrating on the cool metal against his back, surrounded by pregnant women and old men and tiny babies. They talked in whispers, speculating about the trial, sharing stories about their babies, comparing notes about births and pregnancies, men massaging the backs of their wives, women hooking arms with their husbands. None of them knew they stood next to a bomb.

And Felicity.

She was coming toward him, holding hands with her fiancé. Just as she lifted her gaze to his, Mather's barrel-chested guard with the dove insignia on his shoulder stepped in front of Kieran. "How are you here?" the man asked him, one eye narrowed.

"I've been hanging out in the forests," Kieran said. To his own ears he sounded like he was reciting from a script. "I needed to be alone to prepare for my testimony."

"You had dozens of people searching," the man said angrily. "We thought you'd been kidnapped!"

"I'm sorry," Kieran mumbled. *There's a bomb inside me,* Kieran wanted to tell him. *They made me swallow a bomb.*

The man waved a sophisticated detection device over Kieran's body and patted him down manually. Finally he lifted a walkie-talkie to his lips. "Pastor. He's clean."

"Bring him to me," Mather said.

"Let's go," the guard said and took hold of Kieran's elbow.

He pulled Kieran through the entrance and down the aisle to-ward the stage. The music was already playing, and Kieran had to weave through crowds of people. When he passed by a group of Empyrean kids, one of them called out, "Kieran! Give Mather hell!" He could only wave and walk by, but he wanted to scream, send them all running. He felt as though his personality were splitting down the middle as the guard pulled him up the steps to where Anne Mather sat on a chair. Behind her, up on a dais, sat six old peo-ple who Kieran assumed were the Central Council. The old doctor had his knobby hands on his knees, and he regarded Kieran with a sideways stare.

"Kieran," Mather said sternly, "where have you been?"

"I'm so sorry." Kieran looked behind him. People were settling into their seats. The front row was full of small babies, and two rows behind them sat the Peters boys with the stern couple who had adopted them. One of them raised a hand to Kieran. *Run!* Kieran wanted to warn them. *Please, please, please.*

The little boy smiled.

"I remind you that Waverly is still missing, Kieran, and I need to stay out of the brig if I'm going to help you find her," Mather said.

Kieran nodded, trying to hide his confusion. Jared had saved her, so where was she?

To the guard standing next to Kieran, Mather barked, "Take him to the witness box. He's first on the roll."

A bead of sweat tumbled down Kieran's forehead and he batted it away as a guard led him to a dais off to the side. He sat in a tall chair behind a glossy black podium and waited for his life to end.

Run

Waverly sprinted up dozens of flights, spurred by terror. She gripped Jared's com unit in the palm of her hand, afraid to drop it and send it falling down the immense stairwell to shatter into a thousand pieces. When she couldn't run anymore, she sat on a stair halfway between two levels, panting, when something caught her eye, and she looked above her.

A camera. There were cameras in the stairwells now. How had she forgotten that?

With shaking fingers, she flicked at the darkened com screen and it blinked to life, showing only two words: *Enter Passcode*.

Mynx . . . with some numbers. That's what he'd entered. He'd probably never have let her see him typing it if he hadn't been planning to kill her. Jared's thumb had barely moved over the number keys, she remembered, and she'd been sure that 1 had been the first and third digit. She shuddered and typed in *mynx111*. Nothing. She tried *mynx11*. Words blinked onto the screen: *Final try before shutdown.*

A door banged open on the landing above her. "Waverly," a man called. She looked up through the metal grating of the stairs and saw the dirty black soles of two feet, then a second pair, then two more. Four men. "Come with us now and we can protect you."

She started down the stairs but saw another two men on the landing below her. To her left was a doorway. The sign read LEVEL 36, but she was too scared to remember where it led.

She looked at the com unit in her hand. One more try.

As the men hemmed her in, she typed *mynx121.*

The com unit blinked to life, and she cried out with relief. In the upper right-hand corner of the screen was a single button: *Blackout.* She enabled the application and, with a boom, the lights in the stairwell went out. She was surrounded by thick, impenetrable blackness.

"What the—" said a man above her. She heard the pounding of a half dozen males rushing toward her. Frantically she felt for the doorknob and darted through the door, running. The com unit gave her just enough light to see by, and she pointed it at the floor, hoping the faint gleam wouldn't register on surveillance. She turned at the first corner she came to and ran without a thought where she was going.

I need to get off this level, she realized. If she stayed here, they'd be able to tighten a ring of men around her until they had her trapped. She turned the corner and headed for the central stairwell, hoping they didn't already have searchers there.

She heard the murmur of alarmed voices ahead of her; there must be people waiting outside the elevator, just around the corner. She pocketed the com unit and the corridor was plunged in thick darkness.

"Another blackout!" a woman was saying. A small child whimpered, and she whispered, "Hush, sweetheart."

"God, I hope they figure out what's going wrong," said another, older-sounding woman.

"The ship is over forty years old," said a man. "Things are bound to go wrong."

Waverly slowed down. *It's so dark, I don't need to hide,* she realized. *I just need to be quiet.* She held her breath and eased around the corner. Their voices were close now.

"Some people think that the stowaway is doing these blackouts," said the younger woman.

"They caught him," the man said. "The Pauleys are still on the loose."

"Ugh. That man is too dim-witted to come up with something like this," said the older woman. "It couldn't be them."

"Ginny isn't stupid," said the younger woman. "Crazy, but not stupid."

Waverly crept by them, within feet of where they stood. Her breath was shallow and slow, and she felt light-headed, but she didn't dare breathe deeper. She ought to be across the corridor by now. She held out two fingers in front of her, waiting to bump into the wall, but it didn't appear.

I'm moving diagonally. She turned a little farther to her right and her fingers touched the wall. She found the edge of the door and slowly drew her hand over the bumpy metal until she found the doorknob. She eased the door open, holding her breath, willing the hinge not to whine, and slipped through. She slithered down the stairwell, one stair at a time, gripping the outer railing. There was no sound in the blackness. She was free.

She went downstairs until she could smell the rich dampness of the tropics bay and entered the corridor, which was thankfully dark. When she reached a doorway to the rain forest, she slid into it, pausing to listen. Not a sound. There was no one around. She'd escaped!

She tucked herself into what smelled like a nest of palms, pulled out the com unit, and huddled over it, reasonably sure that she was invisible. She reentered the password and it blinked on.

Now let's see what this thing can do. She bit her lip and got to work.

PART FOUR

Good-byes

Morality is of the highest importance—but for us, not for God.

—Albert Einstein

Buddy

When Seth awoke, he was alone. He could still see the indentation of Waverly's head in the pillow, so he knew he hadn't dreamed it. He blinked. His eyes felt tacky and dry, and so did his mouth. He lifted a finger and croaked, "Hello?" He saw the shadowy shape of the nurse stand up and walk over to him.

"Waverly?" he asked.

"She'll be back," she said softly. "How are you feeling?"

"Thirsty," he managed to say.

She picked up a plastic tumbler from his bedside table and lifted his head with a gentle hand at the nape of his neck. The water was cool and soothing, and he gulped down the entire tumbler. "More?" he whispered.

She gave him two more tumblers full, and the more he drank the better he felt. Finally, when she set his head back on his pillow, he could look around. He was hooked up to an IV that snaked into a vein near his elbow. He looked for his other arm to check for an IV and remembered that it wasn't there.

"Your fever is really high," the nurse said, then grunted once and slumped over.

Seth stared at her, waiting for her to lift her head back up, but she didn't move. "Hello?" he asked.

"Hi!" called someone from behind her. A tall figure stood in the front doorway. Seth blinked. What he was seeing couldn't be real: Jake Pauley with a grin on his face.

The nurse toppled out of her chair, drooping forward and onto the floor in a heap. Seth saw the hilt of a knife jutting from her back and a growing stain of blood spreading over the thin fabric of her shirt.

"What did you *do*?" Seth shrieked.

"She wasn't a friend," Jake said with a shrug as he started across the room. "I knew Thomas would get you here!"

Seth looked around for help, but the only other person in the room was an emaciated-looking man lying on his back, the only sign of life a slight rise and fall of his chest. Seth tried to sit up, but he felt lopsided, off balance, and so very weak.

Jake leaned over Seth, studying his face. "You look like shit."

"What are you doing here?" Seth finally asked him, his eyes bugging in their sockets. He drew away from Jake until he felt the safety railing pressing painfully into what was left of his shoulder.

Jake smiled, showing a speck of clay-white food between his incisors. "I'm busting you out of here."

"No!" Seth said, infuriated. "I can't walk! I'm not going anywhere with you!"

"Aw!" Jake settled himself into the chair vacated by the nurse, resting his feet on Seth's mattress to avoid touching her body. "You're just mad because I left you in the brig. That wasn't personal."

Seth stared at the man. He'd always known Jacob Pauley was

insane, but his total lack of concern for the woman he'd wounded or killed, his cheerful demeanor . . . He was worse than crazy.

"We better get you out of here," Jake said, looking around the room. When he spotted the wheelchair next to the old man's bed, he bounded toward it. "Let's get that tube out of your arm," Jake said as he wheeled the chair even with Seth's bed. Without warning, he yanked the IV out of Seth's vein. "Put your arm around my neck."

"Why did you kill her?" Seth asked through sudden tears. That nurse had been kind to him. She'd saved his life.

Jake lifted Seth out of bed, groaning with the weight. Seth felt a sickening dizziness, then suddenly he was upright, sitting in the wheelchair, gripping the arm with his good hand, leaning far to the left. "I need that IV," he said with a thready voice.

"We'll get you some meds soon. I just want you to see this."

"See what?"

"It's a surprise!" Jake said and wheeled Seth out the door.

The corridor was quiet, and Seth wondered how Jake could be walking out in the open so fearlessly. From his pocket the man pulled a small object that looked like a pen and pointed it at the surveillance camera as they passed by. Jake noticed him looking and explained, "It's a laser. It whites out our image. Ginny thought of it."

Seth wasn't well enough to be sitting upright. His arm—the missing one—felt suddenly enormous, as though it had swollen to the size of an elephant's leg, and he tried to readjust it, but that only caused an agonizing ache in the stump.

Jake pressed the elevator button without fear, and when the doors opened, he hummed a little tune as he pushed Seth through.

"I felt bad about leaving you behind on the Empyrean. I really did," Jake said, but there was no depth to the statement, as though he knew he *should* feel guilty and so he tried to. "But I'm here now, buddy."

Buddy. Seth was filled with such hopelessness, he let the man say what he wanted, take him where he wanted. He only half believed this was really happening. *It's a fevered dream*, he told himself. *Wake up.*

The elevator bell rang, the doors opened, and Jake wheeled him down the corridor toward some closed double doors. The corridor smelled of corn pollen. *We must be outside a granary*, Seth thought distantly. A man was lying facedown on the floor with a knife sticking out of his back. Seth's stomach turned.

Jacob smiled. "She's a dead aim."

"Who is?" Seth asked.

"Ready?" Jacob said.

"For what?"

Jacob pushed Seth through the double doors. Seth blinked, unsure at first where he was. There were rows of corn planted directly in front of him, but to his left he could see a banner hanging from the ceiling that read COURT IS IN SESSION. It was draped artfully underneath a large porthole that showed a sparkling night sky. Lights hung near the ceiling, too, and as Jacob pushed him forward, Seth saw that the lights were trained on a stage that he could glimpse only intermittently from between the tall stalks of corn.

"What the hell is this?" Seth asked in a whisper. He heard voices speaking in hushed whispers, hundreds of them. It was all so surreal. "Where are we?"

"That kid who put you in the brig?" Jacob intoned softly. "Remember?"

"Uh, yeah. I remember," Seth said, irritated. "His name's Kieran."

"Well, you're about to get your revenge."

"What do you mean?" Seth tried to twist in his wheelchair to look at the man, but the motion sent a jolt of agony from his stump up through his shoulder and into his neck. "Are you going to hurt Kieran?"

Jacob answered with a gleeful chuckle. "Can you walk a little way? It's not far."

Seth stared in the man's eyes, his unhinged, dim-witted eyes, and nodded. He wasn't sure that he could walk, but the only chance to stop this lunatic was to stay with him. So, on shaky legs, Seth stood, forced himself to touch this disgusting human being to steady himself, and stumbled along with the killer Jacob Pauley, into the cornfield, blinking against the threat of losing consciousness.

If I can save Kieran, he told himself as he watched his feet, one after the other, hitting the ground. He had to watch them because he couldn't feel them. *If I can save him, that's something good I'll have done. And maybe people will know I wasn't bad.*

His heart jumped inside his chest as he willed himself to live long enough for this one last thing.

Then, with no warning, the overhead lights winked out.

Search

Waverly left her hiding spot in the tropics bay and started toward Kieran's signal, feeling her way in the dark. Luckily it hadn't taken long to figure out the tracking program on Jared's com unit. The design of the thing was amazingly simple. Waverly took the starboard outer stairwell, listening for Mather's guards. She could hear their echoing voices, but they were far enough away that she couldn't even see their flashlights. When she reached the same level as Kieran's signal, she opened the door and went into a quiet hallway on the granary level. The ship seemed deserted; she hadn't run into a single person, so she figured it was safe to use the com unit for light.

She hadn't gone far when she noticed that Kieran's signal was now behind her. She turned back and stopped outside a door to what looked like a storage room. *Now what?*

Don't get myself killed, that's what, she told herself. She only hoped the lights wouldn't come back on at a bad time. She knew they operated on a timer, but she didn't know how long the darkness would last.

She pulled Jared's small gun from her waistband and looked at it in the dim glow of the com unit. The rifles she'd used before had clearly labeled safety catches, but this one wasn't labeled. Assuming Jared had kept the safety on, she shifted the button toward the muzzle, then tried opening the door. It was locked. Holding the com device in her teeth so she could see, she pried the faceplate off the locking mechanism and, careful not to touch anything metal, crossed wires until the door clicked open. She waited behind the door, listening for any noise from inside, but there was nothing.

"Kieran?" she called, her voice wispy in the dark. She waited, listening to the thick silence, until she couldn't wait anymore, and looked into the room using the light from the com device. At first glance, the room appeared empty of people. Had Kieran been untied and the rope left behind? She stepped inside.

A whimper sounded from below, and Waverly shone the light down.

"Serafina!" Waverly cried.

Just then, the lights came back on. She startled and looked around, relieved to find no one else in the room. But where was Kieran?

Blinking against the sudden brightness, she rushed to her young friend who was writhing on the floor, tears streaming over her plump brown cheeks. "Honey!" Waverly tore at the knots that bound the little girl's hands and ankles.

As soon as her hands were free, Serafina lunged at Waverly, wrapping her arms around her neck and pulling her into a tight, terrified embrace. Waverly held her, rocking back and forth.

"Sweetie." Waverly knelt down and waited for Serafina to wipe the tears away so she could read Waverly's lips. "What did they do to you?"

But Serafina grabbed hold of Waverly's hand and pulled her to the door. She started running down the corridor, tugging Waverly along after her.

"Stop!" Waverly said. She grabbed hold of the little girl's shoulders, waited until Serafina's black eyes fixed onto her lips, then she mouthed, *Where is Kieran?*

Serafina groaned in exasperation and pulled Waverly farther down the corridor.

"Are you taking me to him?" Waverly asked, feeling stupid.

Serafina pointed down her throat, then patted her pudgy little girl belly, made an expansive gesture with her hands, then threw herself to the floor and played dead.

Waverly stared at her, totally lost. "Did Kieran eat something bad?"

Serafina nodded exaggeratedly and repeated the pantomime.

"Poison?" Waverly said slowly.

Serafina shook her head, moving her hands out from her middle in a gesture that suggested . . .

"Are they going to blow Kieran up?" Waverly asked in a horrified whisper.

Serafina started crying and nodded.

"Where is he?"

The overhead speaker crackled, and Waverly heard Dr. Carver's voice. "Pastor Mather's impeachment proceedings will begin in five minutes. Anyone who wishes to be present is advised to come to the granary immediately."

"Oh my God," Waverly said under her breath. She'd forgotten all about Mather's trial. By the time she recovered herself, Serafina had run ahead toward the granaries. "No!" Waverly cried and chased after her, but she couldn't move fast enough. Serafina was already darting past a man who was lying on the floor. As Waverly neared him, she saw there was a knife sticking out of his back. She gritted her teeth and pushed past his blank stare and through the doorway after Serafina.

The air was filled with the sounds of a milling crowd. She was at least thirty feet behind the last rows of chairs, concealed by tall corn plants. The room looked different, and it took Waverly a moment to realize that the first time she'd been here, the fields had been planted with wheat. But the crops had been rotated since then, and now tall, green cornstalks reached up toward the lights, their tassels looking like skeletal fingers. Waverly had an unsettling flashback to her first time on the New Horizon, when she was a hostage and forced to come to this room for Anne Mather's church services. Now it was a courtroom, and the colorful fabrics, the tapestries, the theatrical lighting had all been stripped away. In their place was a bare stage upon which sat the church elders in black robes. In the middle of the stage sat Anne Mather, awaiting her charges, and to the right was Kieran, sitting inside a witness box. Thank God she wasn't too late!

Serafina dove into a row of corn and Waverly went in after her as the sound of a gavel crashing against wood tore through the air. Waverly finally caught up with Serafina deep in the cornfield, grabbed hold of the little girl, and mouthed, *Run!* All she could think of was Serafina's mother, long dead, and how she'd asked Waverly to look after her daughter. Waverly kissed Serafina on the forehead, then looked intently into the little girl's eyes and mouthed, *I can't let you get hurt!*

Serafina grabbed hold of Waverly's face and stared silently into her eyes until Waverly felt herself calming down. Serafina's irises were a deep brown, flecked with gold, and they were large, still, deliberate, and soulful. Serafina had something more to say. Waverly took a deep breath. *What is it?* she mouthed.

Serafina stood away from Waverly and made two fists that she held at her sides, puffing out her arms and scowling from under lowered eyebrows—an unmistakable impersonation of Jacob Pauley. Waverly nodded. *The big guy,* she mouthed. *The mean guy.*

A quick nod, then Serafina mimed taking something out of her pocket and pushing a button.

"The big guy has a detonator? He controls the bomb?"

Serafina nodded again. Next she held her two fingers close together, then mimed pushing the button again, and ended with the expansive gesture Waverly had come to understand meant explosion.

Waverly shook her head, confused.

Serafina held up her two fingers again, then spread her arms wide to make her fingers far apart. Then she pushed the imaginary button, and this time, nothing happened. No explosion.

Waverly stared at the little girl.

"Jacob has to be near Kieran? For the detonator to work?"

Serafina nodded, going limp with relief.

"You're amazing." Waverly kissed her. "Now get as far away from here as you can."

Serafina didn't have to be told twice. She sprinted for the door, jumped over the feet of the man lying on the floor, and disappeared down the corridor.

Waverly peeked up through the corn toward the stage. She saw Kieran sitting in the witness box, listening to an official-looking man reading the charges against Anne Mather. Kieran was tiny from here, but she could see he was panting, and he wiped at his brow with the palm of his hand.

What do I do? She wrestled with a wave of panic that threatened to take over her mind. *I could scream. But then Jacob would detonate Kieran for sure. He must be waiting for Kieran to give his testimony.*

Waverly craned her neck over the corn tassels to her right and saw what looked like a rustling in the corn about thirty yards away. She started toward it, moving slowly, edging past each stalk, trying not to touch any of them. She knew she ought to be afraid, but it wasn't fear she felt. She smelled every honey-sweet kernel of corn, felt every prickly leaf as they brushed the skin of her arms, was aware of every hair on her head and every twitch of her nerves. She heard every nuance in the voice of the judge as he read: "You are accused of crimes against humanity during the initial attack on the Empyrean . . ."

None of that mattered to Waverly now. She was calm—she had to be—but she knew the truth: *If Jacob sees me coming, we're all dead.*

Light

The lights had just winked back on, and Seth looked at the stage through the spaces between the cornstalks. Jacob had acted worried when the lights turned off, though he made no comment, and he'd pushed Seth recklessly in his wheelchair to the granary. They'd felt their way through the cornstalks, Jacob half carrying Seth, listening to hundreds of alarmed voices reacting to the mysterious darkness. Then they'd crouched in the corn to wait. When the lights came back on, Jacob had stood up briefly to check their position relative to the stage and said under his breath, "Perfect."

Seth's entire body was trembling, and he felt the strength in his legs start to give, so he lowered himself to the ground and sat there, panting, his head resting on his knees. He already felt the absence of the IV medication; his pain had doubled, and he felt weak and terribly ill. *I could die right here*, he thought. Tears slipped from between his eyelids when he thought of Waverly and how she'd cried on his shoulder. It was both a comfort and a torment knowing that she would grieve for him.

The murmur of the crowd faded away, and he heard the gravelly voice of an old man, but he couldn't make out the words.

Seth lifted his head to watch Jacob, who had taken an eager step forward, crouching in the corn, a boyish smile on his face. *He's been looking forward to this,* Seth realized. *He thinks this is going to be the biggest moment of his pathetic life.* Seth could hardly bear to watch, but he studied every nuance as Jacob licked his fleshy lips with a white tongue. For the moment, his hands were empty.

Seth's stomach heaved, and he spit a flavorless dribble of greenish fluid between his knees. When he wiped his mouth with the back of his hand, his face was numb.

No. No. My God. He'd tried wiping with his ghost limb. He lifted his real hand to wipe his face, which wasn't numb after all, and toppled over, rustling the corn around him. He flopped onto his back, looking up at Jacob, who was scowling at him, annoyed.

Jacob sliced across his neck with a flat hand, telling Seth to be quiet, then turned to look at the stage. Seth realized the noise of the crowd had faded away. An old man began reading criminal charges in a slow, rhythmic monotone. "Anne Mather, you are charged with crimes against humanity . . ."

He gazed at the overhead lights. They cast a yellow-white halo, and he could imagine his soul fusing with that light, dissolving into a trillion photons. *It wouldn't be so bad,* he thought, *if I die, and a part of me goes on, I could follow Waverly around, live inside her hair and whisper in her ear.*

Sharp raps of a gavel meeting wood jerked him out of his reverie. The room was filled with sudden silence. It rested over Seth like a pillow, and for a moment he thought it was smothering him. But no. That's not what was happening. Somewhere along the way his lungs had begun to fill with what felt like fluid, though he didn't even have the strength to cough. He gulped air, swallowed it into his stomach, pulled at his throat with his ghost hand. He hadn't expected this. Somehow he'd thought his heart would simply stop. He hadn't expected dying to be scary.

Don't be scared of dying, he told himself. *Be scared you won't stop Jake from killing Kieran.* Seth took tiny breaths, lots of them, in and out, in and out. He rolled his eyes back to Jacob's hands. The man held no weapon, so there must be some time left. Seth concentrated on breathing, forced himself to fill his lungs to their breaking point, hold, and release. He did this a few times, trying to force the fluid back, to stretch his lungs out, buy back room for air.

Suddenly an old man's voice filled the room. "Kieran, in your own words, please, tell the story of the first attack on the Empyrean."

"I was . . . ," Kieran began, sounding shaky. "I was in the shuttle bay. I saw the whole thing."

There was a long pause, so long that Seth could hear a few confused murmurs among the listeners.

Seth saw that Jake was pulling something out of his pocket. It looked jury-rigged, slapped together with tape and wire and putty, but there was something neat-handed about it, as though it had been lovingly crafted. From it extended a small metal antenna, and on the face of it was a glaring red button.

Not a gun, then. A bomb.

Jacob held the detonator in one hand, a finger poised over the button, waiting for Kieran to go on.

He's waiting for a theatrical moment, Seth thought with loathing.

Seth reached up toward the device with his good hand, but Jacob was so far away, and Seth was flat on his back, melting into the earth. Kieran started talking again, but Seth couldn't focus on his words. All he could think about was getting that detonator away from Jake.

If he kicked at the device, he might trigger a detonation, Seth knew. He tried to sit up, but his stomach muscles seized and he was overtaken, his head swimming as the ground dropped beneath him. His body was in rebellion, and he couldn't move.

"Run," he whispered. "Kieran." But Kieran just went on talking. Not even Jacob had heard. Seth tried to yell, but it only made him heave, and more of the green fluid came up.

It felt strange to be losing control like this, and for a few moments Seth could only stare at a browning leaf that hovered over his face, stare at it as his mind emptied, and his only thoughts were located in his drowning lungs. He felt the ghost of his arm reaching up, up, stretching five, ten, thirty feet to the ceiling to touch that light overhead. The burning bulb felt hot and healing to his phantom fingers, and he cupped the light in his palm as the photons fell over his skin like rain. Hundreds of voices raised in an ancient melody, ancient words. *Dona nobis pacem.*

He was hallucinating.

He *must be* dreaming because right in front of him, emerging from the green leaves just over him, was the infinitely lovely face of Waverly Marshall.

She knelt about four feet away, crouched low, peering at him from between the stalks, leaves framing her face like a fairy crown. She looked as surprised to see him as he was to see her. Her dark pink lips parted as she held a finger to them—*be quiet*, she was saying. Was she real?

Seth opened his mouth to tell her to go, save herself, run, please, but her eyes lifted to Jacob's face, and they narrowed with a hatred that was focused like a laser.

God, he loved that girl.

Waverly lifted a gun, flicked a button on the side of the barrel, and aimed it at Jacob's middle. Seth could only watch as she cocked the hammer.

A sharp, metallic click snapped through the air like the crack of a whip.

Jacob Pauley's body jerked with surprise. "You little bitch," he said just as she pulled the trigger.

The gunshot exploded, silencing the angels. Seth heard screams, but they were distant, too far away to help.

Jacob collapsed, his knee landing inches from Seth's face. The device he'd held dropped onto Seth's belly. Seth watched, helpless, as Jacob's bloody fingers batted the gun out of Waverly's hands. He heard it land somewhere off to the left—too far away to save her. "I'll kill you," Jacob snarled through a gurgling throat.

Run, Seth said, or did he only think it? But Waverly's eyes were on the device, which was still on Seth's stomach. She bent to pick it up, but Jacob's fist swung at her head, punching her in the temple. The blow was weak, but it was enough that she collapsed onto her hands and knees. Jacob's bloody fingers closed around the device again, his slimy thumb fumbling at the small red button on the side.

With his real hand, Seth took hold of Jacob's thumb and bent it backward. The man's grip was slippery with blood and the device slid from between his fingers again. Seth took hold of it and, with his last ounce of strength, flung it as far as he could. He heard it land somewhere past his feet, toward the stage.

Waverly had recovered enough to see Seth throw the device, and she bolted to her feet and screamed over the tops of the cornstalks, "Kieran! Run! Get out of range!"

Seth heard a thud and looked just in time to see Jacob grab Waverly by the shoulder and push her down. She fell to the ground, dazed, her face right next to Seth's. Jacob began crawling toward the device, one bloody hand held against his middle.

Seth opened his mouth to speak to Waverly, but she rolled away from him, pawing at her pocket with both hands. From it she pulled a small rectangular object. *What is that?* he wanted to ask, but suddenly he was choking on fluid that bubbled up from his throat. He turned his head to spit it out, then watched as Waverly disappeared into the corn, craning her neck, searching for Jacob. Seth wished he could help her, protect her, do anything at all.

Once again his body took over his mind, and he found his thoughts dissipating into his tingling fingertips, his shaking legs, his numbing face. *A little more time!* He reached again for that overhead light. He thought somehow if he could close his ghost hand around that light that it would give him enough time to say good-bye.

He was still reaching for the light, just starting to feel its warmth, when it winked out.

Run

"I was . . . ," Kieran said into the microphone, which was cold and unyielding against his lip. Doctor Carver had just announced him as the first witness; somehow he'd stood and found his voice. "I was in the shuttle bay. I saw the whole thing."

And he closed his eyes. Ginny was going to kill him now.

He waited, pressing his stomach into the podium, hoping the feeble wood might shield some of the audience, knowing it would only splinter into shrapnel. His every muscle braced for violent death . . . and nothing happened.

"Uh . . ." Kieran searched the crowd for Felicity and found her gleaming hair right in the middle. Unlike the other women, she wore no hat or kerchief on her head, letting the beauty of her hair shine without shame. He silently thanked God she was far enough away that the blast probably wouldn't reach her. Her fiancé held her hand possessively, glowering at Kieran.

They were waiting for him to speak. They all were.

My last words, he realized.

"I haven't known what to say today," Kieran finally said, focusing on Felicity. He wanted her kind, sweet face to be the last thing he saw. "Until recently, I've thought of this crew as the enemy. But I don't really think that's the case."

An infant cried out, and he saw a woman in the middle of the audience lift it to her shoulder, patting its little back until it settled down.

"You attacked the Empyrean because you thought we'd done you harm, and maybe some of us did. Horrible things happened that day," he said, remembering hundreds of Empyrean crew members spiraling into space. Had Mather meant for that to happen? Did it matter what she meant? "My father died that day," Kieran said, as though he were remembering again after a long time forgetting. "I watched it happen."

No one in the audience seemed to be breathing. Felicity's smile had changed, and she watched Kieran searchingly. They were all looking at him, totally rapt, and something his father once said rang in his ears: *The truth is powerful. People usually listen to the truth.*

"I loved my dad," Kieran said through a closing throat. "I miss him every day. After losing him, I wanted revenge for what happened to him. But looking at you, all I see are regular people. Families. You love your babies. You've opened your hearts and homes to our orphans. You're not the bad guys. I can't blame you for what happened."

Kieran turned around to look at the church elders sitting behind him, up on a dais, old men and women who had been charged with caring for these people. And Mather. She sat with her fists on her knees, watching him warily, unsure what he was doing.

Kieran stared right into her cold gray eyes and said, "I blame your leaders for what happened that day. I blame the church elders. I blame Anne Mather, and you should, too."

Kieran braced himself for the end, but what happened next was wonderful.

Felicity stood up. Her fiancé tried to hold her down, but she jerked her elbow out of his grasp and pulled an object from under her tunic to hold over her head—a sign written with bold black letters: ANNE MATHER MUST STEP DOWN.

No, Kieran wanted to say, but he was too stunned to speak. What was she doing?

She was only the first. Others stood up, first a few, then many, and they lifted posters and banners and signs above their heads. Some of them held images of Waverly's face with the word TRUTH written underneath in bold black letters. Some of the signs said MATHER = MURDER. Others said DEPOSE MATHER or DEPOSE THE CHURCH ELDERS.

The old doctor's mouth popped open, and he stared in disbelief at the crowd. Mather had turned ashen, and her head wobbled on her neck.

Felicity smiled at Kieran and started singing, all by herself. She had a light soprano voice, but it was true and simple, and resolved from a fearful tremor into an ancient, beautiful melody. Soon other voices rose with hers, and their song filled the immense room.

Dona nobis pacem, they sang, over and over and over again. Kieran knew the simple meaning of the Latin words: *God give us peace.*

Kieran looked around him. Anne Mather sat perfectly still, staring at the crowd in disbelief. The armed guards behind her looked amazed. One of them, a stocky man with a kind face, placed his gun at his feet, looking as though he'd been wanting to do that for a long time.

"Thank you," Kieran whispered into the microphone, and he lifted his hands to the ceiling and called to the heavens, "Thank you!" Then he backed away from the podium, backed toward Mather and the elders. Let them be the ones to die.

Suddenly the song was pierced through with a loud popping sound. Some people in the back cried out with alarm. It took Kieran a moment to realize he'd just heard the sound of gunfire. The song died down. Husbands shielded wives, women folded their bodies over babies. They were quiet as they waited and watched, fearful, and then . . .

"Kieran!" A frantic voice broke through the quiet, and Kieran looked up, startled. "Kieran, run!" someone was screaming. He searched the audience. People were turning their heads, half standing. Way in the back, Kieran saw Waverly's brown head pop up above the cornstalks. "Get out of range!" she screamed, then ducked back under cover.

He stared blankly at the space where Waverly had been. One heartbeat . . . two . . . then Kieran turned on his heels and sprinted for the nearest door. He was in the hallway, running blindly, not even sure where he was going when he heard someone fall in behind him. "Stop or I'll shoot!" a man called.

Kieran knew that booming voice. It was the big guard, the one with the dove insignia, and he could hear his footsteps gaining on him.

Kieran knew he ought to be able to outrun a man of that age, but his heart was already laboring, and he couldn't master his breath. He took in huge gulps of air and pushed them out again, filling his lungs, but it wasn't enough. Already his legs ached and his arms felt floppy. The heavy footsteps of the guard were right on his heels. Somehow Kieran found another ounce of speed, and he pushed himself on, headed for the central stairwell.

Suddenly the lights blinked out, and the hallway was impenetrable darkness.

Kieran heard the man behind him cry out with surprise as he fell with a thud. Kieran ran alongside the wall, feeling with the fingertips of his right hand. He passed by one door, two doors, three . . . When his fingers touched air, Kieran knew he'd reached the corner of the corridor. He rounded it, still jogging, ignoring the wheezing of his lungs.

His eyes ached with the effort to see in absolute darkness. He heard more voices behind him, and he sped up, but he didn't dare break into a full run for fear of falling. Instead he concentrated on silence, his feet padding along the hallway, forcing himself to picture where he was.

When he felt the pebbled metal of the stairwell door, he jerked it open and padded up the stairs, regretting every audible scuff of his shoes. When he reached the shuttle bay level, he bolted into the corridor and turned left, running as quickly as he dared.

Now he walked with his hands extended in front of him, feeling through the darkness until he finally touched the cold glass of the shuttle bay doors. They opened with a whoosh of hydraulics, and Kieran stepped into the vast shuttle bay, feeling the air, trying his hardest to walk a straight line. His steps were halting now that he had no wall to feel along, and he squinted instinctively. His footsteps echoed against faraway metal walls. The room *sounded* big.

He stopped in his tracks and tapped his foot. The echo expanded off to his left, but to his right, the sound was muffled. He must be standing right next to a shuttle.

He lifted his hands up over his head and walked until his fingertips grazed a shuttle's cold underbelly. He smelled the cruddy scent of hydraulic lubricant. *I'm right under the hinge for the cargo door.*

With his fingertips, he traced the seam of the door, covering every inch with his palms until his thumb grazed the casing for the release button. He pulled away the protective shell, pushed the button, and suddenly the room was flooded with light as the ramp lowered to the floor.

If they didn't know where I was before . . . , he thought as he ran up the shuttle ramp and punched the button to close it under him.

Now if Ginny detonated him, at least the blast would be contained within the hull of the shuttle and no other lives would be lost.

Kieran blinked in the pale blue light as he ran up the spiral staircase to the cockpit, where he flipped on the control panel. Immediately a woman's voice called, "Shuttle B-11, identify yourself."

He put on the headset as he settled into the pilot's chair. "This is Kieran Alden. You need to evacuate the nursery school room. The Pauleys planted a bomb there."

"What?"

"Get the kids out of the schoolroom before the Pauleys blow them up!" Kieran screamed.

"Wait," the person said, sounding like she didn't believe him.

There was a long pause. Kieran fired up the engines and released the tethers that held him to the floor. His seat rose up beneath him. What was taking them so long?

"Kieran?" It was Anne Mather's voice. She must have been patched in remotely because he could hear the murmur of the audience in the background. "What's the situation?"

"There's a bomb in the nursery school. You've got to get the kids out of there now!"

"Hold on, Kieran," Mather said, and in the background he could hear her barking orders to evacuate the schoolroom immediately, then she came back on the com link. "How do you know this?"

Kieran tried to explain as quickly as he could, but he had to repeat himself several times before she believed him. Finally he screamed, "You need to let me take this shuttle off ship so I'm out of range!"

"Kieran, I can't just let you take one of our shuttles."

"Well, then you've killed me." He laughed hysterically. He could feel the hard lump of the explosives in his stomach. The skin on his arms and legs felt as though it were trying to ooze away from his middle to take cover.

There was a long silence, then Mather's voice came back on.

"Okay," she said, sounding defeated. "Let him go."

"What?" the man said. "He could ram us!"

"He's not going to ram us," Mather droned. "Are you, Kieran?"

"No!"

"Let him go."

Kieran eased the shuttle into the air lock and held his breath as the huge doors closed behind him, then waited for what seemed an eternity before the outer doors opened. He pushed the joystick forward and the shuttle drifted out of the New Horizon. When he was safely out of the air lock, he sped up and watched in the rearview vid screen as the New Horizon shrank away.

He took in one deep breath . . . two . . . and suddenly he was sobbing into his hands, hysterically gulping air and shaking, his legs and arms and fingers alive with the electricity of his infinite relief.

"Kieran?" It was Mather calling him. "I've just spoken with our doctors. Can you . . . expel the explosives?"

He nodded. "I'll try."

He engaged the automatic navigation system, strapped himself into his seat, fitted a grav bag around his mouth, and stuck his finger down his throat. He heaved and heaved, bringing up his breakfast, and then fluids, until finally the balloons started coming up, one by one. He ignored the growing pain in his stomach, ignored the horrible burn in his throat, until every last balloon had come up, all twelve of them.

The detonator was still there; he could feel it wedged inside him, tearing at his insides. It was too jagged and large to pass back through his esophagus. When he had no strength to keep trying, he pulled himself back to the cabin where he took up the headset. "Hello?"

"Go ahead, Kieran," Mather said.

"I threw up all the explosives," he said. His heart felt weak, and his head swam from the effort. "Not the detonator. It's too big."

"That's progress, Kieran."

"Should I come back?"

"Not until we find the Pauleys. They can't blow you up, but if they activate that detonator, it might rupture your organs. One of our doctors is here with me, and she says to drink plenty of water. It might help move that detonator through."

"Okay." His voice sounded little to his ears.

"We'll find them, Kieran," Mather said reassuringly before signing off.

He turned off his headset before replying, "Go to hell."

A red light on the control panel by the copilot's seat caught his eye, the com screen flashing, *Closed signal.*

He pressed the option for more information and couldn't believe his eyes. Someone was hailing him from the Empyrean on an encrypted channel. He pulled himself to the copilot chair and enabled the signal.

"Hello?" he asked.

"Kieran?"

He knew that voice.

"*Arthur?*" he whispered. The lights on the control panel took on an otherworldly quality, and he dropped his head to his hand. "I thought you were . . ."

"Can you get to the Empyrean?"

"The Empyrean is dead," he said stupidly.

"Sarek and I are *on* it, Kieran. It's not dead."

Kieran couldn't move or speak. They were both alive? His dearest, truest friends were alive!

"Hello? Kieran? Can you find your way to us?"

Kieran shook his head to clear it, enabled the long-range sensors, and found the shadowy form of the Empyrean moving in a parallel course to the New Horizon. "I think I can."

"Get to the port shuttle bay. I'm signing out so they don't hear us."

"Okay," Kieran said, dumbfounded.

Kieran sat in the copilot's seat, staring in disbelief at the blue and red lights in front of him. Twenty minutes ago he'd been sure of his impending death, but he was alive, sitting on a shuttle, about to go home to see his dearest friends.

Arthur and Sarek were alive!

Kieran disabled the com system so he wouldn't be bothered by Anne Mather again, took hold of the joystick, and turned the shuttle toward home.

The End

"Seth!" Waverly hissed into the darkness. She had, only moments ago, turned off all the lights with Jared's com unit. She could hear Jacob swearing as he pawed over the ground, looking for the detonator.

"Seth?" she called back through the darkness. Her hand grazed a foot, and she groped in the dark until she could feel his lips.

She waited . . . waited . . . holding her breath . . . *please please please* . . .

A tiny puff of exhaled air warmed her fingers.

"You little bitch!" she heard from behind. Jacob was still back where Seth had thrown the device. Waverly pulled at Seth's arm, trying to lift him, but he was too heavy.

"I'll get you," Jacob snarled. She could hear him stumbling through the cornstalks, wheezing and gurgling. His gut had exploded into ribbons of blood when she'd shot him. She'd expected him to crumple right then, but he hadn't, and she had no idea where the gun was.

"Run," she heard whispered from below.

"Seth!"

"He thinks I'm his buddy," Seth whispered. She kissed his cheek, his eye, his ear. "He won't hurt me."

"I can't leave you!"

"He won't hurt me," Seth insisted. "Go!"

"No!"

"Get help," he wheezed.

She felt Jacob's hand close around her ankle. "I'll kill you," the man said.

She kicked his hand away, got to her feet, and ran back through the corn, blindly, no idea of where she was going or what she should do.

Save Seth. Help Seth.

By some miracle, she still held the com unit in her hand and decided to risk using the screen as a light source. Its meager glow revealed only her immediate vicinity, but it was enough to keep her from falling. She pointed it at the ground as she followed a row of corn.

After long, terrifying moments, she found the wall, then she turned to her left and followed it until she reached the doorway she and Serafina had entered. She nearly tripped over the body of the dead guard, and she crouched over him to pick up the walkie-talkie that hung on his belt.

"Hello?" she said into it. "Is anyone there?"

"Who is this?" asked a harsh voice.

"This is Waverly Marshall. I need help. Seth . . . he's sick and hurt and Jacob Pauley has him. Please."

She sounded like a little girl, and for the first time in a long time that's what she felt like: a child who needed a grown-up.

"Where are you?"

"I'm at a doorway on the port side of the granary. The guard is dead. I think Jacob killed him. Please. Seth needs help."

"There's a security force on the way," the voice said.

"Okay." Waverly buried her face in her hands.

She couldn't do this anymore. No more scheming. No more revenge. She wanted safety. She'd had it once. She hadn't even noticed it then. *It wasn't real anyway,* she told herself. *I only thought I was safe, but all those years, that's when Anne Mather and the doctor were making their plans, laying their traps.*

Cones of light spilled into the darkness in front of her and she heard the heavy steps of men. She raised her hands to show she had no weapons. "Please! We need to help Seth."

"Where is he?" one of the men asked, stepping forward. She couldn't see him, but he had a deep voice that was somehow gentle, and she took a step toward him.

"Jacob Pauley has him in the cornfield." One of the men took hold of her roughly by the elbow.

"Can you take us to them?"

"I think so," she said.

One of the men took Jared's com unit out of her hands. He looked at it with suspicion. "What is this?"

"It's some kind of computer. It belongs to Jared Carver."

The man's eyes dropped to the dead man on the floor and he cried, "Who killed Robert?"

"Jacob, I think," Waverly said, blinking against his flashlight. She was surrounded by men now, at least five of them. "Please. Seth is so sick."

"Show us where," said the stocky one with the deep voice. He took her arm and walked with her, his grip firm but gentle. There was something about him that appeared kinder than the rest, and she pinned her hopes on him.

"In the cornfield," she whispered. "Toward the starboard side."

"I told the Pastor to raze this field," she heard someone behind her say. "But she wanted things to stay normal."

"All the guns were accounted for," said another man. "We thought it would be okay."

"They're not *using* guns," Waverly hissed, losing patience. "The Pauleys made Kieran swallow explosives."

"How do you know that?" one of them asked, alarmed.

"I'll tell you later. Right now Jacob is looking for the detonator in the cornfield, and we have to stop him before he finds it!"

That got them moving. One of the men stayed behind to issue evacuation orders to the audience. Waverly could hear the voices of the crowd, hushed, waiting for the lights to come back on. Two of the men went ahead, their flashlights illuminating the corn fronds, stopping every few feet to look back at Waverly. She pointed them toward Seth, following the broken stalks she'd left behind in her flight from Jacob.

When they were getting near, she whispered, "Better turn off your lights." She crouched down, and the four men did the same.

"He might have a gun," Waverly whispered to the man on her right.

They moved more cautiously now, but their footsteps through the cornstalks were too loud. She hoped the sounds of the audience being moved out of the granary bay might cover the noise they were making.

If Jacob had found that gun . . .

One of the men walking to her left cried out, "Someone's here!"

"Where?" the man holding her arm asked.

"I stepped on him." The man's flashlight flicked on and he pointed the beam at the ground, but Waverly couldn't see what he was looking at. "He's dead."

Waverly sank to her knees. "*No!*"

"I'm here," someone whispered a couple feet from her right knee. She crawled toward him and felt Seth's clammy forehead, heard his struggling breath. She leaned her forehead on his and cried.

"Jacob Pauley," one of the guards said and kicked at the dead man's arm. Jacob's staring eyes never moved in their sockets as his head wobbled on the ground. Waverly cringed. He was a brute. He was stupid. He was cruel. And she was glad he was dead, but she couldn't stand to look at him like that.

"Central Command . . . we need a med team down in the port-side granary, stat," said one of the men into a walkie-talkie. He knelt by Seth and felt his forehead. "Bad fever," he said, shaking his head.

"Don," Seth whispered.

The other men paused, all of them looking at the stocky man. "How does he know you?" one of them asked sharply.

"I brought him a few meals down in the brig." He was lying. Waverly could see by the way his eyes never moved a single iota as he stared into the other guard's face.

"We've located Kieran Alden," Waverly heard through a walkie-talkie. "He's in a shuttle right now."

"Copy," one of the men responded.

Waverly was glad Kieran was safe, but she was terrified watching Seth's face as he struggled to breathe. His lips were peeled back from his teeth in a painful grimace and she could hear fluid in his throat. She took hold of his hand, squeezed, and was relieved that he had enough strength to squeeze back, if weakly. He rubbed her fingers with his thumb, back and forth.

She rested her forehead on his and whispered, "I love you."

She held her breath until he whispered, "I wanted to say it first."

She smiled. In the middle of all this, he'd made her smile.

Soon two people came pounding through the corn, carrying a stretcher between them. She watched as they slid the stretcher under Seth and strapped him in. She started to follow them back the way they'd come when she felt a hand clamp around her elbow. She turned to see Don blinking apologetically. "We need to ask you a few questions."

Just then, the lights came back on. Squinting, Waverly looked around to get her bearings. She could just barely see over the tops of the corn. Mather was standing on the stage next to a group of guards, their heads ducked away from the bright lights as the last of the audience left the granary.

Waverly gasped. A dark shape mounted the stage right behind Mather. The shape uncoiled like a snake; a hand extended like a fang.

"Look out!" Waverly screamed.

Ginny Pauley opened fire before anyone could react. She shot Anne Mather in the back once, twice, three times.

Mather sat down on the stage, almost as though she meant to.

The guards around her started running, fumbling for their guns, screaming. Ginny turned her gun on the men who had been standing with Mather and shot them, one by one, a single bullet for each of them.

Waverly ran after the guards, racing toward the stage, her vision jarred with every step. She acted without thought, without feeling, not sure why she followed them. They broke through the edge of the cornfield and were now in full view of that crazy, murderous, damaged woman.

Ginny dropped down to one knee, her gun pointed at Waverly. Waverly felt arms wrap around her waist and she hit the ground. A heavy body landed on top of her, and she heard a man's deep voice in her ear. "Stay down."

Waverly nodded, and he crawled off toward the stage. She watched from between chairs as four men opened fire on Ginny, who sank to her knees, hiding her head under spindly forearms, her body twisting in a grotesque spasm. The air exploded with so many rounds of gunfire that Waverly couldn't count the bullets.

And then . . .

. . . quiet.

In the calm that followed, Waverly heard agonized moaning. Four men were standing around Ginny, looking down at her as a fifth man stripped her body of the weapons she'd carried: knives, a machete, a nightstick, and a handgun.

It was Jared's handgun, the one Waverly had brought here.

Don came back to Waverly, stricken, beads of sweat over his brow and the bridge of his nose. He wiped his forehead with the back of his arm. "You okay?" he asked.

Waverly nodded. "What about Mather?" she asked.

"Not good." He took hold of Waverly's arm to help her up. She was unsteady on her feet as he pulled her toward the stage, her legs moving automatically. When she swallowed, her mouth was dry and somehow full of dirt.

The moaning got louder—it hadn't been Ginny moaning after all—and when Waverly looked up at the stage, she saw a pair of legs twisting in agony. She slowed down, but the guard kept her walking. "I don't want to see," she whispered.

"She wants to talk to you."

"No," Waverly said quietly, but she let him pull her along.

So many times she'd pictured killing Anne Mather. She'd dreamed it, over and over, bloodthirsty dreams that woke her feeling disturbed and satisfied, horrified and eager.

But now she'd *seen* it: an unarmed woman gunned down. It didn't matter that the victim had been Anne Mather, the architect of all Waverly's loss, her pain, her transformation into a dark-hearted creature. The act itself had been the ugliest thing Waverly had ever seen, and she was glad now she hadn't been the one to pull the trigger.

"Tom," Mather moaned.

"Thomas," one of the guards said into his walkie-talkie. "You better get here now. Hurry."

They were almost to the stage, close enough that Waverly could see the sheath of blood spreading under Mather as she lay on her back, looking up at the lights with those cool gray eyes, swallowing down the blood that pooled inside her mouth.

"Wave . . . ," Mather whispered. She moaned and closed her eyes.

"Hush," Waverly said. She knelt down and took Anne Mather's hand.

"I wanted . . . ," Mather said softly. She seemed to have no control over her own breath and had to time her words with each tortured exhale. "To say . . . I'm sorry."

Waverly looked at her own hands cupped around Mather's deathly cold fingers. Her sworn enemy, the woman she'd planned to ruin with her lies, whose death she'd fervently wished for—why was she holding her hand?

"I've done so . . ."—Mather panted between words, grimacing in pain—". . . many things." She took in breath sharply, then coughed, great racking hacks that sent foamy blood spurting out of a hole in her chest.

"I brought this," Mather whispered, "on my . . . myself."

Waverly could only look at her. She had no words.

The heavy metal doors behind Waverly opened, and the guard named Thomas stood in the doorway, his face slack with shock.

"No," he whispered and staggered onto the stage. He fell to his knees next to Waverly, then bent over Mather and smoothed the hair off her forehead. "Annie," he said with a whimper. "I should've stayed! I should've known!"

She smiled at him. "No, honey. Don't."

The big, frightening guard bent down and kissed Mather tenderly, her forehead, her eyebrow, the corner of her bloodied mouth. "Stay," he pleaded.

The Pastor opened her mouth to speak, but she coughed again, and suddenly she was heaving, folding in half as a medical team thrust Waverly out of the way and bent over her, fitting a mask over her face, stanching her wounds with mounds of gauze. Thomas refused to let go of her hand and watched her face with minute attention as the medical team traded arcane terminology, describing what was happening to Anne Mather's body. Waverly didn't need to understand their words to know she was dying in the most horrible way.

The color faded from Mather's cheeks, her lips turned blue, her eyes rolled up in her head. Waverly lowered her gaze when Thomas, the Pastor's most vicious protector, wept over her, kissing her forehead, massaging her hand, rocking on his knees.

Waverly turned away. They all did, to let Thomas have a few last moments alone with her.

Besides, the woman was no longer there and there was nothing more to look at.

The Gift

In the infirmary, a medical team fitted a mask over Seth's face, and he breathed in the pure oxygen. Soon his head cleared, and his feeling of panic subsided. Nan, the nurse who had saved his life, was in the bed next to him. He couldn't believe she was still alive.

She had turned toward him, looking sleepy, her skin pale, her lips cracked and whitish. Clear tubes snaked out of her nostrils. She raised her eyebrows as her lips formed the words: "How are you feeling?"

He couldn't speak with the mask over his face; he could only roll his eyes. She nodded in understanding, and he felt a little less lonely. Someone else was suffering, someone who cared about what happened to him.

He motioned for the doctor, the older woman with a knot of gray hair at the nape of her neck. He could barely whisper, "How is she?"

The doctor turned toward the nurse and asked, "May I tell him your condition?"

The nurse nodded once.

"His knife hit her between the scapula and the spine. The blade nicked a lung, but most of the damage is orthopedic." The doctor looked at Seth fondly, and he looked back at her high cheekbones and intelligent expression, thinking she must have been pretty when she was young. "Don't you want to know *your* condition?"

"I'm dying," he croaked.

"I hope not," the doctor said, her tone deadly serious. "You came close. But the oxygen is helping your body stabilize. We've got you back on your meds, and we're watching you."

"Waverly?"

The doctor shook her head. "We'll try to find her, okay?"

He nodded and fell asleep immediately.

When he opened his eyes, the lights were back on. Nan looked very tired, and her chest was wrapped with layers of white gauze, but when he turned toward her she brightened up. "You look better," she said softly.

He smiled.

A tall, thin man brought him a tray with some cut fruit and a bowl of broth. He managed to drink the broth through a straw, and it felt good as it filled his stomach with warmth. The fruit was pink and soft and sweet. He couldn't identify it, but he enjoyed warming it on his tongue before he swallowed it, piece by piece. At the end of the meal, he was exhausted.

"Waverly?" he asked the thin man.

"Let me make a call." The man walked out of Seth's line of sight, but Seth could hear his side of the conversation. "I've got a very sick young man here asking for Waverly Marshall . . . She's sixteen years old, how much of a threat could she be . . . Patients do better when they have family around . . . She's the closest thing he has . . ."

Seth closed his eyes again, and when he opened them, he was looking at Waverly. Tears slid over her smooth cheeks, and the corners of her lips pricked upward into a smile. He felt instantly better.

"Hi," she whispered, and he felt her fingers moving through his hair, rearranging, working at knots, smoothing it back from his forehead. Her touch relaxed muscles he hadn't known were tight, helped his blood move through his veins, soothed the nerve impulses that told him he was still in pain, still sick, still in danger.

"You're going to be okay," she whispered.

He knew she was lying, that they'd told her the truth. He knew it by the hint of terror in her eyes that she tried to cover with her smile. He loved her for that, how brave she was being, and how brave she was trying to help him be.

"Where you been?" he asked.

"They had a lot of questions," she said evasively.

"You in trouble?"

"All I could do was tell them the truth," she said. "So far they can't find a problem with my story."

Seth felt a presence on the other side of his bed and turned to find Don standing over him. "I tried to get back to you in the lab. I could tell you were sick." Don rubbed a chunky hand over his face, looking as though he hadn't slept in days and hadn't shaved in a lot longer than that. "I couldn't risk leading them to you."

"It's okay," Seth said. He was already feeling tired from all the talking. But there was something he needed to tell Waverly before he fell asleep, because he was afraid he might not wake up. He badly wanted to touch her face, stroke her hair, but he was too weak to lift his arm. "Listen," he said to her.

Don got up to let them be alone, and he was grateful for that.

"I don't want you to be alone," he told her.

Her face crumpled. "I'll have you."

"Maybe not," he got out before he had to fight for air. Waverly seemed to have lost the ability to smile. She stroked his hair at a frantic pace. When he could speak again, he said, "I want you to have a family."

She shook her head in a desperate kind of denial and looked away from him.

"The kids they made from you," he said. She wouldn't look at him, but he knew she was listening. "I saw one. She's . . . she's so cute."

Now Waverly did look at him. He saw a hardness in her that he knew would probably never subside completely, but she was with him, listening.

"Kieran is a good guy," he said. "He loves you."

Her large brown eyes searched his face as though trying to divine some motive. "He wants someone else now," she said.

"He'll protect you."

"Seth . . ."

"This place is dangerous." She tried to put her fingers over his lips, but he spoke anyway. "If you're married and pregnant, they . . ." He stopped to catch his breath, then forced out the words, "They'd let you live. For the baby."

"Without you?" she whimpered. "I can't—" She lay her head down on his mattress, but she kept hold of his hand, massaging his fingers, kneading them, kissing them.

When he had the strength, he squeezed her hand. "I need to know you'll be okay."

Her features hardened. "Then live."

Reunion

Kieran's shuttle touched down on the Empyrean in a dark, empty shuttle bay. He'd expected Arthur to meet him, but there was no one. Kieran walked down the shuttle ramp, confused, holding his sore middle. He'd expected relief now that he'd expelled the explosives, but the detonator had lodged inside him, somewhere deep, and it felt like a hunk of broken glass.

He pushed the pain out of his mind and looked around. The bay was completely dark except for the light of a single OneMan hanging near the air-lock doors.

"Kieran." It sounded like Arthur's voice, very soft and distant, coming from the OneMan. Kieran approached, hunched over, gripping his stomach with one hand. "Are you there?"

Kieran leaned into the helmet to speak into the headset. "I'm here."

"Go to the port-side stairwell and walk down."

"Okay." Kieran limped across the bay between the rows of shuttles. He made it to the stairwell and started down the cold metal steps, leaning heavily on the railing. The ship was cold, very cold, but the air was good. He could smell the pollen from the rain forest as he descended the stairs—a huge relief. The ship's lungs were still intact.

He heard footsteps below, then saw a long shadow creeping up the wall of the stairwell. From around a bend, Arthur appeared. His face broke into an immense smile, and he ran up the rest of the stairs and hugged Kieran tightly. Kieran winced, and Arthur pulled away. "You okay?"

"Not sure how to answer that," Kieran said.

"I heard you say Jacob Pauley made you swallow explosives," Arthur said.

"How did you pick up that transmission?"

Arthur grinned. "We're always listening."

"I threw up the explosives. Now I just have the detonator in me."

"So you're safe?"

"I won't explode, anyway."

The two boys took the stairs down three more flights, only enough time to give each other a broad outline of what had been happening. As Arthur opened the door to the habitation level, he smiled. "I've got some pretty interesting news, but first . . ." Arthur paused, seeming almost frightened to ask, "Have you seen my dad?"

Kieran touched his friend's shoulder. "I saw your dad in the brig when I first got there."

Arthur closed his eyes and smiled.

A cramp seized Kieran, and he doubled over.

Arthur grabbed him by the arm to hold him up. "I thought you said you threw up the explosives."

"Not the detonator, though." Kieran groaned. "It's stuck in me."

"Maybe we can get it out. Let's ask Tobin."

Kieran leaned on the wall of the corridor. "Tobin is alive?"

"Yes," Arthur said and cocked his head. "They think we're dead?"

"They *told* me you were."

"I was afraid of that."

Kieran winced with another spasm of pain and pulled on Arthur's arm.

"Come on," Arthur said, "let's find Tobin."

Kieran followed his friend out of the stairwell and down the cold corridor, bracing himself against the wall. Arthur knocked and entered an apartment without waiting for a response. Kieran followed him into a living room that had been converted into a makeshift hospital. There were four beds, each one pushed against a wall, each occupied by one of the sick adults. Victoria Hand was the only one conscious, and she smiled weakly at Kieran and lifted a couple of fingers.

"Tobin!" Arthur called and went down the hallway toward the bedrooms.

"Quiet," Tobin said irritably. He was sitting on the side of a bed, looking spent, but when he saw Kieran behind Arthur, he bolted to his feet. "Kieran!"

Kieran rushed at his old friend and put his arms around him. "I thought you were all dead."

In the bed where Tobin had been sitting was Philip Grieg, the heroic little boy who had saved Waverly and Seth from Jacob Pauley. When Kieran last saw him, his face had been horribly swollen and bruised. Now his features were back to normal, and there was even a healthy pink in his cheeks. "How is he?" Kieran asked as he sat down on Philip's mattress.

The little boy opened his eyes, a faint smile on his lips. "Hi."

Kieran laughed with joy. "He's okay?"

"He has three words," Tobin said with pride. "'Hi,' 'bye,' and 'uck,' when we bring him his emergency rations."

"So he's getting better?"

"He started talking a few days ago." Tobin gave a tentative nod. "I think he's blind in one eye, and he can't use his left hand, but he can hold a cup of water, and he's starting to be able to sit up. Victoria thinks he might be able to walk again someday, but not for a while."

Kieran bent over the little boy and kissed him on the cheek. Philip smiled and said "Hi" again.

"Is that Kieran?" someone by the door asked, and Kieran turned to see Austen Hand standing in the doorway holding a stack of empty ration containers. He dropped them on the floor, rushed at Kieran, and gave him a bear hug. "I thought that was your voice."

"Yeah," Kieran said, grimacing at the way the boy jostled him.

"What's wrong?" Tobin asked.

"He's got a detonator in his stomach," Arthur answered.

"What?" Tobin and Austen yelled simultaneously.

By the time the situation was fully explained, Tobin had Kieran lying on the floor at the foot of Philip's bed. He gave Kieran a pain reliever and stood over him while he drank three entire grav bags of water.

"They said to force fluids, right? We're forcing fluids."

"I can't drink any more," Kieran said halfway through the third bag.

"Yes, you can," Tobin said stubbornly as he squeezed the bag into Kieran's mouth.

Kieran managed to force the rest of the water down and was surprised to find that it actually did lessen the feeling of broken glass in his middle.

"The water should help expand the tubes inside you and help you pass that thing."

"You can't operate?" Arthur asked.

"I'll ask Victoria," Tobin said and left the room.

"Where's Sarek?" Kieran asked Arthur.

"He's in the next apartment over. He's monitoring the repair crew."

"Repair crew?" Kieran asked, surprised.

"From the New Horizon. They're salvaging the Empyrean," Arthur said with a gleam in his eyes. "The central bulkheads were all untouched, and they've even been able to save some of the starboard compartments, too. They're working on connecting everything together with pressurized conduits. They're almost done."

Kieran felt gobsmacked. "You mean this ship is worthy?"

"The Pauleys tore a big hole in the hull, but the girders and underlying structure are still strong," Arthur said.

"But how can it fly with a huge hole in the hull?"

"It's not like the ship has to be aerodynamic," Arthur said with a shrug. "Space is a vacuum, right? So as long as the bulkheads remain strong, this ship can travel."

Kieran shook his head, amazed.

"I remind you, not without some measure of pride, that my father was a member of the original design team," Arthur said, puffing up his chest. With a big smile he added, "German engineering."

Tobin came back in the room with an apologetic smile. "Victoria said opening up the gut is very risky."

"But what if the detonator tears something?" Kieran asked, not sure it hadn't already.

"Perforation. That's the danger. If you start to feel sick, we'll operate." Tobin looked at him worriedly as he fumbled through a pile of medications that were overflowing a small table in the corner, then handed him a vial of pills. "Take two of these every four hours for the pain. And rest."

"No," Kieran said, sitting up. "I want to see Sarek."

"He's a couple doors down," Arthur said. Kieran followed him down the corridor to an apartment near the stairwell. The front room was so cluttered with papers and ration containers that it took Kieran a couple seconds to spot Sarek sitting at the dining table. When Sarek saw Kieran, he stood up from his portable com unit, a half smile on his face. He put his hand out for Kieran to shake, but Kieran pulled his friend in for a hug. Sarek patted Kieran's back awkwardly.

"Good to have you back," Sarek said briefly. He sat back down at the dining table, which served as a makeshift desk for him. Judging from the mounds of ration containers and empty coffee cups, he spent all his time here. "Did Arthur tell you?"

"Tell me what?" Kieran asked, sinking onto the ratty couch next to the table.

Arthur looked like he was about to give Kieran the biggest present of his life. "I've found a planet that fulfills the Goldilocks Contingency."

"Fulfills the what?"

"Read for yourself." Arthur handed him a printout from the mission manual.

The Goldilocks Contingency

New Earth was chosen by the mission designers for its moderate temperatures, its atmospheric composition, its size relative to Earth, and the similar length of its day and year. The sun it orbits, Centauri 8, emits a light spectrum very like the sun's. Of the thousands of worlds surveyed, New Earth was by far the likeliest candidate where Earth-based life could thrive.

Nonetheless, the designers recognize that the mission might, as it nears New Earth, encounter data that suggest the planet is not all we had hoped. It is also possible that another planetary system might be discovered that could appear even more hospitable than New Earth. If the mission crew determines to change course for another system, the mission designers have included a contingency plan for how to survey the target system, how to cope with a course correction, how to manage a slowdown upon approach to the new star system, methods for determining the best possible orbit should the system be reached before adequate deceleration has taken place, etc. . . .

We wish to advise, however, that such a course change should take place only if and when insuperable circumstances have made life on New Earth untenable, for this new course will be fraught with risks impossible for the mission designers to anticipate, and that might challenge the equipment and personnel in ways for which they have not been prepared.

Kieran searched Arthur's expectant face. "Are you telling me . . . ?"

"I've found a planet that can support Earth-origin life," Arthur said with great pride, then added, "most likely."

Kieran looked from one boy to the other. They seemed perfectly serious. "But the mission is for New Earth . . ."

"This planet is closer," Sarek said. "We could be there in nine years."

"We wouldn't have time to slow the Empyrean down . . ."

"We'd have to put the ship into a long elliptical orbit and send out away teams via shuttle," Arthur said. "It can be done. They planned it all out with equations and computer models for a course correction."

This time Kieran couldn't hold himself back. He grabbed Arthur's face and kissed him on the forehead. Arthur pushed him off, rubbing the kiss away while Sarek snickered.

The friends talked into the night. Sarek and Arthur ate a meager dinner of pasta with beans and spinach, but Kieran could manage to drink only broth. He felt the detonator inching through his gut, but the news of this new planet was so exciting he didn't care so much about the pain. Kieran looked at the star charts and read through Arthur's calculations, and the more he learned, the more convinced he became that this was the answer. "This is wonderful," he finally said. "But we can't leave the others behind."

"That's the part we can't—" Arthur began.

Just then, a knock sounded on the door. "Open up," called a gruff masculine voice.

The three boys froze in fear.

"I've been listening to you for the past forty minutes, kids. I know you're in there. Open up."

To Sarek, Arthur whispered, "It's Chris. The crew chief."

"I want to talk," the man said.

Arthur paced the room in short circles while Sarek wrung his hands with anxiety. Kieran could only stare at the star chart laid out on the table in front of him. Already lost. It was already gone.

"Kids," Chris cajoled, "I've known you were on the ship all along."

"We can't trust you! You were going to deny our wounded medical help," Arthur said to him through the door.

"I said that to *warn* you. I've seen your com signal all along from Central Command. I knew you were listening, but I never told my crew."

Sarek and Arthur looked at Kieran, uncertain. "You guys have a gun?" Kieran whispered.

The other two shook their heads.

"I'm alone and unarmed, guys," the man was saying. "I just want to talk."

"I've been listening to him," Arthur whispered as the boys huddled in a triad. "All I can say is, he sounds like a nice man."

Sarek looked at Kieran. "But he could be tricking us."

"He knows we're here," Kieran said. "Everything is lost anyway. We might as well talk to him."

Arthur walked to the door, hands hanging at his sides as though he were ready to draw a weapon, though he had none. He opened the door to a man with light brown eyes, a squarish buzz haircut, and an angular jaw. He had an apologetic smile on his face and held up his hands in a gesture of surrender. "I'm not here for a fight." He slowly entered the room, looking cautiously from boy to boy.

None of the boys moved or spoke. Kieran's heart was pounding painfully in his chest, and his stomach clenched around the jagged lump in his middle.

Chris pointed to a wooden ladder-back chair next to Sarek and said, "May I?"

Kieran had no idea what to say as the man walked across the room, turned the dining chair around and straddled it, leaning his elbows on the back. He was sitting next to the table where all their plans were spread out, plain to see. "I've got some interesting news," Chris said as he chewed on a toothpick. "But first, tell me about this planet you were talking about. Go slow. I'm not as smart as you guys."

Kieran wondered for a few moments if he could somehow kill this guy to protect their plan, but Chris looked strong, and besides, there was something about him that seemed trustworthy, friendly, even. Arthur and Sarek exchanged looks, and Sarek shrugged. "He already knows."

Arthur sighed, resigned, and told the story over again. When he'd finished, Chris chewed off the end of his toothpick and spat it out. "That is certainly amazing news, but I've got you beat." He made dramatic eye contact with each of the boys before he said, "Anne Mather is dead."

A full minute of silence passed before anyone could speak. Kieran asked, "How?"

"Ginny Pauley got hold of a gun. That's why I decided to finally make contact with you."

"Jacob's wife . . ." Arthur said pensively.

The man opened his hands in a gesture of appeal. "If there was ever a time to take over this ship . . ."

"What?" Kieran asked sharply.

"I want to help you take over this ship," Chris said evenly. "Why do you think I knocked when I did?"

"Why should we trust you?" Arthur demanded.

The man grinned and pointed at Sarek's com screen. "Flip to the surveillance video in the port shuttle air lock."

Looking skeptical, Sarek did as he was told. Eight people were trapped in the air lock pounding on the doors, screaming at the tops of their lungs. "Chris! Chris!" one of the men yelled. "Open up! Hey!" Someone else, a woman, said, "He can't hear you. Otherwise he'd have opened it."

"What's going on?" Kieran said, eyeing the man with suspicion.

"It's a bluff," Chris said. He pulled a new toothpick from his breast pocket and stuck it between his teeth. "Soon you'll send this video to New Horizon Command with the message that you'll blow those people out the air lock unless they release all the Empyrean crew."

"Why would you help us take this ship?" Kieran asked.

"Because I've got some of my own people waiting on the New Horizon that I want to bring aboard."

"You mean you want to share the ship with us . . . ," Sarek began. "It's our home."

"I know," Chris said, shifting uneasily in his chair. "That's why I wanted to talk to you guys."

"To ask permission?"

"To inform." To the silence in the room, he said, "I've got a guy on the New Horizon who's working on gathering some . . . refugees. They're people who can't make a life on the New Horizon anymore."

"But Anne Mather's dead," Arthur protested.

"The people who *really* run the show? They're alive and well."

"The doctor," Kieran said.

Chris's eyes darted over to Kieran, and he nodded. "For some of my friends, this ship is their only chance."

"You don't really want us to blow those people out the air lock . . . ," Arthur began, watching Sarek's vid screen, which still showed the frightened, trapped people.

"Hell, no. Like I said, it's a bluff. Those are just the people on my crew who I know won't cooperate with us. Once we get our people over here, we'll let them go."

"We need more than just hostages if we're going to scare the New Horizon into giving us our parents," Sarek said, his steady black eyes fixed on the man.

"You've got an idea?" Chris said.

Sarek grinned.

The Brink

Waverly stood by Seth's bed, her hands gripping the safety railing. His vitals had stabilized, and he looked more restful now. She touched his brow and, even though the com screen over his bed reported that he was still running a fever, she thought she felt a difference. She held her lips to his forehead and kissed, kissed, kissed him.

Suddenly a rude alarm shattered the air. She looked up to see the doctor running toward a ringing telephone.

Seth was so deeply asleep, he didn't even twitch.

"All hands to their quarters," came a hysterical woman's voice over the intercom. "The church elders are needed in Central Command immediately."

The medical staff froze in stunned confusion, then Seth's doctor raised her arm over her head. "Huddle, everyone!" The nurses and other staff rushed to the woman's side and conferred in whispers, then most of them ran out the door to the stairway. Waverly watched as adults rushed down the corridor to the elevators, shouting in panic. When she looked at her hands, she found she was wringing a handful of Seth's sheets.

"What's going on?" Waverly asked Seth's doctor, who came to check his chart.

"Some kind of emergency," she said, though she looked like she was holding something back.

The intercom crackled to life once more, and the same woman's voice called over the speakers, "Waverly Marshall, report to Central Command immediately."

The doctor looked at Waverly. "You better go."

Waverly shook her head. "I'm not leaving Seth." She still didn't know where Jared Carver was, or if he'd awoken. She didn't want to think about what he'd do to her if he got her alone again. Don had assured her she'd be protected, but she wasn't sure anyone would be able to stop Jared from coming for her.

Just then, two armed guards came into the infirmary. An older, scrawny man jerked his chin at Waverly. "Let's go." A pudgy guard grabbed her by the elbow. "You're needed in Central Command."

Waverly knew that she had no choice but to follow them. She looked back over her shoulder as she waited with them for the elevator. Seth's doctor was rearranging his tubes, tucking his sheets under his legs, as though getting him ready for something.

The walk down the corridor to Central Command was quiet, but she could feel the animosity of the guards as they pulled her along. She kept her hands down, letting the skinny guard open the door for her as the pudgy one pushed her through.

Central Command was a scene of chaos. A terrified-looking woman with clipped red hair beckoned Waverly with a shaky wave of her hand. Dr. Carver was sitting in one of the chairs that lined the long row of windows, and the rest of the church elders were gathered around him, leaning on the com consoles. *Murderers*, Waverly thought when she saw them. Selma, the large woman with the piercing blue eyes, nodded hello. The rest of them avoided her gaze.

"What's happening?" Waverly asked, but she was interrupted by Kieran's voice coming over the com.

"If I don't talk to Waverly Marshall right now, we're increasing speed."

"The Empyrean is on a collision course with the New Horizon," Dr. Carver said to Waverly. "He's demanding to talk to you."

The red-haired woman handed her a headset. The chaos that had ruled the room moments before settled into a tense silence as every eye fastened on Waverly. "Kieran?" she said tentatively and sat down at the com screen to study his image. His cheeks looked scooped out, his hair askew, and he glared at her. "What's going on?"

"I'm going to ram the New Horizon unless they release the hostages."

"Try to talk sense into him," the doctor said, but Waverly turned her back on him.

"Kieran," she said. She studied his face, letting him read hers, trying to guess what he was up to. "You can't mean this."

"There's no time to talk about it, Waverly," Kieran said with a weird smile. "I'm going to kill everyone unless my demands are met."

"What . . ."

"Unless every single Empyrean survivor is on a shuttle and ready to dock with the Empyrean in the next thirty minutes, we're going to ram you."

"But the Empyrean is destroyed," she said slowly.

"That's why we have nothing to lose now," he said.

Kieran would never harm anyone, she knew. He was bluffing. He must have some kind of plan. He stared into her eyes, poker-faced, willing her to trust him. *I do trust him*, she realized. *He's going to get us out of here.*

"Kieran, *please!*" She tried to sound desperate, terrified, and found it wasn't difficult at all. She *was* desperate. She *was* scared, because she thought she knew what was happening, that he'd gone to the Empyrean and found it wasn't destroyed after all. Another lie from Mather that Waverly had somehow never doubted. This might be her one chance to go home. If she lost this chance . . . She couldn't think about that now. She just had to make this real. "There are women and children aboard! Babies!"

"I'm dying," he snarled. He sounded insane. "The Pauleys killed me when they made me swallow those explosives. Their detonator is tearing up my guts. I have nothing to lose anyway."

"Where is our crew?" the redhead com officer burst in.

With a cruel smile, Kieran flipped a switch, and the image changed to a bunch of scared-looking people huddled into the corner of a large shuttle-bay air lock.

"Oh God!" The redhead touched the screen with her fingertips, but the image was already back to Kieran's face. "We'll blow them out unless you cooperate," he said.

"Kieran . . . ," Waverly began.

"We'll put these hostages on a shuttle as soon as we know every Empyrean survivor is on the way to us. Including the ones in the brig. When their shuttle lands, we'll change our heading and no one has to die today."

He gave her a small nod, almost imperceptible. *Trust me*, he seemed to be saying.

"No," Dr. Carver said. "We can't negotiate with this . . . this . . ."

"He seems serious, Wesley," Selma said slowly. "The boy is dangerous."

"Wesley's right. We shouldn't negotiate with a madman," tiny Miranda said. She lifted her chin in defiance, and a feather on her elaborate hat jiggled.

"Can't we just evade them?" asked one of the elderly twins, looking at a man with a short black beard who was sitting in the pilot's chair.

"He chose his angle of attack perfectly," the pilot said, his face ashen. "I can't turn this ship fast enough to get away."

"Kieran means what he says," Waverly said to the room at large. "He's been acting crazier and crazier, ever since the first attack."

"He never seemed unstable," the doctor said, stroking his chin with a thumb and forefinger. There was murder in his eyes, and Waverly resisted the urge to cross the room and shove his head against the blast shield. "How do we know you're not in league with him?"

"You have a recording of the only conversation we've been allowed to have," Waverly spat. "I don't know any more about this than you do."

"He's speeding up!" the pilot cried.

The doctor twisted his cane between his fists, looking furious. Little Miranda fingered her beaded necklace. The elderly twins shifted uncomfortably on their stools, and Deacon Maddox stared at his own intertwined fingers. Selma looked from one to the other of her fellow council members, studying them, until finally she cleared her throat.

"I say we send them," she said.

The other elders accepted this with stony silence, until Miranda stirred. "We could be sending those innocent people to their deaths!"

"To save hundreds of our own," one of the twins pointed out.

"The Empyrean has sped up again," the pilot said, his voice quaking.

"You have ten minutes," Kieran said, clearly straining against the increased inertia. He was glaring into the com screen, his jaw set, his lips pressed together with rage. Suddenly he doubled over as though some invisible hand had punched him, but he straightened up enough to say, "Decide if you want to live."

And the screen went dark.

That wasn't fake, Waverly knew. *He's in pain.*

"That's barely enough time to get all of them to the shuttle bay," Selma said.

The doctor nodded as though an idea had occurred to him, and he straightened his back, tapping his carved cane on the floor. "Send them."

The crew looked at him to make sure they'd heard right.

He sat there, smug and certain in his power. "What are you waiting for?"

The Command room burst into a flurry of activity as crew members ran to their com stations and shouted into their headsets, blinking as though they couldn't believe what they were saying.

"I refuse to let go of the assets on the Empyrean," the doctor said to the rest of the church elders. To the pilot he barked, "Turn away from them to buy time."

"What do you think I've been doing!" the pilot shrieked.

Dr. Carver shifted in his seat, obviously feeling like a fool.

Kieran couldn't have picked a better time for this, Waverly thought. *Mather would have known what to do, but these people are in over their heads.*

"I'll go with the hostages," Selma said, lifting her chin bravely. "I'll negotiate for their release."

Dr. Carver cocked his head. "Why you?"

"Who else, Wesley?" Selma barked irritably. "Are *you* volunteering?"

Dr. Carver looked away broodingly.

Selma sniffed and abruptly turned her back on the rest of the elders. "You're coming with me," she said and took hold of Waverly's arm to pull her out the door and into the corridor.

"I need to get my mom," Waverly said as a hysterical-looking man nearly knocked into her, then ran off. The corridor was crowded with harried people, all of them running, making eye contact with no one.

"She's waiting for us in the shuttle bay." Selma pushed the call button for the elevator. All the excitement had winded her, and she wiped at her sweaty brow with the side of her hand.

"Then I need to go to the infirmary."

Selma patted her arm. "Don't worry about Seth. Miriam will bring him."

"Miriam?"

"Dr. Jansen," Selma said as she stepped onto the elevator. "She won't leave him behind."

"*Leave* him? What do you mean?"

"You'll see," Selma said with a smile.

When they reached the shuttle bay, many of the Empyrean kids and the surviving parents were standing outside two shuttles waiting with their ramps open, and more were trickling through the shuttle-bay doors all the time. Waverly scanned the crowd, looking for Seth. Several of the kids waved excitedly at her, and she waved back, but when she saw Dr. Jansen leaning over a gurney, she ran for it, ignoring their eager questions.

"You need to understand I can't predict . . . ," Dr. Jansen was saying in Seth's ear, but Waverly couldn't hear the rest over the din of the crowd.

He nodded dismissively, waving her out of the way when he saw Waverly standing behind her.

"You're awake!" Waverly cried and kissed him.

"They shot me full of steroids for the trip. I feel pretty good," he said and gave a small smile.

"Are you sure you can travel?" she asked him.

"Do I have a choice?"

But Waverly was looking at Dr. Jansen. "Will he be okay?"

"I'll be with him," she said evenly after a brief glance down at Seth, who nodded at her. "The journey won't change anything."

Waverly thought something had passed between the doctor and Seth, but she was distracted by someone shouting, "Attention!"

Selma was standing on a shuttle ramp, her hands raised over her head. "Everyone, get onto a shuttle! We have no time to explain. Be assured our lives depend on this! I'll tell you what we know over the com once we're boarded!"

Dozens of voices rose to ask questions, but Selma disappeared into the shuttle, leaving them no choice but to follow her.

"Waverly!" someone called, and Waverly turned to see Sarah Wheeler running toward her. Sarah looked bedraggled and pale, but she was vigorous, and when Waverly wrapped her arms around her, she felt solid and whole.

"Where have you been?" Waverly asked tearfully.

"The brig," Sarah said disdainfully. "Where else?"

"Where's Randy?"

Sarah pointed at her boyfriend, Randy Ortega, who smiled and waved. He looked excited, as did all the kids from the Empyrean. "I'll talk to you when we land."

The two girls hugged again, then Sarah wove away through the crowd.

"Have you seen my mom?" Waverly asked Seth. He shook his head. Waverly looked frantically around until she saw her mother's dark, shiny hair. Waverly's heart filled, and she called out, "Mom!"

"Waverly! Where have you been?" Her mother rushed at her, wrapped her in a too-tight hug, then pulled away to point a finger in her face. "I've been worried!"

"I'm sorry," Waverly said, knowing now wasn't the time to explain.

Regina wrapped her arm around her daughter's shoulders. "Don't do it again."

Waverly leaned her head on her mother's shoulder and smiled to hear those words. Seth was watching her with a grin on his face.

She felt a small hand slip into hers: Serafina Mbewe had found her. She looked down at the little girl, who raised her black eyebrows asking if everything had turned out okay. Waverly nodded and mouthed the words, *You saved us all.* The full truth of the words hit her when Serafina smiled with childish satisfaction. *She has no idea what she did,* Waverly realized. *But someday she will. I'll make sure.*

Holding the hands of Serafina on one side and her mother on the other, Waverly boarded the shuttle. Dr. Jansen pushed Seth's gurney up the ramp behind her. Once aboard, Waverly felt a hand on her shoulder and turned. "Amanda!" Waverly cried. "What are you *doing* here?"

"We're going with you," Amanda said, and surprised Waverly by winking at Seth. "Hiya, Seth."

"Hi," Seth said and gave Waverly a smug smile, enjoying her confusion.

"Meet Misty," Amanda said to Waverly. She held up a wriggling bundle, and a pair of luminous eyes looked at Waverly from a nest of blankets. The baby's tiny fist was in her mouth, and she sucked on her fingers contentedly, looking utterly at peace in her mother's arms.

"She's beautiful."

Only after she said it did it occur to Waverly that, biologically, this was her own child. But looking at the way Amanda held her, arms folded protectively around the little legs, the way the infant cuddled against her breasts swollen with milk . . . *No*, Waverly decided, *Amanda's her mom.*

Behind Amanda stood a small group of unfamiliar people huddled in the cargo hold. Don stood with them, speaking in low tones, and they were nodding attentively.

"What's going on?" Waverly asked Amanda. "Who are they?"

"Don and Chris arranged this," Amanda said. "We're all . . ." She paused, searching for the right word, "Refugees, in a way."

Waverly looked at the huddled group. There were about fourteen of them, and they all seemed hesitant and afraid. To Amanda, Waverly said, "I was worried they'd hurt you after you helped me escape."

"Anne protected me," Amanda said with a sad smile. "She never trusted me again, though."

Waverly knew how much Amanda had once loved Anne Mather. "I'm sorry."

"Josiah is waiting for me. We'll talk more?" Amanda asked with a hopeful nod.

Waverly nodded, her eyes on the infant as Amanda moved away, hoping Kieran knew what he was doing.

New Mission

Seth slept through the journey from the New Horizon to the Empyrean. The steroids had temporarily masked his symptoms to make the journey possible, but they didn't take away his exhaustion. Waverly had taken hold of his hand as his gurney was strapped to the wall of the cargo hold, and he'd fallen asleep. When he woke, he was looking at the ceiling of the shuttle bay on the Empyrean. Home. He turned his head to see Waverly standing by him and opened his mouth to speak, but she placed her fingertips over his lips. "Listen," she whispered.

He followed her gaze to a man standing at the head of the room. He looked just like Don, but instead of Don's receding hairline, he had a squarish haircut and a strong, angular jaw. Whatever he was saying must be amazing because the room was hushed and every eye was glued to him.

"Any of you who wish to go back to the New Horizon are welcome to do so," the man said. "None of us would blame you one bit. If you stay on this ship you'll be leaving behind friends, all your possessions, and a lot of memories. Worst of all, you have very little time to make this decision. We ran a pretty ballsy bluff to get you here, and a lot depends on what Dr. Carver decides to do in response. Now, about the planet."

An excited murmur ran through the crowd, and Seth whispered to Waverly, "What planet?"

"Wait and see," she said, patting his shoulder.

"The planet can be reached in about nine years." The man held up a hand when the crowd erupted into excited talking. "Please! We have very little time. I'll turn over the description of the planet to the young man who found it. Arthur?"

Waverly cried out with delight, and Seth lifted his head up for a moment, long enough to see Arthur Dietrich taking the microphone from the man.

"Um," Arthur faltered, and there was an uncomfortably long pause, but then Arthur said in his characteristic brainy monotone, "The planet wasn't charted by the mission designers."

"Why not?" called a man from the back. He was immediately hushed by a dozen annoyed people.

"The nebula we just crossed shielded the star system from Earth's telescopes. All they could tell was that it was a likely candidate, which is why I started studying it." Seth heard the rustling of papers through the microphone. He looked at Waverly's face. There was a light in her eyes he hadn't seen in months, and she smiled with such hope and eagerness, he wished he could freeze this moment in time.

"The planet," Arthur went on, "is about fifteen percent smaller than Earth, and its day is 22.64 hours long. The atmosphere has a composition similar to that of Earth, though the carbon dioxide is quite a bit higher. Once we begin planting crops and establishing ecosystems, that level should drop."

He cleared his throat again, and Seth smiled at his extreme nervousness. Arthur had never been one for public speaking, and Seth didn't blame him. The only thing more terrifying than giving a speech was going on a space walk. Seth lifted his head long enough to steal a glance, and he saw Gunther Dietrich, Arthur's dad, standing behind his son, beaming with pride.

"The planet has three moons," Arthur went on, "and about sixty percent of it seems to be covered with water. There are polar caps, but they are small and may be subject to seasonal fluctuations."

"Is there freshwater?" a woman called from the front of the crowd.

Arthur paused uncomfortably. "We can see evidence of rainfall. The oceans may be full of salts and minerals. That will take further study."

"Is there life?" asked an old woman in front.

Another pause. "There must be plant life, since the atmosphere contains oxygen. We see no evidence of large fauna."

"Is there an ozone layer?" a man called from the back.

"We're still waiting on that data."

"What's the weather like?"

"Weather?" Arthur asked, unfamiliar with the term. For some reason, the adults all laughed, along with the man who'd asked the question.

"Are there harsh storms?" the man clarified. "Winds? Is it cold?"

"Right. I've only been observing the planet for a few weeks," Arthur said. "So far the average temperature in the temperate zone is around sixty-five degrees Fahrenheit, which is around eighteen degrees Celsius, if you prefer metric. There are frequent spiraling atmospheric disturbances that begin over the oceans. The largest one I've seen covered about . . ." There was a rustling of paper. "That storm covered about five percent of the planet's surface. When it hit land, it diminished."

"Continents?" called a woman.

"Difficult to say, actually," Arthur said. "I've counted five large landmasses, but there are lots of large islands that cluster around each continent, which can make it difficult to tell where one continent begins and the other ends."

"Does it have a stable orbit?"

"That's on the Goldilocks Contingency Checklist," Arthur said. "I wouldn't have kept studying the planet if I'd seen any possibility of an unreliable orbit."

"Have you named it yet?" called a squeaky little girl's voice.

The whole crowd laughed, but Arthur was kind enough to take her question seriously. "The name should be determined by democratic process."

Waverly raised her hand to ask a question. "What if we change course only to find out a year from now that the planet can't support life?"

This question silenced the room completely. Seth raised his head to look at the stage and saw that Arthur was handing the microphone over to Kieran Alden. Kieran looked bad. He was bent over, obviously in pain, sweating and pale. Seth glanced at Waverly, who had lowered her eyebrows with worry.

"That's the most important question anyone has asked," Kieran said. Seth thought everyone in the crowd must be holding their breath. "This ship is stable for now, but it suffered a major catastrophe. Chris and his crew think that it's worthy enough for a journey of up to twelve years . . ." The crowd erupted into a wave of whispers, and Kieran raised his voice, though the strain of doing so was obvious. "But that's with constant vigilance and maintenance. In other words"—he paused, and people quieted down—"this could be a doomed mission."

"So if we come with you, we could die," said a woman.

"We can't make any guarantees," Chris said as he took the microphone from Kieran, who sat back down, looking exhausted. "The heat from the explosion may have denatured some of the metals in the underlying girders. This ship definitely won't make New Earth."

The crowd accepted this with a dense, worrying stillness.

"This is why we wanted to give you a choice," Chris went on. "All of you have had a hard time on the New Horizon. Anne Mather is gone, but there's no telling what the command structure is going to be. I have Selma Walton here to report on what the church elders have been discussing since the Pastor's death."

Seth was glad to see Selma again. Even from here he heard the jingle of the bangles she wore on her arm. "Thank you," she said. "As of now, Dr. Carver plans to place his adopted son, Jared Carver, in the Captain's chair."

"That thug!" a woman called angrily from the middle of the crowd.

"I have been a loud critic of Jared Carver from the beginning," Selma said, "but I can tell you the rest of the elders tend to go along with the doctor. No one knows what will happen, but if any of you thought that Anne Mather's methods were violent, I can't imagine what life would be like under Jared Carver."

"Damned if we do, damned if we don't," a man muttered.

"Now," Selma said and waited for the crowd's grumbling to diminish, "I'm afraid that we can only give you an hour or so to make this decision. Dr. Carver does not want to let go of this vessel. Our best chance to avoid bloodshed is to run before they can regroup."

Seth looked at the faces around him, many of them crew members from the New Horizon. They looked scared and worried as they processed what Selma had told them, but they also looked determined and very brave. *Good people*, he thought. *They're going to make it.*

Selma put her hand on Chris's shoulder, and he smiled. He had a glint of mischief in his eyes that Seth liked. "Chris is going to take anyone who wants on a very quick tour of the Empyrean to look at repairs and to see the surviving ag and eco bays. And of course Arthur Dietrich, Kieran Alden, and I will be up here to answer any questions."

The crowd moved forward, leaving Seth and Waverly a little more space. Seth could hear Kieran's voice rising above the crowd as he tried to answer questions, but Seth was too tired to pay attention. Besides, he didn't need to know any more.

"We're going to the planet, right?" Seth said to Waverly, stroking her fingers with his thumb.

"Hell, yes," she said.

They smiled at each other. She'd become the vibrant, beautiful girl he remembered from months before, the girl he'd only been able to watch from afar as she gave this ebullient smile to someone else. Now the smile was for him.

He lay back, letting himself drift off for a while, his consciousness floating on top of the murmurs from the crowd. He felt at peace. *If I die now, I'll go happy*, he told himself.

"Oh my God," someone said right next to him. He knew that voice.

"Maya!" he cried out. He tried to sit up, but he felt as though a boulder were holding him down. The steroids Dr. Jansen had given him were already wearing off. Maya smiled hugely. "What happened to you?" Seth asked her.

"I've been in the brig," she said angrily. "They were keeping me there to manipulate Anthony." She extended a hand to Waverly. "I'm Maya Draperton."

"How do you two . . . ," Waverly asked, taken aback, and Seth realized Waverly knew next to nothing of what had happened to him for the last several weeks.

"Maya took me in when I first got to the New Horizon," he explained.

"Your arm!" Maya cried out. His stump had slipped out from under his blanket. "My God! What *happened*?"

Seth had to shake his head. He couldn't talk anymore. Waverly rushed to explain, "He got blood poisoning."

"But you're going to be okay?" Maya asked, looking between Waverly and Seth.

"Yes," Waverly said firmly. "Are you staying on board?"

"Oh yes. You?"

"Definitely." Waverly looked at Maya's swollen belly, but she didn't say anything about it.

"I guess I'll see you both around," Maya said as she rubbed Seth's good shoulder. "I'll come find you in the infirmary."

Waverly looked around worriedly. "Have you seen Felicity?"

Seth could only shake his head.

Suddenly a loud *ping* sounded over the speakers as though a microphone had been dropped. With a shaky voice, Selma cried out, "Anthony? Get up here now!"

Seth caught a glimpse of Anthony, the doctor who had treated him on the New Horizon, as he ran onto the stage and bent to someone sitting in a chair. Seth craned his neck, but he had to lie back down right away. "What's happening?" he asked Waverly.

"It's Kieran," she said, her eyes wide with fear.

Anthony called out, "I need to get him to the infirmary!"

The crowd divided as the man and three other people started to carry Kieran off the stage, but then Arthur rushed to whisper into the doctor's ear. Anthony looked outraged. "*What?*"

Seth tried, but he couldn't hear what Arthur was saying. "Go!" Seth said, pushing Waverly's hand away. "Find out what's going on."

Waverly fought her way through the crowd and pulled on Arthur's shirt, but the boy shook her off, his hands tearing through his hair. Then suddenly Anthony was pushing through the crowd, coming Seth's way. "I need that shuttle!" he yelled. "Everyone clear away."

Waverly came back to Seth, looking ashen. "There's no infirmary here," she said disbelievingly. "Arthur and Sarek tore it down."

"*Why?*"

"I don't know!"

"So . . ." Seth shook his head, uncomprehending.

"They have to take Kieran to the New Horizon."

"But . . ." Seth caught a glimpse of Kieran's face as Anthony and two other people carried him past. His skin looked green, and his eyes rolled in his head. Kieran's mother stood to the side, her face pale as she stared with childlike dread at her son.

"Anthony!" Seth saw Maya rushing past to pull on Anthony's arm. "You're not leaving!"

"He's going to die, Maya!" Anthony said as he backed up the shuttle ramp, Kieran's ankles in his hands. "I need an operating room!"

"No!" Maya stamped her foot.

"I can't just let him—" Anthony started to say.

"I'll go." Dr. Jansen stepped forward. "Anthony, you stay."

Maya and Anthony looked at her, their faces long. "Miriam, we can't ask you to—"

"You didn't." She jogged up the ramp and shouldered Anthony out of her way, taking hold of Kieran's ankles.

"Miriam!" Selma rushed to Dr. Jansen. "What are you doing?"

"He needs a doctor to survive the journey," Miriam said, but she looked so sad.

"But our plans!" Selma lifted a hand.

The two women looked long at each other, then Selma stroked the back of her finger along Dr. Jansen's cheekbone.

"Please." The word was spoken small-voiced by Kieran's mother.

Dr. Jansen broke her gaze from Selma's and started dragging Kieran up the ramp, shouting to the two men helping her, "Strap him here!"

Anthony knelt on the floor to secure Kieran, and the two traded medical terms, sounding to Seth as though they were speaking some foreign language.

Somehow a pilot was quickly found who wanted to go back to the New Horizon, along with a few other people who had already decided not to stay. At the last moment, Selma cried, "Wait!" and ran up the ramp as it started to close. Through the gap Seth could see Selma wrap her arms around Kieran's doctor and kiss her. The shuttle ramp closed, and Seth felt himself being pushed away as the engines fired and the ship lifted off the floor to ease into the giant air lock.

The air-lock doors closed behind it.

And that was it. Kieran Alden was gone.

A falling sensation took hold of Seth, and when he gasped, he realized his lungs had filled with fluid again. The steroids had worn off already, and Dr. Jansen had told him another dose would be too risky.

"I won't let them leave him," Waverly said under her breath, and she rushed from Seth's side, headed out of the shuttle bay.

Wait, he wanted to call after her, but he didn't have the strength.

Anthony came to his side and put a cool palm against his forehead. "Miriam told me your condition."

"Wave—" Seth said. He was in a panic, and he tried to get up. *I can't die without her. I can't do this alone.* "Please . . ."

"You're not there yet, buddy," Anthony said, his fingertips on Seth's pulse. "You've got some time. We'll get her back before . . ." He stopped there, letting Seth understand his meaning. *One breath at a time,* Seth thought and lay his head back on his pillow. *One breath, and another, and another . . .*

Good-byes

"We're not leaving him!" Waverly screamed as she entered Central Command. Sarek Hassan and his father were alone there, huddled over a com screen, staring at it with deep concern.

"Two shuttles," Sarek said.

"Probably a lot of men," his father muttered and put a hand on his son's shoulder.

"They're coming," Sarek said to Waverly.

"Who?" Waverly asked, stepping forward.

"Is that Waverly Marshall?" A hateful voice filled the room, and she rushed to Sarek's side. Dr. Carver sneered at her from Sarek's com screen. "Did you think we'd just let you go?"

"What are you doing?" Waverly asked. Her voice sounded grated and papery, but she forced herself to take a deep breath. *I'm not going to let him make me weak.*

"We're attacking, my dear. What did you think we were going to do?"

Waverly could tell from the background around him that he was transmitting from Central Command. She couldn't see them, but there must be people all around, listening. She remembered what he'd said to her, about how she'd turned the tables on Anne Mather in her brief speech on the New Horizon all those months ago. She glared into his desiccated, scowling visage and said, "You're a murderer."

He shook his head, a patronizing smile on his lips as though she were nothing more than a mouthy kid. "You have no credibility, Waverly, after the way you lied in your testimony. Anne Mather was a godly woman, and you tried to destroy her."

"You *wanted* me to," Waverly said to him. "You got her out of the way and now you're going to put your son in charge. That was your plan all along, wasn't it?"

"Jared," the doctor said with a flick of the wrist. Jared Carver appeared, leaning into the screen from behind the doctor. His features were puffy, and he looked like he was still drugged, but he scowled at Waverly with a fierceness that frightened her.

"You cooked your testimony up yourself, Waverly. You *admitted* it to me." He pulled his small com unit from his pocket—the guards must have returned it to him—and he flicked a button. Waverly could hear her own voice coming out of it, and Jared sneered at her as it played. She looked dispassionately at his twisted features and wondered how she'd ever thought him handsome.

But that *was* her voice sounding out from his clever little device: "I lied during my testimony against Anne Mather," she'd said. He turned the device off with a grim smile.

"You forced me to say that," Waverly said. "You were going to kill me."

"You're the killer," he snarled. "You almost overdosed me."

"I was defending myself," she said.

"You snuck up behind me and caught me unawares," Jared said.

She was frustrated, and though she tried to hide it, she could see Jared smiling with satisfaction. He thought he had her. But then she got an idea. "My confession wasn't coerced? Prove it. Play the whole recording right now."

Jared's features relaxed into a confounded pause. "I don't—"

"It should all be there, right? The entire video file? I doubt you've had time to edit it. So play the whole thing for everyone in Central Command. Prove you didn't coerce me."

Jared glanced around him. Waverly wished she could see the faces he was looking at, but judging from his growing dread, she had him.

The doctor's face appeared again, twisted with insensate rage. "We're going to kill you" was all he said, then the screen winked off.

"We have to turn the ship," Kahlil Hassan said quietly to his son.

The door to Central Command opened, and the man Chris walked in. "They're sending shuttles?"

Sarek and his father nodded.

"We can't leave Kieran!" Waverly said. She turned to Chris, and though she'd never met him in her life, she took hold of his hand in both of hers and pulled until he looked at her. "Kieran . . . he's too important. We can't leave him."

"They're launching OneMen," Sarek called out. The screen he was watching showed a dozen OneMen leaving the two shuttles, all of them heading for different air locks all over the ship.

"Where are your guns?" Chris asked.

Sarek hid his face in his hands. "Only Kieran knows where they're hidden."

Everyone looked at him in horror as they absorbed this.

"Even if only two or three of them make it on board . . . ," Chris began. No one finished the thought for him.

"We can't stop them," Kahlil said. His tears frightened Waverly more than anything else so far. "We've got to run."

"No!" Sarek said. "We can't do that to Kieran!"

"Son," Kahlil said, taking both Sarek's shoulders in his hands, "too many will die. We have no choice."

Waverly stood in the middle of the room, hands at her sides, her mouth hanging open, useless. She said nothing. She knew it was true. They had to run.

Gently Kahlil pulled Sarek away from the controls. The boy went to sit in a chair off to the side, where he buried his face in his hands. Chris sat down in the pilot's seat and engaged the shipwide intercom. "Attention! A New Horizon landing party is almost here. We're about to punch the engines, so get ready for some serious inertia. Please lie down on the floor." He set the message to loop and turned up the volume. "We've got about a minute before they get here."

"Seth," Waverly said under her breath. What would an increase in g-force do to him? She took off at a run back to the shuttle bay. Rather than wait for an elevator, she took the stairs, bounding down the steps two at a time with Chris's voice in her ear.

"Twenty seconds . . . ," he said as she rounded the landing. She'd gone another two flights when he started the countdown. "Minus ten . . . nine . . ."

She reached the shuttle-bay level and sprinted down the corridor.

". . . six . . . five . . ."

She slammed into the doors and pounded on the controls to open them.

The doors slid open. Dozens of people were lying on the floor, looking up at the ceiling, hands stretched to their sides in a surreal pose repeated over and over again. Where was Seth?

". . . three . . . two . . ."

Waverly looked around frantically and spotted the doctor strapping Seth's gurney to the wall.

She started running just as the engines engaged.

She hit the floor before she was aware her knees had buckled.

She sucked in a chest full of air once, again, and then she tried to gain purchase on her hands and knees to crawl the rest of the way to Seth, but her arms were made of lead, and her spine sagged. She had to lie down. The force on her own body was enormous, making it hard to breathe, hard to think. What was this doing to Seth?

Her face pressed against the floor. She could feel the sharpness of her cheekbone digging into the metal beneath her, and the sensation finally broke through her numbness. She cried. Kieran Alden was left behind to face those evil people alone. Her mind ticked through all the possibilities, searching for a different choice, another way to save the ship and Kieran at once. But it wasn't possible. Kieran wouldn't have wanted them to risk any more lives. He'd want them to run. She knew it as well as she knew her own character.

When the inertia let up, Chris's voice came over the intercom. "We've put some distance between us and them, folks. It's not too late to take a shuttle and turn back, but if you want to do it, do it right now."

Waverly struggled back to her feet. Her left knee creaked painfully, but it held her weight, and she limped over to Seth's gurney. He was as white as new wool, drenched in sweat, and his chest rattled when he breathed. She kissed his lips, once, twice, and took his hand . . .

He opened his eyes and smiled. "Don't let go," he whispered.

Beginnings

Kieran woke up groggy under a dim light. To his left his mother sat dozing in a chair, her cheek resting on the back of her hand. Someone took hold of his right hand, and he turned to find Felicity Wiggam smiling at him.

"Hi," he tried to say but sputtered into weak coughing instead.

"Here," she whispered and touched a drinking straw to his lips. He pulled in small sips of ice water, and his mouth and throat loosened.

"Where . . ." He couldn't get any more words out.

"You're on the New Horizon," she whispered. "You were brought here for surgery."

The last thing he remembered was sitting on the stage on the Empyrean, discussing their new mission plan, and being gripped by a horrible pain.

"Your heart stopped when they were repairing your small intestine." For the first time he noticed tears clinging to her eyelashes. "They had to rebuild a defective valve."

This was too much to take in all at once, so he turned his mind to something easier. "Why weren't you on the Empyrean?"

Her mouth tightened with anger. "Avery didn't tell me about the evacuation until it was too late for me to come, too."

Kieran looked at her hand and saw that her ring finger was now beautifully bare.

"Kieran, you've been asleep for three days," she said slowly.

"Three days . . ."

"They're gone. The Empyrean had to leave. I'm so sorry."

She gave him time to absorb the full meaning of the words. The Empyrean was gone. His friends. His home. He'd never see them again.

"Waverly sent this," Felicity said and handed him a printout with a text message on it. He was too weak to hold it for himself, so Felicity asked, "Do you want me to read it?"

He nodded.

Felicity cleared her throat and began.

"Dear Kieran, They sent an invading force to take back the Empyrean. We had no guns and no way to defend ourselves. I'm so sorry, but we had to run. I knew that you would never want us to put ourselves and all the little kids in danger for your sake. At least, that's what I am telling myself right now. I hope you can forgive us someday. It's not what I wanted. I'd hoped that you and I could spend the next ten years rebuilding our friendship. I think good friends is what we were always meant to be. I hope you feel that way too."

Felicity faltered, blushing deeply, and shot a hooded look at Kieran before continuing.

"It might be a good thing that you went back to the New Horizon. Felicity is there, and I think you should steal her away from her fiancé. I know she would be happier with you, and I think you would be happier with her than you ever could have been with me."

Felicity gave a little embarrassed giggle, and Kieran smiled.

"With Anne Mather gone, you can be a voice for good on the New Horizon. Be careful, because Dr. Carver and his son Jared won't want to share power with you. Keep your head down, and stay away from them."

At this, Felicity made eye contact with Kieran but kept reading.

"I love you, Kieran. I'll always love you and remember you for what you are: a completely decent, brilliant man who, just like me, sometimes tried too hard. Live a good long life.

"Remember me fondly, Waverly."

Only when Felicity looked at Kieran did he realize he was crying. His tears had seeped into his pillow and made his ears and neck wet. Embarrassed, he tried to wipe them away, but his hands were floppy and useless, maybe from weakness, maybe from drugs.

Felicity reached for a tissue from his bedside table and, with tenderness, dabbed at the tears in the corners of his eyes. Then she smiled, and with her crystal blue eyes on his, unwavering, she bent over him and gently kissed his lips.

PART FIVE

Gaia

I saw Eternity the other night,
Like a great ring of pure and endless light,
All calm, as it was bright;
And round beneath it, Time in hours, days,
    years,
Driv'n by the spheres
Like a vast shadow mov'd; in which the
    world
And all her train were hurl'd.
                    —Henry Vaughan,
                        "The World"

Sermons

In the slender light of dawn, Waverly Marshall stepped off the shuttle onto the rocky soil and gazed across the hard, glistening ground. Wearing an airtight landing suit complete with heavy boots and a suffocating glass helmet, she walked down a gentle slope of black volcanic rock to stand on the pebbled shore of a vast ocean bay. The water crashed against the beach, a beautiful rushing sound that filled her ears, pounded her chest, ringing all around her. The sky glimmered with a pale pink light, blending into a deep blue overhead. As the orange sun pierced the edge of the horizon, the water glimmered in a line of shimmering brightness. It was the first sunrise she'd ever seen, and it was indescribably beautiful. As the sun brightened the sky, she saw a collection of clouds moving in over the water, long streams of what she guessed was rain falling in gray streaks.

She wished Seth could see this.

She was twenty-five years old now, but already she had a touch of gray at her temples, an annoying trait she'd inherited from her father. She walked toward the test animals in the pen she'd set up the night before. The goats were munching happily on the bale of hay that had been left for them, all three of them perfectly content and healthy. She lifted her walkie-talkie to her lips, which was patched into the shuttle's long-range com system, and hailed the Empyrean. "You getting all this?"

"Everyone on board is watching," Arthur Dietrich answered, sounding tired. "How did you sleep?"

"I didn't." She'd sat up in the pilot's seat in the shuttle, unable to take her eyes off the meteor shower that rained down. The planet was passing through the tail of a comet and the show had been stunning. She didn't regret staying awake for it. She'd have been too tense to sleep anyway, knowing what she was going to attempt the next morning.

"The goats look fine," she said to Arthur, and sent a video image for the crew in Central Command to see. Three goats, perfectly unaware of the momentous occasion they were a part of. With a deep breath she said, "I'm taking off my helmet."

"I'll start the clock," Arthur answered. His little boy's voice had resolved into a smooth, sensitive tenor that perfectly suited his thoughtful personality. He'd never gotten tall, but he was handsome in a boyish, Germanic way, and he'd become one of Waverly's best friends.

Waverly released the locks on her helmet and lifted it off. Was she afraid? Excited? There were so many emotions coursing through her she couldn't begin to name them.

A brief suction sound as the helmet lifted off, then . . .

The air moved over her skin in the gentlest caress, lifting the hair from around her face, cooling her. She breathed in through her nose and out through her mouth. The atmosphere smelled pure and fresh and perfectly safe.

Through her headphones, she heard the distant sound of

applause from the crew in Central Command. She was deeply honored to have been appointed the first human to breathe the air on their new home, and she knew that this image would be seen by countless generations for centuries to come. What had been the words? *One small step for man...*

"Waverly?" Arthur called into her headpiece. "We agreed, no more than thirty seconds."

"Algae never killed anybody, Arthur," she said, referring to the vast deposits of algae in the planet's oceans, churning out the oxygen that would make life here possible. Thus far, no land-based life had been located. "The surveys showed there's nothing airborne here to worry about."

"We agreed," Arthur barked. "Put your helmet back on."

She groaned with annoyance but knew he was right. She replaced her helmet and listened as the air filter kicked into overdrive, clearing out any foreign particles. Compared to the air of the planet, the air inside her landing suit smelled disgustingly stale.

"How does it look?" Arthur asked her. She thought she heard a tinge of jealousy in his voice. As the planet's discoverer, he'd been the first choice for the journey, but then his beloved wife, Melissa Dickinson, the girl who had made life bearable for all the orphaned children on the Empyrean, had gotten pregnant with their first child, and she was too close to her due date for him to leave her.

"It's ..." Waverly was at a loss for words as she took in every shadow cast by every stone, every glistening speck of mica and quartz in the gray igneous rock upon which she stood. The wind made a soft, whispering sound over the glass shield of her helmet, and she longed to take off a glove to feel it moving between her fingers. *Soon enough.* "It's amazing. Beautiful. Big! Can we build a settlement here?"

"We're looking at a nearby site right now. It has a nice gradual hill above a substantial river. It ought to be safe from flooding but manageable for crops."

"Waverly," Sarek interrupted. "Your launch window closes in two hours."

"Okay," Waverly said, "I'll start breaking down."

She unlatched the gate on the animals' pen and herded the goats up the shuttle ramp. They resisted at first, obviously remembering the terrifying turbulence they'd experienced on the way down, but Waverly was able to strap them into their harnesses with relatively little struggle.

Then with a sigh, she looked at the silver container she'd left just inside the shuttle ramp. A part of her dreaded what she had to do next, but a deeper part of her knew that it was time to let go of the past. She unscrewed the lid and stood still a moment, holding it tightly to her chest, remembering. She lifted the container over her head and let the wind carry off the remains. "Good-bye," she whispered.

Then she turned her microphone back on.

"Did you do it?" Arthur asked. He sounded choked up.

"It's done." Waverly watched the cloud of fine dust sail away on the breeze.

"He's the first one to make his home on Gaia," Arthur said softly. "I think he'd like that."

Waverly heard a distant click, and static filled the signal. "Kieran? That you?" Waverly asked.

"I'm here," Kieran said after a pause. The New Horizon was very far away now, and two-way communication was becoming more fraught with cosmic interference and time lapse. They were lucky to still get a signal through. Kieran's voice was deeper now, a little more gravelly with age, but he sounded so much steadier, more fully himself. "Felicity is here with me."

"Hi, Felicity," Waverly said. "Glad you two could make it."

"We wouldn't miss it," Felicity said. Waverly smiled to think that when she and Kieran had been dating, she'd always been worried that he'd notice Felicity was the most beautiful girl on the Empyrean. Even way back then, deep down she must have known those two belonged together.

"You have something to say, Kieran?" Waverly asked, glad there was someone else who could speak. Her heart was still too closed.

She watched as the cloud of dust dissipated over the waves, falling to join the water. To have his ashes scattered on their new planet had been his dying wish.

"Captain Edmond Jones was a courageous, brilliant man," Kieran said, and he sounded as if he really meant it. "He fought for what he believed in, accepted his own shortcomings, and tried to make up for them. The Empyrean colony will forever feel his loss. May his spirit guide the settlers as they begin life on their new home."

"Amen," Waverly said as her gaze trailed along the infinite horizon.

"Amen," Sarek and Arthur echoed, along with all the Command officers on the Empyrean.

In the background, weaving through the static, Waverly could hear the cry of a newborn.

"You guys had *another baby*?" she asked Kieran with mock incredulity.

But he and Felicity had already signed off. Later Waverly would send them a text message to congratulate them.

Waverly signed off the com link. Dry-eyed, she turned and walked back up the shuttle ramp as it closed, and up the spiral staircase to take the pilot's seat. She engaged the engines, and the shuttle lifted off, leaving the ground of her new home. In the coming months the crew would begin the arduous process of bringing supplies down from the Empyrean storage bay, setting up temporary dwellings, and beginning the endless task of learning which plants could thrive in this new environment. The process of terraforming this planet would go on long after Waverly's death, she knew, but she could hardly wait to begin.

The journey back to the Empyrean took several hours, but Waverly enjoyed the view from her cockpit. She flew her craft with the port side facing toward the planet so that she could watch the mountains, the intricate coastlines, the patches of snow and ice over the poles, and the black volcanic soil of the continents rolling underneath her. She would never tire of looking at it.

Soon the Empyrean loomed ahead of her, moving fast. It would maintain an orbit between Gaia and one of the larger moons, slowing itself using the opposing gravitational fields in a carefully choreographed dance designed by the geniuses Arthur Dietrich and his father. Within a few years the huge ship would slow down enough that it could assume a geostationary orbit over the colony and could be used to monitor weather activity on the planet and meteor activity in the solar system, as an insurance policy against cataclysm. Somehow Waverly thought they needn't worry too much. They'd chosen a good home. She trusted everything would be all right.

She guided the ship into the air lock and waited while Sarek repressurized, then she landed the shuttle inside the bay, waving out the blast shield at the crowd collected to welcome her back. Soon they trickled away, back to their duties, and Waverly settled in for her quarantine.

Over the following week, a medical team wearing protective clothing put her through a battery of tests to make absolutely certain she hadn't carried any alien contagion on board. Other teams took soil samples and air samples to search for microscopic life, but all their tests confirmed what they'd suspected: The planet would provide no real difficulties related to infectious disease. Gaia had all the necessary components to support life, but aside from the oxygen-producing algae in the oceans, which they'd found to be harmless, there was no other apparent life.

When Waverly was finally released from quarantine, she saw that once again a crowd had collected at the feet of her shuttle. As she descended the ramp, she waved to Sarah Wheeler, who lifted up her daughter Samantha's tiny arm in greeting. Randy held Samantha's twin brother, named for his own departed father, José.

Waverly scanned the crowd for her own family and saw her mother Regina standing off to the side, holding little Caleb. He jumped up and down when he saw Waverly, clapping his chubby little hands, and Waverly blew him a kiss. Her boy was so excited he could hardly contain himself.

Waverly came cautiously down the shuttle ramp only to be tackled by little Josiah, who rammed his head into her stomach, full force. Her youngest child, he was always the first to demand to be picked up, fed, or cuddled. She never minded, though it made her worry Caleb wasn't getting enough attention.

"Did you get my wock?" little Josiah asked, blinking his huge crystal blue eyes.

"I got it," she whispered and handed him a small pebble that she'd actually found in the conifer bay. They hadn't completed the toxicological analysis of the rocks from the planet, so she couldn't bring him a real rock, but try explaining that to a three-year-old. After a brief visual inspection, Josiah immediately put the pebble in his mouth and thoughtfully swirled it around on his tongue.

"You like it?" Waverly asked, laughing.

He took it out long enough to say, "It's okay," before popping it back in.

"That's my boy," Seth said from behind Waverly, and she whirled. He gave her his characteristic crooked smile. "Destined to be a geologist, I think." Caleb tugged on his pant leg. From behind his back Seth produced a bundle of flowers and gave them to his five-year-old, then picked him up in his single muscular arm. The little boy proudly handed the bouquet to his mother.

After nine years, Waverly was still in awe, still grateful, still amazed that Seth had survived his illness. Over the weeks following the Empyrean's flight from the New Horizon, Dr. Anthony told her again and again to prepare herself, that Seth wouldn't last much longer. Again and again, Seth fought his way back.

Now Waverly rested a hand on Seth's shrunken shoulder. She liked touching him there because she was the only one allowed. He smiled as they walked to the door of the shuttle bay. "Did our Golden Boy make a good speech?" he asked her.

"You didn't listen?"

He shrugged. "I may have caught some of it."

"I know you don't think the Captain deserved to be the first one buried there."

"He was a monster," Seth said quietly.

This was an old argument between them. The Captain had always maintained his innocence, insisting that Waverly's father and Seth's mother, along with their colleague Dr. McAvoy, had acted alone to sterilize the women of the New Horizon. When the Captain learned of their betrayal, he said, he alerted Captain Takemara of the New Horizon, who insisted they be executed for treason against the mission or his ship would attack. Rather than put his crew through the trauma of a public trial, Captain Jones had opted to deal with the criminals quietly. Then Anne Mather took the helm of the New Horizon and began her plans to attack the Empyrean from their hiding place in the nebula, unbeknownst to Captain Jones. Over nine years, he never changed a detail of the story, but Seth didn't believe a word of it.

Waverly wasn't so sure. Whenever Waverly broached the subject with her mother, she was so evasive, and became so angry, that Waverly suspected Captain Jones's story must be true. At the very least, it was clear that her father had been involved in committing a terrible crime that led to a great deal of bloodshed. Over the intervening years, she'd come to accept that she would never know for sure if Captain Jones was a conspirator or not. After a while, it stopped mattering to her. She knew that Seth clung to the idea that his mother had been an innocent scapegoat, and she did her best to avoid the subject altogether. Let Seth have the memory of one good parent. Let her mother believe she'd protected the memory of her dead husband. They'd both been through enough.

So instead of responding to Seth now, she reached for his hand, held it to her lips, and kissed it. He smiled at her as he pulled her along the corridor toward their apartment.

Their apartment was immaculate, just the way Regina Marshall liked to keep it. Waverly's mother had never fully regained her old spark, but slowly she'd emerged from her fog and was helpful and productive.

As Waverly was drying her hair after a long hot bath, Seth

knocked on the bathroom door. "Video call for you from the New Horizon."

She went into the master bedroom, wrapped up in a fluffy white robe, and engaged the com signal. "This is Waverly."

"Congratulations," Kieran said after a pause. His image was grainy, but she could see his smile just fine.

"And to you. I heard a newborn crying. That makes five?"

"Her name is Waverly," Kieran said and grinned as he watched her try and fail to suppress tears.

It was awhile before she could speak again. "Thank you, Kieran. I'm just glad to know you and Felicity are so happy together."

"It was all meant to be," Kieran had said to her with a peaceful certainty.

"Oh Kieran." Waverly laughed, shaking her head. "We'll never agree about this."

"I know. But I can't help it. It's how I see things." He tapped absently on the desk in front of his com console. "You know, if I hadn't swallowed those explosives, if they hadn't operated on me to get out that detonator, they'd never have found my defective heart valve. I'd have died of an infarction before the age of thirty. Tell me you don't see the hand of God there."

She shook her head. "I just don't see the patterns you see."

"Because you refuse to see them," he teased.

"You see them because you *want* to."

He surprised her by laughing. "Maybe you're right."

"What? Is that doubt I'm hearing?"

"Without a healthy dose of uncertainty, faith isn't faith. It's zealotry."

They shared a long, quiet smile before she said, "You know what, Kieran?"

"What?"

"I think you're an excellent pastor."

"But never captain," he supplied for her. Indeed, when the doctor and Jared Carver had been publicly shamed, Selma Walton had taken over the vessel and exonerated Kieran of any blame associated with the Pauleys' bomb plot. Kieran then joined the political faction that insisted the pastor and captain roles be kept separate by law. Seth had been surprised by this, and Waverly knew it redeemed Kieran in his eyes. The two men would never be friends, but she felt they'd at least forgiven each other. Now Kieran smiled at Waverly. "I'll leave those nasty moral compromises for you pagans."

"We're so grateful."

"I'd better go," Kieran said.

"Keep in touch," Waverly said, and he nodded as his signal winked off, knowing that conversations like this would soon become impossible. And no one would know for another thirty years if the two colonies would be able to stay in contact on any kind of permanent basis. Waverly hoped they would.

After a quiet dinner of roasted vegetables and a lovely egg-and-goat-cheese frittata, and an evening reading aloud to her squirming little boys, Waverly crawled into bed next to her husband. Seth folded her into his embrace and she rested her head in the hollow of his shoulder. She fell asleep almost instantly but was startled awake when he said, "That was our first time apart in nine years."

"I couldn't sleep," she said, nuzzling his neck.

"Me neither." She thought he was going to let her sleep, but then he asked, "Was it amazing?"

She smiled in the dark and pictured the dappled water reflecting the sunrise, remembered the caress of the breeze on her skin, the dome of endless, eternal blue over her head. "You won't believe how beautiful."

"Tell me about it," he said and gave her a gentle shake to keep her awake.

In the intimate whispers of a long-married pair, she described the water, the air, the sky, the clouds. They stayed up, resisting sleep, talking into the wee hours, glad to be together, glad to finally be going home.

ACKNOWLEDGMENTS

Once again I want to thank the entire team at St. Martin's, but especially Jennifer Weis, Mollie Traver, and Matthew Shear, who I know fought the good fight for the Sky Chaser books. My agent and friend, Kathleen Anderson, has continued to be a tireless advocate. In addition, I want to thank my friend Victoria Hanley, for her careful reading, and my brother, Michael Ryan, for his wise edits and his absolutely brilliant idea about the oxygen-producing algae.